COLLISION!

by James Broom Lynne

COLLISION!
THE MARCHIONESS
THE WEDNESDAY VISITORS

James Broom Lynne

COLLISION!

Doubleday & Company, Inc.   Garden City, New York
1973

Although most of the locations mentioned in this book exist, the people do not. Any resemblance between them and any living person is purely coincidental.—J.B.L.

ISBN: 0-385-07926-5
Library of Congress Catalog Card Number: 72–96247
Copyright © 1973 by James Broom Lynne
All Rights Reserved
Printed in the United States of America
First Edition in the United States of America

For
PETER HEBDEN
and
NORMAN FISHER

COLLISION!

CHAPTER 1

Monday, 13th December, 19.00 hrs.

In the Eastern Region, some twenty-eight miles from London, a stretch of double track, nine miles of rail as straight as a die, runs between Chelmsford and Shenfield Stations. Drivers and commuters know it well; if they are behind schedule, vital seconds can be gained and employers' times of business respected.

The track at this point allows a maximum speed of 80 mph. It is the main Eastern artery, serving many points, with branch connections covering the whole of the eastern seaboard from London to Berwick, part of the Midlands, northern England and all the seaports along the coastal stretch.

As with most arterial railroads, traffic is diverse on this line. The gantries straddling the track carry overhead electric cables to feed trains to Clacton and suburban services nearer London, heavy and light freight use the line; Cartic 4's, long articulated wagons, take British cars to Harwich en route to the Continent, and occasionally return loaded with foreign cars. Permanently coupled Freightliners, over nine hundred feet in length, use this route, and every day the Hook Continental makes its morning and evening run to and from Harwich; and branching off this main eastern artery, capillaries carry the green Metro-Cammell Railbuses serving branch lines whose traffic does not warrant heavy multiple train units.

A normal, busy main line, sensitive to danger and armoured against the unexpected, and, between Chelmsford and Shenfield, nine miles of track as straight as a die.

Midway along this length of track, a high-density housing estate backs up to within seventy feet of the line. On the other side pleasant, undulating country, well-wooded, wanders away to the far Essex skyline, unbroken by development sores. The A12 Motorway, cutting through that country half a mile away, is fortuitously hidden by rising ground and belts of trees.

The name of the estate is Willow Point, for reasons that were once obvious. Before bulldozers rendered the acreage as barren as a 1914–18 battlefield, willows had wept and hung about the damp places and edged the little stream that was no more, for drainage had emptied the land of natural water to make the ground safe for house foundations.

December 13th was a Monday, a day of the week wage-earners are only too glad to be done with, and Willow Point had begun the process of settling down for the evening. The day, which had started frosty and cold, had seen the rapid inclusion of a warm wet-weather front bringing rain to the south-east region of the country and rendering all except the brightest man-made colours to a monotone of grey-green. A typical Monday; depressing and spiritless with early nightfall.

The Willow Point commuters were home and dry, their working day over with time to spare for the square world of television and the more virtuous activity of do-it-yourself.

Each house was a castle heavily defended against enemies; little fortresses unprepared for war or the wrath of God, but armed against the predictable.

A mixed goods train, thirty wagons in all, took the nine-mile stretch ten miles above the permitted maximum.

Apart from personal motives which edged his throttle hand beyond its usual sensitive judgement, the driver had had to make a series of short, irritating runs between various sidings on the Up line—a stop-go activity designed to allow peak-time commuter services free passage. The end of his journey lay in the London collecting area of Stratford where his load would be branched off to a terminus north-west of Liverpool Street.

It was not unusual for a driver to exceed the speed limit by the odd mile or so; he knew the braking power of his loco and, if he was on a familiar run, he was well aware of potential danger spots, multiple points and curves in the track whose banking called for deceleration.

Electronic safety systems were functioning perfectly, but vulnerable to the millions-to-one chance of human error, a factor which can reduce a highly sophisticated computer's usefulness to that of an empty beer can.

Human error was the only fact which enabled the Inspectorate, an independent investigatory body, to point an accusing finger and take punitive action against an individual.

Ten miles above the permitted maximum.

It was assumed by the Inspectorate that a coupling between wagons five and six, its metal weakened by a bad shunting movement earlier in the day, snapped clean off its main shaft, creating a transverse drag. Speed and inexpertly phased load distribution combined with the skewed coupling to throw the fifth wagon, heavily loaded with aggregate, off the track, whipping its tail of four into the path of the 18.40 passenger train from Liverpool Street.

The 18.40 was jam-packed. Armrests were down in the second-class compartments to allow four-a-side seating. The buffet-car queue stretched down the length of the carriage and overflowed into the coach beyond. Seatless passengers obstructed passage in the corridors of the central carriages. Winter heating was on full blast, despite the muggy depressed weather, and commuters sweltered.

Christmas shoppers had swelled the passenger load beyond its usual capacity of regulars, and those habitual users unable to find seats cursed the casual travellers usurping space unofficially allotted to those whose journey was strictly necessary.

Grumbles and discomforts were running true to form for the month of December.

The impact speed of the 18.40 and the mixed goods was 150

mph—combined speeds of 70 and 80 mph. The Brush-Diesel passenger loco slammed into the dragging tail of wagons with an explosion of sound that ripped into the domestic privacy of Willow
Point.

The diesel ricocheted off the wagons and onto its side, ripping
up track until it caught an obstruction and reared up like a dinosaur
in anguish before describing three complete somersaults and crash-
ing to its death in a great balloon-burst of orange flame as the
fuel tanks ignited. Overhead, ripped electric cables arced with a
spluttering blue flame, intensely bright in the orange glare of the
fire.

It was four minutes before the first coherent telephone message
found intelligent ears. Then emergency rescue forces moved into
action with high-priority signals flashing in all regional hospitals,
fire stations, area police headquarters and railway depots.

In seven minutes the first of the rescue services was on its way,
siren blaring, to the disaster area between Chelmsford and Shenfield, to join those householders with guts enough to face a tragedy
they had neither earned nor expected.

A hiatus of sound—the silence of shock—then a keening, like
a chorus wailing out a thin dirge of despair, swelled out of the
telescoped wreckage to reach the hearing of the estate-dwellers,
shocked into attentiveness by the massiveness of the impact sound;
they spilled out into the street and back gardens, eyes turning to
the funeral pyre of the diesel locomotive.

It was a disastrous intrusion of their privacy. It rendered their
preoccupations with self and domestic pleasures and anxieties so
trivial that, long after the track had been cleared and services were
back to normal, memory remained as sharp and poignant as the
most acute and organising war experience. It gave traumatic
memory-fixations and highlights to many hitherto uneventful lives.
The limelight of press, television and radio emphasised the enormity of the unwitting part they had played in the drama, whose
magnitude surpassed anything they had seen in the second-hand
violence of the nineteen-inch, three-channel world of their sitting
rooms. Yet those who responded with the compassion that is sup-

posed to exist in all men found their understanding of the human condition deepened; belief in themselves strengthened. And for those who held back for reasons, rational or reprehensible, the need arose to invent narrative of action and bravery which could neither be proved nor disproved; so false heroes rubbed shoulders with the real and few could tell the difference. The Press supported both: *'The nearby housing estate responded with the courage and resourcefulness of the kind shown in the Blitz of London'.* The estate was blanketed by heroic descriptions, its inhabitants spiritually decorated, each and every one, with medals for exemplary conduct; including the man fixated on the television programme and who refused to budge from a gripping *Z Cars* episode and the programme which followed. He suffered no regrets or self-recriminations. He was tired after his day's work and reasonably happy to put his feet up and let others do the living and the dying.

CHAPTER 2

Monday, 13th December, Dawn

No. 1/487 locomotive, its two thousand seven hundred and fifty horsepower motor thrumming, linked with the chain of goods wagons under the hand of Driver Coates. In a diminuendo of sound, the wagon's buffer links chimed and clunked into union.

Outside, the rain lashed the train with the full force of a wet December morning, and the promise that it would prevail for the rest of the day.

It was bad for Coates' temper; his three-day rest period had come to an end with a 5.30 am rising from a warm bed. A look at the weather and a wife who wanted nothing but to push breakfast into him and get back between the sheets had set his bad-temper pattern for the day.

Leaving the house at 6.15, he had walked to the goods yard cursing the foul weather and a torpid Trade Union, and paying an infinitesimal vote of thanks to God that the railway marshalling yards lay only half a mile from his house.

The pre-dawn noises of the city of Norwich came to his ears; the strange calls, mournful and depressed, of factories changing shifts; the clankings from the station yards like lengths of chain being dragged by monster ghosts—these sounds echoed Coates' psychic state. He was both angry and depressed as he reached the yards and collected his schedules for the day. Henceforward any incident, however trivial, would become a grievance vehicle for his resentments and aggressions.

Randall, the traffic controller, hadn't helped with flippant remarks about Trade Union guerilla fighters with nothing in their bellies but hot air and black pudding. Angrily he had collected the schedules and left the traffic office to claim his locomotive from the engine shed, his silent and apprehensive second man, Len Spencer, following one pace behind, more out of deference to his senior's temper than from traditional respect.

They had taken their places in the cabin, neither speaking until the control checks had been made. There continued to be the minimum of communication until they had linked up with the wagons, and signal lights gave them the all-clear to move out of the yards and into the black morning.

As Coates switched from electric power to diesel, Spencer attempted a human remark to raise the emotional temperature of the cabin.

'Nasty old morning.'

Coates remained silent and Spencer added: 'Might improve. You know—rain before seven, fine after eleven.'

'That's balls.'

'I've known it to be right. Like red sky at night, shepherd's delight.'

'If I'd had any sense, I'd've gone sick like the rest and been spared your old wives' tales.'

December was proving a bad month for British Rail's south-eastern region. A virulent spread of gastric 'flu had reduced the number of duty-fit drivers and second men to a dangerously low level. Sacred timetables necessitated a system of diagrams—the railwayman's term for his working schedules—which ensured essential rest periods if drivers were to work a longer day and yet conform to Union rules.

Traffic control had worked overtime thoroughly to diagram passenger services, freight movement and rest periods to cover the region so that no normal departure or arrival would be cancelled or delayed, and goods and parcels traffic, now seasonally heavy, would be kept rolling.

To some drivers extra time meant overtime rates—welcome at Christmas when pockets would be emptied to meet the demands of December; to Driver Coates it meant that the bosses had unreasonably trespassed on his private and free time.

The last station clearance light showed green and Coates advanced the throttle. The track gleamed ahead, faint silver in the driving rain.

Forty-eight miles down country the day began its long winter process into a freezing, star-brittle dawn. Frost settled in the Stour Valley and across the flat marshlands to Manningtree Station, perched on the southern bank of the valley. A hundred yards down the line from the platform ramp a track-worker's shed bore a silver-grey covering of frost crystals on its tarred roof. It was cold, bitterly cold and the high-tension cables that straddled the Stour as it widened into the estuary, hummed in the icy airstream.

The man sitting on the only chair in the dark track-worker's hut began a spasm of uncontrollable shivering as the chill of the morning invaded his body to join the unendurable solitude he suffered in his mind.

Relief was near at hand; in his lap lay an old service revolver with three cartridges in its chamber where recently there had been five. It needed but a simple action to put an end to persecution, loneliness and the numbing cold. Instead, he took his last remaining cigarette from its packet and put it between his lips.

As he thumbed the wheel of his lighter and the gas ignited, the gun glinted in the light from the flame. He drew on the cigarette and inhaled deeply, looking at the revolver, seeing it as the connecting link between life and death.

That it had already caused death the man knew. Recently it had spoken in a great explosion that had been more in the mind than in the gun itself. Days, hours, weeks ago—it was difficult to tell in the confusion of his brain—the gun had spoken and a known environment had died; a large part of life, years of problems, family, accustomed routines, all had gone and only flight remained.

But the destination was unknown. He had followed an urgent, blind force of direction that had brought him to the valley and up the railway embankment to the cold haven of the trackworker's shed. That same force was stirring in him again, suggesting a further extension to the distance between his cold body and the thing from which he was running.

He shifted about on the hard chair, feeling the cold biting into his bones. He picked up the revolver and held it close to his face; the eye of the muzzle was round and blank, without expression, but he knew that a few inches below the eye lay the intelligence of a cone-topped bullet with its magical power to end all confusion. But there was no motivation behind the finger curled round the trigger. The energy to raise the pistol and into his mouth with the muzzle pointing to his brain was yet to come.

Motivation, what little he had at that moment, was reserved for the enemy, for the persecutor and those who hunted him.

An old anger stirred, sending a growth of warmth into his stomach. He spoke loudly and to himself. 'I'll not be pushed around—I'm as good as the rest of them. They lie and cheat behind my back—won't face me with it.'

He replaced the revolver back in his lap.

'Oh, no—they haven't the nerve to face me with it.'

A low, distant drumming, a vibration, came to his ears. He lifted his head and listened intently. Now the hut itself seemed to vibrate as if with the tremor warning of an approaching earthquake. The sound increased and the man came to his feet, suspicious and alert, gun raised and ready to fire.

Round the banked track of the line running into Manningtree Station, the 07.20 thundered into the approach, brake shoes spouting fountains of sparks. It roared past the shed, brightly lit carriages flashing the interior of the shed into relief in quick phases, like bursts of fire from a machine gun.

The voice of the diesel spoke. A short high and a low sustained note—a bugle call that cut into the cold morning and echoed across the Stour Valley like the reveille of a ghost legion.

John Amos Davies heard it as he drank his second cup of strong black coffee in the kitchen of the big house. He glanced at his watch: 07.20. The train was on time and its sound would have alerted other commuters in the village that it needed only another hour for their own train to herald its approach to the station.

Davies had no desire to return to a warm bed. The forces that had woken him at five had been welcome, for his sleep had not been of the depth needed to induce the relief his mind wanted. Sleeping the minimum for many days, and keeping up the uncertain balance between the body's need for rest and the psyche's fearful reluctance to leave the action world of evasive and protective movement had taken its toll. At five that morning he had known that the point had been reached when survival was now or never; that the spark of hope was within hours of extinction.

Cynthia, his wife, was asleep in her bedroom, the previous evening's intake of whisky ensuring a period of beneficent oblivion. Davies envied that merciful black-out. It released Cynthia, for a full nine hours out of every twenty-four, from awareness of inadequacies and failures—blessed gift which Davies longed to share.

Life, as Cynthia understood it—caring for children, the right education, advancement of her husband's business life and income, consolidation of their social position in an ordered society and, of supreme importance, the retention of an attractive face and body —life had ceased to have its habitual meaning in a sudden, melancholy revelation on her fifty-first birthday. A look in the mirror, some chemical change, and the last illusion had vanished.

Alcoholic oblivion, with its euphoric precursor, which she regulated, was a curtain, a kindly, thick black-out to be drawn between the day and night of her unhappiness.

Davies could hear Cynthia's unmusical breathing as, back in his dressing room, he selected his clothes for the day—and waited for the post to arrive as he had waited since the moment he had come out of shallow sleep.

The post to arrive.

He remembered other times when the arrival of the post had been a trivial matter: bills that could be dealt with, letters from his sons at school and university, news from friends at home and overseas filled with clannish information. The memory seemed to relate to another age, to a time that was completely gone. Now, he, the house, his way of life, the environment he had in the last five years almost criminally nurtured and sustained, all depended upon a letter due to arrive in a matter of minutes.

The Big House, as it was known to the village, positioned on the hill with feudal ability to overlord all compass points of the parish was, to most people with an eye for land and property values, an asset worth all of forty thousand pounds. Twenty acres of wooded land, lawns, flower beds, orchards, a heated swimming pool and the house itself, eighteenth-century and elegant, suggested that its owners would be privileged, upper class and rich.

Previous owners of the house—rich clergymen, a gentleman farmer, the odd well-endowed military man, a title or two—had impregnated it with history and a façade of gentry reliability.

Davies had bought this façade with its purchase twenty years ago. It had fitted his aspirations, income and an ethos he had worked hard to get. Also Cynthia had loved the house, and, in those long lost days, he had wanted to give her as much of the world it was in his power to give.

In terms of money—the hard cash of reality—the asset of the house was known to Davies down to the last penny. It was also known to his banks and the various finance companies with whom he had mortgaged, re-mortgaged and second-charged the house and all contained in it. It was a black fact and one which he had faced with grief over the last few difficult years; its value, as a personal asset and in terms of cash to call his own, was in the region of seven hundred pounds.

And that was nothing, *nothing,* in the sea of debt which threatened to engulf him; the great angry sea that had been building up in volume, and would soon burst its confines and drown him. The absolute limit of credit had been reached.

His last chance, good or bad, could happen at any moment with the dropping of a letter through the letter-box in the hall. He wondered if he would have the nerve to open it there and then or wait until he had taken his first-class seat on the train.

He looked at his watch as he slipped a smoked-pearl link through his left shirt cuff. The post would arrive in the next fifteen minutes, possibly as he waited in the car to drive to the station, bowler-hatted, briefcased and richly ready to commute for the day; an appearance he would sustain with all the aplomb he could manage.

From the window of the dressing room he could see across the village; down the hill running away from the house he could see a glimmer of a bicycle torch in the morning darkness. It was either the paperboy on his rounds or the G.P.O. uniformed messenger of life or death.

He finished dressing and went to the hall, observing that his knees were trembling. Halfway down the stairs he paused and looked through the long well window; ten miles to the north-east the lights of Ipswich glittered in the frosty air, among them the winking, changing green, yellow and red signal lights of the railways station and marshalling yards. Down there, Locomotive H109 was warming up for its 08.10 departure for Manningtree, Colchester, Chelmsford and London, getting ready to link with the carriages on Platform 2.

In the cabin of H109, George Denning checked the controls. The Dead Man's brake was the last instrument he tested. 'It's a comforting thought,' he said to Joe Wellford, his second man, 'that a ghost'll take over if we both get a call to join the angels.'

H109 was an impersonal, characterless way of describing a Class 47, Type 4, 2750 hp Brush-Sulzer Diesel Electric locomotive. To command a piece of machinery with a tractive power of fifty-five thousand pounds marked the zenith of George's rise from fireman, his status had been little more than that of stoker, in those far-off days when he had ridden the old, wonderful Britannias on the south-eastern run. The dark blue-grey uniform with its BR badges and rank insignia which he now wore was a far cry from the fire-man's overalls and knotted handkerchief in which he had sweated as he stoked the fiery furnace of the hungry Britannia.

It was George's silver jubilee year; it had taken twenty-five years of steady progression from light goods and shunters to his present command of the Brush-Sulzer Diesel Electric. To 'command' such a locomotive was the only status symbol he wanted or laid claim to. 'Locomotive Commander' was the title for driver he had pro-posed to the Railway Board. It was a reasonable description for a skilled man who regularly took into his hands the lives of thou-sands of passengers. On this 08.10 trip alone he would carry some-thing like a thousand passengers, and that was a damn sight more than any airline pilot carried on an individual trip; so where was George's smart uniform with gold stripes and gold-crested cap? The comparison did not rankle; it existed as a talking point to be raised at Union executive meetings or something to be put in the suggestions-box. At the last big Union meeting he had coun-tered Jack Coates' exposition on the anomaly between the salary of an airline pilot and that of a driver with the axiom, 'It's eco-nomics that decide a man's wage, not the number of lives he holds in his hand.' One day anomalies would cease to exist and he was content to wait and press for reform in an undemonstrative way.

'Going to be a nice clear run,' Joe Wellford said. 'I like this sort of morning—frosty and clear. You can see the way ahead.'

Using electric power, George guided the diesel into Platform 1 and gently connected with the coaches; fifteen blue and grey Pullman carriages with guard's van, parcels wagon and buffet car with stand-up bar and seating for thirty in which Maurice, the steward, was getting up steam for the morning's run on coffee and tea.

The station clock's hands moved to 7.50. Early arrivals had be-gun to board the train and take the accustomed, necessary seats that habit demanded, and Maurice, despite the rule of no service until departure time, had taken pity on unbreakfasted regular com-muters and served coffee.

Ahead, where the station canopy ended and the track zoomed into perspective, the sky had lightened. Another half-hour and the sun would touch the eastern horizon. Another twenty minutes and H109 would obey the green light and the guard's whistle and move out of Ipswich to begin the run to London.

For no reason except that it could be called 'testing', and because he liked the sound, George Denning gave a long, loud blast on the diesel's bugle. The sound funnelled its volume due south and across the flat land to the Stour Valley where crisp, cold air currents carried it up to the village of East Bergholt.

Some of the commuters heard it as they attended to the countdown before the station blast-off.

The sound reached John Davies as he watched the letter come through the box and drop to the hall floor.

A mile away from the Big House, on the village boundary, H109's call sign coincided with Elizabeth Marwood's acceptance of another cup of tea from an attentive husband, whose dressing gown and slippers contrasted strangely with the town suit she wore. The change in roles was disconcerting. Taking up from where one left off had its advantages and disadvantages. Sixteen years away from office work, with its typewriter chatter and gossip, seemed a long time, for she had found the life stimulating. She had missed the life and the salary she could call her own. The change was odd and pleasurable; now husband would be housekeeper, and wife, breadwinner. It was a thought she kept hidden from him while she expressed only her reluctance to leave husband and family of two daughters; it was for the good of the unit and a worthwhile sacrifice while father, spouse, lover, her other half, recovered from his major setback. She was now a working wife and felt years younger.

A few houses away, the new estate of fifty ranch-style £5,400 houses began. 'Ranch-style' was an outsize term used to define three-bedroomed open-plan homes with garage for one car. Well-architected, the houses presented a problem to those owners for whom words had exact meanings; without toting a gun or raising a herd of cattle, how could the description be justified? The most a tenant could do with his small piece of land was to keep the lawn in as good a condition as his neighbour's and, like Charles Shelley in No. 4 (Shiloh), leave the Western stuff to his two sons and a couple of cap-guns.

Charlie Shelley was looking forward to his day. Leaving the house an hour later than all his working days for the last ten years was an unaccustomed luxury. The alarm clock in his head had clanged him awake at the usual time, but he had enjoyed coming down to the kitchen and brewing a pot of tea knowing that he had all the time in the world. Now that it was winter and the light summer mornings a distant memory, catching the later train was a kind of victory over the 07.20, whose run to London was like travelling through the night; henceforward the sun would be up when Charlie boarded his train.

Recent promotion meant more to him than an increased salary cheque and an office which he would now share with two instead of twelve. He had joined the 08.20 commuters and could now call the pre-dawn monster the Cattle Train.

It was coming up to eight o'clock and ten minutes before a car-borne fellow commuter, Edward Ferris, picked him up for the run to the station. Now there was a miserable man with a hell of a home life, thought Shelley. It was the man's perpetually hurt face like a whipped dog's that told a story of what? He had no kids, that could be part of the problem, although children could be problems in themselves; you never knew where they might be heading. Also, Ferris wasn't the sort of man you'd expect to see in a pub, but there he'd been on Saturday night buying six bottles of beer and one of ginger wine without a smile on his face; for relatives, he'd said. Charlie Shelley, assuming on his nodding acquaintance with Ferris, had twisted the latter's arm and made him accept a half of bitter. Now, until Charlie could take advantage of his rise in the world and put down a deposit on a second-hand car—a *second* second-hand car, for he never liked to leave Edna, his wife, without their six-year-old Austin Traveller—Ferris would call for him at 8.05 every morning.

It had been worthwhile buying the morose so-and-so a drink. In the pleasant, warm atmosphere of Shelley's local pub, the Hare and Hounds, and with the help of Peter, the benign, friendly 'I'll have no swearing in this house of sin' proprietor, Charlie had managed to induce a smile on the face of the unhappy Ferris despite the humour of Bill the Barley, a regular who suggested that Ferris put a bit of the ginger contained in the bottle 'up her tail'.

Which led Charlie to conjecture that Ferris' trouble must be sex, to judge by the fleeting expression of hurt on his face when Bill offered his contribution to horse-sense.

Sex, thought Charlie; either too much of it or too little. How does a man count his blessings if he gets more or less than he bargained for? His thoughts turned to Edna, scolding the boys into activity at the top of the stairs. He'd got what he bargained for and loved every sexy inch of her and after *fifteen* years. Get that, you unfortunate unhappy ones—fifteen years and still working on all cylinders!

And what was the blessed world doing this morning? As his two secondary modern school sons came into the kitchen, unwashed but fully dressed, Charlie switched on the radio to catch the south-eastern news.

Edward Ferris had turned on the radio for the sole purpose of making a time-check. The news meant little to him; troubles, like charity, began at home and the world's problems were only a microcosm of his own.

The house was silent, alien and neat. He finished his breakfast of toast and tea, and stacked plate, cup and saucer, knife and emptied teapot on the draining board. In a few minutes he would get the car out of the garage, pick up the cheerful Charlie Shelley and drive to the station.

He went into the hall and collected raincoat, scarf, hat, briefcase and umbrella, then called up the stairs to his sleeping wife.

'Margaret—I'm going now!'

There was no response and, as he turned to the hall-stand mirror to make sure that his tie was straight and hat correctly positioned, he bitterly observed to himself, 'there's no place like *this* home'.

The observation held no humour for Ferris. The face he saw in the mirror was that of a man prematurely divested of hope. The face would change as the miles lessened between the village and Chelmsford; from grey melancholy to anxiety, from anxiety to pleasure. The order would be reversed on the journey home in the evening.

Upstairs, in the double bed he hated so much, slept the great offence to his sense of decency and self-respect, yet he would return to it day after day like a masochist taking his daily ration of punishment. But there was a miracle somewhere, ready to erupt from Heaven or Hell and resolve his dichotomy; God knew he had earned his release from bitterness and castigation.

Leaving his grey reflection where it belonged, he walked through the kitchen to the door communicating with the garage. He unlocked the double safety lock he had recently installed—the village had had four break-ins in twelve months—and entered the garage, closing the door behind him.

Now to pick up Shelley. On the strength of a drink he hadn't wanted he'd agreed to give the man a lift. The round-faced, cheerful Shelley was too noisy, randy and full of the joys of Spring for Ferris' taste. The outside of Shelley irradiated a mindless humour that had no place in a troubled world. The man, Shelley—the man you saw—was the icing on a sponge cake. He'd laugh at dirty, sexual jokes and use women like a cheerful rapist. But a promise was a promise; he'd give the man a lift and concoct some reason for denying him lifts in the future.

He drove carefully out of the garage, came out of gear and handbraked the car; climbed out and secured the garage doors, making sure they were safely locked. He looked up at the window of the room in which he had known such degradation and revulsion.

Goodbye, Margaret—in a little while I'll be with Helen.

As he climbed back into the car, he remembered a hand touching the lower part of his body; he shuddered, likening the feel of the hand to that of a snake clutching the most sensitive and nervous part of his being.

One item in the news sounded on Hector Annersley's sensitive eardrums as he drained his teacup in the kitchen of his Raymond-Erith-designed, neo-Georgian house south-east of the village.

'Following the deaths of a woman and child in Claybourne, Suffolk, the police are anxious to interview a man whom they believe can help in their enquiries. He is William Arthur Kemp, last seen yesterday evening . . .'

Then followed a short, guarded account of a gunshot killing on a smallholding. It was the spice of life to Annersley. A solicitor with a fairly lucrative practice exactly on the demarcation line between the City and the East End, he had a taste and philosophy for anything connected with crime and punishment—murder in particular. As a criminal lawyer *manqué*—defence or prosecution, it didn't matter—he felt that he was predestined at some later date (Annersley was fifty years old, and used logic) to walk with princes and top QCs. He *knew* the very nature of the punishment to fit the crime, especially murder, for, as distinct from the plebeian crime of theft, however large, a killing had a more direct line with God, who was always on Annersley's side. At the local Franciscan Friary, where he was a constant, irritating visitor, he was known as the Hyper-Roman Catholic or Super Pundit. On a lesser level he was known as an embarrassing bore.

Murder. A fascinating crime. In a clear case, the victim went immediately to judgement and, before they'd changed the law, in due course the murderer followed his victim. A very proper expiation of his sin. Purgatory was an infinitely more satisfactory way of paying the price than life imprisonment for an average of twelve years or being detained at Her Majesty's pleasure.

And he, Annersley, should know all about it. His teenage son was in a corrective establishment, despite the fine upbringing to which Annersley had subjected him.

Northern Ireland, Malta, the impending coal-strike—his ears went deaf on such uninteresting news. He rubbed his hands briskly together and addressed his long-suffering wife.

'Well—another hard day's work.'

It was the sign she had waited for. Dutifully, she rose from the table, went into the hall and made sure that briefcase, *Daily Telegraph,* umbrella, bowler hat and topcoat were in their designated places. All she had to do now was wait for his perfunctory, loveless, unwanted kiss and the day would be hers alone.

Unaware that the day would bring unaccustomed devils into his life, the ex-Reverend Kenneth Thorneycroft, in his isolated cottage south of the village, switched off the radio as his wife entered the kitchen.

'It's cold,' she said. 'What will the weather do today?'

'Bright and cold at first—rain later. A nasty murder in Claybourne.'

'You nearly had a living there.'

'Yes.'

'We wouldn't have met if you'd taken it.'

'I know.'

She moved to the Raeburn stove and opened it up to full draught.

'A cold, bitter, foul day,' she said. 'I want Spring to come.'

And, perhaps, to be one Spring nearer the day when he would have earned the right to wear the cloth again and do the job for which he was fitted—the cloth he had loved and lost because he had been foolish.

The Claybourne murders hovered over his deeper thoughts. 'I'll never understand murder,' he said. 'Never.'

West of the village, where the houses were old and protected from planners' infilling and development, David Blake backed his car out of the garage with little enthusiasm for the day ahead. It was Monday and he had to teach the illiterate, inept and arrogant. Tomorrow was Tuesday and the same prospect faced him. The same on Wednesday, and then four days in which to recapture that which had gone. If only he could face the prospect of poverty with the same bravado and true stoicism of fifteen years back. How good that would be. He'd grown too accustomed to a cash balance and the luxury of paying for luxuries.

The headlights of his Triumph 2000 spotlit his wife's car as he backed up the sloping drive. He was a two-car owner living in an expensive beautiful house that had known the presence of John Constable. He lived a well-to-do bourgeois life, lived on his reputation and regretted the cost of sustaining it. Where had motivation gone? Gone with the dealers, every one.

He drove away from the house and joined the stream of tail-lights beading the road to Cattawade and Manningtree Station. He was one of the beads in a chain and he didn't mind; it was part of the pattern, a design of living that included so many people he liked and admired. But there was conflict where there should be harmony between the two worlds in which he spent his week.

The day was starting sour because he had to come to a decision and pride was preventing an objective judgement. Those who can, do, those who can't, teach; a fallacious, Shavian statement incapable of withstanding analysis, yet it seemed to contain the essence of his attitude which, on this cold Monday, made the days ahead suspect.

As the traffic ahead slowed down for the right-hand turn at Cattawade, Blake noticed that PC Weston was at the wheel of the car in front.

The 7.45 bus from the village made the level-crossing a bare minute before the Hook Continental Express from Harwich rolled slowly through Manningtree. At the bottom of the crossing ramp, Harry and Mabel Peartree alighted and began the three-hundred-yard walk to the station. It was no hardship for them to rise early.

Years ago, when they were young and in their salad days, they would have walked across the fields to get to the station. Not that the railway had played an important part in their lives; a day trip to the nearby coast once or twice a year was the most they and their good kind could manage in those hard days.

Harry, seventy-three and slowing down, and his wife, a few days short of seventy, had grown into each other, like the graft of different species of apples on the same stock. They were parts of one unit; when one eventually gave up the ghost, the other would cease to function.

They trudged the rising ground to the station in silence, their needs for the day and Christmas gifts packed in carrier bags, each regretting the decision to take a return trip to the big city to visit a married daughter. They were too old, too set in their ways to leave the cosy, warm shell of cottage and village or to expect any joy from a crowded train and a noisy, bewildering city jungle.

They reached the booking hall and, as Harry fumbled in his purse for money to pay for two return tickets, the first of the commuters drove into the station parking area, beating by a short head a Kettlebatch taxi bearing Mr Thorpley, whose daily journeys to and from London were transports of joy.

Beyond the station approach, the main roads grew a chain of car headlights. Of the drivers converging on the station, the most elated was Police Constable Weston, East Bergholt's lawman. He was in mufti, and looking forward to a week of courses at New Scotland Yard. Five days in the nerve centre of crime detection. Since joining the Force, this was the first important step he had taken in his rise to the top. Who wanted to be a village copper all his life?

He had joined the Cadets at seventeen and entered the Force proper at nineteen, pounding the beat with the best of them for three years, and learning every twist and turn of the streets of Ipswich; committing to his memory and instincts all the danger and trouble spots—food and drink to a keen copper—and marking up a good record of justified arrests and convictions. Three years on the beat and then a posting to East Bergholt into a fine police house with pedal bike, scooter bike and patrol car.

Weston now judged his East Bergholt posting to be nearing its end. Two and a half years had passed since he became the village's lawman, and he had applied for admission to Police College; with his O and A levels it was certain he would be admitted and given the automatic status of acting police sergeant. One year's training to full stripes and then—he was quite certain where he was going.

The bright star in his ambitious sky was the Metropolitan Area of London. He'd work it—by God he would work it!—to get posted to London, to any district in the area. Qualities of leadership and crime prevention and detection would soon raise him to the rank of inspector. The progression was quite clear in his mind.

The men at the top would be curious about this man of exceptional ability who, in a few short years, had shown that he was the stuff a top CID man was made of and would invite him to join them at—get this, you who call me the slowest gun in Suffolk—at New Scotland Yard.

From inspector to detective inspector and from that to detective chief inspector and, since success breeds success, a jump to detective chief superintendent.

Here, Weston's dream of the future entered the realms of copper angels and he was content to leave the rest to fate. It would be foolish to aim too high.

Weston drove under the bridge and right into the station approach, conscious, deeply conscious, of the fact that he had begun the next important leg in his journey to the top.

The sky was now pearly grey with a pink flush in the eastern horizon, but it was still dark enough for the man with the gun to leave the track-worker's hut unseen and make for the platform where the commuters were now gathering.

The urge to move had motivated him again. Memories from the far distant past had seeded in his mind. He had to get to London where he would be an unknown face among many; to London where there had been a mother and protection, home and shelter.

He moved up the platform ramp, imagining himself to be invisible, safe from bullies who bore the name Flynn, and he mingled with the people he feared, right hand deep in his pocket, touching the gun. It was what Billy Kemp, the little, bullied boy, would have done before he grew into a man called William Arthur Kemp.

CHAPTER 3

Monday, 13th December, 08.20 hrs.

George Denning took H109 through Bentley Station at sixty miles an hour, well within the maximum speed safety level. Ahead, in the distance, some two and a half miles away, the sodium and arc-lights of the plastics factory at Brantham glittered. He eased the throttle down and the speedometer needle began to fall.

The factory took shape on his right, the tall chimneys belching out the smoke that occasionally tainted the air with the smell of disinfectant. Somewhere in that great complex of machine shops and chemical plants Denning's son Anthony worked as colour-balancer, doing his six-to-two shift.

Denning gave a treble blast on the diesel's bugle. Away in the factory, Anthony Denning heard it, looked at the factory clock and said to his mate, 'There goes me dad.'

The long banked curve into Manningtree gleamed ahead and Denning lowered his speed down to the thirties. The brightly lit signal box showed up on his right. Beyond it, hard against the level-crossing gates, was the usual stack of lorries from Harwich; DFDS and Geest refrigeration trucks and heavy transports too bulky to use the bridge road below the crossing which served lighter traffic.

At twenty miles an hour, the diesel entered the station; the faces of the commuters ranged down the platform like a queue of masks.

Denning applied full brake pressure, his throttle now down to nil and out of gear.

'Nicely,' he said to Wellford. 'What's the betting I'm not more than six inches either side of the limit on the end ramp?'

'Fifty to one against.'

'What's the betting we're dead on time at Liverpool Street?'

'The same—fifty to one.'

'Don't you trust Traffic Control, Joe?'

'It's Acts of God I don't trust—like frozen points, signal failure, engine breakdown. He's got a lot to answer for.'

'Who has?'

'Since the bosses won't take responsibility, it must be God.'

'I didn't know he was interested in trains,' said Denning. 'Landing flaps down—reverse jets and remember Maurice in the buffet bar. A nice, easy soft landing and—' and butter-smooth, he brought the diesel to a halt, not one plastic cup tilting its contents over the lip and onto the tables in the Pullman coaches.

'Four minutes for the workers of the world to unite and board the train.'

Along the platform, traveller neuroses faded; the 08.20 was not only on time but in its hoped-for position. As the train came to its easy, almost imperceptible halt, Maurice had already started mixing coffee and tea for the regulars. Behind him glittered stacks of miniature bottles of whisky, gin and rum, bright display stand-ups, cans of Worthington E. Double Diamond, Bass, Guinness and Coca-Cola. And the pin-up calendar showing a girl, blonde as far as the photographer had been allowed to see, ungoose-pimpled, with dream-like breasts, and ill-clad for the month of December she symbolised except for the furry Santa Claus boots and the Christmas tree in the background.

The steam heater spluttered the first cup of coffee into drinkable warmth as the first boarder to claim seat and place in queue appeared at the counter.

'Strong coffee,' said Maurice. 'Right?'

'Right. How much for the girl in the boots?'

'She charges piece-work rates. Five pounds an hour. Cheap at the price. No charge for a look.'

'I'll just look.'

Annersley boarded the train with two seconds to spare, leaving his car inconveniently parked in front of David Blake's Triumph. *Daily Telegraph* tucked under his arm and briefcase in hand, he began to walk the corridors in search of a pair of ears, his resolute stride forcing the Peartrees to stand aside in a mid-carriage recess to allow him to pass.

He glanced in at compartments, looking for a likely face. He found one he had not yet tried; a Manningtree boarder whose face Annersley recognised but to which he could not put a name and identity. The possibility of a mystery to start the day tingled his palate. He entered the compartment and selected a seat opposite the stranger with a known face.

'Good morning,' he said. 'I'll join you if you've no objection.'

'None at all.'

In three minutes flat, Annersley had introduced himself and learned the name of his fellow traveller. A name to a face and Annersley had it. Newspaper reports of—how long ago—three years? He'd chosen well. A defrocked minister of religion augured well for an interesting run to London.

Mabel and Harry Peartree sat side by side in a mid-train carriage. Harry asked nervously, 'Is this first class?'

A man opposite shook his head.

It was luxury compared with the last train ride Peartree had taken. Then it had been first class and third—a class difference which, with its disparateness of comfort, he had accepted all his life.

'It's second class,' said the man and Harry stirred.

'We're third,' he said and got up to go.

'There's no third class. Went years ago. You sit tight and enjoy the journey.'

The upholstery was good, the armrests comfortable and the view from Mabel's window seat clear and wide. An old station flashed by and she nudged Harry.

'Ardleigh.'

'Ardleigh?'

He'd had a place there years ago. A big house with kitchen gardens and orchards. Five miles from East Bergholt to the house. Spring, Summer, Autumn, Winter, he'd left his cottage at seven to cycle to the big house for an eight o'clock start. Old General Woods had owned the house. Peartree, now the general's senior by ten years, always thought of him as 'old General Woods'. After the general's death Harry had ceased to cycle to Ardleigh. One week's notice and he had sought other employment in his own village; one day in this garden, two days in that; he had kept out of debt and hadn't touched his post office savings. Now he tended his garden, paid a peppercorn rent and actually saved from their joint old-age pension.

'Old General Woods,' he said. Mabel nodded recognition to his memory.

Privilege had come to them in their old age. Their cottage was ancient, picturesque and in the old, protected side of the village. They paid fifty pence a week rent, landlord paying the rates. He had offered to put in sanitation with bathroom and all the etceteras, at the same time pointing out that the rent would have to be increased to meet a new rateable value and the cost of installation. Both Peartrees had asked for nothing to be done. Night soil was no problem for Harry. It was good for the garden and they were used to using the little hut a few yards away from the cottage. The landlord didn't press them, despite his local tag, 'Grab-all Madden'. He was younger than the Peartrees by twenty-five years and could afford to wait. When the day came he would spend a thousand on the cottage and sell it for eight or nine. A good investment; you buy at eight hundred and sell—when?—ten years after purchase for ten times as much? He left the Peartrees and their clopacal hut in peace; the passage of years would see the fruit of his investment.

The new Ardleigh reservoir gleamed in the dawn light. Under its water lay the garden Harry had tended, but the general was dead and the controversy over the flooded land that had raged for months in the local press had passed over Harry's head. He knew that somewhere good farmland had been deliberately flooded, but since it was miles from his cottage garden, its location was as foreign as the places Harry had seen in the Great War.

No. 1/487 locomotive was in the thick of bad weather. Norwich lay behind, the lights of the city a diffused glare in the screen of rain. Screen-wipers lashed the rain driving at the cabin of the diesel.

'Godawful!' said Coates.

'What is?' asked Spencer.

'The NU bloody R, the weather—every stinking thing.'

'We're warm and dry.'

'Wet and bloody stupid!'

Ahead, signals showed red and Coates throttled back. 'What now? A clear run, the TM said.'

'I'm in no hurry. We stop on the red, go on the green.'

The red persisted and Coates brought the goods to a jerky halt. His early-morning temper flared up with the unexpected frustration. Diagrams had indicated an early afternoon duty stopover in which he'd have ample time to attend a meeting of the NUR specially convened by himself.

Sensing the reason for his senior's anger, Spencer said: 'You'll get there in time. We can pick up a bit of time on the straight runs. What we lose on the roundabouts we can gain on the swings.'

'You sound like the bloody liberals who vote go easy at the meetings.'

The red light winked to green and Coates edged up the throttle. He took it slowly towards the complex of points half a mile ahead; here, the loco was pointed off to take the line down to Great Yarmouth via Acle, there to lose three wagons and take on four.

'There's a soft man at Acle,' he told Spencer. 'A soft man I'm going to give the shits to.'

'Soft?'

'A moderate. A coward—a bloody liberal.' Coates raised his voice to an effeminate pitch. 'Demands must be reasonable and in line with the Union's agreed policy—the country's economic state requires great constraint on the part of the workers.' Returning to his normal voice, he added, 'Crap like that!'

'You can be too hard,' said Spencer. 'People's backs get put up.'

Coates grunted his disgust. 'If it hadn't been for the hard men where the hell would you be now? Crawling on your economic belly begging scraps from the employer's table—and getting that by overtime. You listen when I talk to the soft man—get educated!'

On the same topic some sixty miles away, Joe Wellford said, 'I don't want a strike *or* a go-slow. Not now, anyway. With Christmas coming up I need every penny I earn.'

'There's a time to strike and a time not to strike,' said Denning. 'Nothing to do with Christmas or the old lady's birthday. Arbitration's on—the Union Executive knows what it's doing.'

'That chap Coates—'

'The Norwich driver?'

'That's him. Have you heard him ranting on about the lick-spittling soft men in the Union?'

'He's called me one,' said Denning. 'Maybe he's right. He's a hot-belly. He'd make more sense if he farted instead of opening his mouth.'

John Davies' pulse-rate was running high as he deliberately drew the letter from his pocket and ripped it open with his thumb. He used touch only, averting his eyes as if bored by the action of his hands. He drew out the letter, feeling the smaller piece of paper clipped to the main sheet. It felt like a cheque, yet he still couldn't use his eyes. He unclipped the piece of paper and slipped it in his pocket. He watched the frosted fields through the carriage window until they were obscured by trees before painfully directing his eyes to the letter. He read the first paragraph, bending the lower part under so that he couldn't see the closing lines. It began hopefully enough:

My dear John,
   I am so glad you thought of turning to me. Remembrance of things past makes me aware of the quite considerable help you gave so generously when things were bad for me and very good for you.

Davies lifted his eyes and looked through the window. It was a good paragraph—hopeful and understanding—and the cheque, if it was a cheque, lay in his pocket, its amount unseen and proof that a debt of gratitude had been recognised. He had helped in the past, helped without thought of reward, for things had been so good that actions could be undertaken with generosity: there was nothing he needed in return.

He felt the letter in his hands and guessed there would be two more paragraphs, to judge by the amount of space taken up by the one he had read. It *had* to be done. The letter *had* to be read.

Directing his gaze down, he forced himself to read:

   I more than understand your situation. There is much done by men in our position—certain risks that have to be taken with the hope, always, that time is on our side. Much that hovers between the law and the other dreaded, unmentionable thing. Time is of the essence.
   Enclosed is something I sincerely want you to consider as a very long-term loan, since I am sure your pride would not allow you to accept it as a gift. I suggest you use it to open an account away from your present bankers. Having no wish to teach Granny to suck eggs, I'm sure you will know best how to use it to mark time.
   When things are better for you, let's lunch together—there is much to talk about.

Hubert hadn't given him what he'd asked for. The slip of paper in his pocket did not mean instant relief—the relief he'd asked for. It was simply the means to buy time.

He took in the line, *Ever yours, Hubert,* and drew the cheque out of his pocket, wishing a couple of noughts had been added to its value. *A thousand pounds.* It was neither life nor death. His request had been understood and rejected with all debts cancelled out. A thousand pounds when he'd wanted cover for sixty—had asked for sixty thousand at a reasonable rate of interest. Hubert had done the decent thing according to Hubert's sense of decency. He'd given him a thousand with the overt instruction 'now use it to raise the rest'. Or did Hubert mean 'use it to cut and run, dear boy'?

There could be no cut and run, neither could he use it to raise the rest. There wasn't a moneylender or financier in town he could turn to. The ads in the newspapers promising instant loans from twenty pounds to ten thousand were not for him. He had one day left in which to hold his head high. One day in which pure acting ability would see him through the day's activities and tomorrow—he shook his head—there could be no tomorrow.

Something was wrong with his sight. His vision was misty—dark. He stared through the window, dimly recognising that the train had passed Ardleigh.

It was all ended. Things had petered out, finished—and yet, as in a story coming to a tragic end, a character had been inserted to emphasise the tragedy. What could show up death more sharply than the false promise of renewed life to a dying man? The appearance of Monica Inchbald in Davies' life, so casual, an afterthought cast into the pattern of things to make life more difficult to bear, had suggested that there might just be a vital life yet to be lived.

And that, to a man dying of an incurable disease, was irony of the highest order.

To cut and run, a luxurious thought. To cash the cheque —no difficulty there—and away, far far away, to live without caring for an alcoholic wife and a property that crushed his spirit. To let his sons now taste the really hard way of having no Daddy to turn to. To let them all suffer the agonies he had borne in the last few months. To escape with the energy and health that was still miraculously his, despite the immense strains and stresses that now stretched him on the rack.

But he would suffer because they would suffer. He would not be left alone and trouble would be double trouble. It was in the nature of things. There was no way out as far as he could see. No Peter Stuyvesant escape by jet to a carefree, expansive haven—with Monica?—where he could live again. It was not possible, because he was nearly dead.

Death, in every sense, was the reality and the life; a beautiful abstract, beyond his reach. No kiss from Monica—only the kiss of death awaited him.

The thrumming of the wheels accompanied his racing thoughts. A rat turning a treadmill endlessly, furiously. His vision, still misted, took in the sight of a beer can tossed out of a window bouncing and clattering along the side of the embankment. The can was many thousand times smaller than the one he carried.

Two carriages away, David Blake considered the only justification he felt for spending so much time teaching art to the artless; it amounted to £21.36 per day. Ten years ago he'd have laughed at the daily rate. Ten years ago he had been a top gallery man. Exciting years in which even try-outs pushed into the wastepaper basket had been retrieved by dealers, handsomely mounted and framed and sold for rich returns.

A few glorious years of high popularity, the medal of the Royal Academy and supertax pinned to his proud chest. He had arrived at age twenty, while he was still a student. *'Those whom the Gods love, die young'*, club-footed Byron had written. He forgot to add, *'after a long illness'*.

Mondays in London, trying to get through to fourth-year students whose articulation seemed as limited as a comic strip, and Tuesdays and Wednesdays up in Norwich doing the same thing. Three days of solid, unrewarding teaching. Sixty-five-odd pounds per week less tax, by common standards a big reward for three days' labour with subliterates who expressed more of their tiny psyches in fancy dress than on canvas.

Blake stared gloomily through the window. He was forty and felt as square as a sugar cube, if that was the term they used now. The years of recognition and honour had gone. But did that matter? What was the root of his discontent? Looking back, the driving force in those early years had been the utter conviction of the vision transmitted to his hand and made visual on canvas. The first show at the Redfern a sellout, followed by five years of high production and the accolade of the Royal Academy. And then the declining years in which he'd done the old vision to death while other painters claimed the admiration of critics and the love of dealers. He was old hat at forty, and painted fewer and fewer canvases.

What had he accumulated in his formative years to make his painter's vision so original? Certainly he had loved his childhood and the emotional and visual impressions so sharply and beautifully etched in his mind. But what had the last ten years brought? A good marriage and a slow decline. Ten years in which nothing memorable had happened; nothing to be transmuted into expression and communication.

Opposite Blake, Charles Shelley surveyed the world with a bright eye, using his accountant's knowledge to reckon the total wealth represented by the 08.20's commuters. He estimated that the income per capita ranged between £400 and £10,000 above the per capita level of the earlier train. He started at £400 because that was the fantastic size—according to his values—of his salary rise and promotion. The bonus didn't end at an extra eight pounds a week, it went on into the future. Success breeds success, he thought. He had shown that he could rise at the late age of thirty-eight; another twenty-two years of work, assuming retirement at sixty, could well see a series of promotional steps which would bring him as near the top as a quiet man could wish. And success, he told himself, breeds confidence. Take David Blake, the artist who sat opposite him staring gloomily out of the window. He had fame and lived on the nob side of the village. At the same time, you'd expect a successful man like that to look more cheerful. Perhaps, thought Shelley, he's down to his last ten thousand. A *very* worrying situation.

'Going to be a nice day,' he said. 'Nothing like a good start to a Monday. I've seen you in the village.'

'You live in East Bergholt?'

'The east end.'

'Oh, yes.'

The unimpressed reply would have crushed Shelley a few days ago; now, he took it with a smile.

'A chummy crowd on the estate. Nothing upstage about the folk there.'

'I imagine not. What is there to be upstage about?'

The irony was lost on Shelley. 'That's a fact,' he said. 'You're an artist, aren't you?'

'Yes.'

'Is it true you're an RA?'

'For what it's worth—yes.'

'Must be a great honour.'

'It was.'

'I thought you had to be about sixty or seventy.'

'Like policemen, RAs get younger every year.'

'That's good.' Shelley grinned his appreciation. 'Talking of coppers, PC Weston's on the train.'

'Then we're safe from train-robbers.'

'We don't get much crime in East Bergholt,' said Shelley. 'That's the good thing about living in a village. Not like the cities. You get the odd bit of trouble when there's a local dance. You know, the gangs come in from Ipswich and Colchester looking for trouble, for a punch-up.'

Blake made no answer and Shelley continued.

'You come up every day?'

'No.'

'I thought you might be a regular.'

'Thank God I'm not.'

For a moment Shelley was nonplussed; then he said, 'It's not so bad—you get used to it. The wife and I think it's worth the fag of going up and down five days a week for the privilege of living in the country. As a matter of fact, I used to catch the seven-twenty.'

Again, Blake made no comment. His eyes had left Shelley to gaze once more out of the window.

'Gone up a bit in the world,' said Shelley. 'Means I can catch the later train in the morning. Of course I'll have to catch a later train in the evening—the six-forty. You know that train?'

Blake dragged his attention away from the scene outside the carriage window. 'I know it. I shall catch it tonight. It's a sardine tin. It's also hell if you don't get on the train at least fifteen minutes before it starts.'

'Sounds like the five-thirty—that's the one I used to catch. I'll soon get used to the form. You learn a lot travelling up and down. I knew a friendly bunch on the five-thirty—they'd save you a seat —a good crowd. We've had a lot of laughs.'

'Then you'll get plenty on the six-forty—it's a tragi-comedy.' Blake spoke without humour, longing for Shelley to open his *Daily Express* or do-it-yourself magazine and spare him the pleasure of train conversation, but ebullience was running high in Shelley. The buffet car was one carriage away. 'We're running into Colchester,' he said. 'Better get a cup before it fills up. Can I get you one?'

It was a kindness that cut into Blake's introspection. He was tempted to refuse, but Charlie Shelley's open, friendly face smiled at him in invitation.

'That's kind of you, but let me get it—it's your first day.'

'Oh, no,' said Shelley. 'It's my pleasure. I can tell the chaps in the office I had coffee with an RA. That'll impress them.'

'It's not impressive. It's like being old before your time.'

'You mean like getting your gold watch in five years instead of twenty-five?'

'Just like that.'

'I don't see it.' Shelley shook his head. 'I thought it meant you were right at the top. You know—recognition and all that. The tops and you couldn't do better.'

'Have you been to the Academy? The Summer Exhibition?'

'No—not my line.'

'What about the Chamber of Horrors in Madame Tussaud's?'

'I've been there.'

'Then you've been to the Academy.'

Later, as the train ate up the miles to London, Shelley carried nine-tenths of the conversation on topics ranging from the murder in Suffolk and the mysterious glamour world of artists compared with the more mundane but secure world of his employment in a shipping company to a blow-by-blow account of the rustic ingle-nooked fireplace he'd built into his house on the estate.

Oddly enough, Blake's depression and introspection lessened. It was a relief to listen, with occasional responses, to communication on an intellectually uncluttered level. It also enabled him to make prosaic comments which, in the context of his dialogue with Shelley, seemed simple and wise and rendered life and its living, for the space of the journey itself, an uncomplicated affair. And when they parted at Liverpool Street, Blake had unbent enough to promise to save Shelley a seat should he be first on the train.

PC Weston, third carriage from the end, listened to the boys home from boarding school. One of them he knew: Dennis Tilling, The Lodge, Gaston Street, East Bergholt.

'Home for the holiday?' he asked.

'Yes.'

'Where are you off to now?'

'Science Museum.'

Kemp, huddled in a corner seat, went deeper into himself. There was an outer unease in his mind: one connected with the deeper unease, imminent and dangerous. The smiling man talking to the boys spoke in a certain manner; not cultured, not country; it was the way in which he asked questions—innocent questions.

Hand gripped gun in pocket more tightly. There was an urge to use it rising up in him and he didn't know why. He'd escaped—had run away—yet he felt as near to danger as he had been in the track-worker's shed.

Then it came to him. The smiling man wore a blue shirt and

black tie; the way he asked questions. A nervous tic started up in Kemp's right temple.

Weston's eyes left the boys and glanced at the man in the corner. Trouble there, he thought, much trouble. The face was drawn and grey, immediately averted as Weston's gaze settled on him. RIP, thought Weston, remembering a song his father sang, there's another good feller gone west.

Escape again—immediate escape. Eyes averted, Kemp got up and opened the sliding door, edging through a minimum of space. Then he was down the corridor and gone.

Weston watched him go. Some people carry their troubles like a sack of potatoes, he thought. He committed the man's appearance to his trained memory—age around fifty, thinning hair, mouse-coloured, height five eight, weight eleven stone. He filed the information away and thought about the Science Museum.

'They've got the Alcock and Brown Vickers Vimy in the Museum,' he said.

'It's the lunar module we want to see.'

'Yes, but take a look at the Vickers Vimy. Do you know it took Alcock and Brown nineteen hours to fly the Atlantic from Newfoundland to Ireland?'

Dennis Tilling's face twitched into a grin. 'What held them up, sir—string?'

In the driver's cabin, Denning and Wellford watched the distant mound of Colchester draw near. The Town Hall spire gleamed in the sun, which was now above the horizon and striking high ground.

'Don't like the colour of the sun,' said Wellford. 'I know that colour and it's too bright. There's rain coming in.'

'Not before we reach London.' Denning gave bugle warning as the diesel approached Colchester Station. 'With luck, we'll run ahead of it.'

As H109 entered Colchester Station, Maurice poured Scotch from the miniature bottle and handed the glass to Mr Thorpley.

'All right, sir?'

'Coming up to par.' Thorpley peeled off a pound note from a crisp roll and handed it to the steward. 'You must have one with me.'

'Very nice of you, sir. I'll save it till we get to Liverpool Street. Regulations and all that.'

He took the price of a Guinness and gave Mr Thorpley his change. 'Back on the four-thirty, sir?'

'No—the six-forty. I have an aunt to see—a difficult aunt. The Scottish branch of the family.'

'The Monday one?'

'The same. A very difficult woman.'

Maurice grinned. 'Then I'll see you, sir. On the six-forty. I'll set you a couple aside. Avoid the rush.'

'I thought you did the four-thirty run.'

'I swapped. Do a bit of Christmas shopping. Charlie'll do my usual run.'

'I don't know what I'd do without you and Charlie,' said Mr Thorpley. 'You both seem to understand my needs.'

Like a well-trained bloody servant, Maurice thought. With customers like Mr Thorpley, mind you, you didn't mind giving the old 'Yes, sir—no, sir—three bags full, sir.' And it wasn't just for the extra bunce you earned by acting obsequious. There were bastards who treated you like dirt, those that never thanked you, the complainers and the queue-jumpers. Maurice disliked the jumpers, they were clots and slow-witted. They'd see a queue ranging from the left in decent order and promptly take up position on the right. So he ignored the stupid buggers and denied them the slightest acknowledgement that they existed.

Maurice was fifty, with black, balding hair and a mobile face whose range of expressions had been developed over many years of practice. Before BR economy cut down on dining facilities he had been head steward of a Pullman dining car. There he had learned how to call an old cow Madam and pigs Sir—and all done with a smile and thank you for your patronage, Your Highness.

There was an art in dealing with habitual complainers. You'd listen to their grumbles about the food, inspect the source of their grievance and agree to do something about it, instead of ramming the plateful into their silly mugs. Then you'd take the dish back to the galley, rearrange whatever was on the plate and return with the chef's compliments and apologies and hope that Madam or Sir will now find the dish to their liking. That was in the good old days.

The good passengers made life worth living and the job worth having. Many of them were themselves doing jobs they didn't particularly like, yet made the best of it and found time to crack jokes.

It was difficult to place Mr Thorpley. Obviously he had money, and he spoke in an educated voice. He dressed well and viewed the world with a kindly eye. Maurice had tried many times to ferret out of him the manner in which Mr Thorpley earned his wealth, if earn it he did, but it was always the aunts. It was worth having another go, though.

'Hard business day ahead, sir?'

'A very hard day. I have to control my aunts' financial affairs. Also, I seem to have more aunts than most people.' Mr Thorpley switched the conversation to other trivialities. 'I haven't seen the dreaded solicitor bore this morning.'

'He passed through,' said Maurice. 'He only pesters the buffet when he can't find someone to talk at.'

'And then he bores you?'

'Don't give him a chance. I expect he's found a victim.'

Mr Thorpley glanced through the window. 'Better set me another to one side, Maurice—before Genghis Khan and his army invade the train.'

Annersley was enjoying himself. He had steered the conversation round to the recent de-canonisation of saints. As a Roman Catholic he welcomed the action of the Vatican, he told Thorneycroft. Really, these odd, insignificant pedestrians cluttering up the saintly order of things. The coinage had been debased, didn't Thorneycroft agree? Of course, the Pope's action had deprived the Anglican Church of a number of worshipful figures—poor old George and Christopher for instance, always held in low regard by the Mother Church but of special significance to the Anglicans. Mm?

Thorneycroft said: 'I don't concern myself with haloes. To be Christian is all I ask of any man.'

He asked earnestly, fervently; he prayed for it. The fact that men were not Christian was a fault he partly laid at his own door. Vanity was the great sin. Individuality and its quest, the vice from which they suffered.

Annersley looked through the window and observed with an expression of distaste the unbroken parade of commuter faces lining Colchester Station's platform edge.

'Have you noticed how the style, the class of person changes with the Colchester influx?' he asked. 'And Chelmsford is much worse.'

'Different environment—different problems.'

'Quite,' said Annersley. 'Exactly what I mean. A pity they let them on this train. To paraphrase Scrooge, "Are there no cattle trucks, no galleys?"'

Knowing the form, Mr Rae had been the first of the Colchester commuters to head the queue at the buffet counter, while Sellars, his regular train companion, had begged two side-by-side seats in the non-smoking section of the car.

Mr Rae now observed, as he looked suspiciously into his coffee, 'The ability to adjust to a new condition is one of man's greatest gifts—to British Railways.'

'Rule Britannia!'

'Now that was a train. Do you remember, in those days, how coffee was served in real china cups—green glazed china cups— *with saucers?*'

The train clattered over a series of points and the level of Mr Rae's coffee angled dangerously. He lifted the cup by its brown plastic holder and balanced the level before it could dribble over the side.

'That wouldn't have happened in the old days of steam,' he said.

Sellars nodded. 'No slosh—only smuts coming through every nook and cranny.'

He folded his *Daily Telegraph* into a neat rectangle, anxious to settle down to the crossword, aware that his companion was gazing into the distance and down memory lane.

'Ninety-four tons four hundredweight, with a tender weighing over forty-nine tons,' said Mr Rae; 'and a tractive effort of thirty-two thousand pounds. Four six two—seven P six F.'

Sellars frowned his puzzlement. 'What's that?'

'Made at Derby,' said Rae. 'One of the finest steam locos ever —the Britannia.'

'What does four six two mean?'

'Four bogies, six driving and two rear wheels.'

'To say nothing of the noise and the soot and the breakdowns.' Sellars shook his head. 'You'd have done well as the man walking in front with a red flag, Reg.'

'Like a true pioneer.' Mr Rae went silent, listening to the beat of wheels on rail. 'The voice has changed,' he said, at length. 'The voice of the railroad has gone modern. Welded stretches of rail— you might as well be in a bus on the A12. But the sound of an old loco! Poosh-poosh! Poosh-poosh! as it climbed a gradient. Beautiful sound. And the diddley-dong—bungely-ding—diddely-dong—the beat of wheels on the track. No more—all gone.'

He belonged to every railway preservation society in the United Kingdom and couldn't explain the mystique. He would say, 'Either you are or aren't—it's as simple as that.'

It was the heroism of the old days that appealed to him. The smokestacks of the locomotives breathing out fire, steam and smoke; the blackened face of the fireman beneath the knotted handkerchief cap; the open cabins in fair weather or foul. It was man against the elements and the driver was the skipper—a real captain.

'And what is it now?' he asked, rhetorically. 'A push-button affair in which the driver is only partly responsible for the safety of his train. In fact we're dangerously near the time when a driver will be unnecessary. Trains will be so automated that—well, do you remember the old departmental stores where they put your bill in a cylinder and shuttled it to the cashier? Click—zip—and compressed air sent it on its journey up and along and ting! That's how it'll be. Passengers will enter a cylinder and the mastermind at the station will push a button and an electrically impulsed automatic track braking system will ensure required stops, just as automatically controlled checkpoints will operate against the danger of collision. We'll be computerised to our offices and homes. All humanity gone!'

Sellars found trains boring. 'What the hell?' he said. 'I'd have thought safety was the great thing. You can have the old mizzen masts and galleons—I'll travel Jumbo jet.'

'You've missed my point,' said Mr Rae. 'The railways will be geared for safety—and we will have—what?'

'Safety?'

'Bigger and better accidents. Shall I tell you what I wait for?'

'Stephenson's Rocket?'

'I wait for the first Jumbo jet to crash. It's the way things are going—the laws of chance. You won't find—on paper that is—a safer aircraft than the Boeing 747, yet—and mark this—by the laws of chance at least one of them will come to a sticky end. It's in the nature of things. Four hundred passengers on board. Consider it. A safe aircraft, every possible contingency catered for, but it will happen. Bigger and better accidents—*that's* my point.'

Sellars wasn't impressed and said so. Rae turned a triumphant face on him. 'Name one type of aircraft that has never crashed —just one.'

Sellars' lack of interest in aviation equalled his ignorance of railway affairs. 'There must be one,' he said.

'Not one. I've done my research. The number of Jumbo jets in service will rise, and so the chances of an accident will increase. Speed and safety don't go well together. You can't have your cake and eat it. Slower vehicular transport means safer transport. We're going too fast.'

'It's the human error that's at fault,' said Sellars.

'Granted,' said Rae: 'And why? I'll tell you why. The human factor is inhibited by mechanisation so that when it's called upon to make a decision, a judgement, it's unable to cope.'

'You're a thundering Jeremiah.'

'A prophet of doom. Yes—I accept that.' He looked at his watch. 'We seem to be running on time. Good—I don't want to be late this morning.'

Sellars grinned. 'Speed's of the essence, then?'

'We're travelling no faster than the Britannias on this very same run. A safe speed on this stretch of rail.' He looked out of the window and pinpointed their location. 'A few miles outside Chelmsford. Time for the crossword, I think.'

Across the aisle from Rae and Sellars, Edward Ferris felt a mounting anxiety. In a few minutes the train would slow down for entry into Chelmsford Station. There, like a neap tide, commuters would surge on board, thrusting and predatory for seats. Somewhere in that flood Helen would be jostled and pushed, or perhaps there would even be no Helen, and he wanted desperately to see her. As always he had saved the seat beside him in a state of acute embarrassment, even going to the extent of lying when asked if the seat were free and furnishing the empty place with cup of coffee and newspaper.

He wanted desperately to see her. After the weekend's misery he needed her presence to reassure him that a good life existed somewhere.

Oh God—oh God! The morning train prayer was always the same. Oh God, let her catch the train! Oh God, don't let a belligerent call me a liar and take the seat I've saved for her!

Oh God—oh God!

'Train's gooin' too fast,' said Harry Peartree. It was impossible for him to focus on the flashing, dazzling strip speeding past the carriage window. Now and then, when the track embankment dropped its level and a long view of the Essex countryside ap-

peared, it seemed that the train had slowed down and Harry's
mind and eyes received a picture of fields, trees and horizon that
satisfied his comprehension. But then the flashing strip would appear again with its illusion of fantastic speed and his resentful
mind was troubled again.

'Too bloody fast!'

Looking at the angry old profile, Mabel could see little evidence
of the man she had married fifty-one years ago. It was as if there
were two men: the young man of twenty-three, joyful and lusty
still in his relief that he had survived the last two years of the Great
War, and the present, grumbling, hard-working, fretful old man
for whom she felt a motherly, all-forgiving, protective affection.
He must have been other men between the years, but she couldn't
remember him at forty, or fifty, or even sixty. The years had gone
by unnoticed, the process of living affording little time for
reflection.

Mabel Peartree was not given to introspection; she had old
Harry's dictum to support the wisdom of letting one's mind alone.

'Thinkin's bad for the mind, girl. Ent no time for it.'

But she couldn't help thinking as the miles peeled out under
the wheels of the train. Harry operated in two strictly regulated
areas; she wondered which he was in now. In the first area he was
both master and labourer, fiercely independent and individual to
the point of non-cooperation, and in the second, the day's mascu-
line labour done, he took his chair by the Kitchener stove, to be
waited upon, receiving his bed and board without lifting a hand,
expecting, and always getting, her devoted attention. He hadn't
washed a dish in his life, Mabel thought, and that's how it should
be; it lessens a man to wear an apron.

She switched her mind from Harry to the prospect before her;
it would be nice to see Peggy again, and her son, Colin. It would
be nice to see all her children again; to have them gathered under
the cottage roof like the old days. But they were scattered, all five
of them, and living their own lives, sparing the odd day to visit
the old ones in Bergholt. On these visits Mabel wondered if they
had been wrong in rejecting Mr Madden's offer to build them an

inside toilet; she knew her grown-up children disliked the fly-buzzing closet at the end of the garden. Peggy never complained, but then she was the best of the lot. Of the five daughters she had always shown the greatest patience in bearing with Harry's irascibility.

Wine. She thought of wine because Peggy always flattered her father on the excellence of his home-made wine, which was, sometimes, good. Every year he would put down twenty gallons—why should he pay through the nose for shop muck? Beetroot, blackberry, carrot, parsnip, rhubarb—*'That gits yer gooin, girl'*—anything the good earth gave up under Harry's green fingers could be turned into wine. Good earth, that is, enriched with the weekly collection from the privy. From pea-pod to wheat and raisin, all Harry's bottles were subjected to his rigid discipline—'No atastin' o' that for four year.'

As if he had homed in on Mabel's thought process, Harry said: 'The general give me a glass o'—claret, 'e called it. Muck, it were —muck! Tart as vinegar.'

'What made you think o' that?'

'What?'

'The general.'

Harry frowned, the claret-memory forgotten. 'They flooded 'is land—orchards an' all.'

The train was taking them further and further away from the cottage and the familiar and trusted furniture of their lives. There was only one advantage, thought Mabel, in risking life and limb on a perilous journey to the hell called London—it would be good —oh, so good! to get back to the glowing Kitchener stove and the mantelpiece with its china dogs and presents from Clacton and Felixstowe and Lowestoft, and Harry uncorking a bottle of wheat or parsnip wine.

'But it'll be nice to see Peg again,' she said.

'She should've come down to Berg'olt—it ent far.'

'There's her family to look after.'

'They gotta car, ent they?'

Mabel leaned back in her seat and closed her eyes. The rhythm of the train was making her drowsy and she was thinking too much. She dozed a little while Harry sat by her side, resenting every mile of the journey away from home.

As George Denning throttled down for the Chelmsford stop, Wellford said: 'Don't think we're going to beat the rain after all. Funny thing, that—if the wet's travelling at, say, forty miles an hour and we've averaged more, how come it's overtaking us?'

'Search me.'

They passed the signal-box on the right and Wellford acknowledged the hand waved from the window.

Commuters were stacked down the platform's edge and Denning said: 'I'll never get rid of the feeling that someone's going to play at silly buggers and jump on the line just as I'm pulling in.'

'A feller did that at Holborn Tube last week. Funny, that—why do they pick the Underground?'

'Search me.'

'Tell you one thing—' Wellford scanned the faces lining the platform's edge: 'You get better-looking birds at Chelmsford than Colchester.'

'That's a fact.'

'I wonder why?'

'You wonder too much, Joe—the rain, suicides, birds.'

'I've got an enquiring mind.'

'Is that what it is?'

Edward Ferris said: 'The coffee's cold, I'm afraid.'

'It doesn't matter—it's still drinkable.'

Looking at her, feeling her close by his side, he felt the unpleasantness of the weekend falling away into the background. He had spent two days crawling across a desert of recrimination and contempt and had found his oasis.

His East Bergholt–Chelmsford neurosis receded also. Fortuitously, the train had stopped to her advantage, the carriage door immediately facing her the most convenient for access to the buffet car.

'Helen?' He felt the love shining in his eyes. She returned his look with a smile, the grey-blue eyes looking into his. 'Thank God you caught the train,' he said.

'I always do.'

'I know, but—accidents happen. You know how it is. Things at home—hold you up.'

And let you down. How he hated and resented the Clan. They had ganged up on him over the weekend. Under the pretence of family unity and the ties of marriage, Margaret's father and mother, her brother, his wife and two children, the whole brood had descended on him Saturday morning for a free weekend in the country.

To be an alien in your own house was humiliating and, since no secret was sacred, he had had to bear with the knowledge that they knew every detail of his life with Margaret. His impotence following her miscarriage two years ago was known to them and made known to him by all the means available to the malicious. Even the question *'How are you feeling, Eddie?'* was loaded up to the sexual hilt and, *'Everything all right, then?'* filled with implications. And all the implications were true. But the poison did not come from him; he had taken in the venom when he married Margaret, for he had married a clan of people foreign to every aspect of his nature. To hope for the best was a philosophy guaranteed to make life hell, but it was the only way he knew. He had been sexually moved by Margaret—something rare in his pre-marital days—and he had been grateful. It disproved a nagging fear that had been with him for many years. He'd taken advantage of the offer, hoped for the best and married into impotence and a malicious clan.

'How was it?' Helen asked.

'The weekend? Not too good. And yours?'

'The same. Why wasn't it good?'

'Her family came . . . Helen? Why was it bad for you?'

'A big row—worse than usual.'

And there they left it. They smiled resignedly, understandingly, and talked of less dangerous things. Approaching Romford Ferris said: 'The best thing about Monday is that I'll see you after a weekend without you.'

Helen didn't answer. She stared down at the coffee in the plastic cup and wished that she could break a lifetime of social inhibitions and tell him that now was the time to end with the ritual, the habit of convention, the rut routine of living, and cut adrift, together and on the same raft. An attempt by her husband to claim by force his conjugal rights—she knew the euphemistic word for *that* act— paralleled so aptly by Soames Forsyte in the TV saga, had been successfully warded off by a knee arched up suddenly and painfully into an unsuspecting groin. She could not tell Ferris this; not Edward who moved her to pity and the desire to receive him into her body; it would cause him pain and embarrass her.

Ferris, too, drew back from relating the events of the weekend. He could not tell her that on Saturday night Margaret had reached for him and commented, 'When's this maggot going to get a backbone?'

Never! he told himself. Never with Margaret and yet, even with her, the mechanical success would have pleased him.

They drifted into office talk. Mundane talk accompanied by the mutual comfort of flanks touching as they sat side by side.

Mr Thorpley, now on his third miniature whisky, observed them from the buffet counter as he had watched them for many weeks with liquor-sharpened perception.

'They don't seem to be getting anywhere,' he said to Maurice. 'Who, sir?'

'The inhibited couple. The frustrated ones.'

'Ships that pass in the night,' said Maurice. 'I've seen a lot of them in my time. A lot of other things, too.'

'Interesting things?'

'Used to be a lot of shenanigans in the old days. A couple of tarts plied their trade between Liverpool Street and Clacton in the late forties. Early evening and night trade.'

It was a possibility that had never occurred to Thorpley. Time-and-motion study seemed to suggest that it wasn't possible; the ergonomics were all wrong.

'That's on the level,' said Maurice. 'Where there's a will, there's a way.'

'How many runs would they make?'

'Up and down—maybe six. Five days a week.'

'Did they do well?'

'Seemed to,' said Maurice. 'You can't believe everything you're told, but one of them's supposed to have bought houses in Frinton—very select area.' Maurice shook his head with regret at the passing of time. 'Things were easy in those days. The old Britannias pulled the coaches—Beeching had yet to come. More free and easy, if you see what I mean. You could even ride free if you knew the dodges.'

'And now?'

'All mechanised—very efficient. Collectors know their job. Now one man does the job of four. Comfortable carriages—buffet service—nice uniforms. Everything for passenger comfort and quick turnover.'

'But no organised BR brothel?'

'That'll be the day, sir.'

'Indeed it will. I can imagine the station announcer—"The train now standing at Platform 9 is the four-thirty for Norwich—calling at Colchester, Manningtree, Ipswich, Beccles and Norwich. Refreshment and brothel services are available on this train." '

'Can you imagine the posters?' asked Maurice. 'You know that one—"Don't just sit there—eat something"?'

'I can just see the change in the wording,' said Mr Thorpley. He looked into his empty glass. 'Have I time for another, Maurice?'

'If you've room for it, sir.'

'I have the room—and it's a very difficult aunt I have to see.'

The crossword addicts were hard at work, preference ratio standing at ten *Daily Telegraphs* to two *Times*. The *Times* puzzler was in a class apart and knew it. He played chess while the others played checkers; he arrived at the answers by pure reason and knowledge; the others relied on instinct, smatter-knowledge and the helping hand. The *Times* puzzler was a solitary—an intellectual loner. On the return journey, the *Telegraph* crossworders would nip through the *Evening Standard* cryptic puzzle in fifteen minutes or so; the *Times* reader would complete his morning puzzle with the calm deliberation of one who has thought about the clues and looked up a few reference books.

Elizabeth Marwood, sitting at a table with two *Telegraph* men, caught on to a puzzling clue impeding the progress of the crossword.

' "There's skill in this hunting lady: seven letters." Got to begin with A and end on an S.'

The answer slipped into Elizabeth's mind.

'Art,' she said. 'Artemis.'

The men looked at her admiringly. 'A brain. Should have known it.'

They ballpointed in the letters with relish.

'There's one here. "Hardly a feline trance: Nine letters." C, two spaces, A, four spaces and ending in Y.'

Again the answer slipped into Elizabeth's mind.

'What about catalepsy?'

'Brilliant! Quick as a flash.'

The men were interested. One of them asked, 'We haven't seen you on this train before. Colchester?'

'No. I got on at Manningtree.'

'We're Colchester.' He said it as if admitting to a nationality. 'Are you going up for Christmas shopping?'

'No—I've got a job. Starting today.'

'So you'll be a regular?'

'If all goes well.'

'That's great. What do you think, Frank?'

'We need a brain on the train, only don't help us too much.'

A few miles later, names had been exchanged. Frank Martin was an accountant in a large rag-trade house and John Paton a clerk in a shipping office. She found them pleasant company; a foretaste, she hoped, of the casual, easy world she was about to re-enter. They drank coffee and polished off the morning's crossword.

'What train will you catch tonight?'

'The six-forty.'

'Right. I'll hold you a seat in the buffet car. I'm always the first on the train—you ask Frank. You can take your time—no sense in hurrying to the station when your friendly seat-holder has got there first.'

'Is it a crowded train?'

'Sardine-packed by six-twenty. Worse on Friday nights. Weekend trippers, kids coming home for a weekend with Mummy and Daddy. Hard on the regulars.'

Frank Martin said: 'You'll get to know the bad habits and evil ways of regular travellers. We try to make the daily journey bearable. Regulars hold seats for other regulars. We declared war on the casual traveller years ago. When there's some show on up in London—the Boat Show or the Motor—exhibitions and events like that, we step up operations.'

'Why?' asked Elizabeth.

'Extra passengers, and I *mean* passengers. They don't know one end of the train from the other. Queue up on the wrong side of the buffet counter. Tell you what hurts a regular most—when you find some shopper sitting in your accustomed seat.'

'You feel like shooting him,' said Martin.

'What about the annual WI Conference?'

'Pure hell. They fill up the carriages with their flower hats and chatter like hysterical monkeys.'

'The Chelsea Flower Show.'

'More hats. The Agricultural Show—what about that one?'

'All moo, baa and mangel wurzels—and chaps with hands like bunches of red bananas.'

'And sometimes,' said Martin, 'the coaches are booked solid for parties of school kids. That really hurts. I've heard regulars swearing like troopers because their carriage—their seats—are occupied by a swarm of kids.'

'And what have we got now?' asked Paton. 'Christmas, and tired shoppers taking our seats and clotting up the corridors. There ought to be a law protecting the commuter.'

'So what do you do?' asked Elizabeth.

Paton grinned. 'We make the best of it.'

The ethos of commuter travelling was easy to define; to make heaven out of hell. You sought the company of others, struck up relationships and shared the common neuroses which by their nature made you sensitive to the cares of your fellow. You understood his anxiety as he left his place of business in the evening and raced across London to catch the train. Many hazards lay in the path between office and station and five minutes late in the last sprint up the station escalator could mar his journey on the train. Paton was the scout of his group. His office was near Liverpool Street Station and he could be relied on to get to Platform 9 before the 5.45 from Ipswich rumbled in. Even at the platform's edge or at the starter's gate (a commuter's simile for ticket barrier) the hazards might, and very often did, continue. The train could be half an hour late in its arrival and the queue would build up behind the irritating notice that the train was being cleaned and apologies for the inconvenience. Then the impatient regular would watch the cleaners with their dustpans and brooms move slowly down the trains, his senses keyed up to take in the slightest irritation, to winkle out the lurking queue-dodger who hovered near the starter's gate as if waiting for anything but the train, and then slipped surreptitiously into the queue.

Paton explained: 'They rely on the passive British public not to object. It takes nerve to tell a man, "Take your place in the queue".'

'Why?' asked Elizabeth.

Paton grinned. 'He might say, "What are you going to do about it?" And the answer's—nothing.'

'They do it in the buffet queue,' said Martin, 'but they don't get away with it. On the six-forty, Charlie, the steward, is hot on them. Eagle eyes, Charlie has. Just ignores them. They don't know he's watching, but he is. Eventually they give up or get served round about Chelmsford and that's thirty miles from London.'

'So it's one extra seat in the buffet car?'

'If it's not too much bother.'

'None at all. Welcome to the club. That's six seats to hold. Let me see—briefcase, hat, umbrella, evening paper, raincoat—that's five articles plus me. That's six. One article per seat. Consider it done. I'm the man the casual traveller hates—and I love it!'

The lavatory was a safe refuge. Now and then someone tried the door, but it was only when a thunderous rapping sounded on the door that Kemp came to life, withdrawing the gun from his pocket.

The knuckles again rapped on the door.

'Tickets!'

Kemp made no sound of relief. He slipped the gun back in his pocket and slid the bolt.

'Sorry to disturb you, sir.'

'I didn't get a ticket.'

'Where'd you get on?'

Where? It was a question he couldn't answer. There had been a station at which the train had stopped. Colchester.

'Colchester,' Kemp said.

The collector produced his pad of ticket receipts. 'Just make the train?'

'Yes.'

'Return or single?'

'Single—I'm not coming back.'

'One pound exactly—one hundred new pence.'

Kemp dug into his trouser pocket and clutched all the money he had: two crumpled pound notes, a few coins. He handed a note to the collector and waited silently for the receipt. The collector grinned at Kemp. 'Hope I didn't get you off the throne.'

'No.'

'I don't like knocking at toilet doors—might be a duchess inside —you never know. Got a seat on the train?'

'No.'

'There's a few up front.'

'I'll stand.'

And hide in the lavatory again. He wanted his world to be small and protected.

Rhythmically, the train ate up the miles to London. Conversation and thought monologues littered the coaches like debris before the wind. Some dialogues flourished, others died as topics were exhausted and enthusiasms waned.

'I see the rain's caught up with us.'

'Thought it would. The day started too bright.'

'One advantage over the old steam days I give you—the coaches are more comfortable and the windows command a better view.'

'And no hot smuts in the eye.'

'Sometimes comfort must be sacrificed for beauty. Take the Tal-y-Llyn Railway in North Wales. Primitive and beautiful. Hard seats and smoke galore. I've a book on the subject—you might like to read it.'

'Any love interest?'

'Only the love of trains.'

'You teach all the week?'

'Three days.'

'I was good at drawing when I was a kid. It got strangled at birth.'

'It's just as well.'

'Eh?'

'Some of the students I teach—little talent and great encouragement. A bit of infanticide might have helped the art scene.'

'How do you understand an abstract? You know—Picasso—that sort of thing.'

'Take too long to explain. Just keep looking and learning. You listen to music?'

'A bit.'

'Most of it's abstract.'

'It is?'

'Patterns of sound suggesting moods, actions—even scenes. If you want realism in sound you just record sound effects.'

'. . . totally opposed to priests of the Mother Church marrying. If they don't like the rules they can get out. I'm sure the Anglican Church would be happy to receive them.'

'Why do you suppose an ex-Roman Catholic would be welcomed by a reformed church?'

'A matter of authority. You might say the earth of the Church of England would be enriched. But the nux of the matter is that we don't want sex-involved priests with one eye on the chalice and the other on bed.'

'And that is the view of the Pope?'

'I would say very much his view. Sublimation is of the essence. To be a servant of God, in the priestly sense, one must canalise the whole of one's energy into serving Him. A priest cannot do that cluttered up with family and possessions and a weekly ration of sexual intercourse. Neither must he covet his neighbour's wife, goods and chattels. You take my point? The Franciscan takes the vow of chastity, poverty and obedience—the very essence of Christ's message to the apostles. And it's the only way. To be totally selfless.'

'A man can marry and still serve God.'

'I agree—but in a very humble way. Like me.'

'Is that my third or fourth, Maurice?'

'The fourth.'

'Enough for one morning, I think. I'd better go to my seat and get ready for the exodus.'

'See you tonight then, sir.'

'God willing—He seems to be on my side, so it's very likely.'

'You're wearing your uniform tie and shirt, Mr Weston.'

'It's glued on. Is that a school shirt?'

'Yes.'

'Then we're in the same boat. Are you doing the other museums in South Kensington?'

'No—we want to get to Lambeth—the War Museum. Might get to Madame Tussaud's and the Planetarium, though.'

'You've got a full day lined up—like me.'

'Is it your day off?'

'Coppers don't have days off. Sometimes they're off-duty but they're always on call. I'm going to New Scotland Yard—a week's course in crime detection and procedure.'

'Have you seen the Black Museum?'

'No. Might see it this week.'

'I bet it's interesting.'

'Like the War Museum, full of horrors. And while I've got you pinned to the seat, Dennis Tilling—was it *you* called me "the slowest gun in Suffolk"?'

'I didn't.'

'Come on, now—confess. Make it easy for yourself and you might get a light sentence. Only ten years' hard if you cooperate.'

'Lunchtime, Helen?'

'Of course.'

'The bad taste of the weekend's going. Seeing you made all the difference. Look—the gentleman drunk's on his way to his seat. I wouldn't like his liver.'

'He seems happy enough. I wish I felt the same.'

'One day—soon.'

'You say that every week.'

A course of action to cover two points—the station and the office. A taxi to the bank; cash Hubert's cheque, then to face Max and flannel through the day counting the minutes to tomorrow. And tonight? Tonight I must face Cynthia with the truth and see the panic in her face as I rip away the last bit of security from her life. It has to be done. The process of recovery—if she recovers— might as well start tonight. Will I have the nerve to face Max and the others when tomorrow comes? Will something snap tonight or during the night? If death came without the precursor of pain and suffering. Snap! Like that and—nothing.

Sixty thousand—oh God! Where can I get it?

'Didn't beat the rain after all, Joe.'

'No. Bethnal Green showing up. Landing flaps down.'

'Get the thermos filled at the canteen. Make it strong but milky. Look at those poor maintenance buggers working on the track. Wouldn't like that job.'

'The feller with the hooter's on a cushy one.'

'Highly specialised job. Takes years of training to see a train approach, raise hooter to mouth and give warning. Better tell Coates about the underprivileged hooter-blower. Get him to raise the question of danger money. Takes talent and courage to face bull locos in all kinds of weather with only a hoot between you and a horrible death.'

'What's his pay?'

'Seventeen quid sixty a week, plus overtime . . . We're going to be bang on time. That should please the customers.'

'You reckon Peg'll be on the station ter meet us?'

'She said she would.'

'Why couldn't she an' Ted've come ter Berg'olt?'

'She likes us to see her family in London.'

'Same as comin' down ter Berg'olt. Gittin too old for this lark. Come next Christmas I ain't a gooin on this trip agen.'

'You said that last year, Harry.'

'Then I'll bloody well say it agen. Got better things ter do than spend money gooin up ter London.'

'It's only once a year, it won't hurt you.'

'Ten ter one Peg won't be on the station.'

Collect briefcase, fold *Times* into regulation carrying order, put on hat and don overcoat. Keep up the pretence and nod to fellow travellers as you leave the carriage. I am John Amos Davies, a partner in a reliable, secure and important company of brokers. Given time and solvency I would consider making a new life with Monica. Or is that, like solvency, the dream of an adolescent? I am John Amos Davies, in the best of health and as near death as any man. And in no time at all I will be known simply as a number in one of Her Majesty's prisons. Until that day you will see me as I intend you to see me—a man of property, a man to be respected and envied. On your knees, you safe secure buggers!

Sixty thousand . . . Oh, God—where can I get it?

He'd creep up behind me, twist my arms back and bite the lobe of my ear till the blood came. I hope he died in the war. I hope a German bayonet went into his belly and out the other side. If I saw him now—if Flynn came through that door—I'd let him have it with all barrels. He wouldn't dare face me now. He'd cringe and beg for life but I'd take careful aim and fire once—twice—three times until I was sure he was dead . . . Too many Flynns—they can change the way they look in a second. You'd shoot one and two would spring up out of his blood. They're everywhere. Only one place where you could close the door against the bullies. Only one door and I'm getting nearer to it. Leave the door alone! Stop trying to get in! Find somewhere else to piss!

' "Sounds like someone out of place in, but essential to, a church"—four letters, no clues.'

'What about "nave"?'

'What about nave, she says. Trouble is, she's so quick we don't get a chance to show how brilliant we are.'

'If she'd waited three seconds, we'd have got it.'

'Next thing we know she'll shame us all by completing *The Times* crossword between Colchester and Chelmsford.'

'My old mum told me to beware of clever women.'

'Your old mum was jealous. A bit of the old Oedipus.'

'Remember that clue a few weeks ago—a Greek cat?'

'How else would I know about Oedipus? I didn't start my education until I started doing crosswords. Like another coffee? There's time before the smoke shows up.'

Put down the lid and sit for a bit. There was that scene in the film with those two actors who always played together. Rome–Istanbul express. *The Lady Vanishes,* that was it, and these two hide in the toilet and take it in turns to sit on the bog.

When was that? 1937 or thereabouts, and what was I doing? I was seventeen and picking up girls in Hampstead with Jack Parker and scared to death of doing anything. Lily changed that. The girl next door; she was willing. Up in the Fields–Highbury Fields. I wonder if Mum knew? She knew everything. Must have. Lily Hummerstone. She was wearing a mackintosh. It must have been a chestnut tree–hundreds of them in Highbury Fields. Never felt cold in those days. It must have been winter. Couldn't have been later than seven in the evening and it was dark–a bit rainy. You didn't get Flynn bullies when it was dark–only at school when it was playtime in that stinking, bloody playground with iron gates. Lily? She'd be well over fifty now–she was older than me by three years. Mum must have known Lily and me did it. Mum? . . . Mum–why can't I have a room of my own?

'The greatest mistake the Church made was to drop the Latin. Now the average Mass sounds like a nondescript Anglican service. Latin is a universal language. Go to Mexico, France–anywhere in the world–any Catholic church, and the congregation is bound by a common language–Latin. It's coming down to a level, if you grasp my meaning. Formerly, the Latin Mass transcended the ordinary; one spoke and heard the language of God. Thank heavens we have a strong Pope, otherwise the next thing will be canned transubstantiation and a descent into an easy-going religion, if one can call it religion, of a renegade thousand-and-one mediocre Churches masquerading under the name of the Christian faith.'

'You hold very strong views.'

'A Roman Catholic should. Faith without strength, without obe-

dience to a higher authority—in our case His Holiness the Pope—
such faith is as futile as a french-lettered sex act!'

'As futile as a priest with one eye on the chalice and the other
on bed?'

'Exactly. May I ask what your profession is?'

'Publishing.'

'How very interesting. What sort of books do you publish?'

'Theological, philosophical—very dull.'

'I can't believe that. Perhaps you have *other* ambitions?'

'Mr Weston? That murder at Kettlebatch—you know the one—
the body in a trunk—did you get the man that did it?'

'The case is still open, son.'

'Did you see it?'

'The body?'

'Must have been gruesome.'

'No—I didn't see it, thank God. The Kettlebatch officer did.'

'What would you do if you found a body?'

'Notify HQ and see that nothing is disturbed. Keep villains like
you three away from the scene of the crime. I may be the slowest
gun in Suffolk—'

'It wasn't me called you that.'

'Who did then?'

'My father.'

'Here we are, Joe—green all the way. Platform Nine.'

'Passengers, will kindly extinguish reefers, cigarettes and pipes
and fasten seat-belts. Do not leave your seats until train has come
to a halt.'

'You'd make a good air stewardess, Joe. A blonde wig, a couple of tennis balls and you'd be there.'

As the train lessened speed Kemp emerged cautiously from the
lavatory, right hand deep in his raincoat pocket. Before emerging
he had scraped and washed away as much as he could of the mud
caking his shoes and trouser cuffs.

He glanced through the window of the door facing the lavatory and saw the dense sprawl of East London crawling past the train. It was a comforting sight; like coming home after a long absence. Narrow streets and hiding places, anonymity and people who minded their own business and left you alone—unless they were Flynn.

Deep in that sprawl of London, north-west of Liverpool Street, lay his childhood and the safety of home. Protection. A house in a row, a number 19, whose door he had to kick because he was too small to reach the iron knocker. And inside the house, if it was Monday—was it Monday today?—the smell of washing and the lunch of cold meat, pickles and mashed potatoes and a mother who always had a suggestion when he complained, 'I haven't anything to do, Mum—can I make something?'

He knew, or had known, that it was not there any more—the fresh, breezy smell of washing day, the cold meat and potatoes— even the house itself might have gone. But the secret must still be there; the environment must remain, a sanctuary into which he could crawl and hide from persecution.

The station approach tunnels cut out vision and his feeling of safety increased. He would like to spend the rest of his life in a warm dark tunnel, safe from inquisitive, accusing eyes; safe from open, night fields bristling with frost and the urgency of running, running until lungs and heart felt as if they would burst.

He came out of his reverie as a compartment door slid open behind him. Fear came back and he jerked his head round. There was nothing to justify panic. Along the corridor other doors were opening to emit commuters anxious to get to the front of the train for convenient exits. He moved along with the tide, mingling, until the stream was stopped by an obstruction.

Behind him, a voice said: 'This'll do nicely', and Kemp saw the black tie and blue shirt. There were three rounds in Kemp's revolver. His hand tightened on the butt, index finger curling round the trigger. If the man touched him—Kemp felt a sudden sweat bead his forehead. No—look away—get away! In a moment or two he'd be free—a face in a crowd. Keep free of death. Somewhere, in another life, another time, there had been too much death and he was running away from it.

Thorneycroft had borne Annersley's egotistical monologue with fortitude and patience. Now he listened to Annersley expressing his delight at having had such a pleasant journey to London.

'Good conversation makes this daily grind a pleasure—if one has the good fortune to talk to a fellow traveller with wit and understanding.' And then, as Thorneycroft took umbrella and briefcase from the rack, Annersley said: 'I hope we meet again. In the meantime,' he paused significantly with an understanding look— 'and as I always say, no matter what we have done, God is always with us.'

Ungraciously, Thorneycroft thought to himself: *'Not with you, my friend—the Devil's your fellow traveller.'* Aloud, he said, 'Yes— I believe that to be true.'

'I hope we meet again,' said Annersley. 'Are you returning tonight?'

'I shall catch the six-forty.'

'Good—so shall I—I'll look out for you.'

He watched Thorneycroft's tall, thin frame edge past passengers collecting coats and baggage from the racks. I can just see you, my friend, he thought, chasuble and all, dispensing your Anglican version of the faith with naughty thoughts racing through your head. What a mockery you made of chastity and the marriage vows. But I must have charity. The poor fellow's suffered for it, God knows. When I get to the office I'll see what I can dig up about him. An interesting chap.

Harry and Mabel Peartree waited for the exit rush to lessen before collecting their carrier-bags and stepping out into the cathedral-like cavern of the station. Completely unknown territory lay outside; puzzling, impossible networks of Underground trains and moving staircases; buses that jerked to a stop and barely gave you time to get on before speeding away. No time to ask questions; no time to ask for answers to be repeated; it was all quick and go and don't come again. London's for the thrusting and the Devil take the hindmost.

They stepped down on the platform and moved towards the ticket barrier, Harry fumbling in his coat pockets for their tickets.

'Can't find 'em. Had 'em on the train.'

'The man took them,' said Mabel. 'The inspector came on the train and took the tickets.'

'He giv 'em back. Tore 'em in half and giv 'em back. They won't let us through the gates.'

With relief, Mabel saw their daughter bearing down on them.

'Peggy!'

'Hello, Mum—Dad.'

'Dad can't find the tickets.'

'I giv 'em to the man and he tore 'em in 'arf.'

'It doesn't matter—you'll find them later.'

'They'll want to see 'em at the gates.'

'No they won't. You got seats all right, then?'

'Dad thought we was in first class. Got him worried.'

Peggy Harris, coming up to fifty and the youngest of the Peartree girls, steered them patiently through the barrier and into the concourse where people seemed to move in every direction like ants scattering and looking for order after a nest has been ruined by a spade.

'We go on the Tube to Holborn, then change and get a train to Holloway.'

'I don't want ter go on a moving staircase,' Harry grumbled. 'Last time I nearly went arse over tit.'

'You'll have to, Dad, there's no lift or stairs.'

'What about a bus?'

'Takes longer—besides, it's raining. You'll be all right.'

They were out of place both in speed and appearance. They moved slowly, cautiously, suspicious of the movement around them, disliking the noise and the bustle of posters advertising breasts and crutches.

Mabel said: 'Dad doesn't like the Tube. What's a taxi cost?'

'To Holloway? About fifteen bob. Waste of good money. He'll

be all right. Ted'll get you back to the station tonight in the car. He'll be home just after five. That do you, Mum?'

Everything had increased its speed since last Christmas. Ticket machines shot tickets out like quick green tongues and, just beyond the machines, the escalators rumbled twice as fast as last time—you could tell that by the way people had to run onto them to keep their balance.

'You give me your carrier-bag, Dad—that'll give you two free hands. Just walk on as if you're going along a street and grab the rubber rail. I'll be behind with Mum.'

At the station activity quietened down. The rush hour had been met and coped with. The ants had left one hill to go to another.

Denning and Joe Wellford left H109 to collect the diesel now backing onto the train they had brought in. They would not see H109 until their last run of the day—the 18.40, when they would walk along the same platform to man the loco for the run to Ipswich.

'That's got Monday morning over,' said Wellford. 'Funny thing that—nobody likes Monday. If it was Friday the thirteenth and not Monday the thirteenth, I might understand it. Nothing wrong with Friday. I don't get it.'

'There's a lot you don't get this morning, boy.'

CHAPTER 4

Mid-Morning, 10.00 hrs.

The cheque was drawn on one of those quiet banks which never seem to advertise, and whose façades suggest exclusivity like a secret safe set in a wall behind a genuine Rembrandt. Davies knew the bank, just as he knew the name of every bank in the country—large and small.

Hubert had been discreet despite the paucity of his contribution to the Save Davies Fund; the cheque requested the bank to *'Pay Bearer or Order* One thousand pounds'. No names, no pack-drill. Thank you, Hubert—thank you for presenting me with a test of initiative. Adventure Ltd. I am the Chairman, Board of Directors, Secretary and the whole damned staff of Adventure Ltd. Davies could almost taste the irony of his thoughts.

Traffic lights halted his taxi by a large poster hoarding. A Pan-Am 747 streaming through the eternally blue upper air caught his vision. He read and digested its message, *'Escape to the wide air yonder—by Pan-Am'.* Was that Hubert's recommendation—Cut and run? Or had Hubert written between the lines, *'You've a thousand pounds in cash—let's see you turn it into sixty thousand by the end of the day'.*

How much is a thousand pounds?

As one year's interest, a thousand pounds should call in a loan of ten thousand at 10 per cent. What could be bought for one thousand and sold for sixty? Nothing. A 60 to 1 winner, *that's* sixty thousand. A straw in the wind and nothing more. No more betting. He'd followed the classic pattern and wagered money, other people's money, on the markets and, just as classically, failed to make a killing and repay it. He had lived on the dream of wiping the slate clean.

The taxi drew up outside the discreet bank and Davies paid the driver. He entered the bank with cold authority and presented the cheque with the instruction, 'I'll take it in tens.'

'Very good, sir.'

The cashier gave the cheque a quick inspection and referred to a slip of paper to the side of his counter.

'In tens, you say, sir?'

He took a block of ten-pound notes from his drawer and thumbed quickly through the numbers, withdrawing the amount expertly without disturbing the neatness of the stack. He thumbed a double check on the number he had counted and slid them across the counter with a smile.

'One thousand, sir.'

'Thank you.'

So easy, thought Davies. Hubert could walk into this bank and cash sixty thousand, the only question asked being, 'How will you take it, sir?'

He fitted the surprisingly small stack of notes into his wallet with the air of a man who had withdrawn his day's expenses and nodded to the cashier.

'Good morning.'

'Good morning, sir.'

Now what? Davies left the bank and hailed another taxi. He had one more day of status quo in the business house. He would go there in his customary style, bid staff and secretary good morning and enter his office, Canaletto print, mahogany desk, executive suite of sofa and armchairs; an office that suggested an opulent sense of security, and see what the day held for him.

As he came out of the bank, he felt rain on his face. He looked up at the sky; it had clouded over, obscuring the sun with a screen of unbroken grey.

There was enough sunshine in Mr Thorpley's inner life to compensate for the outer lack of it. His destination was a four-storeyed house in St John's Wood, a sizable property and one of many owned by him in various London districts.

'Aunt' was the term he used to describe the lady in charge of each of his houses. She kept house or, as Thorpley might put it, '*Keeps a house*'. Keeps it in order; sees that it is clean and, most important, sees that the tenants are quiet, discreet and pay their dues on the nail.

He had told Maurice that he had to see a difficult aunt. This was partly true; Mrs McCartney was very conscious of her value and rights, and her embrace was that of a friendly and loving anaconda—Mr Thorpley had a long memory, a pleasant memory, of her embraces.

A possessive woman, he thought as the taxi bearing him northwest skirted Regent's Park—affectionate in her way and very conscious of the amount of cash he pulled in every week from the St John's Wood house.

His week of aunts was spent in visiting his houses: two in Fulham, one in Baron's Court, two in West Kensington, two in Bloomsbury and one in St John's Wood, the best of them all. In each house he was known by a different alias; only Mrs McCartney had known him by his real name for many years. In each house he had his own personal flat filled with almost identical ephemera, the most constant of these being a good supply of Scotch.

The taxi passed Lord's cricket ground, took two left-hand turns and came to a stop outside a house in a tree-lined avenue.

'Number twenty-seven, guv.' The driver reached out and hooked his arm and hand round, unlocked the door. 'Didn't I bring you 'ere a couple of weeks ago?'

'You may have.'

'Soon's you gave me the address I remembered.'

Mr Thorpley walked up the short path, noticing the curtain twitch in one of the ground-floor windows. He produced his key and unlocked the front door. A quick nip to sustain his alcoholic balance and he would summon the lady of the house.

It was with a conscious air of authority that PC Weston entered the New Scotland Yard building in Broadway. He would have felt differently had he been in uniform; in plain clothes, despite the police shirt and black tie, it was on the cards he could be mistaken for a detective sergeant or an officer attached to that glamorous section, Special Branch.

He showed his pass to the constable stationed at the entrance doors and requested direction.

'C Department—fifth floor—room one-o-eight. Better hurry up, lad—you've got seven minutes.'

As the lift whined upwards Weston had a vision of promotion. The journey from East Bergholt to New Scotland Yard was a long haul, but why not—why not? Others had done it—others had come up from the sticks and the beat. He had all the basic qualifications, indeed, he had more than most; eight O levels and one A was higher than the requirement and, although he just touched the minimum height allowed in the Force his record after five years' service was good if unexciting.

Room 108 was filled with officers in mufti. Weston entered and looked for a familiar face. A wave of a hand caught his eye and he saw the round, beaming face of Rogers from Colchester in the far corner.

'Are you going back tonight?' Weston asked.

'Not me, boyo. Christmas comes but once a year. Do the wife a bit of good having me out of the house for a week.' Rogers smiled broadly. 'Do me a bit of good, too, I shouldn't wonder.'

'Well—watch it. London's a place of wicked temptations.'

'Like Colchester? Tell you what happened last week.' Rogers chuckled. 'Some poor feller going to a drag party. Parks his car in the Library car park—you know the one. He's pretty proud of the job his wife's done on him—blonde wig and eyelashes. He walks down Culver Street and wants to pee. Sees the lavs opposite the toy shop on the corner. This chap's bladder's pretty full, you understand. So what does he do—mm?'

'I can guess what's coming.'

'It's round about eight o'clock and dark. Not many people about. He can't go in the Gents' like that so down he pops into the Ladies'. There's a girl down there. She doesn't like the look of the legs or the size of the shoes. So up she goes and, as luck would have it, Bernie Underwood's taking in Culver Street on his beat. She makes her complaint and, as the poor bastard comes out of the lav, Bernie takes him and lugs him off to the station.'

'He's been charged?'

Rogers nodded, the smile fading from his face. 'Bernie deserves a kick in the balls. I mean, what would you have done in that feller's position?'

'I wouldn't have been in it in the first place. Anyway, maybe the man's got a record. Any man putting on drag is weird. A real kink.'

'You've no sense of humour, Steve. None at all.'

Exactly on the stroke of 10.15, Detective Chief Superintendent Greenlaw entered the lecture room. He arranged his notes on the lectern, raised his eyes and scanned the men standing to attention. He held their gaze in silence for a moment, then smiled and said: 'Be seated, gentlemen.'

He scanned them again, briefly, as if committing to memory every one of the thirty faces.

'Your week of phased courses will be spent in this section of the Yard, C Department, which deals with all aspects of crime; the Flying Squad, Special Branch, Criminal Records Office, the Forensic Science Laboratory and the Fingerprint Branch are all within this department. I am Detective Chief Superintendent Greenlaw and I am attached to C Department; it's my job today to introduce you to your week of study. . . .'

Looking at Greenlaw, Weston saw the face of experience—the face of a copper who had made it. Few officers had not heard of Greenlaw. The last eight years had seen his star in the ascendancy with an imposing list of successful cases, all of which had hit the headlines. Tenacity, patience, perception and strength—essential qualities in a policeman—these were the natural endowments of Greenlaw. But he was also a hard man and expected others to drive themselves as far as he drove himself. Critics of Greenlaw would offer the failure of his marriage as evidence of his rigid devotion to duty, adding yet another paraphrase to the done-to-death, 'No greater love hath any copper than he who lays down his wife for his beat.'

With the ease of a man who tells a familiar story, Greenlaw launched into an account of the function of C Department, and Weston listened, determined that this course was a corner-stone in his rise from police constable to something approximating the status of Greenlaw.

She steered them across London, bearing with patience a grumbling old Harry, and a Mabel who followed her daughter's directions with painful attention.

They walked down the Holloway Road, as ugly as Mabel remembered it. In the drizzle it looked even more depressing than her last Christmas memory.

'Not far now, Mum,' said Peggy. 'We'll have a cup of coffee when we get in.'

Harry shook his head. 'Rather 'ave tea.'

'Tea, then—whatever you want, Dad.'

It was better when she got them in the house and settled them down in armchairs. She made a pot of tea and fussed them into restfulness, and prepared to spend the day listening to memories and a tally of village happenings that now meant so little to her. There was also the contents of the carrier-bags to be sorted out; the wrapped Christmas presents; the jars of jam and horse-radish made from roots grown by Harry and grated and packed in vinegar by Mabel; the photographs taken last summer by Florence, the oldest Peartree girl; and, to the old people the most interesting information of all, a necrology of those who had passed on in the village since they were last in Peggy's Islington house.

At twelve o'clock Harry slipped off into a doze. Mabel watched him for a while, then joined Peggy in the kitchen and helped prepare lunch, noting with approval that her daughter had stuck to tradition: cold beef, mashed potatoes and pickles; food Harry expected to be on the table every Monday. The only thing missing, to his mind, was the smell of washing day and the sight of clothes hanging on the line. Instead, he went to sleep to the roaring sound of Peggy's washing machine and spindryer.

Eight miles away, in the City, Elizabeth Marwood had already settled down to her first task which had been designed to help her understand the nature of the company's business. The office manager had been very kind, and spoke about amiable crews and happy ships.

The offices were light and large, the typewriters were quieter and electric, girls smarter and certainly less cowed than they had been. The men, too, looked nicer; their hair was longer, suits smarter. She looked down at her suit; perhaps she was too severely dressed; well—she could soon change that.

A man in his late twenties came to her desk with a smile on his face.

'Mrs Marwood?'

'Yes?'

'I'm Chris Johnson—from Africa and India.'

'Africa and India?'

'The department. Look—some of us always take a new girl to lunch on her first day. It's a sort of custom that's grown up. I hope you won't refuse.'

She looked at him wondering why she didn't feel an age-gap; why she did not feel twelve years his senior. Being referred to as a 'new girl' was nice.

'Say you'll come.'

'I don't think I can refuse—if that's the custom.'

'In this case, it's not just custom.'

'How many of you will take me to lunch?'

'Just three of us—and all gentlemen.'

Later, as she drank the coffee, which tasted real and had been brought to her, she felt a flush of contentment. A little later, guilt edged in as she thought of her husband alone in the house at East Bergholt; alone with his sense of failure. Take your time, Hugh, I've saved the day and myself into the bargain. I promise I will not turn into a dominating bossy female. I've liberated without burning my bra in public. Didn't I promise to comfort you in sickness and in health? Well, I shall earn twenty-five pounds a week—isn't that a comfort? I've the best of both worlds and I intend to enjoy them without rancour—do you understand that, Hugh? Without rancour. Mortgage repayment, insurance premiums, the basic expenses, the weekly blood-letting, is now in my hands. So take your time, Hugh—the time will come when you'll be able to pitch in and we'll work it fifty-fifty which is how things should be. You'll be removed of the necessity to support me and remember, should anything happen to you, I'm in harness again and earning a good wage. That's better than an insurance policy worth two thousand pounds in the event of your death. These things must be talked about; it's not morbid, just a fact of life—and death.

She was looking forward to lunch with Africa and India; it was years since she had been entertained in the context of a woman who was her own mistress with time to call her own. Looking out of the window she saw that the morning sun had quite gone and it was raining hard, rendering the view across the Barbican a drab, monochromatic city landscape.

Like a bedraggled grey homing pigeon, Kemp trudged the last hundred yards to the Angel, that busy cross-section of streets and roads marking the boundary between Islington and Finsbury. It still resembled the Angel of his childhood; the buildings were the same, only the shop fronts and names above them had changed. Rosenblooms, in which his mother had bought him a grey suit, was now called the Risoli Grill.

He crossed City Road and entered Upper Street. To the left, a road forked off. To Chapel Market, he remembered, and then to Liverpool Road and Palmers Place and Madras Place, St James Street and the school with the iron railings.

Like clips of old film scenes from his childhood flashed into his memory, driving out the immediacy of the terrible confused recollection he had left behind in the darkness of the cold Suffolk night. Only the man was there, in a dilapidated, run-down smallholding; the child, Billy, was walking the streets of Islington along safe, tested roads that led to another time into which he could escape. He *was* that child disguised as a man and the gun in his pocket— he gripped the butt firmly—was a cap gun. The thought cheered him, he had enough money to buy several boxes of—what were they called—amorces—that was the word—another name for caps.

A cinema on the left, the Regal. It used to be called the Blue Cinema, he remembered. And, a few hundred yards along on the right-hand side, the Ritz, which was a cut above the Blue. *Three Smart Girls*—that was the title of the first film he'd seen there. The memory was so clear he could almost hear Deanna Durbin singing and his mother humming a tune from the film on their way home to Ringcroft Street.

No. *King Kong* had been the first film he'd seen in the Ritz. The Army planes diving and wheeling on Kong poised on top of the Empire State Building; the great simian hand reaching out and catching one of the planes as it came in with machine guns blazing. And then the dying Kong, riddled with bullets taking one last sad look at—Fay Wray?—then tenderly, with the last of his strength, placing her gently down to a place of safety before toppling off and falling to the street below.

'*Night winds calling melancholy.*' Why should those words come into his head? '*Where the drooping holly—*' Another Ritz memory? Crosby . . . '*Mourns my tragedy—*' *The Big Broadcast* and his mother had bought a gramophone record; 'Please' on one side, 'Here lies love' on the other. '*All my thoughts are jumbled, everything is blurred.*'

Kemp gave voice to his memory and sang quietly in a weak imitation of Crosby.

'*Please—lend a little ear to my plea—tell me that you love me too. Please, won't you hold me tight in your arms, I could tell you all of your charms.*'

The Lives of a Bengal Lancer and Kemp had pummelled the plush on the top of the circle balcony until the dust rose. Cooper being gunned down at the end of the picture, dying heroically and for a good cause. The Jack at half-mast.

How real the faces were. Franchot Tone and Gary Cooper, Bing Crosby and Deanna Durbin, the grizzled mask of King Kong dying high above New York, persecuted and murdered by people who didn't understand what it was like to be persecuted.

Glamour faces receded into the past and out of it came the grinning evil face of Flynn. Kemp felt again the teeth nipping the lobes of his ears, a sharp pain added to the stretched ache of his pinioned arms. The misery of playtime in the paved yard of his school in Islington; the torture of apprehension as he kept his eyes open for the approach of any one of the bullies, but especially Flynn. And the fear of using the school latrine; Flynn would wait and commit painful, depraved things on your privates. Sometimes Manzi would join Flynn and make him watch Manzi bring his thing to twice its size and squirt. Even now, Kemp felt sick as he remembered Flynn making him do it to Manzi.

Kemp suddenly felt hollow, emptied of strength. A tremble started in his knees and spread upwards. He was cold and hungry; cold through hunger. Ronald Colman in the closing sequences of *Lost Horizon,* going home, going to where he most wanted to be. Forever plodding upwards through the ice and mountains, on and on until he reached the valley and eternal life. He'd seen that at the Ritz, too, and he'd liked the girl in it waiting for whatever his name was to return to Shangri-La.

He found a café near Highbury Corner, and sat on a high stool looking out so that he could see across the road to the near distant trees of Highbury Fields. He drank strong tea and chewed at a crusty roll, oblivious of the others in the café and the transistor belting out pop; he was staring at the memory of a little boy paddling in the pool in Highbury Fields or collecting conkers under the chestnut trees. Oblivious, too, of the news flashes; that the police wished to interview a man in connection with a double murder in Suffolk. But had he heard it he would not have connected the man with himself; he was a boy in the windy, sunny days of pre-war years.

He chewed on the roll and heard nothing, saw nothing but the words and pictures of the past, oblivious to the repeated requests of the man on the stool nearest him that he be given a light.

Davies rejected the proffered cigar with, 'Thanks—you know I don't use them.'

Max Viscenti, senior partner of the Company, returned the cigar case to his pocket, clipped the end of the cigar he had selected and leaned forward as Davies clicked the table lighter into flame.

'A change in plans,' Viscenti said. He drew on the cigar until its tip glowed. 'I'm off to Bonn—twelve o'clock flight. Hope it doesn't put you out. A few days, that's all.'

'When will you return?'

'The 22nd.'

'You'll miss Accounts Day, Max.'

'I know. I want you to see to that. All right?'

All right? Was an extension to his life all right? Deliberately calm, Davies said: 'Why Bonn?'

'Fund transfer—our Swiss bankers don't like it.' Viscenti smiled. 'But then, they're supposed not to like it.'

'I'm sorry I wasn't able to do it.'

'Not your scene—mine. When I threaten it has point. I told Geneva I'd go elsewhere for better rates.'

'And did you?'

'I did—and I'll get them. It'll cost me five thousand in the right pocket. What the hell—spend five thousand and save a hundred thousand.'

Looking at Viscenti's Italianate features—the golden tanned dark face, volatile and sardonic—Davies felt his own face colour with a flush of relief. He relaxed his muscles and leaned back in the chair, savouring the partial peace that had come to him. The one day's grace had turned into nine.

'Just hold the fort,' said Viscenti. 'Make lots of money, or at least don't lose any.'

Viscenti had the knack of making adversaries feel like sitting birds. Davies felt this as Viscenti's perpetually mocking face smiled at him across the table.

'I hope you enjoy your visit,' he said. 'Will you mix business with pleasure?'

'I always do.' Viscenti leaned back in the chair and drew on his cigar. 'You should do the same, John. You catch the same damned train every evening unless I twist your arm. Plums and peaches still grow on trees, you know.'

'I know. I haven't had a peach for a long time. Perhaps when you get back, Max, we'll go fruit-picking together.'

Viscenti said pointedly: 'Things all right with you?'

'Manageable.'

'Good—I was a little worried. People talk, John.'

'Things were tight for a while, that's all.' Davies smiled and returned the interest. 'How about you, Max? The *Sunday Times* wasn't very complimentary.'

'A pin-prick. The voice of envy. My answer will be in the *Observer* in a couple of weeks. A whole page devoted to the Great Viscenti and his rise to power. That'll make the City sit up.'

And in two weeks the City will sit up and notice that John Amos Davies was in real trouble. Max wouldn't be content with saving the partnership's name; he'd see that Davies was not only discredited but taken for the last ride into ruin. But right now he had a few more days of grace.

'You wanted to see a statement of my accounts, Max?'

Viscenti shook his head. 'When I return.'

'Have you told the other partners I shall be acting for the firm?'

'They know. We can have a round-up on the 22nd.'

'Right. There's a little more work I'd like to do on my accounts.'

A little more work on the glaring absence of sixty thousand pounds. He could ask Viscenti. He could say, 'Max—here's a thousand—I need sixty thousand. Don't ask me why. Just give me terms for the loan of sixty thousand.'

And Max would look at him for a long time, suspicion as lively as a panther in heat, then shake his head. What would he say? Something like, 'No trouble about the sixty thousand—I'll give you terms—but I'll have to ask why?'

And there was no cover left. He'd exhausted every disguise known to a money manipulator. He must think of the reprieve— the extra days in which miracles could happen.

'Well, Max—have a good trip.'

'All my trips are good,' said Viscenti. Self-satisfaction glowed in the dark face. He got to his feet and made for the door, where he paused, then turned. 'One thing you might do for me, John, in the next day or so. Take the Inchbald woman to lunch. I want the Inchbald holdings—every one of them. You can get them. Better still, see her today.'

'I'll try to manage it.'

'Not only is she a ripe plum and juicy eating, she's also interested in you, John—or are you tired of women?'

'No—and I am interested in Monica Inchbald.'

'Then make it today—tonight, too, if it's in the cards.'

'You read my mind, Max.'

Max nodded. 'It's a gift I have. I've read the Inchbald's, too. Bed.'

'Then I'll do my best.'

'You do that, and I'm sure Miss Inchbald will do the same.'

Seeing Max's amused smile, Davies said: 'And it's as simple as that?'

'These things are. I believe in fanning sparks into flame. It's the arsonist in me. In any case, the Company apart—' Again the smile, cynical, amused. 'I've never known you to turn down a bite into a ripe plum.'

'Perhaps I've lost my sweet tooth.'

'Then pretend you've got it back. We want Monica Inchbald. Give me a glowing report when I return. Okay?'

'I'll see. Perhaps you'll hear the bang in Bonn.'

'The bang?'

'In lieu of a glowing report.'

Alone in his office, Davies cradled his head in his hands and tried to see through the tangle of worry. Nine days instead of one. If it was a small mercy, it was hard to see where the heavenly pity was being applied. Perhaps the mercy was Monica—the last gift of a benevolent God; an erotic version of the last meal given to a condemned man.

Suddenly, it was a meal he wanted very much.

He reached for the switch on the inter-office communicator and spoke into it: 'Get Miss Inchbald on the telephone, will you?'

The strange thing about Charles Shelley's new job was that he seemed to have less to do for more money and under better conditions. Hitherto he had worked with twelve slaves; now he worked with—you couldn't call them slaves—executives would be a better term—two *other* executives in a room that was the same size and proportion as the previous one. He had understood that progression meant added responsibilities and harder work. Less for less, more for more, that seemed to be the real morality for work. Delegation was obviously a large part of responsibility; he was now in a position to pass on snaggy problems, all he had to do was give them to one of the lesser men, ask that they be done without delay, and then check the result for accuracy and pass it on to higher authority. He was getting more for less. Somewhere, the can—that large receptacle called blame—had grown larger, the lettering on its side '*C. Shelley*' proportionately bigger. And that's what more for less meant. It was the price for carrying a larger can.

He looked out of the window and saw, down the street opposite, the municipal Christmas tree at St Paul's, its fairy-lights twinkling in the rain. '*Happy Christmas!*' shouted the shop on the corner and Shelley thought, 'The same to you.'

Over coffee with Holden and Greaves, his fellow executives and great fellows, he wondered how David Blake was getting on with his art teaching. One lunchtime he'd go along to the Tate Gallery and have a look at one of Blake's paintings. It didn't seem right to know a man and be ignorant of his work. Life was broadening; until this morning the Tate Gallery was merely the name of something you saw listed in the sights of London, like the museums.

'How do you get to the Tate Gallery?' he asked Holden.

'Bit difficult from the City. Take a bus to Westminster—number eleven and change, then a one-five-nine down Millbank.'

'I thought it was Trafalgar Square.'

'That's the National.'

'Yes, of course.'

'Are you going there?'

'Thought I might some time. A chap I know has a couple of paintings there.'

'In the Tate?'

'He's an RA. One of the young ones. Like policemen they're getting younger. A nice chap—we travelled up together this morning.'

But no Tate today, thought Shelley. Today I go shopping for a pre-Christmas present for Edna and the boys. I shall blow ten quid on luxuries and to hell with the flag. It was a day to celebrate; a day to remember.

He didn't mind the larger can.

Coming round to lunchtime, he phoned his wife and reported on the job so far.

'And don't forget, Edna—I'm catching the later train. The six-forty. I'm getting a lift from Edward Ferris. Should be home a little before eight. . . . No—everything's fine—couldn't be better.'

As he replaced the receiver, Holden said: 'You seem pleased with yourself.'

'I am and I know why. It's because I'm a peasant. I was born one and I'll always be one. I like my job and can't see much wrong with my wife and kids. I'm healthy and I like Christmas. I even like catching trains before dawn comes up.'

'You are a peasant,' said Holden. 'I find the job boring, I haven't got a wife and kids, I've got piles and I hate Christmas. And I loathe getting up in the morning.'

'So what does that make you?'

'A sophisticate and don't you forget it.'

The 10.30 from London to Ipswich was approaching Colchester. The rain now covered the south-eastern half of England and extended up into the North.

Just outside Colchester, as the clock in the driver's cabin came up to 11.25, Wellford said: 'How long for the stop-over in Ipswich?'

'We take the sixteen-fifteen up to London—say three and a half hours.'

'What'll you do?'

'A bite to eat and a long nap. What about you?'

'I dunno—a couple of pints—walk round the town.'

'Come home with me. The wife'll feed you.'

Colchester landmarks showed up through the rain; the spire of the Town Hall and the elephant water tower. Denning throttled back and entered the approaches, obeying the speed limits as the track curved the diesel towards Platform 2.

As Denning brought the loco to a halt, Wellford said: 'What about that meeting of Coates' in Ipswich? I thought you might be going to it.'

Denning made a sound of disgust. 'That rabble rouser! Bloody little Napoleon! One day he'll come up against the big boys. Then we'll see how small he is. Big fish in a little sea, that's Coates. He's got a following in Norwich and thinks the whole world's behind him. He'll get no change out of Ipswich. A good dinner and a nap's more important than Coates.'

There was little passenger traffic and the lights winked green dead on departure time.

'Twenty miles to go,' said Joe Wellford. 'If you think it's all right, George—about the meal.'

'She always makes enough for four. You're welcome.'

Up country and to the east, Coates was doing badly. He'd harangued the traffic manager at Acle and received short shrift in the argument that followed, had shunted on three wagons and was now holed up at Great Yarmouth, out of schedule and fuming with high temper as Control sorted out a mix-up of goods movement.

Len Spencer huddled deeper in his shell as Coates ranted on about the soft men and the inefficient.

'If I miss that meeting,' Coates said, 'I'll throw my bloody hand in!' He opened the side door, lowered himself down to the track and strode purposefully across the points toward the traffic manager's office.

Spencer watched him go with miserable interest. Another day like this and he'd ask for a transfer—anywhere. There was nothing to tie him to Norwich or anywhere in the south-east region. He'd no family, he was as free as the air, so why should he suffer the bad temper of a man he was rapidly coming to detest. He'd hoped that underneath Coates' irascible nature lay something worthwhile. That hope had now gone. The outside of Coates was Coates all the way through.

Spencer watched him reach the traffic manager's office and disappear through the door. Another row and Coates would emerge blacker in mood than ever.

Hope you miss your bloody meeting, thought Spencer—it'll get me off the hook. I've had enough of you for one day. His spirits rose at the thought. He looked at his watch—11.00. The meeting had been convened for 12.45. The chances of making it were thinning. There was the possibility of a clear run to Ipswich like the one last week when they had reached Ipswich in an hour. Unless there had been a change in goods movement, which meant veering off the main line and into the sticks, it was still on that Coates would address the meeting he had convened.

Coates appeared outside the TM's door; Spencer could see by his stance that he was still angry. The TM was there, too, indicating a lineup of trucks in track five.

Coates lurched away from the office and made for the diesel. As he climbed aboard he said, viciously, 'Beccles—bloody Beccles!'

Thumbing the diesel to life, he jerked into gear; it forced Spencer back in his seat with a jolt.

'Easy,' he said. 'Easy, Ted!'

'Five bloody gravel trucks—track five. Why weren't they on the diagram?'

'I don't know.'

'I'll tell you why—they don't know what they're bloody well doing!'

Beyond the lights he brought the diesel to a jerky stop at the checkpoint and waited for the points change. When it came, he muttered: 'Take your bloody time!'

He reversed the diesel into track five, head craned out of the side window to watch for the shuntman's signals. A hand was held up to halt.

The shuntman was walking towards the diesel, then clambering up to speak to Coates through the cabin window.

'Your name Coates?'

'What is it?'

'You got this meeting in Ipswich. I'm with you all the way, boy —best of luck. Wish I could be there. Who do they think we are.'

'Bloody lead-swingers—now get off my loco and get shunted!'

The man looked offended. 'Just wanted to wish you luck, mate.'

'All the luck I want from you is those trucks coupled.'

'Sorry—no offence meant.'

The shuntman disappeared and Spencer heard his heavy boot-steps crunching away down the chippings.

'All the time in the world,' said Coates. 'They've all the time in the world. That bloody peasant would lick the boots off Marsh if he thought there was tuppence in it.' He leaned out of the cabin window. 'Get a move on, you bloody cripple!'

Coates shunted the trucks brutally. Spencer's face showed concern and Coates glared at him.

'What are you worried about?'

'Don't like to see a good driver abusing his engine.'

'Balls! I know what I can and can't do.'

Forward to the checkpoint, then track change and reverse to track four, on to turntable and out again on the main line to Beccles. The operation took twelve minutes and, as they cleared Great Yarmouth Station for a promised clear run to Beccles, the time showed 11.15.

'What's at Beccles?' asked Spencer.

'Rail sections trucks—three for Ipswich. Overload—so we get the bloody lot to carry.'

'You'll make the meeting.'

'I intend to.'

Two miles out of Yarmouth, Coates edged the diesel up to full throttle and beyond the permitted speed. Spencer saw a 60 sign flash by and looked at the speedometer—70. Well—that wasn't much above, but it was still wrong. Thank God they were approaching a stretch where even the foulest-tempered driver had to obey the rules. Nevertheless, as they thrummed along the restricted length of track, Coates was still running the loco ten miles an hour above the limit.

In ten minutes they had made Beccles and pointed into a siding where the overload trucks were waiting. The traffic manager came across the track to see them. His message was brief and to the point.

'Sorry, men—a hold-up. Three-quarters of an hour should see you off. They're re-routing chemicals and Army stuff—priority—three wagons—okay?'

Coates' face darkened, frustration bottling his rage; Spencer watched him and hoped the cork wouldn't come out. There could be no meeting now—Praise the Lord, thought Spencer, maybe now Coates would keep to his promise and throw his hand in—if he wasn't all piss and wind. The trouble was that he, Spencer, had to spend the time waiting and the run from Ipswich to King's Cross in the company of a man whose temper would certainly worsen as the day dragged on. A transfer was definitely on, and he'd pull no punches in stating his reasons and to hell with the consequences. Tomorrow he'd see the bosses and tell them he'd had enough. He hoped his reasons would convince them that he had a case.

Meanwhile, he had a difficult day to get through. He snatched a look at Coates seething in silent anger, his eyes staring out through the driving window, loathing everything he saw.

It was coming round to the lunch-break, and Blake was in an uncertain humour due entirely to the scoring of points over his group of four students. It was one of the luxuries of the school that a tutor seldom had more than four or five students in tutorial periods. The practise had come down from the Graphic Design section and he, for one, approved of the change. While he was still available for consultation by students not in the month's tutorial group (it was surprising how little they wanted to consult) it meant that both students and tutor came under personal influence. Previously a tutor's time had been spread out, diffused, among twenty or so students; and since most of them were quite content to do their own thing the tutor's only hope of being noticed was to stand behind them and either make encouraging noises or deprecate the direction in which concept and technique were going.

The morning had been spent mostly in discussion. It had started in the life class, then moved to the tutor's room where Blake had, pointwise, proved that hard-edge painting—which he loathed—was a cul-de-sac without future or value. It had been explored to the very end, had been an interesting experiment, could be recorded in the history of painting but was nothing more.

He had at least put forward an argument which the four students had been unable to refute. Also, he had damned the subculture of pop and Andy Warhol and the tiny world of imagery his students found so satisfying and complete. He told them: 'Include it by all means, but don't make it the whole of your existence or it will let you down. You've closed your minds to the past and, by so doing, you closed the door to your future. In five, ten, twenty years—fads and fashions will change. You're as Conservative as Ted Heath. Bigoted and stuck with the trappings of conformity—your dress, your thoughts, your music, your images—you're regimented. For God's sake show some originality or join the Army, the Salvation or the other thing, and do something useful!'

The students hadn't liked it, but they'd taken it and, as they filed out in silence, Blake knew that he'd earned a nickname that would eventually reach his ears. But he'd made his point and had enjoyed doing so.

Just as he was about to leave the tutor's room, Sally Eversley, one of his group of students, came back. She knocked on the door and entered, her large, dark eyes expressive of something she needed from him.

'Yes, Sally—what is it?'

'You worried me—when you talked to us. I think you might be right.'

'Perhaps I put it too strongly. I wanted to make the point that it might be wrong to put your trust in what proves to be a fashion.'

'That's just it—in the absence of anything else—well, you've got to hold on to something. All my friends, they're like me—my age, the only—well, the only mature people I know are like my parents.'

'There's always me,' said Blake, and smiled.

'Oh—you're different, but I don't know you. Not the way I know my friends. I'm not involved with you, if you see what I mean.'

'You should be—I'm your teacher—I'm supposed to lead you along the right path.'

'That's really why I came back. You made the others angry—said you were straight.'

'That's modern for square, isn't it?'

Sally nodded. 'But I don't agree with them,' she said. 'I believe in what you say. I do, really.'

'Then what's your problem?'

'I'm twenty and you're forty.'

It puzzled him for a moment. The age-barrier question was one he recognised as a fact without the concomitant desire to close it.

'There's nothing wrong with that,' he said. 'I'm not asking you to marry me.'

'That's just it.' The dark eyes were full of sincerity. 'It's a question of involvement. Why wouldn't you ask me to marry you—or anything else for that matter?'

'To begin with, I'm married already.'

Sally shook her head. 'Nothing to do with it.'

'Perhaps I don't want to marry you—or anything else for that matter.'

'Because you've put up a barrier. You're my teacher and you're forty. We don't put up the barriers.'

'You're lecturing me, Sally.'

'No. It's the way we talk to each other. And that's not just a fashion. I want to be taught by you so I want it to be good teaching—and why can't we call you David? Students call teachers by their Christian names in other schools.'

'The Principal is against it.'

'But are you?'

'Not really—I don't think it matters.'

'Some of us nearly choke when we call you Mr Blake. That's straight.'

'I'm sorry—I can't change the rules. It's as much for your protection as mine.'

'Against getting involved, Mr Blake?'

'Say that again and call me David.'

'Against getting involved, David?'

The use of his Christian name loaded the question. The 'mister' ruled out sex involvement; the question might have been purely political. The re-phrasing had turned it into a love cliche, as horny and corny as 'this thing is greater than both of us'.

'You see what I mean,' he said. The barrier between them was wafer-thin. He saw that she was good to look at; that he could touch her if he wished and the caress would not be rejected. His thoughts thickened the atmosphere in the room. The large dark eyes regarded him with an intimacy that he didn't entirely dislike.

'Oh, Sally,' he said. 'Oh, Sally, Sally, Sally!'

Adding to the intimacy, she mimicked him: 'Oh, David, David, David!'

'So what do we do now,' he asked.

'See what happens. I want to be taught by you. If I'm involved and you're involved perhaps my work will be more significant.'

'A terrible word.'

'It's the only one I can think of—it'll have to do. Anyway, a few of us want you to have a drink with us, today.'

'Sounds like a quiet revolution.'

'We've made a list of the teachers we can ask. You're the first. We've also made a list of the teachers we can't ask.'

'Why take the easy ones first? Why not try to convert the hard cases.'

'They're too solid—too far gone. Can you imagine Mr Widmer or Mr Rushton drinking in a pub with unruly art students?'

'I can't imagine either of them drinking with me.'

'So you'll come with us at the lunch-break?'

'You're determined to break down the barrier, then?'

'I thought I had already.'

She really is beautiful, thought Blake. She had the style and looks to back up her direct manner; confidence in the way she knows she is made.

'Are you seducing me?' he asked.

'Something like that—it's all part of involvement. Why do you use such silly words?'

'You learn them when you take up teaching.'

CHAPTER 5

Involvement was taking a different turn in Gracechurch Street. Edward Ferris and Helen had finished a sandwich and coffee lunch in a café and were now both depressed. They had met with a show of affection; the result of a momentary loss of inhibitions, a loss that had allowed them to plunge into the implications of their relationship. While their euphoria lasted they had discussed, too frankly, methods of coping with the immediate future. He had started the discussion with the word 'divorce', since that word contained all that he desired. It meant a divorcement from the Clan, from a way of life he dreaded going home to. For Helen, the word held the same meaning.

Then, as they implemented the necessity of divorce and all that it meant, fear of legal action and social criticism laid a cold, skeletal hand on their enthusiasm. Could they stand the talk and gossip in the office? How much would it cost him, as the guilty party in the divorce? Alimony was a problem and how far could he, in all conscience, drop out? Mortgage repayments on the house came to forty pounds per month. What was the legal position since the house was joint owned between him and his wife? The complications grew more numerous and heavy.

For Helen the case was more simple. It had its difficulties, its unpleasant aspects, but it was legally easier for a wife to leave her husband. She needed Ferris to supply the answer. She needed him to make the decision, then only would her lesser problem be revealed in its true value.

She said: 'Other people seem to manage it.'

And other people sailed alone round the world or climbed unclimbable mountains, thought Ferris. I'm frightened of my own shadow. I haven't the courage to be happy—only to be dull and unhappy.

'Perhaps,' he said; 'perhaps it will reach the point where it really is unbearable. Breaking point, I mean.'

'I reached it this weekend.'

'Don't tell me.'

'I must. He tried to make love to me. It wasn't very nice. If you said to me now—"Don't go home tonight—we'll make it now and never go back." If you said that—'

'I want to say it.'

'Then say it!'

Exasperation was in her voice. She leaned across the table, looking into his face.

'Say it, Edward! We'll write letters now. Give them both the shocks they deserve when the morning post arrives.'

'It's not as easy as that. There's stuff I need in the house. I can't just not turn up. She'd call the police long before my letter got to her. Or she'd raise Cain at the office. You don't know her.'

'Do you think Ivor would take it lying down?'

'Why can't we just go away somewhere—a long way off?'

'You know the answer to that.'

They were too respectable. Too conditioned by a false sense of social responsibility and a fear of trouble disturbing the quiet muddy waters of their life. Their gambler's instinct had been strangled at birth. Only miracles were acceptable. The death of Ferris' wife would have been welcomed by him as an Act of God and, if He contrived at the same time to remove Helen's husband, a double miracle.

In conscious expression of this, Helen said: 'So we wait for a miracle?'

'Something will happen. I love you, Helen.'

'And love can be starved out of existence.'

'Soon.'

Mr Thorpley took the fine bundle of notes—mostly of five-pound denomination—from the hand of the angry aunt and said: 'A good week—how much of it was casual?'

'Fifty-five.'

'I approve of casual letting,' he said. 'Like Bed and Breakfast. In fact, it might be a good idea to put a card in one of the ground-floor windows announcing B and B. You can always tell the serious applicant that we're full up.'

Jean McCartney, in her early fifties, overweight and florid, looked at him with stony hostility.

'You don't seem happy this morning, Mrs McCartney. Any trouble?'

'None in the house. I see to that. You've a lot to thank me for.'

'That's why I pay you so handsomely.'

'That's your opinion.'

'Thirty pounds a week, tax paid and all found, isn't a matter of opinion.'

'I've friends who get forty.'

'I expect they supplement their income by old and tried methods. Why don't you do the same?'

Mrs McCartney glared at him.

'I don't mind you entertaining a few friends,' Thorpley added, 'as long as you don't neglect your duties. I'll need lunch.'

Mr Thorpley's once-weekly lunch in the house was an aspect of her relationship with him she didn't totally resent. She took pride in the preparation of food. Somewhere, a long way back, a wrong turning had taken her away from her true vocation. The path strewn with easy money had seemed more appealing than domestic science. Nevertheless, despite the rigours of her chosen profession, she had kept in touch with matters concerning the kitchen.

'What can you offer me today?' he asked.

'I've made a pâté. There's smoked salmon if you want it. Escallope of veal—Napolitaine or Bolognaise, please yourself. Lemon sorbet, avocado—three cheeses—Sage Derby, Camembert and gruyère.'

'Bolognaise I think for the veal. I'll have both the pâté and salmon. Just the cheese to follow.'

'It'll be ready at one o'clock.'

'Good—time for a little something while I count these.' He waved the bundle of notes at her. 'Be a good woman and pour me one, will you? Three fingers—stevedores' fingers and—' seeing her expression of resentment at his orders, he added: 'if you can bear with a tyrannical landlord, pour one for yourself—I know what topers you Scots are.'

'You can talk—you old lush!'

'Ah! That's better. I can't bear bottled-up anger. It's like the old rhyme "Where 'ere you be let your wind go free, lest the bottling of the wind be the death of thee." '

Mrs McCartney poured three fingers for Mr Thorpley and three for herself. He took the glass from her.

'Here's to the days that were, Mrs McCartney.'

'I want more money.'

'Put it to arbitration. Haven't you a Union you can appeal to? Let me see now—there's Transport of Delight and General, the NUF, the Allied Trades—you girls really should get together. You're open to exploitation by wicked bosses like me. Just think what strike action would mean.' His smile grew broader. 'A go-slow wouldn't help, I'm afraid.'

Mrs McCartney's anger bottled again. She marched out of the room, whisky glass in hand, slamming the door behind her.

He turned his attention to the week's rents. The average was £150 and the pile under his hand was five pounds above. A good week made possible by the innovation of casual letting. Three rooms in the house could be rented by the hour or by the night. He must introduce the same scheme where possible in his other houses.

He slipped a rubber band round the stack of notes, then pencilled the amount in a little black notebook on whose cover was printed the legend, *'Cash Book'*. He drank a third of the Scotch in his glass and took a sheet of paper from the top shelf of the bureau. It was headed *'Official Charities'*.

He ran his finger down the list, noting the dates pencilled at the side of each entry.

Soldiers, Sailors and Airmen. Yes—it was time their turn came round. God knew that he, Peter Thorpley, had cause to thank their existence. Servicemen on leave always seemed to have one thing and one thing only on their minds and he had seen, in his own small way, that their minds were relieved of anxiety.

He took an envelope from the drawer and addressed it to the Sailors, Soldiers and Airmen Association, etc., etc., peeled three five-pound notes off the stack and put them in the envelope. Completely anonymous. No compliments slip. No message from a wish-to-be-unknown donor. My heart is one of ten per cent gold, he told himself. Tomorrow, in the Fulham house, I will again collect the rents and send ten per cent of the total to the next deserving cause.

It was the advantage of being a man of means; you could be generous—really generous.

He sealed the envelope and propped it against the little clock on the mantelshelf. Ten minutes to one. He drained his glass of Scotch and moved to the sideboard for another little one before Mrs McCartney came in with his excellently cooked lunch.

Annersley looked at the menu and ordered roast lamb with its supporting cast of vegetables, followed by fruit tart and custard. The morning had brought little of interest in the way of business. No criminal with a fascinating problem had turned up, neither had he been consulted by a fellow lawyer. He had attended to a few conveyances he had under way, dictated three threatening letters and then spent a rewarding hour on the telephone.

There was no doubt about it, his fellow traveller on the morning train was an interesting man—and what a fool! The naivety of the man! A good living in a decent parish and he had to fall for the wife of a fellow cleric and a *canon* to boot. Even so, thought Annersley as he timed the hiatus between ordering and receiving his lunch, there are ways and means of effecting a liaison without bringing in the sensational Sunday newspapers. Passion with patience, that was the motto Thorneycroft should have adopted. Annersley liked the motto. He put it into Latin and it sounded even better. *Passio cum Patientia.* If he could he would work it into his conversation with Thorneycroft on the six-forty.

He took out his pocket-sized memorandum book in which was jotted down cryptic shorthand items, mostly the beginnings of jokes he had heard and wished to remember for future telling, and wrote down the motto. *Passio cum Patientia.* A pity Thorneycroft was not RC, the Latin would have meant more to him.

On the opposite page an item met his eye causing him to scowl. *Dec. 20—Michael—home for Christmas parole—meet with shoes.* The scowl left his face slowly and he sighed, closing the book and returning it to his pocket.

We all have a skeleton in the cupboard, he thought. Thank God Michael had committed the offence out of the county and had had the wit to play down the fact that his father was a solicitor. There had been no fuss and, all praise to the Virgin and the Saints, the case preceding Michael's had been ripe and juicy enough with rape and robbery to throw his son's offence into a minor key, not worth the court reporter's salacious pen. There is a God who watches over us, Annersley ruminated, he allows rape and violence to be committed that his servant on earth might be lightly punished.

Rape and violence. Mr Annersley frowned and thought deeply into the Latin. *Passio cum Patientia. Passio* suggested violence. *Passio.* You would use that to smash in a skull; the action of a raging passion not necessarily linked with the sex act. Why not *Perturbatione Patientia—In Perturbatione Patientia.* The first translation sounded more prosy but the second was more accurate, although it did perhaps suggest a nun's love for Christ.

He took the memorandum out of his pocket, turned to the page and wrote the new translation under the first. Again—*meet with shoes* caught his eye.

The shoes were most important. Regularly, boys from the reform school at Hollesley, a little way outside Ipswich, used the morning train on their parole or release. Apart from looking a brutal lot you could always tell them by the regulation shoes they wore. Made in the school itself, Annersley understood. He wouldn't have his son coming home with that mark of Cain on his feet. He would take a pair of shoes to the gates of the school and see that the boy changed before entering the life of law-abiding society. He'd take a pair of shoes and a stiff lecture.

Annersley's lunchtime thought process suggested a theme for the lecture as he ate his way through the roast lamb and vegetables. God and the Law. Had not God protected his reputation by allowing rape and Grievous Bodily Harm? Fortuitous, the unbelieving might say. The mysterious ways of God are hard to understand. He sees beyond and behind time. Heavenly schedules had placed the rape at a certain time and in a certain place, just as it had been ordained that Michael would succumb to the forces of evil on a certain date in a certain place. Everyone had appointments in Samaria.

His thoughts changed key. But Thorneycroft's naivety! What had he hoped to get away with? A faked suicide with clothes left on a beach. How ridiculous. That in itself constituted an offence not only against the cloth but against the law. How would he, Annersley, have counselled a love-sick vicar? *In Perturbatione Patientia* to begin with. Perhaps if the lady had left her husband and arranged some noticeable act of adultery coupled with allegations of mental cruelty. These things can be arranged without infringing the law. Then a little patience, my friend and you will come into your own.

He had all the details at his fingertips. The time, the place and the denouement. It was first-class entertainment to talk to a man about whom you knew so much and who hoped you knew little. One was invested with the power to speak with significance and, who knows, the man might wish to confide—to tell all—to use one as a father confessor, and that was really first rate.

The 6.40 would be a most interesting train. He must get there in good time and hold a seat for his unsuspecting friend.

The unsuspecting friend sat in a little office in an old building in Bedford Street by Covent Garden. From his window, Thorneycroft could see the clothes hirers entering and leaving Moss Bros., but apart from that there was nothing worth looking at.

For some reason his journey with Annersley had stayed with him, like a sour taste that lingered on the palate. The solicitor's words had twanged the strings of Thorneycroft's conscience or had reawakened feelings of guilt; it was difficult to determine what he had done. He had certainly deprecated most of what Thorneycroft stood for—as if knowing full well the nature of that stand.

He stared down at the galley proofs he had been correcting. Boredom was making him unobservant. Twice he had retraced his corrections only to find many he had missed through sheer lack of interest. The subject of the proofs would interest Annersley. *The Church and the State—Attitudes to Crime and Punishment.* A good subject but so dully written as to make the book virtually unreadable.

He put down his red ball-point pen. It was time for lunch and the prospect was as boring as the work he would have to get through before catching the 6.40 back to Aline.

Aline. Her sacrifice had equalled his and it had not brought peace of mind. Happiness was always just around the corner. It was there, not far away; sometimes it seemed within reach in those rare moments when they came to terms with the conditions of their life together. Moments all too rare. Inevitably, thoughts of the future came in to depress the happy times. To live for the moment —consider the lilies of the field—take no heed of the morrow. He and Aline had done just that and hadn't considered the future. I behaved like a stupid child, thought Thorneycroft—Aline, too. We were unsophisticated to an extreme. When I was a child, I thought as a child—and look where it got us. I am a fish out of water. As dishonoured as any soldier stripped of rank.

He suddenly felt very tired and buried his head in his hands. Michael Chinner, senior partner of Chinner & Rockwell, publishers of religious and ethical works, saw the figure of dejection as he entered the outer office.

'Cheer up, Kenneth. Man's born to suffer as the sparks fly upward.'

Thorneycroft raised his head.

'Angst—world weariness.'

'Sorry to hear it. Hope you're not too tired to see someone this afternoon. A chap at SCF. We've had the offer of an interesting book. It's well written if you're about to groan. It's action stuff and should sell.' He placed a thin manuscript on Thorneycroft's desk. 'Specimen chapter and synopsis. I thought you might read it at lunch. It's good.'

'Who wrote it?'

'Joseph Carter—the man I want you to see. You'll like him, I think. A long history and all good stuff. With the Friends during the war. Since then has devoted his time to Save the Children and Freedom from Want.'

'A good man with a vocation,' Thorneycroft said bitterly. 'I envy him.'

'Have you heard from the Bishop?'

'Yes.'

'What did he say?'

'Nothing I didn't know already. That I could serve God without wearing the cloth. That reinstatement is out of the question. Perhaps in the years to come, etcetera. I want to be back in harness, Michael—I haven't changed.'

'But circumstances have. Lie low, Ken—it's a nasty term to use, but you know what I mean. The Press would hound you to the grave if the Bishop was foolish enough to readmit you. Not that he can. You've a good life with Aline.'

'I want it to be better.'

'Then give up baying at the moon—it's holding you back from

making the most of your life. What do they say—there's better men outside the Church than in it? I believe that to be true. Like Carter, the man I want you to see. He doesn't need a dog collar to help him serve humanity.'

'It's a question of authority.'

'Carter has all the authority needed to carry out his work. Perhaps more because he doesn't wear funny church clothes. In some dark regions the Church is still considered a political body and therefore undesirable and dangerous.'

'Obviously I haven't his virtues.'

'That's probably true. I know *I* haven't. I'm vain and greedy, have intellectual pride and consider the needs of the body before the needs of the soul.'

Chinner's words hit home, although he had only stated a commonplace fact. Thorneycroft said: 'Thank you, Mike—thanks for holding a mirror up to my faults and failings. But the fact remains, I am nothing without the Church. I can do nothing, be nothing without its sanction and approval.'

Chinner was silent for a while. He watched Thorneycroft get up from his desk and stand by the window looking out on the wet street. At length, he said: 'It's not that you haven't courage or the personality to take part in the Christian marathon. You've the mind and brain to add to the effectiveness of the Church. What I would question is the quality of your faith.'

Thorneycroft felt the stab of the words pierce his back.

Chinner added: 'It's a poor pacifist who goes armed to his tribunal. All the years I've known you, Ken, I've never heard you doubt your own faith. You've deplored the lack of it in others but you've never speculated about the value of your own. I suggest you examine it as, no doubt, the Bishop has.'

Thorneycroft heard Chinner leave the room, gently closing the door behind him. He stood there for five minutes, feeling a chill playing about his heart, watching the figures, umbrella'd and wet, scurrying along the street below. Various measures of faith lived

in those figures. There were those without and those with. Which
was he?

The clock in the Scotland Yard lecture room showed 12.45 when
Detective Chief Superintendent Greenlaw closed his book of notes
and said: 'Thank you, gentlemen—we will reassemble in Room
forty-nine at two fifteen. Before you go to the canteen, however,
I suggest you go to the reports room and check on anything that
may have come concerning your area.'

Thirty police officers in mufti rose and scraped back chairs and,
as they filed out of the lecture room, talked to each other in voices
that clued them to their place of origin. Weston, whose natural
dialect came from Essex, hard vowels and clipped consonants,
exchanged words with a constable from Somerset whose S's
sounded like lazy bees.

The lecture had been elementary stuff, but that which PCs in
country parishes are likely to forget in the routine prosecution of
their particular functions. Apart from the occasional accident,
petty crime or apprehension of a summons dodger, their life con-
sisted of patrols, endless paperwork and the passing on of information to other areas.

Greenlaw had sketched in a true picture of their activities before
coming to the point of his lecture. 'In no way,' he said, 'am I depre-
cating the activities of the so-called village constable. His is an unexciting but human job. I speak from experience when I say that
it consists of being polite to all and having a sense of territorial
pride. He likes his manor kept clean and he does it by being on
call for twenty-four hours a day and establishing a personal relationship with the people in his territory. Detectives like me can
be as rude as we like, but not your friendly fuzz, the village
constable.'

When the expected laughter died down he continued: 'But it
happens, too often for comfort, that a major crime occurs in his
area and he will be the first police officer on the scene. Now, since
his actions may well determine the future of the investigation, it

is supremely important that he is completely up to date with vital procedure and information. The purpose, therefore, of this series of lectures is to make this vital link a fully informed and efficient officer.'

On the way to the reports room, the man from Somerset said: ' 'Tis a bit like a Western. There's this sheriff who's never drawn a gun on anyone living in this town that's never had any trouble. Then a fast gun rides in and threatens to take over the town an' everyone looks to the quiet sheriff to take the gunman.'

'And the sheriff ends up on Boot Hill?' asked Weston.

'Not in this Western. He goes up to Dodge City and gets Wyatt Earp to teach him the fast draw and when he comes back to the quiet township he looks the same but he isn't. He plants a slug right between the gunman's eyebrows.'

'The inspector doesn't look like Wyatt Earp. The kids in my village gave me a nickname—"The Slowest Gun in Suffolk".'

'That's rich. Any truth in it?'

'I'm no slower than the next man.'

The reports room was large and crackling with electronic noise and the strange language of radio transmission and reception. Selected reports for the class were assembled on a desk. Weston scanned through the area titles and photokit pictures. Nothing for him. Then Somerset nudged him.

'Something for you. A nasty one. Your county anyway.'

The report came from East Suffolk Constabulary and was couched in stronger more direct language than the guarded BBC announcement in the seven o'clock news.

It gave details of the double murder 'of wife and daughter, William Arthur Kemp, Sallows Farm, Claybourne, near Ipswich. Believed armed and in the vicinity. Officers are advised to approach this man with caution. Kemp is aged fifty-one with thinning brown hair grey at temples, five feet eight in height, eleven stone in weight, with scar above right eyebrow, top left central incisor tooth missing. If observed, do not approach but advise area control.'

As Weston read the report, his mind went back to the train as it approached Colchester; the thrumming of the wheels, the boys sitting opposite and the cheek he'd received from Dennis Tilling. It seemed to have no connection with the report he held in his hand until his mind's eye left the three boys and rested on the man huddled in the corner seat.

The coincidence was too great to be ignored. The scar above the man's eyebrow had shown livid in his strained face. And there had been mud on his shoes as if he had used rough places to get to the station. Claybourne lay thirteen miles north-east of Manningtree, Weston knew the area well. The man could easily have bypassed the River Orwell west of Ipswich, then over the A12, into the country and down to the Stour—which he could have crossed at Flatford or on the bridge road from Cattawade to the station.

Weston had to test the strength of his hunch against the possibility of making a fool of himself. In Suffolk he wouldn't have hesitated; New Scotland Yard was a different proposition. But if the man Kemp had been on the train and was now in London it wasn't Suffolk's pigeon.

He said to Somerset: 'What you said just now—about the sheriff getting into the gunfight. I think I'm in it. I don't know—I may be wrong.'

'Better safe than sorry. What have you got?'

'A murder not far from my patch. I believe I travelled up with the wanted man. The description fits. And he looked like a wanted man.'

'The streets are full of 'em,' said Somerset.

'What do I do?'

'You're in the nerve centre of crime detection and you don't know what to do?'

'I might be wrong.'

'Coppers often are. Go and see Greenlaw—it's what he was talking about this morning. No harm done if you're wrong.'

Detective Chief Superintendent Greenlaw listened to Weston's report with interest, chin cradled in hand. When Weston had finished, he reached for the telephone.

'Let's see what we've got in so far.' He spoke into the receiver, 'I want the latest on the Suffolk murder. That's right—Kemp. All you've got.'

Replacing the receiver, he said: 'How far is Claybourne from—where did you say he got on?'

'Manningtree, sir—about thirteen miles.'

'So it's possible it's our man. Anything suspicious in his manner?'

'Nervous. Looked tired and in trouble. There was something else, sir. You know the way some people look at you—I mean, if they think you're a copper.'

'I know,' said Greenlaw. 'As if they've smelt something nasty.'

'That's it, sir—this chap looked at me like that.'

'But you were in mufti.'

'Blue shirt and black tie, sir—it's enough for some people. Anyway, he didn't stay in the compartment for long. After shifting about a bit he got up and went out. I didn't see him again until the train pulled into Liverpool Street. In the corridor near the front of the train—if looks could kill I wouldn't be here.'

Greenlaw nodded. 'We'll see if description tallies with your memory.' He looked up as the door opened. A shirt-sleeved constable came to Greenlaw's desk and handed him a red file.

'That's as much as we've got, sir. The last report's just come in. Road checks and a pretty intensive search of the area's under way.'

'Any conjecture?'

'Only the classical one—suicide. The old pattern.'

Greenlaw turned his eyes on Weston. 'The average wife murder ends in suicide—nine cases out of ten. Makes our job easy. Just look for the body.'

He opened the file and scanned the report sheets.

'Doesn't seem to be much doubt in their mind.' He unclipped a sheet from the file and said: 'Let's have your description again, Weston—we'll see how observant you are.'

Weston cast his mind back, taking his time. He recalled his opening conversation with Dennis Tilling and the boys; then his observation of the man in the corner.

'I reckon he was fifty or thereabouts, thin, brown—sort of mouse-coloured hair—height five feet eight—weight around eleven stone—black shoes with mud on them—gaberdine belted raincoat—standard beige colour—scar above right eyebrow—'

'Eyes?'

'Dark brown—nearly black.'

'Have you read a description before?'

'Only one in the report room, sir.'

'Is your memory coloured by the report?'

Weston shook his head emphatically. 'No, sir.'

'Anything to add to the description? The colour of his shirt and tie—socks?'

'The shirt might be light grey or white. No tie—the collar was undone. Didn't notice his socks, sir.'

Greenlaw handed the description report to Weston. 'Not bad—you'll see your man tallies with the report. Any sign he was armed?'

Weston frowned in concentration. The huddled figure in the corner—what was he doing? Nothing but expressing some obsessive anxiety, his left hand twitching as it lay on his thigh. Where was the other hand?

Weston came out of his trance and said: 'His right hand was in his raincoat pocket.'

'All the time?'

'Yes, sir. When he got up he used his left hand to open the sliding door—and kept the other in his pocket.'

'Later—when you saw him again in the corridor?'

'Nothing, sir—except to see his face again. I can't add anything more.'

Greenlaw looked up at the shirt-sleeved constable. 'Any pictures yet?'

'No, sir. Should be some stuff coming through from Suffolk—I've asked for photos.'

'We'll take a chance and speed things up. It will also be an experience for Weston. Take him down to the department and make up a picture. No harm done if it's the wrong man. We can check our village PC's powers of observation with the pictures from Suffolk. All right, Weston?'

The reference to 'village PC' stuck in Weston's gullet. 'Yes, sir,' he said.

Sensing Weston's hurt, Greenlaw said: 'It was meant kindly, lad. Met. coppers are called worse names.'

Mollified, Weston followed his guide along the important corridors of New Scotland Yard. In a few short hours he had made the jump from routine village life to an experience denied most constables; an experience likely to improve his status—if all went well and he had not been mistaken. Regionally, it could do him much good and bring him that much nearer to the CID.

Kemp left the café and walked slowly down Upper Street. It was well past school time. The handbell would have rung a long time ago. Flynn, Fenton—Fatty Fenton—the Ley brothers, Ginger and Jack, Mowbray and Manzi would be under the watchful eye of Mr Hanley. It took guts to play truant. He'd soon reach Highbury Fields; no one could find him there.

The photokit man added the last piece to the composite portrait and said: 'Well—there he is. Anything like?'

Weston studied the picture. He wished it were in colour instead of clearly defined half-tones. Colour was so important: a grey thin face differs from a rosy or tanned thin face. The face was too static.

'There's no expression,' he said. 'I want to be sure. The man was strained, anxious, frightened, if you like.'

'Can't manage that, I'm afraid.' The photokit officer handed Weston a box of felt pens. 'What about putting the expression in yourself? A couple of worry lines here and there—perhaps a bit of colour in the hair. Draw on this acetate overlay. Better still, you can use one of our artists if you don't trust your own talents.'

'I'd rather have the artist.'

'O.K. That's me. I'm no Picasso but I've done some good work.

You talk about how you thought the man was feeling. And forget what you've heard since you got here. Forget that he might be a killer—okay?'

'I don't think he'd slept—he looked very tired, but his brain was working pretty hard. He was nervous—highly strung—shifted his eyes when I looked at him. Huddled in his seat as if—well—as if he wanted to hide—'

As Weston talked the officer worked on the photokit overlay.

'. . . hair was dull, thin—mouse coloured—hadn't shaved—stubble was a mixed grey and ginger. The scar above his right eyebrow was pretty deep and livid—about one and three-quarters of an inch—'

'Straight, curved, at an angle?'

'It started near the left of the brow—about half an inch away and rose to an inch above—I think.'

'Right . . . Is this better?'

It was very much better and Weston said, 'That's very good—it's like him. Could you put him in an open-necked shirt with a raincoat collar pulled up?'

The artist worked quickly, with a direct, decisive line and Weston saw his man emerge. 'That's him,' he said. 'That's the man I saw.'

'Not bad.' The artist grinned. 'Now we'll see how good you are—we've got pictures of Kemp and we don't need photokit. Thank God people keep their snapshots. Copies were transmitted by radio.' He left the assembly table and fetched a blue file from pigeon-hole shelving on the far wall. He came back, opening the file.

'Take your pick from these.'

The enlargements were taken from snapshots and in bad definition. Weston studied them carefully. He mustn't make a mistake or allow the desire to be right to frame his decision. The last of the photographs convinced him.

The camera had evidently clicked before the man's face had put on its happy-snap smile; before he could wipe off an expression of exasperation.

'It's him,' Weston said. 'I'm sure.'

'Any doubt at all?'

'No—it's him all right.'

Looking at the photograph again, Weston wondered if future events cast shadows into the past. He supposed the photo had been taken a little time ago, perhaps a couple of years, but the camera had caught Kemp at a naked moment, showing the face of the man he would be.

'Well—you've put the finger on him all right,' the photokit officer said. 'Now it's *cherchez l'homme* and all that.' He looked at Greenlaw's runner. 'Greenlaw in charge?'

'He's in at the start—I expect he'll fix it so that he takes over.'

'Then you've a busy time ahead. He'll push hard.' He smiled at Weston. 'You, too—you don't need a week of lectures—you're getting it practical. Lucky man. All you'll need when Greenlaw's finished with you is sleep.'

Highbury Fields was deserted in the rain. At the Barn end, Kemp sat on a bench that was partially sheltered by an old chestnut tree from which drops of water steadily dripped.

Using the last ounce of energy in his legs, he had crossed the busy cross-section road and traced a weary path beyond the swimming pool to those playing fields so redolent with memories. It was a sort of peace, sitting on the bench and armoured against prying eyes—like the time when he had missed school for a whole day and lost himself in the Fields, safe from parental eyes and informers.

He closed his eyes against a feeling of dizziness and let his head fall back on the wooden bar of the seat, his adam's apple protruding through the stretched skin of his neck.

The dizziness was in his brain. It joined with the desire to sleep, to give up, enter oblivion—forget self. To curl up and die. To sleep away all that had happened. To go down and down into the darkness of the past; to the dreams of his mother and Ringcroft Street and the back garden with chickens clucking.

He wasn't far away from the street. When strength returned to him, he'd go there—to the garden of number nineteen. It was Monday and it would be cold meat and pickles and the lingering fresh smell of washday with the clothes flapping on the line.

Kemp slept, the rain and drops from the tree falling on his upturned face.

CHAPTER 6

Lunch-hour, 13.30 hrs.

Davies looked into the eyes of Monica Inchbald and wondered if she had meant what she said. It had been three years since anything like it had happened. In his state of life-and-death anxiety it was incongruous that a sexual opportunity should present itself.

'I'd like some more brandy,' she said.

'Of course.' Davies beckoned the waiter. 'I didn't anticipate you exactly, Miss Inchbald.'

'What does that mean—Mr Davies?'

'Money, women, investments—the combination sums up a type quite unlike you. You haven't mentioned money once.'

'When you've as much as I have, there's little point, John. I've never known a man called John. I like it. I like you. Do I shock you by obeying impulses?'

'A sort of shock. Like receiving a marvellous present.'

'You haven't unwrapped it yet.'

'Will I get another shock?'

'I hope so. Most men I know would have said "Shall we go now?" at least four minutes ago.'

'It's an aspect of karezza—you know, prolonging the delight.'

'I know. I like the face you put on things.' She reached across the table and traced the worry lines on Davies' forehead with her forefinger. 'It's a good face. Controlled and charming but, brother! The war that's going on underneath that face.'

Davies smiled. 'Everyone has a private war.'

'I haven't.' She looked mock-regretful. 'My sweet life's simple. I'm rich—I give to charity—I want what I like and I don't consider the lilies of the field. Tell me about your war.'

'Average financier's worries.'

'Oh dear—that means money trouble, doesn't it?'

'Yes.'

'What a waste of time. It's also bad for sex.'

'Perhaps that's why I haven't said, "Shall we go now?" '

'You're married, of course. Is that any hindrance?'

'No.'

'Good. Shall we go now?'

'That's for me to say, Monica. To be fair, I don't like your name. I've always classed it with the Muriels and Olives of this world. Ruby too—'

'Chanter and Ringwood, Bellman and true—what's in a name? In a little time you'll be calling me "Darling". That's much better because I don't like my name either.'

Looking at the gift facing him across the table Davies savoured the sexual excitement building up in him. It was good to feel the primitive energy of the attraction, would be good to obey the impulses she so powerfully transmitted. Yet there was this other thing tugging at his strength, this appalling anxiety that had to be solved. Was it because of the threat to his very existence that the attraction to Monica was so strong? He had heard that men under sentence of imminent death suffered the wildest of sex urges.

Monica said: 'To set the record straight, John, you can tell Tony Viscenti he can handle my money. Does that set your mind at rest?'

'Yes—and I'm glad. Thank you for making it easy.'

'There's a condition—I want you to be personally responsible for my affairs.'

'Viscenti won't like it.'

'Then it's no deal.'

'In that case, I will be personally responsible.'

'It's quite a lot of money—thanks to my dead American daddy. Do you know, I can't even remember him. I wish I did, he's brought me great happiness.'

'Am I a father-substitute?'

'Probably—I don't know. Does it matter? Do you want to hide in me?'

'It's a nice idea.'

'Then that makes me a mother-substitute.'

'You sound like the Intelligent Woman's Approach to Sex.'

'I am intelligent, I like sex and I approach it enthusiastically. And I am not an easy lay.'

'I neither said that nor thought it.'

'What do you think?'

'If you weren't so obviously happy, I'd call you a poor little rich girl who buys on impulse. Since there's practically nothing she can't buy, she shops in the sex market and, to make shopping more interesting, she makes her offer before finding out if the article's for sale. Are you ever refused?'

'Aren't you afraid of annoying me?'

'No, because you know I like you very much and find you intensely attractive.'

'I thought for a moment you were going to accuse me of shop-lifting. Rich women do it, you know—for the thrills.'

'So do women starved of affection—it's a way of bringing attention to themselves.'

'Do you think I'm starved?'

'I don't know yet. Are you?'

She considered it silently, at first looking deep into his eyes, then shifting her gaze to some point beyond him. She really is beautiful, Davies thought. She has a full, soft mouth and slightly crooked smile, and eyes that alternately mock and then go misty, as if filled with tears. But then the mistiness goes and the eyes go bright with mockery again. Self-mockery?

'If you want something, it means you're without it,' she said. 'You're something I haven't got and I'd like to have you.' The eyes went bright. 'Are you for sale or shall I steal you—I could always say I had a blackout?'

'You've bought me already, Monica. If there's any stealing to be done I'll do it. Let's put an end to ambiguity. Shall we go, now?'

Cynthia Davies had eaten no lunch; there was neither time nor hunger for food. She sat in a high-backed winged armchair, a half-empty bottle of gin on the pedestal side table close at hand. Habit had moved her to switch on the television set which she now watched, only dimly comprehending the images on the screen.

Her attempt to conquer post-alcoholic depression had begun early, the need for the daily transfusion more urgent than it had ever been. Formerly she would have sliced a lemon in the kitchen, taken ice and tonic water from the fridge and calmly, deliberately —like a conscientious barman—prepared a balanced one-third gin to two-thirds tonic. The ration would change later when gin would predominate.

But ritual had broken down. Coming out of oblivion at 10 am, she had bathed her despised, ageing body, given orders to Mrs Clark, her daily woman, and only held out against the hunger for alcohol until 11.45. There was no motivation to fetch ice and lemon; no energy for the uncapping of tonic-water bottles; desire and an incredible fatigue had carried her only to the drinks cabinet to withdraw an unopened bottle of gin and a glass.

There was a film—its title escaped her—in which a character drank until a *click!* happened. A click in the head when life suddenly became bearable. She waited for that click, encouraging its appearance with deep draughts of gin. But there was only sound from the television set. No *click!* Instead, her perceptions seemed to be narrowing down into a minute world encompassed by the taste of juniper and failure.

Somewhere, tears were at hand. She wanted to cry for herself; to weep tears of sorrow for the entire, unhappy world of which she was the chief pivot. There was nowhere to go—who wanted a reject? What could she do? Redundant—as redundant as a senile, old-age pensioner. What use could she make of the old values? The time-filling social grace of 'come round for drinks'; the gatherings convened in the name of sweet charity when she would mix with other Lady Bountifuls and Paternalists of the county—all had gone, for she had no further time for them; the hard outer shell covering the soft vulnerable person had dropped away, her nerve-ends exposed and deadened only by the sacred contents of the bottle.

Overnight, a change had altered her pattern of behaviour; a change she could not put a name to. Mrs Clark had appeared at the end of her morning's work and asked if Mrs Davies needed anything, and Cynthia had replied, without visually acknowledging Mrs Clark's presence, 'Just go.' Formerly, she would have assumed her kindly employer's face and thanked the woman and hoped to see her again next morning.

'Just go.'

She wanted life to go, but a hair-thin lifeline held her to heartbeat and mechanical, bodily response. More gin and she might be human again. More gin and, perhaps, the end would come. The house was filled with the means to end it all; John had three guns in his room; she had enough barbiturates in her bedside table to make the going-out easy.

The lifeline was a fragment of hope founded on memory. It was make-believe and she knew it, but, because she desired it, she could imagine a resurgence of John's sexual interest in her when he would take her with all the intensity of—she reached for the glass and drained it—was it *so* long ago? When was the last time—five years—six? Even then it hadn't been much on his part; an act reluctantly and dutifully given.

His few nights away from home—where did he spend them? And with whom? But John had never needed nights; days were just as good in which to display and enjoy his sexual energy; in the past she had received and enjoyed it. There was no celibacy in him—none at all. He exploited his potency as his right and was too proud to expend his sexual urge in a private world of erotic fantasy and self-fulfilment.

Someone, somewhere, felt his body against hers. Someone, too, received the sympathy and kindness of which she was deprived.

The woman, girl, would be young and not a tart or a willing under-ling, his standards would take care of that; it would be someone worthwhile, worth bringing to bed and loving as she, Cynthia, had been loved.

In the bath she had looked at her body and hated it; loathed its lack of youth and seen with disgust the number of grave-spots on the thinning flesh.

'I've done with you—finished with you.'

She thought aloud, looking out across the lawns and trees of the garden drab in the grey light and drizzling rain.

More gin. Once, it had been real Dutch courage. A few drinks and troubles had lightened, had been laughed over, reduced to their true perspective—made transient and ephemeral. She filled the glass, spilling a little on the polished top of the pedestal table.

'It will take the polish off,' she said.

Using the cuff of her cardigan she wiped away the little pool of gin. The practical action took her momentarily out of herself.

John's face and behaviour had expressed a great anxiety over the last few months. At first she had thought that it was his concern over the loss of their life together, their intimate life in which sex and sympathy were the main ingredients; she knew, now, that it was something else.

'Nothing to worry your head about, Cynthia,' he had said in an-swer to her request for his confidence. He had said that many times in the years and she had taken it to mean that millions were lost or gained in the City every day, the spectre of ruin constantly walk-ing those mean streets. John wasn't a loser; he had been born to win with his perfect pitch for money. Failure happened to others —lesser men.

So it all came back to herself; she was going downhill and he could do nothing to save her. Sympathy, love, sex—she had ex-hausted them.

The image of a child flashed on the television screen and trans-mitted its vision to her memory. A child who loved horses. Cynthia —seven years old and her first pony, a grey called Misty, twelve and a half hands. Dead now, of course—long since dead. Poor

Misty. Gymkhana collecting rings—Misty and Cynthia waiting their turn. Rosettes to pin to the bridle. Like snapshots in a photo album, Cynthia watched the child grow up in a series of flashes; how unrelated the beginning seemed to the end!

Her glass was empty again. As she reached for the bottle, a sudden, sharp pain in her chest halted her movement. She pressed her left hand against the centre of the pain, gasping against the attack. Pleuritic? A pleuritic pain? A few years ago when she had had pleurisy—it was that sort of pain—nearly.

The pain gone, she continued with her action of filling her glass and settled back in the chair. Apprehensive of its return, she was unprepared for the savagery of the next attack. When it came, she had to clench her teeth and close her eyes.

It went slowly, reluctantly. Then she felt an urge to cry for help. The telephone was near; she could ring John or her sons or Dr Mansell or a hundred so-called friends. She made a half-movement toward the telephone standing beside the gin bottle, then checked her action. There was no point in anything—in doing anything. A few kindly words of advice, crocodile sympathy and a charitable visit—the tomb would still claim her.

There were now two pains to contend with: that which stabbed her chest and the deeper, spiritual pain which far surpassed the physical. There was nothing else to do but drown both.

As she reached for the near-empty bottle, the television screen flickered and moved with the sounds and signs of a life that was fast becoming unrelated to her own existence.

'It's getting late,' Helen said. 'I've got to go.'

The Barbican complex was good for lunchtime lovers. They could wander into the arcades out of the rain; the pubs were numerous and warm, places where they could sit for the whole lunch-hour over one glass of beer.

She and Edward Ferris preferred the comparative quiet of a café to the noisy, ebullient atmosphere of a pub. They had lingered over a second cup of coffee trying to recapture that uninhibited moment at twelve-thirty. The first moment of meeting was always the best, but then the moment died. They had managed ten minutes of hand-holding under the table; ten minutes in which they had hoped that mutual pressure of grip conveyed all they wished to put into words. There was so much to say and all of it was dangerous.

They left the café and walked to the office block north of the Barbican, to the great steel and marble structure which daily claimed their labours, Edward Ferris to the fourth floor and Helen to the fifteenth.

They walked apart without touching hands; gossip was too lively an office vice to risk being seen by the many waspish employees.

'We'll meet tonight,' Ferris said. 'Perhaps—I don't know—perhaps something will happen at home. I'm sorry I'm so weak and afraid. I shrink from rows and she convinces me I've the courage of a mouse whenever I stand up to her.'

'It's all right, Edward, I'm like that, too. We're both mice waiting for the cat to pounce.'

The confession cheered them up; it was, at least, a sort of intimacy. Her hand sought his and pressed it. 'I can at least count my blessings,' she said. 'From tomorrow, Ivor will be away for three days. I'll pretend he's left for good and enjoy being alone.'

'I'd like that, too,' said Ferris.

It was not what he meant. To have freedom of choice; to say no to a life of misery. To end an involvement that negated the very meaning of life.

'I'd like to be alone with you,' he said. 'That's what I really meant to say.'

The Albert, a hundred yards away from the school, was known as the 'students' pub'. Combined with the Technical College, whose subjects seemed unrelated to art except in the visual appearance of the supporters of each culture, the number of student regulars made up for the conspicuous absence of average pub-users. In the Summer vacation the clientele slowly changed, reaching its peak at the start of the Autumn term, then those customers acquired would drop off more quickly than they grew until once more the Albert would reacquire its students' pub identity.

Blake accepted his second pint of bitter from the hand of Sally Eversley as Malcolm Bryant, the most aggressive and unreachable of the fourth-year students, reached the end of his diatribe against established methods of the school's hierarchy and its attitudes rooted in infant-school-teaching morality. He ended on a personal note: '. . . so you support them when you accuse us of living in—what did you call it—a subculture?'

'It is a subculture.'

'And it's offered as an insult.'

'No—a criticism of something which occupies the major part of your lives to the detriment of a culture that is wider in its concept and experience. Doing your own thing is fine—if you've worthwhile experiences to draw on.'

'That makes you bloody conceited then.'

Blake drank deeply from his glass.

Bryant said: 'You know what I mean?'

'I think I do. You'd better explain for the benefit of your friends.'

'I mean, what bloody experiences did you draw on when you did your own thing. How old were you—twenty? How you must have lived, Mr Blake—all that real sex and blood and tears. I'm twenty, Mr Blake. How was your bloody subculture when you were my age?'

'Do you want a straight answer, Malcolm?'

'Yes, please, Mr Blake.'

'Say that again using my Christian name—and say it as if you mean it.'

'Yes, please, David.'

'In the first case there wasn't a subculture that demanded special gear to set me apart from the straight men; a subculture that demanded electronic noise and second-hand love and pacifism—' Blake stopped, not quite sure whether to go on.

'And in the second case, Dave?'

The use of the diminutive stung Blake. 'In the second case I was born a bloody sight better painter than you'll ever be. Born with perceptions I didn't ask for but had. Born with an environment that encouraged from birth what I was to do at twenty. Your development stands at the point I'd reached at the age of twelve. And it's my bloody job to help you close up the years and I have to fight not only you but the subculture that draws on nothing that wasn't done better in the 'twenties and 'thirties by commercial artists with talent and the desire to make money. You're so bloody ignorant, so unread, that you think picking your nose is something you invented!'

His voice had risen; it reached across the pub and halted the buzz of conversation. Bryant's face had paled under the impact of Blake's words. Sally's eyes were fixed on Malcolm's face, seeing the hurt in it.

Blake hadn't finished. 'And as a further sign of the difference between us, I've said what I damn well like to you and you're hurt and resentful. You say what you damn well like to me, and the whole of your tribe backs you up as if you're the word of God, and you expect me to take it lying down.'

Conversation buzz slowly mounted in decibels. Bryant's face went back to colour, the hurt expression changing to one of contempt. He reached for his glass, drained it, his eyes never leaving Blake's face.

'You're good, man—very, very good. Born with all the advantages—great. But what do you do now? Where's the evidence of your superior experience. Man—you died years ago. The fire went out and that's the worth of your bloody culture.' He pointed a finger at the glass in Blake's hand. 'I paid for that drink. When you let it out I hope you piss blood!'

'That's the first original thing I've heard from you,' Blake said. 'It's a damn sight better than your message of love, and the glory of your own thing.'

'Liberal cant—and you don't get my point. You tell me, Mr Blake —what are you, a painter or a teacher? Where's the value of your experience? You don't get us at all, do you? You're like those bloody old soldiers who remember and that's all—like those bloody memorials with the names of the clots who died in the war engraved on them. I've seen your stuff in the Tate. Do you know what they are?—memorials—and they don't mean a thing because that's where you stopped dead. To the memory of David Blake—died in action, Royal Academy.'

The group surrounding him were in total hostility. He looked at Sally Eversley, seeing her now as the lure to the confrontation, and he was frightened. Their aggression reached out and hit him like a physical hurt. Somewhere he was wrong and somewhere he was right. A sickness was in his stomach.

He forced composure into his voice and said: 'I know I've gone too far. I've said many things that are only half-true, half-meant. We're none of us sure where we stand. I want you to be the success it's in many of you to be. I get angry and frustrated when I see our future threatened.'

Bryant said: 'Success? What's that? You mean better, more successful and richer than the next man with a bigger house—more cars and deep freezers—bigger and better orgasms? Is that what you mean?' Holding court, he turned his eyes on the students: 'Now he'll tell us he didn't mean that? He'll quote some abstract ideal of the dedicated artist pouring his soul—every bloody bit of it—into his art. Uncommitted and unrelated to anything but the artist's revelation of his buggered-up psyche.'

'I could tell you something like that,' said Blake.

'And that's why you don't get it. Now I'll teach you, teacher. Art's a bloody small part of what it's all about. You heard of love, teacher? Of course you have—for you it means having it off with someone regular and you both wear chastity belts as tight as a pig's arse and the size of a wedding ring. Next comes patriotism—love of country—or so you call it, but you don't mean country—you mean nationality. And what about religion? God? God wears the Union Jack, knows a bit of Hebrew and Latin but votes Tory and Labour and lives in Lambeth Palace, the Vatican and, when he takes time off, nips down to Chequers. He's always on the side of the British, right or wrong. But the best one of all is success. Personal success and fuck the next man.'

'The way you're fucking me now?' asked Blake.

'I'm teaching you the way you tried this morning. A frontal attack, brother, as nude as anything you've seen in your life. We don't want the back-culture you push down our throats. We've seen the effect it's had on the world. Only—we've got the essence—the message. We love but we don't hoard it away from others. We've got God, too, and we call it love and it's for everybody. And love of country—that, too—but country covers the whole bloody world, so we've patriotism—right? And in case you want to throw it in, most of us use grass—tea—or if you want to be pedantic, marijuana, because we're just as animal as you and your bank manager and need something to bear with the bloody stinking world you and your kind invented!'

Words couldn't come to Blake. The injustice of the diatribe as directed against himself and the truth contained in it had built a dam against his stream of defence. He was shocked, too, by the vehemence of Bryant. After three terms of Bryant's refusal to go little beyond the minimum of communication had come an explosion of feeling that took him out of the category in which Blake had placed him.

Words finally came with difficulty.

'You've been unjust, Malcolm,' he said. 'If I told you that I agree with you—in the abstract, it would carry no conviction. You've typecast me.'

'Vice versa—you've typecast me and mine.' Bryant looked at his watch. 'It's five to two and I quote: "Students must keep rigidly to time allotted for breaks." Come on, children, we mustn't keep teacher waiting.'

They began to leave in a bunched group, emphasising their solidarity, Bryant playing the leader to the last by ushering them out with a protective arm.

'About love,' said Blake.

'The big thing, teacher.'

'You've shown little of it for me.'

Bryant's face lost its contempt. He watched the last of the students go through the swing doors, then turned his eyes on Blake.

'Why do you think I told you what a shit you are?' he asked. 'Do you think I'd tell Widmer or the Principal and all the other dead-beats what I told you? Do you think I'd bother to rake out their ashes and start a fire when I know they've no chimney? Why do you think I've given you the right to kick my teeth in and reply in kind? The other kids took in everything we said—'

'You said.'

'Okay—everything *I* said. They got the message. Now you sort out whether I hate or love you. You just bear in mind one thing— we're concerned with things that concern us. Things that don't, we ignore. You haven't been ignored. You take it from there. See you later.'

'I doubt if you will.'

'Happy Christmas then—whatever that means.'

Coates brooded silently and alone in the Ipswich canteen. Through the window he could see his locomotive with its chain of goods wagons on track 7. It, the rain, and faulty schedules had ruined his day. The meeting had been cancelled in his absence and two drivers had said to him, with faces whose expressions denied the sentiment of their speech: 'Sorry to miss the meeting, we were looking forward to it.'

Spencer was somewhere in the town, spending stop-over time by shopping for a bourgeois Christmas and filling the capitalists' stockings with workers' money. Father Christmas was a high Tory who gave with one hand and took away (with interest) with the other. Coates would have none of it. His wife could spend the money she earned any way she bloody well pleased on the nieces and nephews, uncles and aunts she thought so highly of. To hell with all of them—the poor fools didn't know when they were being fleeced.

And the stop-over itself—what a damned mess-up. Extended now until 17.50, when he would be allowed to move his goods out of Ipswich, and down the line to London in a series of sidings stops to allow the white-collar worker trains free passage in the rush hour. The extra money was another crumb from the bosses' table. It was great on paper. Canteen food and a cot to kip in—we mustn't have tired drivers, must we? Driving time was limited by agreement between the Union and the Popes of British Railways. Great on paper, like all their blasted agreements.

He looked again at his locomotive. Four end wagons, loaded with aggregate for King's Cross; two chemical and three Army junk wagons to be shunted off at the same station; then a mixed bag of freight. Thirty-two wagons in all and Coates hated the lot.

The canteen door opened to admit a driver and his second man. Coates recognised them and felt hostility flame up. The driver was a big, florid man, six feet two of loud geniality, contemptuous of sacred cows and tender feet. He caught sight of Coates and nudged his second man.

'Somewhere cosy,' he said. 'Nothing like a cuppa and intelligent chat.'

'What about over there with Mr Coates?'

'Mr Coates? . . . That is a bloody honour.'

The driver forged over to Coates' table beaming his pleasure.

'Coupla workers join you?'

Coates glowered and turned his eyes to the window.

'Have a good meeting? I said to Roy here, I'd like to go to that meeting, I said. Shouldn't wonder if the hall was jam-packed and spilling out in the street, I said. Didn't I, Roy?'

'Sure.'

'An' then a standin' ovation—five minutes at least. I bet you got them going, boy. A real rabble-rouser. You straightened 'em out, didn't you, boy. Eh? Didn't you put steel into their backbones? When's the strike, then—tomorrow—next week—Boxin' Day.'

Coates remained silent, bottling his anger.

'You're exhausted, is that it, boy? An' no wonder—gettin' up and talkin' to a couple of thousand angry men. I don't know how you do it—straight up—I don't know how you do it. A special gift, is it? Me, I couldn't lecture a village idiot. Takes it out of you, does it?'

Coates snapped into speech. 'Shut your bloody mouth!'

'Or you'll shut it for me. I know—I don't know when to stop. I'm a stupid clot. I am—straight up—an' I feel it when I talk to an intelligent man like you with your understanding of politics. You're book-taught, so they tell me. What I mean is—you're a self-made man—self-educated, an' all that. It's a marvel, isn't it, Roy—eh?' He took a noisy sip of his tea, straining it with annoying force through his bottom teeth.

Roy said: 'A bloody marvel! It's like you said, you feel small when you meet a man like Mr Coates. After all, not many men would condescend to mix with the humble after leading thousands of men like Mr Coates has.'

They false-smiled their admiration at Coates, heaping him with laurels as worthless as cabbage leaves.

'You know there was no damned meeting,' said Coates.

'No meeting?' The florid face expressed great consternation. 'No meeting?' Enlightenment replaced concern. 'Ah—I know what happened—the authorities put a stop to it. I bet they got Special Branch out. They recognise a dangerous man when they see one. Don't you worry, boy—they can't keep a good man down. Look at Marx—Lenin—Stalin—look at the trouble they had. They don't like clever men like you. Put 'em down, they say—Ted Heath's good enough to lead the country, this man Coates is a real leader. Put him down. That's what they say.'

Coates clenched his hands into fists. 'I'll put you down, you fat sod!'

'I shouldn't try it, boy. Besides, you'd be soiling your hands. You're for great things. When you come into power you can 'ave me shot—up against that engine shed over there. Up the Liberals!'

'Shit!'

'As the sewage worker said, an' he wasn't far wrong. That your loco over there—on track seven?'

'You know damn well it is.'

'Keeping to diagrams? That's a silly question. They wouldn't bugger a man like you about. They're too scared. Me an' Roy now —that's a different thing. They don't care how much they bugger us about, although we had good diagrams today, didn't we, Roy?'

'Never better. Signals right all along the way. No taking on over-loads. Roses all the way.'

'So we've got normal stop-over. I'm a contented man.'

'And stupid,' said Coates. 'You sit on your fanny and let the management bleed you—you're a hole in the workers' pocket. All you can do is take the piss out of a better man. You're a traitor to the working class.'

The driver sighed. 'I know, Mr Coates. I can't help it if I like Ted Heath, bless his little blue bootees. I can't help it if I'm happy with my lot. I save a quid a week and I'm on the credit side. I'm no good to the country—neither is Roy here.'

'What'll you do when you come to power, Mr Coates? I mean, will you put us down like he says—you know, up against a wall and bang—bang—bang?'

'I'd black-list the whole bloody bunch of you,' said Coates. 'Shooting's too clean for scum like you. I'd put you in a labour camp on Dartmoor and sweat blood out of you until you behaved like men.'

'Dartmoor, is it?' The driver expressed interest, leaning forward with a look of pleasant expectancy. 'I like the West Country. Spent a fortnight there this summer—with the wife. Lovely place. Well—that's something to look forward to, Mr Coates. Up the Workers, an' a happy Christmas to one and all.'

Coates rose from the table. 'Up yours,' he said.

As he closed the door behind him he heard them burst into thigh-slapping laughter. Rage burned in him like acid as he crossed the tracks to his locomotive. It seemed he had no place to go except the cabin of the diesel. He would sit there, nurse his resentments and doze off until wakened by Spencer in time for the next leg of his day's work.

Sleep ebbed away from Kemp and he became conscious of the rain falling on his upturned face. He came back to the world retaining the reality of his dreams. So convinced was he that he was in his sixteenth year and making it with Lily against a tree in the Fields, he disbelieved the hands lying in the lap of a gaberdine raincoat —denied that they were his or that the raincoat covered his body.

The girl was Lily Hummerstone, whose breasts were the first he had ever touched.

'Lily?' He spoke to her across the Fields, through the rain and into his dream. Saw again her wide blue eyes as she reluctantly allowed him to unbutton her dress. 'Lily—let me!'

The feeling had been incredible; so soft and smooth and secret that he had sobbed with the force that had swept through him. He raised his hands from the gaberdined lap and held them up, palms uppermost. What else had his hands held? Memory of Lily faded as he looked at the stubby hands with thick broken fingernails.

Reality was damp and cold. He felt his hair, wet and straggled on his scalp; and there, perhaps three-quarters of a mile away, was his mother with a warm towel ready to dry the young wet head and feed him with hot, sweet milky cocoa and buttered toast.

He got to his feet and felt the trembling in his knees and a resurgence of fear. He put his hand in his pocket and felt the reassuring roughness of the gun-butt. Gripping it tightly, he turned his face to the north and home. After a few stumbling steps he got into his stride and made for Fieldway Crescent which led to the Holloway Road and Ringcroft Street.

Greenlaw said: 'As complete a history as any copper could desire.'

The dossier on Kemp had been compiled with great speed but no lack of detail. Suffolk CID had found the quest for information easy. The dead woman's relatives in Stowmarket had been contacted shortly after midnight and the compilation of the dossier begun. Photos had been produced, copies and enlargements taken, and images of these wired south to London, north as far as Hull and west to Cambridge.

A conference room had been commandeered by Greenlaw and now Weston, three detective constables, a detective sergeant and a squad-car controller sat with Greenlaw and analysed the dossier.

'If Weston is correct and Kemp is in London we must ask ourselves *why* he's come here,' said Greenlaw.

'You can lose yourself in the smoke,' Detective Sergeant Clay offered. 'Just a face in the crowd.'

'The suggestion that he was mentally unbalanced comes out very strongly in the information given by the wife's relatives. I don't know if that can be trusted. Relatives aren't particularly noted for impartial judgement. The dead woman's brother says Kemp wasn't an easy companion. Inclined to brood. Thorny. Well—I know many people like that.'

Hesitantly, Weston said: 'Perhaps he didn't intend coming up to London. I mean—if he'd travelled across country and just happened on Manningtree—'

Greenlaw cut in: 'How easy is it to get on the station? That is—without going through a ticket barrier?'

'That's no trouble, sir. There's no barrier as such. In any case, if you come across the fields you can very easily get on the line a bit beyond the station and walk back to the platform.'

'So you don't need a ticket to board the train.'

'No, sir—you can pay when the ticket collector comes round.'

Clay had been studying the dossier; he now said: 'I've been looking at his connection with London. He was born here, in Islington, stayed there until his mother died, that was in 1950. Then he went to Stowmarket to work. Met his wife there.'

'What does that suggest?" asked Greenlaw.

'What does a man on the run make for—safety or what seems to suggest safety? I hate to mention the word psychology but this man isn't a criminal in the accepted sense of the word. He sounds like a case of diminished responsibility and all that—wife and child murderers usually are. I don't like them the better for it, but the point is they haven't killed for gain so there's no getting away with the loot. They're simply running away—as simple as that, sir.'

'Or they hook a big toe in the trigger guard of a shotgun, look down the barrel and pull the trigger,' said Greenlaw. 'Which is what Kemp might have done. We've only Weston's identification to prove he's in London.'

'I'm convinced it's the man I saw, sir.'

'It's a very ordinary face,' Greenlaw said. 'He wore ordinary clothes. I'd say the scar is the only reliable bit of evidence we've got. But then I've got one too, above my right eyebrow.'

The scar was less noticeable than Kemp's—his had been livid against the white-grey pallor of his face; Greenlaw's was only slightly darker than his ruddy complexion.

'But I believe he is our man,' he continued. 'At least, I'm prepared to back the hunch.'

'What's the next move, sir?' asked Clay.

'A general squad-car look-out in Islington—we can work out an area coverage—say a couple of miles' radius from—where did the chap live?'

'Somewhere off the Holloway Road—midway between Highbury Corner and Drayton Park.'

Greenlaw turned to the squad-car controller. 'How many Pandas can we put out?'

'Ten, if need be.'

'Issue photos of Kemp and send four cars out on the road. Instruct them not to intercept if recognised but inform HQ and wait for instructions. A radius of two miles—Highbury Corner at centre. Got that?'

'Yes, sir.'

'And don't forget to warn them that Kemp may be armed.'

'Very good, sir.'

The controller left and Greenlaw looked at Weston. 'I want you with me. I think you'll learn more this afternoon than a whole week of lectures. Also, you've seen our man or, rather, you've seen a man like Kemp. Now—you three,' Greenlaw pointed a finger at the detective constables, 'I want you to hang around the immediate area. Use your eyes—cafés, parks—anywhere. Ask a few questions and show Kemp's photo. But no action. Report anything you see but keep away from him. Any questions?'

'No, sir.'

'Off with you then.'

As Kemp came out of the trees bordering the Fields, the sound of an ambulance in the near distance came to his ears. Or was it a police car? He prickled with suspicion and stepped back into the shelter of the trees; he had felt protected in the deserted Fields— it would take a little time before he had the courage to make the home run.

CHAPTER 7

Afternoon, 14.30 hrs.

It had dawned on Elizabeth Marwood that she was attracted to other men. Whether it was because their interest in her had awakened a reciprocal interest, she did not know. It must be part of the process of liberation, she reasoned; a revived interest in sex and something quite different from the mechanical responses of a body geared to obey a pattern of physical stimulation (How else could marriage survive? she thought-whispered to herself). She had watched their hands, observing texture and imagining being touched by them. She had responded to the challenge offered by their physical presence; she could plot them accurately—how they would react to chance, to a touch, but they were still a challenge.

Over lunch, knowing that the men from Africa and India found her attractive, she had considered her own responses very carefully and clinically, imagining intimacy with them and enjoying the experience.

On the morning train, too, she had noticed how Paton and Martin had looked at her. You talked and eyes and mouth were watched. But eyes wandered and conjectured; X-rayed beyond the outer covering and found the hidden places. Not that she had considered Paton or Martin as anything but amusing train companions.

So how should she now consider herself? As Elizabeth Jones,

spinster of this parish, back at the beginning with a reasonable pick of men before her? As Elizabeth Marwood, mother of two children under a holy vow of matrimony, comforter in sickness and in health, for richer or poorer with no men before her? And that rhymed, she told herself, a rough rhyme to describe a state of poverty. But that was how it had been. She would love and honour, but obedience was another thing altogether; not only did she attract men, she was attracted to them. She would do nothing about it, of course, nothing *actual,* that is. Thought—that was something else and private to herself. If it stayed in the mind no one would be hurt. It was one way of having your cake and eating it.

If only Hugh had had a productive day. If only the editor of the local newspaper had contacted him with an offer; a features page, perhaps, that wouldn't tax his energy too much and might even revitalise him. It was bad for a man to rely entirely on a small private income derived from the labours of others; it made him a parasite and Hugh was conscious, miserably conscious, of this.

She stared at the foolscap sheet in her typewriter. Damn that inheritance and the chance it had seemed to offer! Hugh wasn't a writer, he was a newspaper man, pure and simple. A break-through, he had called the legacy—the chance to write all those frustrated novels and plays. Four years ago. Four years of rejection slips and letters of rejection, vague encouragement and distinct discouragement leading to nervous breakdown. Damn, damn the inheritance!

Elizabeth looked at the analysis she had been typing and forced herself to concentrate. It was hopeless. She had daydreamed and angered herself into inefficiency. Ripping out the foolscap sheet she began again, forcing husband, family, the men from Africa and India, sex, hands and self from her mind.

Two glasses of after-lunch port had combined with the day-so-far's intake of Scotch to put Mr Thorpley into a state of drowsy drunkenness. He watched Mrs McCartney clearing the table with sleepy, humorous eyes.

'A perfect lunch, Mrs McCartney. Why you chose to cook men's geese instead of Cordon Bleu dishes I can't imagine. I'm sure you were always better slaving over a hot stove.'

'That's my business. I'll not be head cook and bottle-washer to some git of a man.'

'Some of us are quite lovable.'

'Not you—you're too bloody rich.'

'I am, aren't I?' said Mr Thorpley. 'I give it away and pay high wages but it keeps accumulating.'

'You've had too good a run.' Mrs McCartney poured herself a glass of Thorpley's port and drained the glass.

Watching her, he observed: 'Without so much as by your leave. Too good a run, Mrs McCartney?'

'How you've managed it all these years, I don't know. You've never been raided. What do they think you've got here—the YWCA?'

'Friends in high places, I suppose—also I'm a gentleman.'

'My foot!'

'It's true, you know, Mrs McCartney—I can prove it. Look at my attitude to you. I could treat you as if you were nothing but a draggle-tail—a scrubber—but I'm always the perfect gentleman and employer. Do you deny it?'

'Every bloody word! I'm worth fifty a week and you know it.'

'I had in mind sixty.'

Mrs McCartney put down the tray she was about to carry to the kitchen as Mr Thorpley's words hit her.

'Sixty?'

Mr Thorpley nodded. 'However, I'm prepared to take your estimation of your worth. Fifty it is as from next week.'

'You said sixty.'

'Did I? Must be the port.'

'A gentleman would keep to his word.'

'A gentleman never doubts a lady's word. You said fifty and fifty it is—and money well spent, Mrs McCartney. You keep a good table and an orderly house. Now, I shall nap. I'll have tea at four —that will give me ample time to catch the six-forty.'

'Why the hell you don't live in town I don't know,' said Mrs

McCartney. 'Travelling up every day's a waste of time. What do you go home to?'

'The life of a gentleman,' said Mr Thorpley, and composed himself for sleep.

He closed his eyes and heard Mrs McCartney leave the room, and the quiet thud of the door as it closed behind her. The life of a gentleman in the great Tudor house he had bought ten years ago was exactly the status he enjoyed in the parish of Kettlebatch. The duality of his life was the easiest thing in the world to live with. He had never refused a single invitation to a vice-president's list —perhaps it was the inclusion of 'vice' that attracted him, moved him always to contribute never less than fifty pounds to the Youth Club, or the Local Amenities Council or the Kettlebatch Cricket Club's kitty. His gardens were opened regularly to the public and the proceeds donated to the Red Cross, and twice a year he allowed his grounds to be used by the Church Restoration Fund for their Spring and Autumn fêtes. Everything to do with the house was so nice and gentle and generous—he was the original, lovable nob. The vicar had indeed told him so in public when he had opened the last Autumn fête. The speech was crystal clear in Thorpley's memory:

'And last but not least, my dear friends, our thanks to Mr Thorpley for his constant goodwill and kindness. Such men make the world a better place and give us hope that the finest human virtues are indistructible. Truly—and I hope he will forgive me—the village voice comes near the truth when it uses our benefactor's pet description "The original, lovable nob" and I will add, "on whom God has cast his heavenly light".'

Good sense has prevailed throughout my life, he thought, as he daydreamed into sleep. After the war how much did I have? A nest-egg of three thousand pounds; I was demobbed a major out of Intelligence with eight hundred and what did I do? The sensible thing, of course. I bought a house in London and stocked it with what men most desire. Immoral? Most certainly, but how else is it possible to multiply three thousand eight hundred pounds into a modest fortune of some twenty-five thousand without exploitation?

He daydreamed on and thought of Christmas presents for the flock of people to whom he owed gifts. Maurice deserved a good one, *and* the other steward, Charlie. A fiver or a tenner? How beautiful it was to have money! But mustn't be ostentatious. He would make it a fiver, a token appreciation of the service rendered on the return journey when the miniature Scotch would be placed to the right of the buffet counter immediately the bar opened.

All passion spent, he thought, and I am happy and contented. I want neither man nor woman, but I love them all.

Three-quarters drunk, he slipped into a deep afternoon doze, counting his blessings as if they were sheep.

The benison of an afternoon nap was also being enjoyed by George Denning and Wellford in the sitting room of George's house in Ipswich. May Denning had given them a solid lunch of steak-and-kidney pudding, *real* mashed potatoes and greens, followed by treacle pudding and custard.

May, in the kitchen, heard George's snores in unison with the quieter sleep-rasp of Wellford's, and likened the sound to a chicken coop. An afternoon noise, drowsy and associated more with a bee-buzzing hot afternoon in summer than a midwinter's day.

She looked at the kitchen clock; another twenty minutes and she would wake them with a cup of tea that George would greet with his usual 'Good old corpse reviver'.

It was good that he and Joe Wellford got on so well; a pity that Joe would have his own loco next Spring when he would qualify as driver. But very nice for *him,* though—he'd make a good driver and no wonder, he'd been under George's care and influence long enough to learn what it was all about.

She looked at the clock again. Anthony should be home by now —his shift ended at two o'clock. Like father like son, she thought; he'd have gone into the Buck's Horns for a drink with his mates before coming home to the dinner she was keeping warm in the cooker.

Another seven years and George would retire. There was no apparent insecurity ahead of them; old age would descend upon them for good or ill and there was nothing to do about it.

A quiet, settled life with George was all she had ever wanted . . . The arrogant, perky call of a diesel's bugle came drifting across from the station to interrupt her thoughts. It was a sound she knew so well, part of the furniture of her mind. Many times she had fitted the two-note call to *'Denn-ing!'* as she waited for George on his return runs from London; times when the train had run late and she had anxiously looked out of the window and seen how fog obliterated all sight. But, eventually, George's bugle call had come blaring across the town, the voice of George despite the fact that it might be some other hand pressing the button on the controls.

She picked up the *Radio Times* and turned to the TV programmes for Monday. *Panorama* at eight o'clock, then the news, and at nine-twenty *The Troubleshooters* which George called the Ulcermakers, a programme he enjoyed because it so aptly illustrated the life he would hate to lead.

The 6.40 from Liverpool Street would pull into Ipswich at 7.55. George would walk through the door at 8.30. Half an hour or so for supper and they would settle down in the armchairs and help the Troubleshooters spend millions of television money.

She filled the kettle and put it on the cooker.

Monica leant on an arm and looked down at the closed eyes of John Davies. The bedroom was dark and secret but with sufficient light for her to observe how still he was; not exactly tranquil but resigned to tiredness, a blessed tiredness.

She said: 'Are you asleep, Mr Davies?'

His mouth twitched into a smile. 'No, Miss Inchbald. I've abandoned myself to the magic of the moment.'

'You're a good lover.'

'So are you.'

'Do we have a future?'

Davies' eyes opened and looked gravely at her. 'I submerged it in the here and now—in you.'

'That's very sad.'

'I'm a sad man with an uncertain future.'

'I'm hardly your past. How can you have no future when you're part of mine?'

'Difficult.'

She lay down close beside him, her body touching his from cheek to leg. He passed his hand down from her shoulder, along the clean smooth line of back to the rounded buttocks, then up again, his hand leaving her back and curving under to touch the soft obstruction of her breast.

'I'd like one,' he said.

'The same again?'

'Not yet—I meant a future. I've gambled it away, Monica. It's like having terribly good health; so good in fact that you never really consider that it might be expendable and use it and abuse it until something inside conks out. And then you realise just how frail you really are.'

'Are you ill?'

'Oddly enough, I'm not. I should be. I'm told people's hair can go white overnight—or they get ulcers and have nervous break-downs. I haven't gone silver-haired—I haven't ulcers and, up to meeting you, I'd have welcomed a total breakdown so that I'd never know again who I was and who my dependants were. Meeting you has made—well—you know the cure for old age in the Middle East? They bring a young girl to an old man. Her youth wakes up all sorts of glands in the old man so that after he's taken her he feels years younger.'

'But you're not an old man.'

'I'm fifty-one.'

'You could be forty-one.'

'No—it's a fact. I've a drunken, unhappy wife and two very large sons and I passed the fifty-one mark last month. And I feel years younger.'

'That's good, isn't it?'

'Not in my case, because it isn't true—I only feel ten years younger. An illusion. You're an illusion.'

'I'm real. You feel me.'

'I have and you're beautiful. I can't believe my luck—just as I've found my bad luck hard to believe.'

'If you want to tell me about it—the bad luck, I mean.'

'I'll tell you a parable,' he said. 'How beautiful your breasts are.'

'Is that the parable?'

'I was side-tracked. There was once a man who made money for other people. Much money and they were well pleased with him. Then he found that while these people were growing richer and richer, he was growing poorer and poorer.'

'He sounds a nice man.' Her lips moved against his shoulder. 'Why do you smell so good?'

'I don't know. This man now . . . he had some money, too—not much but enough to try and do for himself what he did for others. So he did all the right things with spells and magic but it didn't work and he lost everything, so what do you think he did?'

'Shacked up with a rich heiress?'

'No—he began to use the money that belonged to the people he'd served so well. He said to himself, "Dai, bach—that's Welsh —what you will do, boy, is that you will use their winnings to cover your losses. You have had bad luck, hoggan drug. You will make money with their money and not only pay them back but make enough for yourself to clothe your body in rich garments and give rubies and diamonds to the woman you love.'

'I don't need any more, John.'

'But do you know what happened? . . . Oh—there was weeping and wailing in Bethesda! He took bigger and bigger chances until there was nothing left and the day was nigh when the people for whom he had made money would call on him and say, "Dai, bach—what has your golden touch brought us in the way of dividends—eh, boy?" So Dai travelled to see an old friend and told him if he did not have a big bag of gold by morning he would be torn limb from limb—and the old, very dear friend clapped him on the shoulder and said, "Who am I to turn away a good and trusted friend—here's a penny, Dai, bach, and do not spend it all at once." '

'Poor Dai. What happened then?'

'On his way back to be torn limb from limb he met a beautiful frog and shared his last crust of bread with her. Perhaps he liked frogs—I don't know—and she turned out to be not only beautiful but very, very rich. But, and this is important, he'd fallen in love with her before she told him that he would have his bag of gold.'

'There's still a difficulty, though,' said Monica. 'She's a frog and he's a human. I take it she fancied him. I think she loved him. . . . So what did he do about it?'

Davies was silent for a moment; then he said: 'Do you understand the parable, Monica?'

'Partly. It's very Welsh. John Amos Davies—your name sounds both Jewish and Welsh.'

'It's Welsh. My family tree reveals Reubens and Isaacs and Seths —biblical. The Welsh loved their bibles. I wish I were Jewish—I might have handled my affairs more intelligently.'

'Love affairs?'

'No—business. My Welsh canniness took me just so far. Jewish wisdom might have saved me. I've always felt there's something beautiful in their race—some quality other races haven't got. I wish I had it.'

'At least you've been circumcised.'

'How did you know?'

'I wonder.'

He felt her hands wandering over his body, curving round and down. Restraining her hand he said: 'Did you understand the parable, Monica—the implication?'

'Just that you're short of money. I can't understand why—there's so much of it.'

'But none of it is mine. I'm very serious, Monica. I must tell you something—if I'm to survive I will have to appropriate a fairly large sum of your money. Do you understand?'

'How much?'

'About sixty thousand. It's what I mean about the bag of gold. I've until the twenty-first to get in the clear. I'll just do it—with your holdings. You must understand the score. I will manipulate your money and get in the clear by the twenty-first.'

'Can you do it by then?'

'I think so. It'll be touch and go, but I think I can do it. I don't love you for your money, but I need it desperately.'

'What will happen if I withdraw?'

'I know Viscenti. I know my creditors. Max will hush it up, then crucify me. I'm broke, Monica. Utterly broke.'

The tip of her tongue traced a line along his breast-bone, then up along the side of his neck and round to his lips.

'Monica—are you outraged?'

'Outraged—violated, shamed.' She rested her lips on his, softly and quiescent. Speaking against his mouth, she said: 'I will come to your office tomorrow morning at ten o'clock and assign to you full authority over the Inchbald holdings and you will be rich and I'll be richer and we'll croak like frogs in love. Now be quiet, John.'

A breast was very near his face. In the dim light he could see the erect nipple set in the darker hue of the areola. He parted his lips and gently tongued its tip, feeling it enlarge and harden under his touch. Her hand came round and pressed his head deep into her, desiring him to hurt as he loved her.

Her other hand found him, coaxing and gentle at first, then, as she felt him rise, she tightened and roughened her grip.

'Come into me,' she said. 'Please, John—come into me!'

He felt her leg rise up and bend over his hip, her hand urging him into her and then all sensation converged in his pit as he entered her for the second time in a beautifully incongruous afternoon, the sword of Damocles hanging over his head forgotten in the silken heat that claimed all his thoughts and sensations.

There was a composite man in Helen's mind as she settled down to the afternoon's work. He had the gentleness of Edward and the aggressiveness of her husband, Ivor. He resembled Edward physically, grey eyes, slim body, fair hair, but, inside, the lion that was Ivor prowled and growled.

She had seen only the lion and not the rapacious monster in Ivor when she met and married him. She had wanted to be eaten, had been consumed many times and regurgitated with equal regularity until the process had tired her. The metaphor was odd, she told herself, for she, too, had appetites needing attention. But somewhere along the line, her own had been dispersed by the urgency and brutality of Ivor's leaving her with nothing but an intense feeling of outrage. With Edward it would be different. There would be consideration and gentleness and each would feed at the same source with mutual love. If only some small measure of assertiveness would enter him; some power of decision to cut across the petty, social considerations that seemed to dominate his life. *Our* lives, she corrected herself. No—it was his life; hadn't she told him she was ready to cut and run at a moment's notice? If there had been children to consider she would have understood his reluctance to burn his boats. Yet there was this fear of insecurity; this reluctance to give up ridiculous possessions and a miserable way of life that had taken years to achieve. The fear of trouble; that mysterious, dreaded element which bound unhappy people together. Fear of castigation, the words of criticism from vicious tongues. It was fear, fear, fear. It dominated their lives. Again she corrected herself—*his* life, although his fear was transmitted to her when she was with him so that she shared his uncertainties and misgivings.

Was there no way out? Was there nothing more to their relationship than train journeys and lunchtime meetings?

She looked at the wall clock. Three-thirty. Ivor would be home now preparing for his journey tomorrow; inspecting shirts for missing buttons and looking, actively looking for cause for complaint. And nursing a solid knot of anger as he remembered her successful defence ploy on Sunday night. She hoped pain accompanied the memory.

Then Miss Chambers, in charge of the typing pool, called her to the telephone. It was Ivor.

'I've decided to leave this afternoon.'

'Oh, yes.'

'Does that change your plans at all?' A sarcastic edge to his voice.

'No.'

'There's little enough to keep me at home. There's nothing here I can't get elsewhere.'

'I'm sorry.'

'If you were you'd do something about it.'

'I can't.'

'I've done as much as any man to make our marriage work—'

'I don't want to talk about it, now.'

'Then you'll damn' well listen! What sort of woman are you, anyway? You've never wanted for anything. I've always kept my side of the bargain. Christ knows I've had reason for going off with someone else—but I haven't.'

'Perhaps that's what you should do. As you say. There's nothing at home you can't get outside.'

'That's typical of you. You make no effort to make our marriage work. Last night was typical, too.'

'It was, wasn't it? Rape's typical, too.'

His voice came back to her, quiet and deliberate. *'I'll be away three days. If I find you at home when I return I'll take it to mean that we're still husband and wife in the real sense. If you're not at home, I'll take it you're not coming back and* you *can take it that you won't be welcomed back.'*

'I can answer that now.'

'I don't want your answer now. You think about it for three days. It's up to you. I've done all I can.'

'Have you? . . . Yes—I suppose you have. The fact that it isn't enough isn't a reflection on you.'

'You don't want a man in bed with you—you want a psychoanalyst shaped like a Teddy Bear.'

'That's true, Ivor—I'd like that. I must look for one.'

'Damn you!'

She was trembling as she put down the receiver. It had reached the ultimatum stage at last and truths had been told. She wanted a Teddy Bear psychoanalyst—what did *he* want? Something he could get away from home—a tart—a prostitute; it was what he had always wanted from her. She shuddered as she imagined herself giving him what he wanted in the way he wanted it. There was no gentleness in the vision; touch was a searing grip of sharp claws. That couldn't be sex; it lacked the happiness contained in 'coming together'. To Helen the phrase held no double meaning—it contained no euphemism; it meant the simple coming together of people in love and respect.

To Ivor, the part was the whole.

Edward was gentle and hesitant. His love-making would be kindly and unobtrusive. At least she had a choice between the lion and the lamb.

But later, as she took the letter file to the department head for signatures, she realised that she had no choice; it seemed to be Ivor or nothing. Edward would *never* make his decision . . .

She returned to her desk and, having no pressing work to get on with, turned her mind to other things. Taking her Christmas shopping list out of her personal file she pondered on those names in the list for whom she had yet to buy Christmas presents. For some reason it did not occur to her to strike Ivor's name off the list, despite the fact that it came before Edward's.

Five floors above, Edward Ferris viewed the growth of the afternoon with mixed feelings. On the one hand it was getting nearer the time when he would again be with Helen. On the other hand it brought him nearer the trek home and repetition of the weekend's misery.

He could see no way out. Margaret would strip him of everything: pride, possessions—everything, if he stepped out of line. She would sue for divorce and tell harmful lies in the divorce court.

'He isn't capable of—conjugal relation, my Lord.'

He could hear her sharp voice ringing throughout the courtroom.

'Perhaps you would tell the court precisely what you mean, Mrs Ferris.'

'Certainly, my Lord. He's impotent, if you see what I mean. He's not a man.'

'*You mean he is incapable of sexual relations?*'

'*Yes, my Lord.*'

Ferris's cheeks flushed. The figures he was totting up blurred and he lost the tally. He began again, but the divorce court judge's voice was loud.

'*Mr Ferris—your wife has claimed that you are sexually incapable. Do you agree with her statement?*'

'*It's not that I'm incapable, sir—it's that—*'

'*Yes?*'

'*I can't with her.*'

'*But you can with other women?*'

'*I don't know.*'

'*Mr Ferris—have you consulted a doctor? The reason why I ask is that I would like to determine whether you have done your utmost to preserve your marriage.*'

'*I have not been to a doctor. I did not consider it necessary.*'

'*Not necessary?*'

The judge's face was stern and disapproving. '*I understand several of Mrs Ferris's relatives are in court to testify. What is the object of their testimony, counsel for the plaintiff?*'

'*To prove that Mrs Ferris has been a faithful wife and has done everything in her power to make a man of her husband.*'

'*Very well—I will admit their evidence.*'

And more lies would be told to prove his incompetence.

Ferris considered the evidence against him; it was overwhelmingly in his wife's favour. He could not even claim a noticeable sexual urge outside his marriage, no sex fantasy in which he could indulge an unsatisfied desire. With Helen, it was a case of love in its purest sense; the sexual side was, somewhere, part of it, but something to happen later. When words and expressions failed to communicate the power of his love then sex would take over and say all that needed to be said.

He was sure he would not be impotent with Helen.

'*What are the grounds for this petition, counsel for the plaintiff?*'

'*Adultery, m'lud.*'

'With whom?'

'A Mrs Helen Thomas. It is alleged that on several occasions
the defendant, Edward Ferris, had carnal knowledge of Mrs
Thomas.'

Margaret would never petition on those grounds, even if they
were true. She would use methods more likely to humiliate him; of
these, his impotence was the most hurtful. Never again would he
hold his head high.

He had not told Helen of his disability. Incompatibility had been
enough, his unhappiness ample evidence that his marriage was
a failure. With someone like Helen the disability would vanish
and potency return. True, it had never been strong; it had been
stirred by Margaret's uninhibited desire and methods of seduction.
Had they not started a child?

But Margaret had aborted at six months. Another crime to lay
on his doorstep; his spermatozoa were crippled little tadpoles, incapable of mating decently with a healthy ovum. *Her* words; Margaret's words coloured with terms learned from one of the many
sex books in that top drawer of the bedroom chest. *The Psychology
of Sex, Married Love,* the art of this and the art of that all jostling
with the devices of sex, the off-putting paraphernalia of conception
and contraception. The dutch cap in the round flat box of talcum
powder, the vaginal jelly, the pills and the box of fifty condoms.
The collection made him feel a little sick. It looked like the gear of
a prostitute. It reduced love to a surgical operation.

'I'm only trying to help you, Eddie,' Margaret had said.

Help by showing him pornography? He had been really sick;
fetching up the supper she had cooked.

'Doesn't it move you?' she had asked.

On the settee he had looked at the glossy German paperback;
at the great close-ups of the sex act and its variations; the horrific
world of sex organs blasting his vision.

He had vomited; the sick rising in a quick flood so that it left
him in a fierce spout that spattered down on the obscene pages of
the book.

The vileness of the memory hit him still. The pictures had seared
their image on his brain, like obscene operations, nothing to do
with love: not with Helen, not with him. Whose idea had the pornography been? Had Frank, her brother, the amateur psychologist,
worked out that little plan? He could imagine the report she gave
him and his reaction.

*'He was sick, Frank. The old prude was sick all over the
naughty pictures.'*

*'Doesn't affect me that way. Light blue touchpaper and retire
immediately.'*

'You're a real man, Frank. Perhaps if you had a word with him.'
And Frank had.

*'Hear you and Maggie are having a bit of difficulty. What's
wrong, old man?'*

'I'd rather not talk about it.'

*'We've always been open with each other, Maggie and me. If
she says there's something wrong, Eddie—'*

'It doesn't concern you.'

*'Pardon me, old man—Maggie's my sister, so it does. She lost a
baby, you remember that. The sooner she gets one in the oven
again, the better.'*

'You don't have to tell me that.'

*'Okay. Why don't you get medical advice? Nothing to be
ashamed of. You were put off by the miscarriage, is that it?'*

'I don't want to talk about it.'

'What about AIH?'

'AIH?'

*'Artificial insemination by husband. Feller I know did it. Wife
conceived in three months. If you can't manage it one way, it's
sensible to try another. All you do is go along to the doctor's surgery—both of you—and Bob's your uncle.'*

'What happens?'

Ferris remembered the grin on his brother-in-law's face and the
harsh chuckle.

'You take yourself in hand, Eddie'

The Clan was filthy-minded. He loathed them all and he had to go back to them.

One half of the street of houses he had known had gone, replaced by modern houses like a rude interjection on his memory. Number 19 still stood, the last of its line, and he wondered why it should have been spared. Kemp stood outside the house and related it to his memory, noting the changes. A reeded glass door had replaced the heavy, artificially grained door he had kicked as a small boy, because the knocker was too high for his reach. He remembered the worn patch his boots had made six inches above its bottom. And in the front garden there had been a mysterious hump, brick-built and cemented over, standing some twelve inches high on which he would sit for reasons he couldn't remember. It was no longer there.

The lamp-post on the pavement outside the house—the old one —had gone, replaced by a straight up and down concrete shaft topped with a sodium light. The post he had known had been of cast iron with a bar right-angled out from the base of the lamp it-self. He had tied ropes to it and used it as a swing like all the other kids.

There was no sign of his mother. No sign of Alfred Thackeray with whom he had collected conkers. Where were the winter warmers? The cocoa tins punched with holes containing smoulder-ing rags which you swung round your head to get them glowing? And the long whips which you made yourself and cracked like a lion tamer; his, eighteen feet in length, had been the best in the street, producing a report as loud as the explosion of the Little Demon bangers he and Alfie had put through letter-boxes when the firework season came round.

There was no one in the street and that was strange. The Smiths, the Hummerstones, the Mowbrays, the Palmers, the Browns, where had they all gone? Lily, where was she now? And her father Fred, always out of work for some reasons that had never bothered the little Kemp. Were they all dead and gone? He walked slowly up the street without fear; without the fear that had stayed with him until he had turned off into Ringcroft Street.

The two boys, Cox; he hadn't liked them and they hadn't liked him—Number 23. Bobby Rance, whose name was really Gladys and his first sexual memory; showing her the game Alfie had introduced him to. In her father's garden shed he and Alfie had shown themselves to her—and she had too, and that was all. An adult action they had supposed it to be and could see no point in it other than that it was forbidden for reasons quite beyond them. Bobby lived in Number 30. There was no sign of her. Number 40, where the quiet ladies called Foster lived, a favoured house for *Knock Down Ginger*.

In his mind Kemp attached thin string to the Foster's knocker, then carefully paid it out and round to the next house whose knocker received the other end. Now he carefully lifted the knocker and banged it once, scuttling with Alfie into cover. He saw the door open, tighten the string, raise the knocker of the Misses Foster's house, snap and summon one of them to their door. That had been a good game with variations; it was possible to start a chain reaction along several houses if you had the nerve.

He reached the end of the street and felt a return of unease. He turned on his heel, back to the sanctuary of his house. Passing Number 37 he saw again the fire engines outside and the shrouded figure the firemen had brought out of the house on a stretcher— the first time he had seen death.

Again outside Number 19 he thought into the house and its rooms. Down the passage from the front door; parlour first left, then a dark room occupied by a shadowy father, then three steps down into the kitchen and scullery. A cupboard in the lobby just before the kitchen; a pantry cupboard and the memory, oh so early, of getting into the cupboard, closing the door and falling asleep to wake hours later with his mother in hysterics because he could not be found.

The rain fell gently on him and it was like the bad-weather days when he and Alfie had played matchstick boats along the running gutters of the street.

He could find nothing in the street, yet he couldn't leave it. Madras Place ran along one end, Palmer's Street at the other. He could walk to Liverpool Road and take James Street to the school he'd attended. Would Flynn be there? The boy who crept behind timorous little boys, gripped them tightly and then bit the lobes of their ears? How he hated Flynn and the bullies who forced the gentle cowards to fight each other. Hated them and the teachers with their unjust canings. He wouldn't go there again, not back to something he detested and had left years ago.

The front door of Number 19 fascinated him. He felt he would like to kick it again until his mother opened it. What lay beyond? Did the same wallpaper hang on the walls? Was the lavatory still in the garden with its noisy, frightening cistern and cut squares of newspaper which could be rolled and smoked?

It was all beyond that closed door; the whole scene of Alfie and street games, the cupboard in the lobby, the shadowy father who didn't seem to live there very much. It was safe there; there, no bullies lurked. Nothing lurked. The door closed behind you and you were home and dry.

Nothing seemed to change in the street as the day waned into early twilight. The drizzle fell softly, persistently, seeping through Kemp's clothes. He didn't feel it. His mind was now totally occupied with his childhood. He brought out his toys while his mother prepared tea. If the weather cleared, he and Alfie would go out into the street and crack whips.

Kenneth Thorneycroft returned to his office at 3.30, his mind filled with an image of the world's starved emaciated millions and the wish that Jesus had been more generous with loaves and fishes. Joseph Carter was all that Chinner had claimed. A naturally good man with no devils to fight except the ever-present monster, man's inhumanity to man.

Carter had said: 'I'm a Christian in a funny sort of way. What I mean is, when I find myself faced with a few thousand starving Africans and I've food only for a couple of hundred I relate it to Christ's super dilemmic performance. The great conjuring trick like the loaves and fishes. I don't get a great laugh out of it. I suppose if I'm pushed I'll admit to being a Christian.'

Universal man is born not made, Thorneycroft told himself. I was born parochial and nothing could be smaller than that. Carter's parish was the world and its inhabitants; its millions his family.

It was a bad day for truth. It had started with the acid, torment-ing RC proselytiser on the train whose words had stung him; Chin-ner had told him home truths and now Thorneycroft had a comparison to hold up to his own image, a living comparison that rendered his own life pitifully small.

The book would probably be the best in the Winter list. Carter intended laying blame on the right doorsteps, directly and unam-biguously, ignoring politics and sophistications, going to the heart of the matter and naming the guilty with the naivety of a man of absolute honesty.

Looking out of the bus window in Oxford Street, Thorneycroft saw the glittering travesty Christmas had become. Selfridges bla-zoned its Christmas greeting of goodwill to all men with a sub-liminal message, *'Forget the agonising world of cruelty and starvation and indulge yourself; eat, drink and be merry, for tomor-row you've a year to recover before the next Christmas spending spree.'* Xmas was the true spelling of Christmas. Christ had left it, the unknown quantity X remaining. X Mass, that's all it was.

Completely dissatisfied with himself, he stared at the decorations strung across the entire length of Regent Street. He saw the pretty, sparkling face of corruption; the window dressing of arch-hypocrisy.

The bus stopped at traffic lights. Buskers—clarinet, accordion and drum—were playing 'Away in a Manger'. They played well, touchingly, and Thorneycroft felt his eyes mist as they always did when he heard this carol.

. . . The little Lord Jesus lay snug in his bed . . .

It was all so basically simple, like Carter who had been given the gift of simplicity. Why was God so sparing in his beneficence that he gave nothing to Thorneycroft?

The bus moved on, the carol fading away until lost in the noise of the traffic.

Am I man or priest? Thorneycroft asked himself. What is the balance of power between the man of greed and common passions and the man of God, for I am both these men? Do I think more of possession than nonpossession?

One eye on the chalice, the other on bed, the solicitor had said. Is that the story of my life so far? Is it? questioned Thorneycroft as the bus turned into Haymarket and he rose from his seat and went down the stairs.

He stepped onto the pavement and turned left into Panton Street, feeling the steady rain on his face. He crossed Leicester Square, noting that the picture houses were advertising the usual mixture of family, sex and violence films. Movies for all tastes; even voyeurs, sadists and masochists had to be catered for in the annual celebration of Christ's birth.

The starlings were roosting early, heralding early nightfall. He stopped for a moment and listened to the high-pitched twittering of the birds in the trees. In the context of Leicester Square and its mechanical sound their song sounded hysterical and neurotic as it accompanied the frenetic sound belting out of a disc boutique across the square. He recognised it as one of the numbers from *Jesus Christ, Superstar.*

Christ had made the charts in a big way. He had become a pop hero and now stood in the ratings equal with Elvis, Dylan, Jagger and Che Guevara.

A prophet of doom passed him as he turned into Charing Cross Road, sandwich boards proclaiming that *'The Wages of Sin is Death'* on one side and *'Jesus said "Love your enemies"'* on the other.

That I cannot and will not do, Thorneycroft told himself. I can only hate and despise them; wish them off the face of the earth and out of my life. I hate their noise, their protests, their judgements.

Carter had said: 'Evil? The evil that men do? Oh—I've accepted the fact that evil's with us for all time. I'm not an idealist. There will never be Utopia—Christian or Humanist.'

'Then why do you care for people?'

'I like doing it and you couldn't have a more selfish reason. I suppose I was programmed at conception, you know, like psychopaths. You wouldn't have surgeons if they didn't have a psychotic love of the knife.'

'Do you pray?'

'All the time. Oh, God—let that bloody plane through with medical supplies and food. Oh, God—put some compassion in those stinking politicians and get them off their haemorrhoidal bottoms. Would you call that prayer?'

'Of a sort.'

Love has died in me, Thorneycroft told himself as he took New Row through to Bedford Row. He passed a porn shop and gave a fleeting glance at the obscene goodies displayed in the window. Even that kind of love has become a loveless function. Life, love, was whimpering out.

And Aline was unhappy because love no longer sustained her. They had run from the world and found themselves in a cul-de-sac. Continuing the metaphor, he imagined turning away from the high, impregnable wall facing them in the cul-de-sac, and finding that in their one-minded romantic flight from reality they had failed to notice that another wall had been hastily erected at the other end of the street. They were trapped and could go neither forward nor back.

Paraphrasing Carter's admission of prayer, Thorneycroft said: 'Oh, God—pull down these bloody walls and let me out!'

The tinkling of bells attracted his attention to a group of young Hare Krishnas shuffle-dancing along the opposite pavement.

'Hare—hare—ha—ha—hare!'

Shaven heads and fan pigtails; light saffron robes spoiled by the need of extra protection against the weather—bovver boots, which contrasted oddly with the sexless garb of the faithful. Faith was no protection against wet and cold.

But their vanity! Thorneycroft stopped for a moment and

watched the group shuffling up the street. They sang about their loneliness and love-losses; their tiny revelations, *bête-noires,* all aired in demos and song, as fashionable as the gear they wore. Their protests were all on the surface; the thing to do and nothing more. Funny clothes to divert the attention from inadequacy.

Like a clergyman's dog-collar, thought Thorneycroft. Like me and my kind.

The bell tinkle died away as the group turned a corner. Puppies huddled together for warmth and that's a cliché, Thorneycroft told himself. Groups were formed because of fear of individual action. Who wanted to be a solitary figure in a hostile landscape standing against the injustices of the world?

Joseph Carter wanted to be a solitary—or couldn't help it. He didn't rely on an uncertain God or his earthly ministry. He loved and fought alone.

The pace of thought had quickened Thorneycroft's step. He found he was walking fast but without objective, for he had passed his office building and was now in Southampton Street and making for the Strand.

Slowly, he retraced his steps to Bedford Row, aware that something had happened to him, a sea-change whose nature was indistinct. He was aware that his personal devils had changed from the abstract to the real—Annersley, Carter and Chinner—strange devils when two of them were such good men. It did not occur to him at that moment to add his own name to the list.

A bottle of scent, French and ridiculously small for £4.50, a microscope, Japanese—Charlie Shelley had tried it in the shop, magnifying a hair from his own head to the thickness of a twig—and two Scalextric racing cars at £1.15 apiece; the result of a lunchtime spending spree. £10.25 the lot. He'd also bought drinks for his fellow executives—double whiskies all round—and that was another £1.32. A grand total of £11.57. The boat had really been pushed out and Shelley had enjoyed it. It was difficult to be oriental about good luck; difficult to look the other way as if nothing had happened.

He had felt an instant camaraderie with Holden and Greaves; already they were on Christian-name terms. In Shelley's previous department it had been mister this and mister that, as if its members had to compensate for their lowly positions by the use of the respectful prefix. It was more casual in the executive room. It was also friendly, sophisticated, inclined to verge on the bawdy, and full of laughs.

It had been a great day and one worth celebrating with a round of drinks and the purchase of pre-Christmas gifts.

Regarding the scent, microscope and racing cars, though, however, on second thoughts and maybe—perhaps it would be better to salt them away until Christmas Day. Added to the known gifts already purchased and stored away in the bedroom chest of drawers, they'd boost the Christmas giving by their unexpectedness.

A bottle of Cinzano Bianco—that, he could take home. He would buy one on his way to the station. Edna would like that. Ice and a slice of lemon—it was Edna's favourite drink.

It felt like having money to burn.

Keith said: 'What's your travelling time, Charlie? From door to door.'

'An hour and fifty-five minutes. If the train's on time.'

'Nearly four hours spent on travel every day. Is it worth it?'

'It's worth a lot more just for weekends and summer evenings. We've got the coast sixteen miles away—Frinton and Clacton. Good country all round us. Sticks before smoke any day. You're Ilford, aren't you—same as Bill?'

'Swinging Ilford. Point is, Charlie—it's near London. You can get into Town in no time. Same for the country. Best of both worlds.'

'I want the best of one and I've got it.'

'What happens in Buggolt, Charlie?' asked Bill. 'Wife-swapping?'

'Bergholt,' Charlie corrected. 'Don't know about wife-swapping on the estate. There's a rumour it happens in a house in the old part of Bergholt. I wouldn't know.'

'Ilford's a den of vice—crawling with sex and savagery.' Keith closed his eyes and shook his head. 'We wife-swap and gamble and we've more company directors and criminals to the acre than anywhere else in the south-east region. The Montmartre and Las Vegas of Essex. They say we put the sex in Es. Trouble is, Charlie —I've never found the vice. What about you, Bill?'

'Brothels, gang hideouts, blue films in garages, the drug scene— Sodom and Gomorrah. Ilford's roaring with lust but all I ever get is the sound of lawn-mowers and the bloody traffic on Eastern Avenue. And the only wild pair of tits I see are blue and covered in feathers.

'Pecking the tops off milk bottles.'

'Lovely birds in Ilford.'

'Nothing like it in Buggolt—just crows and larks and—what about vultures, Charlie?'

'It's a good village,' said Shelley. 'If you want religion you've got Church of England, Methodist, Roman Catholic and Congregational.'

'What about the demon drink?'

'We've got seven of the best pubs in Suffolk—the very best.'

And that's true, thought Shelley. If you pub-crawled you could begin by taking in the Hare and Hounds, then the Beehive followed by the Carriers Arms, the Red Lion, the King's Head and the White Horse; and on the outskirts of the village, if you had any space left, lay the Royal Oak.

Of all the pubs, Charlie preferred the Hare and Hounds and the King's Head. Jim, the proprietor of the Head, was a real benefit to the village; his energy in promoting sports and the hilarious annual pram race round the village (with stops at every pub for half a pint) was real country stuff. Shelley reckoned that the King's Head had more darts in it than Robin Hood and his gang had arrows in their quivers. Did the big city have anything like that?

'You won't find pubs like them in London or Ilford,' said Shelley. 'Suburbanites don't know what they miss by not moving out to the country. They want the best of both worlds and end up getting neither.'

Charlie considered what he said. It sounded snide. He added: 'Maybe I'm lucky. I suppose, given the chance, most people would want to live in beautiful surroundings.'

Constable's country stretched all round Shelley's house and garden; the Dedham Vale and the River Stour, Flatford and beyond the mill, the estuary at Manningtree. And over to the west—Charlie's namesake—the village of Shelley, then Boxted, Higham and Stoke by Nayland. Rich rolling country as rural as you'd want in which you could hear the musical brogue of Suffolk. Beautiful houses—beautiful people.

The best country walk of all was down Donkey Lane to the river. You left the estate and went the length of Gaston Street into the old village—the heart of East Bergholt—past the house in which Randolph Churchill had lived and amused the villagers, then right at the old church with its bell-cage on the ground, and into the road leading to Flatford. After two hundred yards you turned right into Donkey Lane, narrow and thick with dog-roses and red campion, elder and spindleberry, warty oaks and beech, warm and sun-trapped on a summer's day, down to the vale.

At the end of Donkey Lane, Dead River—a bad name for one of the best spots—was an offshoot of the Stour; you could look into its dark green depths and see pike and ling drifting and lurking under the weeds and yellow water lilies. Quiet, warm, beautiful.

Then over the bridge and left along the Suffolk bank of the river until you came to Dedham. You stopped for a while and rested, then returned to Bergholt along the Essex side of the Stour to Flatford Mill, taking in the old scarred willows weeping over the river and the water lilies breaking the surface in spots of bright yellow.

Beautiful. You couldn't ask for more and yet—the one bad spot was Flatford, not in itself but the way in which it was used. Each year the tourists and trippers raped it with noise, litter and carbon monoxide. You could see to Flatford Mill, thought Charlie, paraphrasing the music-hall song, if it wasn't for the trippers in between.

And the strange thing about living in a beauty spot was that you took on a sort of ownership of the place once you lived there. You changed status from visitor to owner; it was yours and you resented it being mucked up by hordes of trippers in cars and coaches.

So you avoided Flatford itself during the high season. You knew they would mass together, contained in a small area of teashops and car parks. You avoided them like the plague because they did something to your sense of peace and well-being. The only way to affect tolerance was to imagine them as poor deprived beggars living in city bed-sitters, so why grudge them a day's outing in God's fresh air?

If only they'd keep away, thought Charlie, then Flatford really would be a beauty spot.

His thoughts went back to July. The sheer beauty of a Saturday morning under early-morning sunshine and a rowing boat from Flatford to Dedham with not a tripper in sight because it was early. A dancing, summer morning; seeing a heron, a pair of kestrel hawks hovering high in the sky; larks ascending and the sound of bees; the lap and stir of the water as the boys dipped their oars and sculled to Dedham; coffee from a thermos as the boat idled under a willow.

'You still with us, Charlie?'

'No. I'm floating down the Stour in a rowing boat and glad I live in the country.'

Holden grinned at Greaves. 'You know what I like best about Charlie, Bill? He's simple.'

'No neuroses—hang-ups—fixations—fetishes.'

'Except East Buggolt. He'll have to watch that.'

'He's a buggoltophile.'

'You wouldn't think it to look at him.'

It was friendly in the executive office, thought Charlie again: it was full of laughs, sophisticated and bawdy.

The office manager brought his afternoon cup of tea over and sat with Elizabeth.

'And how's your day going, Mrs Marwood?' he asked.

'Very enjoyable.'

'I'm glad to hear it. I hear you've made a hit with Africa and India.'

'They made a hit with me. Office work has changed since I last had a job.'

'In what way?'

'People are more friendly. Better relations between the top and bottom.'

The OM smiled. 'It certainly applies to this firm—I don't know so much about the others. Perhaps we're lucky.'

'Even the tea tastes like tea.'

'That's my doing, I'm not afraid to admit. A long time ago I saw a film promoting tea. The commentary was in verse and one line stuck in my mind. 'An earthenware pot is the best of the lot'— so Mrs Hudson, the tea lady, puts her Twinings Assam, a good leaf, into three ultralarge brown Betties. Would you like another cup?'

Later, he again came to Elizabeth's desk with a folder on which her name had been neatly lettered.

'I wonder if you would like to share in this firm's amenities, Mrs Marwood. There are a number of things, and all, I think, worth taking part in.'

The charter-flight club, the private insurance scheme, an office weekend in Boulogne, an investment scheme cropping a 15 per cent harvest—Elizabeth was astonished at the generosity.

'It sounds too good to be true,' she said.

'The other thing is the office party. Friday the 24th. We have a very good buffet lunch laid on, drinks and all the rest. Christmas tree with presents. You *must* come to this, Mrs Marwood.'

It was all this and heaven, too. I shall probably become a bad wife and mother and kick over the traces, thought Elizabeth. I must learn to control happiness, conceal elation and show tiredness and what a drag it all is. A stoical martyr with reluctantly told stories of office injustices but, oh well—that's life.

The world outside was proving to be better than the one inside. She felt a fondness for home and the familiarity of loved possessions (children and husband apart); the safety of knowing where everything was. But there was also the boredom and routine, the cooking and washing up; the endless tasks that comprised the burden of marriage.

Now she could shed the burden for five days out of every week. She could afford to have a woman come in every day to clean the house, cook husband a midday meal and do the shopping. Two hours a day for five days at 30p an hour—£3 a week. If that was the going rate in the village it was money well spent. 75p for the amenities she had bought from the office manager plus £5.00 a week for travel; so far she had spent £8.75 and was left with a balance of £16.25. Income tax and National Insurance had now to be considered? £4.50 in all? Now she was down to £11.75; her spirits depressed accordingly.

Lunches had to be bought, plus occasional coffees (drinks were out of the question) and those couldn't be bought for less than 50p a day; £2.50 for the week unless she lived on sandwiches.

The balance now stood at £9.25 and, so far, she had allowed nothing to the family. Clothes for the children and holidays; £4.00 per week and that *had* to be—it was part of the deal. The residue of £5.25 rattled in her mind like loose change.

But was it quite so bad? £262.50 p.a. personal spending money wasn't exactly a packet of peanuts. Then a sickening thought struck her; would she have to pay National Insurance on the daily help— *£2.15 every week?*

£5.25 diminished to £3.10. Thank God she didn't smoke! The job offered her in Ipswich at £18.00 per week had compared unfavourably with £25.00 in London. But if she cut out the daily help and the cost of travel and added the resulting figure to the Ipswich salary it amounted to £26.00. Calculations and conjecture proved strange, disturbing facts.

Elizabeth Marwood's head buzzed with budgets; then she raised her eyes from the column of figures, looked round the spacious office and liked, actively liked, all that she saw. It pleased and entertained her. Everything had been designed and pledged not only to office ergonomics but also to please the eye and senses (that word had taken on a new meaning) of the employee.

To please *me,* she thought, and I am pleased with everything that's happened today. I feel liberated. I am my own woman and I like it. If that is the real reason why I'm working again, then that's good enough. I don't have to justify it entirely in domestic terms. Enough that a little more security has entered the family's life. I must state a figure and stick to it. On thee, my house and family, I bestow my £5.35 personal spending money or what is finally left of it.

Elizabeth's spirits rose again. She looked at her watch; there was time to call on Africa and India and learn a little more about the Company's business.

Mrs McCartney's kitchen clock showed that it was time for Mr Thorpley's tea. She infused the China tea and cosy-covered the pot, set out cup and saucer, spoon, sugar bowl, milk jug and a tin containing Dundee cake and carried the tray up to his room, muttering to herself that she couldn't see why she had to wait on him hand and foot.

Three of the rooms were being used by girls she could trust; good, hard-working, reliable girls as discreet as they came and quiet about it. Such girls brought class to the profession and Mr Thorpley owed her a debt of gratitude for seeing that none but the best rented rooms in his property.

She opened his door, balancing the tray on one hand like an expert waiter, and approached a Thorpley sleeping dulcet in the armchair. She cleared her throat, wondering why she didn't shake the old devil awake instead of carpet-slippering about in his service.

The sleeping face twitched and slowly animated into wakefulness.

'Tea,' she said, briefly.

'Is it so late?'

'Just after four.'

Mr Thorpley yawned and stretched. 'The house is so peaceful and quiet I wonder if we are paying our way.'

'Three rooms are occupied at the moment, although my girls don't really start work until four. I suppose you want me to pour your tea?'

Mr Thorpley nodded. 'It's a luxury for which I pay through the nose.'

Mrs McCartney emitted a sound of derision and Thorpley smiled.

'Luckily the pot can't call the kettle black, Mrs McCartney, so any remark apropos immoral earnings, etcetera, would come very much amiss.'

'I had no intention.'

She poured Thorpley his cup of China tea, handed it to him, then unlidded the tin and showed him the cake.

'It's Dundee. D'you want any?'

'Did you make it?'

'Of course.'

'Then I will. You may be an ungrateful, argumentative Scottish fishwife but you know how to bake cakes. Won't you join me in a cup of tea?'

'That Chinese muck? I'll make a pot of good honest Indian.'

'I didn't know there were any.'

'Any what?'

'Honest Indians. I've always found them devious.'

'Who's calling the kettle black now?'

'I am. I prefer the rugged dishonesty of the Scots.'

Mrs McCartney watched Mr Thorpley break off a piece of cake from the thin wedge she gave him, followed its transit to his mouth and waited for his nod of approval.

'A very good cake,' he said. 'You feed me well, Jean McCartney.'

'I always did, didn't I?'

Thorpley looked at her, his mind turning back the accumulated calendar leaves of years. 1948 and the joy of a good civilian suit and the feel of demob pay joined with his modest bank balance.

The world was his oyster and he had three thousand eight hundred pounds with which to open that oyster, which, in the light of 1948 conditions, seemed to him as tight as an inveterate virgin's legs.

Mrs McCartney had been young in those days—hadn't we all? thought Mr Thorpley—and he, with no desire or palate for the trials of marriage, but attentive to those desires which could not be put down (cold baths and a run round the block only made it worse) had found her telephone number, propositioned her, learned her address and transacted business with her on a high level of delight. Thereafter, for a number of years a relationship flourished between them on a particular plane of intimacy and non-intimacy in which Mr Thorpley learned how he could put his money to work.

Knowing that she had started him on a trip down memory lane, Mrs McCartney said: 'I taught you all you know, you old tight-wad.'

'To our mutual advantage,' said Thorpley. 'I'm just better at business than you. My success story isn't one of from rags to riches —from pros to princesses is more like it.'

'You've done well,' she admitted. 'I didn't think when you first came to me you'd one day be teaching your granny to suck eggs.'

'I did though, didn't I?' Thorpley grinned. 'If it wasn't such a respectable, damnable magazine, the *Reader's Digest* would publish my story as a model to all ambitious youngsters.' He looked steadily at her, the smile fading. 'Apart from the cash side of our relationship all those years ago, Jean—I enjoyed you, you know? I was even jealous when I allowed myself to think about your other friends. I was utterly faithful to you, if such a statement can apply to our relationship and the conditions under which it flourished. Yes—you always did feed me well. I've not forgotten. Now that I'm old, I revere the memory.'

'You're not so old.'

'I'm as old as I want to be. I hankered after all passion spent when I was quite a young man. Sex is troublesome. Profitable, but troublesome.'

'You were keen enough when you first came to Park Road.'

'I was, wasn't I.'

'And all the times after that.'

'You were very satisfying. Like Tigger in *House at Pooh Corner* I'd found what Thorpleys like best.'

'I don't like to see a man turning into an old queen. One of the girls asked if the quiet, well-mannered gentleman who called every week was a customer.'

'What did you tell her?'

Mrs McCartney hesitated before replying. 'I had to keep up appearances.'

'You mean, you told her I was?'

'Well—I've got my pride. Helps me keep my end up.'

'What an apt expression!'

'I don't enjoy being treated like a maid!'

'For a moment I thought you were going to say "maiden". You're quite right, of course. You've my permission to spread stories about my prowess. Nothing kinky, mark you—good, solid he-man stuff and how I pay you sixty—I mean, fifty pounds a time. That should do your reputation a power of good.'

'That's a funny sort of lie. If I spread that around you'll have them lining up for the same treatment.'

'You can tell them it's a waste of time. That I'm hooked on you and have been since nineteen-forty-eight, and that no one else will do, and Jean—if ever I decide to be young again, I'll prove my words.'

She could see he meant it; his flippancy was only on the surface. Other forces demanded that he accept the celibacy of his self-imposed old age. He wasn't a queen, she knew that; it was a little goad she used more for her own comfort than his discomfort. She remembered his visits in the old days with pleasure, and that was hard to find when pleasure had been her stock-in-trade. The coinage of joy is easily debased.

She saw him growing uncomfortable under her gaze and hoped that her message was getting through. She wanted him to throw off the apparel of quaint senility he'd adopted and romp back into the old days. She fancied the old bastard and that was an end to it. It infuriated her that he behaved like the Queen of the May. She was only fifty, and as capable as any of giving a man of her choice a good time, so why didn't the old goat rise to the bait?

The message got through. He smiled away his discomfort. 'It's true, Jean. I don't know why precisely—there's probably a medical reason for it. It's all passion spent and I'm quite happy. I drink too much and shall until I die, which could be put off if I signed the pledge. If it's any comfort to you—if it were not so, you'd be the first and last I'd turn to.'

Something stung her eyes. It couldn't be the beginning of tears, there was nothing to cry about. No woman had been rejected for better reasons.

She said: 'I'll top up the pot.'

'No—bring the whisky and we'll toast the Campbells of Argyle.'

'You'll not drink to those bloody bastards in my presence!'

They were back on their old footing.

'Departed friends, then,' said Mr Thorpley. 'The Macdonalds of Glencoe.'

Kemp's attention was claimed by the sound of footsteps coming along the street. He turned his head away from the door and peered through the darkness.

A schoolboy carrying a briefcase. He was too tall for Alfie; too well-dressed in dark blue raincoat and school cap.

Kemp knew it wasn't himself, yet the embodiment of the boy coming home from school might have been the young Kemp, but bigger, stronger; a boy immune from the bullying attacks of Flynn and the others.

Billy Kemp coming home from school; coming home from *hated* school.

He watched Billy turn into the short path up to the glass-reeded door of Number 19. *Just kick the door, Billy—Mum will let you in.*

But the boy had his own key; could come and go as fancy pleased him. The old little Billy had had keys; keys with hollow barrels into which you packed the scraped heads of matches, inserted a snugly fitting nail with the point filed flat, then banged it hard down on the ground. The key-banger. But never a key to open the front door. Even when he had grown tall enough to reach the knocker he'd still kicked the bottom of the door. *Do you know about key-bangers, Billy?* What a lot he could show the boy. Winter warmers, the long crack whips, the wooden tops sent spinning up the street and the matchstick races in the gutters when it rained.

The boy closed the door slowly behind him, pausing for a moment to look at the man standing under the lamp-post. And Kemp returned the look as the door closed, mentally watching the boy walk down the passage and the three stairs leading to the lobby and kitchen.

Colin Harris, fourteen, a good student to the pleasure of his parents, walked down the short passage, descended the three stairs and hung his raincoat on the peg-rack, looping the handle of his briefcase over the same peg. Behind the closed door of the kitchen he could hear the buzz of voices that told him the ancients had arrived.

He opened the door and put on the smiling face his mother had instructed him to wear on his return from school.

'Hello, Gran—hello, Grandad.'

The old grumbler was sitting in the wooden armchair his mother had found in the attic when she and her husband had moved into the house twenty years ago. It looked as antique as Grandfather Peartree himself.

Colin nerved himself for the kiss Gran would bestow on him and the smell of something old and scented; then the arms-length inspection and the comment that he had grown.

The cheek-kiss, the scent, the arms-length inspection came.

'How he's grown, Peg. He's gooin' to be tall.'

'How are you, Gran?'

'Mustn't grumble, boy. I leave that to your grandad.'

'Grandad?'

Colin behaved to the letter of the polite law Peggy Harris had insisted upon. He advanced on the old man with hand extended, taking the dry grip and shaking it three times before releasing it.

Peggy Harris said: 'Now you're home we can have tea. School all right?'

'It's okay. Came top in French. Easy.'

'You hear that, Dad? Colin came top in French.'

'French?' Harry Peartree made a rapid incursion to a far-flung memory of the Western Front. 'Wee—wee—parley voo. I spoke a bit o' French—you 'ad to out there.'

'Out where, Grandad?'

'The war, boy. The Great War. Up to our arses in mud.'

'*Où est la guerre?*'

'Eh?'

'I've read about it.'

'That's all people do these days.' Harry's memory lingered above the mud of Ypres and Mons. 'They ought to 'ave bin there.'

It was to be high tea. Tinned salmon and a bowl of lettuce, trifle with a thick top layer of whipped cream, the solid fruit cake baked by Mabel the day before and a big plate of buttered bread.

They took their places round the table and began to eat.

Back at the lamp-post, Kemp said to himself: 'What's for tea, Mum?'

Other children had meanwhile walked the street and entered their houses. Now the street was empty again. But sound had come as television sets were switched on and radios volumed up on music alien to Kemp's memory.

Hot buttered toast and jam. The fire in the kitchen burning glitter-bright and warm; the smell of rain-soaked clothes drying. School over for another day. One day nearer leaving age and the beautiful world of the adult.

Suddenly, all thought concentrated in his hand and the hard object it held deep in his raincoat pocket, feeling the roughness of the butt and the contrasting smoothness of the trigger as his index finger curled round it.

Why was he here? Why had he come?

What's for tea, Mum?

'There's a funny-looking man leaning on the lamp-post outside,' said Colin.

'What was he doing?'

'Nothing.'

'That's all right, then,' said Peggy Harris. 'It's a free country and a cat can look at a king.'

Detective Sergeant Clay rendezvoused with Detective Constable Williams outside the library at the junction of Fieldway Crescent and Holloway Road.

'Any luck, Sarge?' asked Williams.

'No, I thought I had a dozen times.'

Williams looked at his watch. 'The big man's due here at five-fifteen.'

'Greenlaw?'

Williams nodded. 'The village constable's coming, too.'

'How many cars out?'

'Four, and my bloody feet hurt. A cup of tea wouldn't come amiss.'

'What d'you think of him?'

'Who?'

'The village constable.'

'Too bloody sharp. Imaginative. Too much mind over matter. It's my bet Kemp's lying in some ditch with half his head blown off.'

'Nothing to go on,' said Clay. 'Every second man you see wears a gaberdine raincoat and has a hand in his pocket. Do not approach but keep under observation and advise HQ. I could have done that a dozen times today.'

'All the same,' said Williams, 'I wouldn't mind a position identification and seeing the village constable make the approach since he's the only one who's seen the man.'

'Poor bugger.'

Annersley was now in full possession of the facts and the whole sordid story lay on his desk in the shape of press cuttings ranging from the restrained style of *The Times* to the lurid prose of the tabloid dailies.

To define true madness legally was well-nigh impossible, yet the action of Thorneycroft at the height of his passion (how else could he, Annersley, describe the man's action?) was pure insanity. What lay beyond the pretence of the suicide pact? Such action demanded foresight. If they, the guilty couple, had decided to surrender identity and go to the farthest corner of the globe, there to start a new life, if their affair had been accompanied by a crime which had earned a sizable profit, some financial swindle, then the pretence of suicide and flight would have some sense about it. But to be tracked down and ignominiously found in Scotland! But Thorneycroft was no Ronald Biggs; he hadn't even robbed the charity-box in his church.

Annersley had searched the newspapers' reports for evidence of motive, but both parties admitted only that 'they were in love'. A puerile reason, thought Annersley. Both Thorneycroft and the woman had been bound over for two years.

'I wish to remain in the service of God' was the other statement reported in the Press. Such men did great damage to the Christian faith, even if that faith was the ineffectual offshoot known as the Church of England. Reluctantly, as Annersley's thoughts wandered, he admitted that the Anglican Church *had* produced one or two outstanding men. He remembered the deference shown to the Holy Father by Archbishop Ramsey when the Anglican leader went to Rome; he had seemed so awestruck he'd have kissed the boots of the Pope if he had been so instructed.

Boots. Boots suggested shoes and Annersley's mind switched to his delinquent son. Tuesday, December 23rd, and Christmas parole. This time we *will* communicate, thought Annersley. Even if

I have to tie the little swine down in his chair. I will not have my questions answered by a question or an insolent 'So what?' The punishment to fit the crime must be accepted gladly by the boy. There is no escape from punishment except that granted by a merciful God. Expiation is of the essence and criminals must take the knocks. Thorneycroft was certainly taking his.

A cup of tea was brought to him by Briggs, his clerk, who announced that a Mr Samuel Hall would like to consult him.

'About what, Briggs?'

'Some charge—criminal, I suspect. He's out on bail.'

'How much bail?'

'Five hundred.'

Annersley's face showed appreciation. 'Does he look as if he can afford a bail that size?'

'Twenty times that size, I'd say.'

'Then show him in, Briggs.'

The impartial legal mind was brought to bear on Mr Hall's problems. The charge was one of receiving and Mr Hall was perfectly open. He had received stolen property knowing it had been nicked. To be honest, he'd been doing it for years. Okay, the law had caught up with him; he'd heard from friends in the business that Annersley was a sharp legal eagle and knew the ins and the outs of the criminal courts. He had money, had Mr Hall, and didn't fancy a spell inside.

Annersley asked his questions and Mr Hall answered with open candour, even supplying Annersley with a typewritten list of the stolen goods, the receiving of which comprised the total nature of the charge.

'Normally,' said Annersley, 'a verdict of guilty would earn you something like two years. There are certain loopholes, Mr Hall, but it will cost a pretty penny, I'm afraid. Apart from my own fees you will need the services of a barrister. I know just the man— excellent fellow but his fees are high.'

'The sky's the limit,' said Mr Hall. 'It'll cost me a bloody sight more if I do two years' bird.'

'We don't want that to happen to you.'

'You can get me off the hook?'

'A fifty-fifty chance, I would say. Who represented you in court?'

'Nobody. I gave the magistrate a spiel. The coppers opposed bail but the beak overruled 'em.'

'Was Dorland the magistrate?'

'Tha's right.'

'Then I can understand the bail. He made many mistakes last year so he's anxious to make amends. Good. But you should have consulted me beforehand. From the facts you've told me bail might have been fixed at a lesser sum. Now—let's go into your case in greater detail.'

At four-thirty Mr Hall left his new-found friend and comforter, convinced that Annersley would get him off the hook. The onus of proof lay on the shoulders of the police. The case was clear and, despite Mr Hall's self-confessed guilt, Annersley was convinced the plea of innocence of the fact that the goods he bought had been stolen would carry the day. It was really quite an easy case to handle and a profitable one. He'd agreed immediately to a retainer of £200.

A valuable client, Mr Hall; no doubt he would tell his friends. The criminal class had always interested Annersley. A pity he hadn't been called to the bar; *Annersley QC, Criminal Lawyer,* a fine title to be die-stamped in gold on a book of his famous cases.

He looked at his watch—4.45—there was time to consult a friendly and approachable member of the police force with whom he could discuss the case against Mr Hall and, perhaps, contrive to widen the loopholes, since Mr Hall's 'sky's the limit' budget more than suggested that rough places could be made plain.

Since 3.30 the old man had reiterated the question many times.

'You sure Ted'll be 'ere on time?'

Sick of her father's fretting, Peggy Harris said: 'Soon enough to get you to the station on time, Dad.'

'Don't like last-minute rushes. People leave things too late.'

'The train's not till twenty to seven. Plenty of time. Ted's never late.'

She cleared away the tea things, leaving a place laid for her husband; there was a chance he might be home early enough to snatch a cup of tea before driving the old ones to Liverpool Street. She looked at the kitchen clock—quarter to five; he should be home on the stroke of five; if he left for the station at five-thirty that should give them all the time needed to get on the train and for Ted to see them settled down in their seats.

The telephone rang in the sitting room and the boy said: 'I'll answer it, Mum!'

'Never spoken on one of them phones,' said the old man. 'Reckon I'm not likely to start now.'

Colin returned and said: 'That was Dad. He'll be a bit late but not to worry.'

'How late?'

'He didn't say. A bit late, that's all.'

'Ted not comin'?' Harry asked.

'He's coming, Dad. Be a bit late, that's all.'

'Don't want ter miss that train.'

'You won't.'

A little later, the old man pulled out his watch and counted the minutes to the train's departure.

'You sure, Peg?'

She'd had enough and snapped at the old man, 'No, I'm not. I'd better get you to the station.'

Defending him, Mabel said: 'Dad doesn't mean to fret, Peg—it's just his way.'

'It always was.' She softened a little and added: 'It's all right, Mum—I get train-catcher's nerves, too. Ted'll be sorry to miss you. We'll be driving down to Bergholt on Boxing Day. He'll see you then. Now let's get your things together. It's not a long walk to Holloway Station.'

Aware that he was the cause of his daughter's irritability, the old man said: 'I don't mind forkin' out for a taxi.'

'You know how much it'll cost you?'

'I fergit.'

Peggy laughed without humour. 'Nearly a pound—if you're lucky. Tube's quicker, anyway.'

She hustled them into their coats and hats, collected return Christmas gifts and stuffed them into a carrier bag. 'You're going back lighter than you came, Mum.'

'That'll give me a free hand to help Dad up the moving staircases.'

Harry Peartree shook the boy's hand and said: 'Parley voo, boy.'

'Oui, mon grandpère. Guardez la guerre.'

Now that the old man felt he was on his way, a smile creased his face. 'Speaks it like a bloody native,' he said. 'Like a real Frog.'

The boy saw them to the door and out of the house, then went into the sitting room and watched the man standing under the lamp.

Kemp also saw them leave the house. The old man reminded him of his own grandfather who had died in the house in the attic room. The old lady with him and the younger woman sparked off no recognition. His grandmother had died before he was born and the younger woman was nothing like his mother; she was too stout and looked older. He returned her look as they passed him, seeing in her face all the elements of suspicion and persecution from which he had fled. He saw it for a moment only, then her face had gone from the light and away down the dark, wet street.

He looked back at the house. A light still shone in the passage; he could see it through the rectangular fanlight above the door.

He had nowhere to go. Home was somewhere and, like hope, the image of that home he had come so far to recapture was rapidly fading. Yet he still looked to the house to give him a sign, some indication of the direction he must now turn his thoughts and actions.

He had a gun in his pocket and no one to play with. Alfie and Bobby, the Cox brothers, Lily Hummerstone—all had gone and he was alone except for the boy who must still be in the house.

If he kicked—knocked—on the door, perhaps he could come out and play in the rain.

He stared at the door willing the boy to come out and talk to him. They could go to Starr's, the sweet shop round the corner, and buy sherbet dabs, tiger nuts, aniseed balls and the big gob-stoppers that changed colour as you sucked them. He was wet and cold—chilled to his very core, yet the butt of the revolver in his pocket felt warm in his grasp. Perhaps if he fired it the sound might wake up the street and restore it to the place it had been with children cracking whips and spinning tops, swinging on lamp-posts and whirling winter warmers round their heads. A big bang, like a little Demon which cost only a ha'penny or a Thunderclap which cost more but made old ladies jump and set the dogs bark-ing. A big, big lethal bang and a repetition of the best day in his adult life, D-Day plus three when grey-green uniformed Flynns had gone down under his rapid fire. There was that one behind the sand-dune—just the helmeted head—and he'd fired a sweeping fifty rounds and decapitated the bully. He'd been exultant—had come into his own—for one brief, exciting day he'd paid off old scores. He'd stood as high as any man; a towering figure of vengeance as he'd blasted the enemy. For one day he hadn't been afraid but as bold and brave as the screen idols of his child-hood. He'd had mates, too. All Alfies, every one of them—all gang-ing up on the bullies and winning hands down. If he hadn't had that bullet in the foot, he'd have swept through France and Ger-many decimating the world population of Flynns like the Black Plague.

Cap-gun Billy and No. 65704, Kemp, William Arthur. They were the same animal. The little boy firing his cap-gun under cover of a privet hedge in Ringcroft Street and the man with the gun on D-Day plus three were one and the same.

Come back, Alfie Thackeray—come back and help me. Together we can beat them off. We'll kill the lot and pick up girls on Hamp-stead Heath and have a feel round—you remember. Oh—those were good times! There was Renee and that girl Jean, and—Lily. You didn't know her, Alfie. I kept it a secret from you, from Mum, from everybody. It was never the same. I blacked out—do you know that? When I came I blacked out and she held me up. Up against that tree—I told her I loved her. That was before. She wouldn't let me until I said that.

And after that I couldn't look at her. She lived at Number 21— next door. She loved me all right—she'd never get anyone better than me. I bet she loves me still. She may be married with grown-up kids but I bet she remembers me and what we did against that tree in Highbury Fields.

Bitches and cows! Nothing but bitches and sows and cows! Just that one day after D-Day, then back again to bitches and sows and cows—years of it, Alfie! Last—when was it?—night? I let them have it. I killed everything, the Flynns and all that happened between Lily and the shit that's fallen on me until now.

A bang to end all bangs, that would stir things up in the old street. Like the old days. And, just like the old days and because his bladder was full, he became a little boy again, turned his back on the house and urinated into the gutter.

The boy saw the man turn his back on the house and use the gutter. For a moment, he didn't believe what he had seen, then, as the man turned back to his original stance, Colin saw the hand securing fly-buttons.

He looked cross the darkened room to the telephone. He'd often wanted to try the 999 call, but emergencies were rare in the street. There'd be no harm done if he dialled the number. A patrol car might come and move the man on—nothing more. The operation would be good for the English essay he had to do; dress up the fact with a bit of drama and it might be good reading. He'd have to miss out the bit about peeing in the gutter.

The man was sinister all right, the way he stood there under the lamp doing nothing but looking at the house and getting wet through. As the boy watched, the man raised his left hand and wiped his face clear of the rain, making separate movements over each of his eyes as if to clear them of tears.

Colin picked up the receiver and dialled. In his excitement—

there was a flutter in his stomach—he fingered a wrong digit. He restored the dialling tone and dialled correctly. After two call phrases he was through.

'Emergency—which service?'

'Police, please.'

'Hold the line.'

The connection seemed to take minutes and the boy was tempted to put the receiver down. Then the ringing tone ceased and he was committed. 'Police.'

'Police.'

'I—I want to report a man lurking outside the house.'

'What number are you calling from?'

'610 4343.'

'And your name, madam?'

'Not madam.' The boy wished his voice had broken. 'My name's Colin Harris.'

'And your address?'

'Nineteen Ringcroft Street, Holloway.'

'Thank you, Mr Harris. What has the man been doing?'

'Well—nothing. He was standing there when I came home from school at four-fifteen. It's a quarter past five now and he's still there—just looking at the house.'

'Can you describe him?'

'He's wearing a raincoat—no hat—thinnish face—a bit old. He must be very wet.'

'Have you seen him before?'

'No.'

'I'll just check on your number—610 4343?'

'That's right.'

'Well, keep watching. We'll send a patrol car round. Thank you for your cooperation, sir.'

He replaced the receiver feeling a little sick. He'd started something he didn't want to finish alone and there was no one else in the house. Returning to the window, he imagined what his mother would have said.

'You dialled 999?'

'*It's what you're supposed to do if you see something suspicious.*'

'*And did you?*'

'*Yes.*'

'*Well—what?*'

'*Just something unusual.*'

All the man had done was turn his back and pee in the gutter.

A few yards from Holloway Road Station, a taxi cruising back from a journey outside the Metropolitan area caught Peggy Harris' eye. It suggested an immediate relief from the ardours of ferrying her parents to Liverpool Street. She hailed the taxi and got it. She would ask the old man for half the fare—the rest could come out of her pocket; it was worth it for the pure luxury of putting the responsibility into other hands.

'This is somethin' like,' the old man said. 'We should've got one before.'

'They're hard to find in Holloway.'

' 'Bout a quid, you said?'

'Something like that.'

The desk sergeant at Holloway Road Police Station took the written message from the constable on telephone duty, read it, then went to the hatch of the radio room.

'Any patrols near Ringcroft Street?'

The communications girl looked at her pad. 'Four on special lookout. Regional request. Priority. CID.'

'Which one?'

'The Suffolk murder. Man wanted for questioning.'

'That one. Wait!' The sergeant frowned. 'Alert all four and tell them to stand by.'

He crossed quickly to the report desk and scanned the priority list. He muttered 'Christ!' to himself and rapped out an order to the constable on phone duty.

'Get that number—the one in Ringcroft Street—and look lively!'

The urgent ring of the telephone cut into the silence of the sitting room and the boy started with the shock.

He went to the phone and lifted the receiver.

'Is that 610 4343?'

'Yes.'

'Police here, madam. Sergeant Woods. I understand a call was made from your number reporting a man behaving suspiciously outside your house.'

'It's not madam. I phoned you.'

'Mr Colin Harris?'

'That's right.'

'How old are you, Mr Harris?'

'Fourteen.'

'Are you sharp-sighted?'

'I think so.'

'Right. Now listen—I'm going to read you a description of a man. Then I want you to go to the window and see if it checks with the man outside your house. Got it?'

'Yes?'

'Is the light on in the room?'

'No. I didn't want him to see me watching him.'

'Good lad. Now listen carefully. This is an official report and you will hear every word. Ready?'

'Yes.'

'Wanted for questioning, William Arthur Kemp, aged fifty-one, height five feet eight inches, thinning brown hair, weight eleven stone, last seen wearing a gaberdine belted raincoat green-grey in colour. Hatless and tieless. Scar above right eyebrow. Believed armed—' the sergeant interrupted his reading. 'Do you know what that means, Mr Harris?'

'I think so—you mean he's got a gun?'

'I mean he might have a gun. It also means he might be dangerous. Understand?'

'Yes.'

'Then here's the rest of the description: Black shoes, light grey or white shirt. Possibly right-handed. Observed keeping right hand in raincoat pocket indicating presence of weapon. Officers are advised to observe and report. Do not approach until advised. Have you got that—Colin, isn't it?'

'Yes, sir.'

'Now go to the window and report.'

'I can use Dad's binoculars.'

'Even better—now jump to it. I'll hold on.'

The car containing Greenlaw and Weston arrived on time at the Public Library. Williams and Clay had begun their report when the radio in the car bleeped and Greenlaw picked up the receiver.

'Greenlaw.'

'A report in from Holloway, sir.'

'Yes?'

'Report runs as follows. Man acting suspiciously in Ringcroft Street. Telephone check with complainant suggests description tallies with William Arthur Kemp wanted for questioning.'

'Right—give me link-up with Holloway.'

Greenlaw looked at Weston. 'Could be our man. Not far from here.'

'Where, sir?'

'Very near. Williams—Clay? You heard the report—I want you under cover at both ends of the street. Don't be seen. I want identification first and no fireworks—keep in radio contact.'

The radio bleeped its link-up with the Holloway Police Station and Greenlaw began clipped, concise instructions to be issued to patrols in the area.

Weston felt like a passenger with nothing to do. He watched Williams and Clay move off to their observation points and listened to Greenlaw issuing his commands. He felt out of it, sitting in comfort with one of the Yard's top men.

Greenlaw signed off and turned to Weston. 'I've got a job for you.'

The net was closing round Kemp as he waited for the past to come alive in the rain, but nets have holes and Greenlaw knew it. Somewhere along the line of detection and apprehension someone, somewhere, had to make the first and most dangerous confrontation. Greenlaw had no qualms; Weston would have to go in and establish identity.

At five-fifteen Thorpley looked at the whisky remaining in his glass and roused his slightly drunken, drowsy thoughts into shape for his journey home. He was pleased with his day at the office. The business was running well and the evening traffic had already started to judge by the increasing use of the front door.

The rest of his weekdays would not be so rewarding. There wasn't a housekeeper in any of his other properties to touch Jean McCartney. Each house contained his own very private room furnished with things kept clean and aired ready for his visits; the same brand of whisky, the same type of furniture and bric-à-brac, the same colours and texture; all homes from home, but lacking the one essential—Mrs McCartney. To the other housekeepers he was just a rich old creep with the taste of a fairy; they didn't know where he came from or where he went on leaving the house; neither did they care.

To Mrs McCartney he could say anything and she would do the same. It was a pleasure to tell her of his life as a country squire or to talk of the past, and it was pure delight to pull her Scottish leg, knowing that all he told her she would keep to herself; locked up as securely as a devout nun's virginity—a definition used by Mrs McCartney, who never asked the religion of anyone she liked lest they should confess to being Roman Catholic.

Once he had told her that as he grew older he felt the need for religion and, seeking in his mind for a faith most likely to permit him to retain his method of earning a living, he had hit upon the Roman Catholic Church—and what did she think?

She had told him her thoughts in a form of violent ultimatums ranging from exposure to the police to the immediate withdrawal of her labour, her anglicised voice lapsing into broad Scots.

Thorpley had his own concept of God; it was no less vague or distinct from the average man's but it was very personal. It was a concept of an all-seeing, all-forgiving, totally benevolent Being who judged not and only wondered how any of those that came to the Gates managed to get through such a ghastly experience as life on earth without committing murder and treason and all the variously named earthly crimes. Mr Thorpley knew that his concept was theologically ridiculous, but it was the only one that made any sense to life. To add to the value of his Deity, Thorpley had arranged the universe to fit into the pattern of his thinking. There was more than one God and more than one heaven. Somewhere along the line of after-life you had a choice of asylum, a choice of territorial bosses. One boss was to be avoided, the nameless one who owned the Earth.

He had expounded his views to Mrs McCartney, who had listened to his finely modulated voice and ideas with interest. When he had finished, her comment had been, 'There's no fool like an old fool.' Nevertheless, in the days that followed she found herself liking Thorpley's God. *He* cut into the lingering sense of sin acquired during a rigorous Scottish Presbyterian childhood as efficiently as a first-class psychiatrist.

'The Catholic Church is out, then,' he had said. 'I'd rather risk eternal damnation than lose you, Jean McCartney. As for exposing me to the police—I've always considered them my friends. The result of law-abiding forbears rich enough to make their own laws.'

He drank the last of his Scotch slowly. His next would be on the 6.40 at approximately one minute past the time of departure. Maurice would roll up the shutters of the buffet bar and begin to serve the long queue of commuters, and Mr Thorpley, passing through on his way to a first-class carriage, would lay down his fifty-pence piece and pick up glass and miniature whisky in one precise co-ordinated movement, thanking Maurice's consideration with a little nod of the head.

Mrs McCartney entered, the opening of and the knock on the door coinciding.

'You'll be going in a minute or two?'

'Another five minutes. I've been thinking how nice it would be if you could be in seven places at once.'

'What does that mean?'

'The other housekeepers can't cook.'

'If you're suggesting I do a shuffle and bang around the houses just to get you a meal when you visit them, you can think again.'

'I was just expressing a hopeless wish.'

'Do you want me to sort them out?'

'My wishes?'

'The other housekeepers.'

'That might be an idea, Jean. You ought to have a title—a bit of authority. Brothel Supervisor-in-Chief. How does that sound?'

'I don't need a title. Just give me authority to sack them if I see fit and I'll get them up to standard.'

Mr Thorpley shook his head. 'It wouldn't do, Jean. You're no diplomat and I don't fancy a number of angry resentful women roaming loose. I'll have to compress my visits to the houses so that I can spend more time with you. In fact, it might be an idea if I make this house my base. Life won't be so varied, but I grow lazy as the years advance. I'm sure you won't object in view of the increase in salary. Fifty pounds a week isn't bad, you know.'

'Sixty.'

'Sixty pounds a week, then—as from the beginning of next month.'

'It ought to be back-dated six months.'

'As I've said, join a Trade Union. Think of a suitable one—you can put it to arbitration.'

Then, suddenly, Thorpley shuddered. It started at the base of his spine, travelled up and settled between his shoulder blades. He frowned as he felt his lower jaw tremble. Mrs McCartney saw the change in his face.

'What's wrong with you?'

'Somebody walked over my grave.'

'What's funny about that? They do it every day to me.'

'But never before to me.'

'A chill on the kidneys, that's all. You ought to stay here—there's enough bedrooms.'

'Against routine. I like commuting up and down. Besides, the neighbours would talk, quite apart from the embarrassment your designs on me might cause my libido.'

'Libido? What's that?'

'Libido,' replied Mr Thorpley, choosing his words carefully as always, 'is that by which we profit. Without it Freud wouldn't have had two pennies to rub together, or, to put it more personally, without it all those long years ago I wouldn't have enjoyed you, Jean McCartney.'

'A fancy name for sex.'

'Roughly.'

'Do you want me to call a taxi?'

'No—a friend is meeting me and driving me to the station.'

'One of your friends in high places?'

'Very high.'

The car, a black Cortina, was waiting outside the house when Thorpley came down the five steps to the pavement. The driver reached across and opened the door and Thorpley climbed in.

'You're on time, Walter—very decent of you to drive me to the station.'

'My pleasure. It's a nasty night and we don't want you catching cold.'

'I rely on you, Walter, to keep me free from infection.'

'I'll always do my best—you know that.'

'You're a good fellow.'

Walter knew his London and all the short cuts, missing out on roads he knew would be snarled up with rush-hour traffic. A pleasant man in his early fifties, round-faced and rugged in an unaggressive way, he had known Mr Thorpley for a number of years; years in which each had developed a healthy respect and liking for the other.

'Mrs McCartney all right?' Walter asked.

'In the best of Scottish health—rude.'

Walter laughed. 'Looked up her record the other day. Makes good reading. Not that she was nicked that often.'

'It must read like ancient history.'

'A bit. There's this report how she took off her high-heeled shoes in Hyde Park and sprinted in her stockinged feet followed by an over-zealous PC. He copped her, of course. Usual charge—soliciting. Two-quid fine.'

'If she was apprehended now, she'd hit the constable over the head with her umbrella—*and* get away with it.'

'We'd see to that.'

'Amen.'

Walter drove the Cortina down the entrance ramp to Liverpool Street Station and pulled up in the permitted area. Mr Thorpley reached into his pocket and drew out a foolscap envelope containing twenty-five pounds, a Monday duty observed with pleasure and received by Walter with gratification.

'A little something to help pay the rent, Walter. Same time next Monday?'

'On the dot—and thanks.'

'Only too glad to help. I value our friendship.'

'Long may it continue.'

Mr Thorpley climbed out, pleased with his day and anxious to board the 6.40 and start his ascent into increased euphoria with Maurice's help in the buffet car.

'Good night to you, Walter.'

Once he had seen Thorpley go through the doors to the booking office, Detective Inspector Walter Snow slipped into gear and headed the Cortina up the exit ramp. It was 18.00 hrs and he was on duty at 18.30.

It was in Davies' mind not to return to East Bergholt but stay in London with Monica, but loyalty and gratefulness fought an unequal battle. Hope had presented the end to yet another road. Tomorrow would see the transfer of the Inchbald holdings to Viscenti's and, with careful but speedy manipulation, his incredible dilemma settled once and for all with the promise of a future that shone with hope.

The problem, the main problem now, was Cynthia. Suddenly she represented the obstruction in the road that had been opened up. Cynthia, the house, East Bergholt, the importance and sanctity of the unit he had fought so hard and criminally to preserve now meant—how much? It was hard to estimate.

He had told Monica that she had brought back a sort of youth to him and it was true. And with the return of youth had come the revelation of possibilities that he had believed were gone for ever.

He remembered opening Hubert's letter and reading into it the implication that he should use the money to cut and run, and the conjecture that followed. The new life. To live again. Let the hard life be for others. If life could suddenly present such incredible delight as this black Monday had given what other good fortune awaited the taker.

Davies reached for the telephone and dialled Monica's number. After three rings she came on the line.

'Monica? It's John Davies here.'

'John.'

'I had to ask—how real was this afternoon?'

'Very real. Where are you now?'

'In my office wondering at my good fortune and wanting not to catch the six-forty back to trouble.'

'Then don't catch it. Come back here.'

'It's the suddenness of it all I can't quite believe. My life hangs on the fact that all we did together isn't just for an afternoon.'

'Tell me what you want?'

'No end to you and I.'

'That's what I want. You can't put a time to it, John. I'm not a one-night stander. I've immense liking for you and we make love very, very well. I don't know how long it will last—who does? It would be very silly to tell you that I love you.'

'Premature.'

'Foolhardy, but you never know. Why do you have to go back tonight?'

'Cynthia. I've got to be there. Sometimes Cynthia goes over the mark and—it's difficult, you see. Also, I have to tell her I'll be away for the rest of the week.'

'You're going away?'

'To London—to be with you.'

'Nice.'

'How often can I see you?'

'I've got a spare bed—several in fact.'

'I'm not interested in spare beds.'

'Neither am I.'

'Are we gambling, Monica? It's all happening so quickly, yet I want to throw everything over. You're the chance of a lifetime, yet my training whispers: *"Caution, John Amos Davies".'*

'John—let's talk guarantees. You'll have my money, which is a hard thing to say and, as far as I can see you'll have me. That's good collateral, don't you think? So no gamble and—John, you didn't tell me everything about your money problems and I don't want to know. If handling my financial affairs helps you get out of trouble, that's fine by me. I don't want to know how you do it. Tomorrow I come to your office and do all that I have to do. We'll settle the dreary business side to our relationship and Viscenti can cope with making my vast fortune even bigger. Does that sound all right to you?'

'Incredible and heaven-sent.'

'I'm an angel without wings. I'd like to say I love you, John.'

'I'd like to tell you the same thing.'

'But it would be foolhardy.'

'Premature. Perhaps one day.'

And it was on. The future extended for years. Davies replaced the receiver and watched, in his mind, the firing squad being told to unload and retire with the apologetic officer unpinning the white disc over Davies' heart and removing the blindfold. Amnesty. Freedom. To live with pleasure again.

Cynthia wouldn't care very much; at least, not more than she had for many years now. The bottle had become her lover, comforter and nearest and dearest. There was little to commend their relationship except the conformity of social image and class behaviour. But that was over and other conformities would take their place but with the advantage of a new lease of life.

The changes would be great; perhaps he would earn the enmity of his sons, and the whole social façade of the class game he had played for years would crumble and show the wattle and daub disguised as weathered red brick. In a few hours the house, the image, the frail unity of family had become virtually nothing, a fantasy that had dominated his life.

And now the reality was as fantastic as a miracle. He remembered the beer can tossed out of the carriage window; his fear as he opened Hubert's letter; his forced appearance of calm as he entered the bank to exchange the cheque into hard cash and then —the afternoon he had spent with Monica. Was it all true?

The collateral of love and money was the best in the world. Blessed Monica and dear Hubert with his thousand pounds which was now gift money to be squandered. He opened the drawer of his desk and drew out the flat stack of notes. It was good to have money to spend again. He would leave five hundred with Cynthia before catching the 8.20 tomorrow morning and tell her to spend it any way she liked. That would please her; she liked spending money and he'd be leaving her with a bang, not a whimper. Five hundred pounds would buy her at least a hundred and fifty bottles of love, comfort and nearest and dearest.

He would not now be hammered. To save the firm Max would not have to fork out and cover the deficit. Viscenti, the tiger, wouldn't need to drop his feline smile and take John Amos Davies, whose head was now held high, to the very end of dispossession and ruin. Max would have too much respect for the Inchbald holdings and Monica's insistence that her assets were in John Amos Davies' hands for him to consider cover for sixty thousand anything more than a slight mistake, and more than rectified by Monica's concession.

It was as good as a 'show of money' to an underwriter.

Better than a thousand-pound bet on a 60 to 1 winner. Many thousand times better.

Cynthia. Goodbye, Cynthia. I'm sorry, but we have nothing further to give to each other and nothing to take. Tonight I will tell you I have to join Max in Bonn and shall be away for five or six days.

What will become of you? What will become of me if I stay with you? I want to live; this morning I wanted to die.

It was time to get to the station. He put the flat wad of notes in his inside jacket pocket, rose from his desk, donned overcoat, hooked rolled umbrella on his arm, told his briefcase to go to hell and went out and through to the offices beyond, bidding a cheerful good night to those employees staying over to catch up on work.

Luck was with him all the way. Emerging from the great building a taxi idled past. He hailed it with upthrust umbrella and thus started the journey home.

The telephone had rung during the afternoon but its call had barely touched Cynthia's consciousness. She had moved from the chair only twice since she had taken up her alcoholic vigil in front of the television screen a little before midday; once to use the lavatory and then to move with peculiar uncertainty and weakness to the drinks' cabinet. She had found no gin, but a two-thirds-full bottle of Scotch.

It was dark in the room except for the blue-white glare of the television screen which highlighted Cynthia as she sat in the high-backed chair, bottle clutched in her arms.

She was now fighting more than her daily, composite level of self-disgust and pity. At irregularly spaced intervals the pain in her chest struck with the sharpness of a knife. After each attack it seemed that she dwindled down into a state of nothing, a limbo in which she was freed from herself and in which she was quite content to stay. But, inevitably, she climbed back into self to face yet another agonising anticlimax.

It was in one of these returns that she had seen the pony being bridled and saddled on the television screen; had been reminded of Misty, her first pony, and of the joy she had felt when the horse-box had delivered him to her parent's house on her seventh birthday.

'Poor dead Misty,' she said, and then the pain hit her again and she was totally absorbed in containing the agony as it lanced into her chest.

This time, the limbo into which she descended seemed to last longer. She was *aware* that it was lasting longer and, for the first time, felt capable of movement within it. In some inexplicable way she could see up, down and round the limbo.

How pain-free and careless it was! Nothing mattered in this neutral world where heat and cold played no part. It was a soft world but entirely protective. Nothing could reach her. No one. She was invulnerable to hurt. John? Who was John? Did he want to touch her? But he couldn't—no one could touch her. She was many times removed from them all . . . Oh let me stay here.

Misty—John? Don't call me back. I want nothing—nothing.

Both ends of the street were under surveillance by Clay and Williams, stationed at the corners but out of sight of the man under the lamp.

From where he stood with Detective Chief Superintendent Greenlaw, Weston could see the motionless figure welded to the lamp-post and highlighted by the sodium glow of the lamp.

'Williams and Clay will be near at hand, Weston,' said Greenlaw. 'I want identification from you—nothing more. Is that understood?'

'Yes, sir.'

'Walk down the street as if you lived in it. Chink your keys as if you're getting ready to open a door. If you need a better look, drop the keys near him and pick them up. You get the idea?'

'Yes, sir.'

'Turn into the street and walk down past the odd numbers. He's outside nineteen. Take your time and make sure he's the man—right?'

'Right, sir.'

'Get moving then. After you've seen him, report to Detective Constable Williams at the bottom of the street. He'll radio contact me. On your way.'

The street was empty of life. A few cars were parked on either side of the road; another half an hour would see all parking space filled with cars. As it was, the spaces were sufficient to afford a sight of the man under the lamp from both ends of the street.

The sound of his footsteps sounded unnaturally loud in Weston's ears as he entered the street and began counting off the numbers. It was like a countdown before blast-off.

51 . . . 49 . . . 47 . . . 45 . . . 43.

There was nothing else in the street; nothing but himself and the man under the lamp. Identify and keep moving. Nothing more. Act like a street resident returning from the office. Perhaps he should whistle or something. Jingle keys, Greenlaw had instructed.

39 . . . 37 . . . 35 . . . He fumbled the bunch of keys out of his pocket and let them chink. A car turned into the street. A Panda? No—that wasn't the plan. He had to walk past the figure under the lamp, identify and report to Williams.

The car slowly coming up the street was a distraction. Weston saw the man turn his head as the car, its lights switched from head to parking, leave the left-hand side of the road and make for the kerb by the lamp.

25 . . . 23 . . .

Kemp watched the figure coming down the street. There was something familiar about the man's walk; erect, confident, a bully; similar to Flynn, who swung his arms like a soldier when he advanced on you. There was also the tinkle of keys.

That was another of Flynn's tortures. He would select the largest key from the bunch he carried and force you into a corner. What he did then was painful and humiliating.

He'd never let Flynn do it again.

Standing again as tall as any man, Kemp's hand tightened round the butt of the revolver. The past had come back; it was walking toward him unaware that it was the last bullying confrontation.

23 . . . 21 . . . 19. Flynn had dropped his keys; had bent down to retrieve them and straightened up looking at Kemp.

'No!' said Kemp. 'No!' He jerked into a convulsive movement, his hand coming out of the raincoat pocket and Weston saw the glint of light on metal. Then a great roar burst out at him and a gigantic pain fisted into his stomach. He clutched at the pain and went down on his knees, crying out against the agony that burned into him.

At the window, the boy saw the four-second-long action like a series of quick cinematic cuts. The flash and roar of the gun, the man going down as the car came to a halt outside the house and then the man going to the car in a crouching movement and thrusting the gun through the driving window.

And for a split-second Colin saw the shocked face of his father staring at the gun. Then the sound of a rear door slamming shut, and the scud of tyres as the car accelerated away from the kerb and up the street.

The boy was shocked into frozen immobility, his eyes taking in the man lying on the pavement, his mind slowly comprehending that the stranger under the lamp-post had driven off with his father.

Strap-hanging on the Central Line to Liverpool Street, David Blake relived the events of the afternoon. Bryant had played a lousy trick on him; an elaborate trick to prove that tutors, teachers, lecturers, call them what you like, had relationships all wrong; they had assumed a position which could not be justified in contemporary terms. 'Relationships, man, have changed. Equality, right? I do my own thing so okay—you, Teacher, you implement; you help me find the value of my own, my very own thing. Not your thing—I don't want it. If I want Surreal or I want Dada—or both—Warhol, Rauschenberg, hard edge or soft, it's what I want and you, Teacher, you help me get there. No preconceived notions on your part of what's wrong and what's right. You've skills born of experience—big skills. I say teach me to realise my concept, not carry on the trad of yours. Now, that *is* equality.'

Blake had been reluctant to take his afternoon class. Room P114 had been full when he entered it after a dull meeting in the staff room.

As he came into the room student eyes shifted from easels and drawing boards, rested on him for a moment, then returned to their work.

He walked slowly round the room, embarrassed by the silence of the class. He paused for a moment by Malcolm Bryant's easel, conscious that Bryant was acutely aware of his presence.

Blake looked at the large canvas on which was slowly emerging the entwined shapes of two forms. For some reason the colour, the forms, the emotive force of the painting struck him as more positive than any of Bryant's previous work.

Bryant stood back and considered the canvas, tugging at his bushy, fiery ginger beard. He looked sideways at Blake and grinned.

'It's called "Love". Lousy?'

'You know I don't think that. Why haven't I seen it before?'

'Bryant works in mysterious ways. We see you one day a week. We're here all the time. Widmer puked when he saw it. So what's your view—dislike on principle?'

'Is that your practice?'

Bryant was silent for a few moments. There was enough paint on his brush to widen a small area on the left of the supine figure. He moved forward and carefully applied the paint, then stepped back and evaluated the result.

'It needed that,' he said. He looked at Blake, mock-rueful. 'We sounded off today—we really sounded off, didn't we?'

'Yes—we each exposed our prejudices. I don't know if we're better off for it.'

'I thought it was great. Real contact.'

'And the rest of the class?'

'Mixed. Fear, guilt, resentment, pity—you name it. If you want a laugh, there's been a knife between my shoulder blades since we got back from the lunch-break.'

'So which of us came off best?'

'Both. What happened at the staff meeting?'

'Virtually nothing. Widmer sounded off about discipline. The

Principal took the liberal view. Opinions were probed and the status quo remains the status quo. What did you mean about fear, guilt and pity?'

'Fear that you'd report the set-up in the pub. I felt guilt—how's that for confession, man? Pity—that was for you. Like kicking a man when he's down.'

'And the knife between your shoulder-blades?'

'You've got to have a scapegoat and I did the talking. The knife doesn't hurt, if you're concerned. Were you scared to come back to P114?'

'Yes.'

'We wondered about that.'

Blake knew the whole class was listening to the conversation; he also knew that it was the understood idea. Something had to come out of it; the confrontation was still on but at a different level. A message had been given to him and he'd yet to understand it.

He looked at Bryant's painting. Something was wrong with the volume of the mounted figure. He said: 'It's just a suggestion—maybe you want it that way, but I feel the mounted figure is too heavy, too aggressive.'

Bryant considered his criticism, pulling at his beard. He cocked his head on one side occasionally glancing at Blake.

At length, he said: 'Why too aggressive—too heavy?'

'If it's love you're after—love between two people—each should have equal weight. Each should be equally aggressive and submissive. Or perhaps you think it isn't a mutual act.'

Bryant smiled broadly. 'That's the best I've heard today. You're right, man. You got the message.'

Across the room Sally Eversley looked up from her drawing board. The silent coldness slowly evaporated from P114.

Blake continued: 'As it stands, your painting suggests rape. If you think that's how love should be, then I wish you luck in finding the right man or woman.'

Bryant grinned. 'I'm not gay, so it's got to be a woman.'

Ignoring the fact that Sally and some of the students had left their work and made their way to Bryant's easel, Blake said: 'You've told me I've got the message, now you tell me what that message is because I don't think I *have*.'

'Sure.' Bryant unscrewed the top clamp of the easel, removed the canvas and replaced it so that the supine figures were now upright. The result surprised Blake. Now the volumes were exactly balanced. A man and a woman close together, making total contact, the heavier form of the man balanced by the darker tones surrounding the woman.

'Great joke,' said Bryant. 'Old as Widmer. People and pictures get hung up the wrong way.'

'I see,' said Blake. 'The message is clear.'

'Haven't finished yet.' Bryant again went to the canvas, removed it from the easel and replaced it with the heavier figure now supine. Now the respresentation was female domination.

'Wrong?' asked Bryant.

'It's a painting for all seasons,' said Blake. 'You pays your money and you takes your choice.'

'Which way up do you like it?'

'With the figures standing. That's love.'

'And it's all a question of choice. You're with them or you're with us. You're on top pulling rank and muscle or standing up face to face with a bunch of ungrateful, untalented students.'

'You were on top at lunchtime.'

'Reaction—self-defence. We don't want it. None of us want it. We have no choice but to react. The school's overloaded with deadbeats. You know that as well as anyone. You're the best painter on the staff.'

'That wasn't your message in the Albert.'

'Reactionary method. Old as Jesus. You got over-allied with Widmer & Co. We want help—not force-feeding.'

The train drew into Bank Station and Blake came out of his reverie. Walls have ears, he thought, and art schools are no exception. In a brutally oblique way he had been told he was the students' choice and, at the same time, had been given guidance should he accept the post of Head of Painting. If he did, and the thought frightened him, he would have to contrive the dismissal of the poor deadbeats and remould the whole of the painting school.

On the other hand, he could throw up the whole damned thing.

CHAPTER 8

Late afternoon, 18.05 hrs.

The queue under starter's orders at the ticket barrier numbered two hundred as the station clock came round to 18.05. The ticket-collector, multi-coloured pullover showing underneath his Hardy-Amies-designed uniform, performed little kill-time actions which infuriated those anxious to get on the train and find a comfortable seat. Now and then he looked down the length of the train to see how far the cleaners had progressed. As soon as he received the all-clear, he would trundle the apology board *'We regret the inconvenience caused while the train is being cleaned for your comfort'* to one side of the barrier, then deliberately, slowly, hoist the blue and white destination board onto its hooks, open the gate and, as Lord Bountiful of British Railways, indicate that the passengers may now come forward and have their tickets inspected and punched.

In the coaches projecting beyond the ticket barrier, and into the station concourse, non-buffet regulars, knowing the form, had entered the train; they would now spend the minutes before departure anxiously scanning the station for expected fellow travellers.

The old hands knew it would be a crowded train. The proximity of Christmas meant an increase in shoppers and that meant parcels and interference of established habits. The balance between a comfortable journey and the disagreeable rested on a razor's edge. The impossible culmination would be Christmas Eve—a Friday this year; the 18.40 would be archetypal in its hellishness.

The station's speakers were carolling Mantovani Christmas music, externally showing the benign face of the season. *'God rest ye, Merrie Gentlemen—'* There was neither merriness nor rest in the concourse, despite the Christmas tree sparkling with fairy lights and the unconvincing Father Christmas rattling a collecting-box under its boughs. The day was running out its imperfect course in a wet and dank evening. Home was the object; little time for charity and seasonal well-being, apart from the journey-length pleasure of train acquaintances when the day's tensions would be relieved over the *Evening Standard* crossword and club humour that would run high in the buffet car.

At the head of the queue, John Paton felt no anxiety. He had in-spected the queue building up behind him and judged them to be amateurs. He would be first at the barrier—you couldn't get away with entering the train beyond the barrier and creeping down the corridors to the buffet car; the collector twiddling his thumbs was a turfer-out and Paton had seen him stop a corridor-creeper and order him back. It was too embarrassing to risk. Paton had seats to hold and he knew he'd get them. The average age of those be-hind him seemed to be around the sixty/seventy mark. First through the gate and a quick sprint—zing—zing—zing! and the seats in the buffet held. A quiet word with the steward round the back of the buffet galley and Paton's reputation as reliable front man would be sustained.

On the other side of the station, platforms numbered from 10 up. There, suburban travellers jostled and banged and strap-hung. Paton was glad to be in a race apart; it was not a class difference but a simple environmental fact. One set of commuters undertook long distances as part of their daily grind, while the other com-muted within the Greater London radius. The long-distance man had time to establish relationships, the great bonus of a sixty or so miles distance between home and office; the short-distancer had too little time to strike up train friendships.

But each was alike in one respect—the constant irritations attending rail travel; overcrowded trains, insufficient excuse for delays and cancellations annoyed the commuter, although loud-speaker techniques showed a slight improvement. If a delayed, frustrated traveller was in a resigned state or in unusual good humour, the announcement 'We regret the late arrival of the eighteen-ten train from Yarmouth—this was due to signal failure' might make him smile with tired but cynical amusement; in bad humour, he was likely to observe, 'The whole bloody railway system is a signal failure!'

But everything's on time tonight, thought Paton, and all's right with the world.

He accompanied the station speakers with a perfectly matched whistle as they blasted out 'The Holly and the Ivy', and thought of Elizabeth Marwood. A nice woman (he nearly thought 'bird', which indicated the direction of his mind). A very big cut above the average and didn't pull the little-woman act. With a girl—woman—like her you felt everything was even-steven as far as jokes, ideas and just about everything else was concerned. A married woman mixing it up with severely married men. A man could go places with her and what a thought that was. Twelve-year itch? Paton questioned himself. A damn good scratch, man, and look the other way. You can look at the fruit and that's all.

He noticed the 'gentleman-inebriate' emerging from the station bar. Now there was a man who knew his form; Paton and his friends had observed him on the morning run and had learned from Maurice and Charlie the tally of his whisky consumption for the day's journey. But he's never drunk, Paton observed to himself; true, he wears a set smile and doesn't move away from the bar even though his first-class seat is only a carriage or so away. Perhaps after Colchester he staggers to his seat for the remaining miles to Manningtree to collect his hat and coat.

'The train now standing on Platform nine is the eighteen-forty. Calling at Chelmsford, Colchester, Manningtree and Ipswich. Buffet service is available on this train. . . .'

Interpreting the announcement as permission to board the train, the queue stirred into life, picking up suitcases, parcels and carrier-bags and making a general movement to the barrier. The effect was only to impact the queue and the collector at the gate continued to kill time.

The station clock showed 18.10 before the collector nodded to an unseen sign down the platform and came through his gate to remove the apology board. He took his time, the eyes of the queue following every movement. Then he hoisted the destination board, took up position and beckoned the queue forward.

Paton, seasoned traveller and top commuter, went through the gate, season ticket flashing at the collector. He was first again, beating by a short head the corridor-crawlers now weaving a quick path to the buffet car. He took a table and a half at the far end of the carriage, marking each seat with expert speed by placing newspaper, umbrella, briefcase, hat, raincoat and his own bottom on the chairs. In four minutes flat all the other seats were marked by lesser champions.

It was to be a full train. A fine night would have made a difference; casuals might have caught a later train now that shops were keeping their doors open for Christmas shoppers until seven o'clock, but a day of incessant rain and damp clothes, parcels and carrier-bags getting soggy had worn energies thin and they wanted home and comfort.

Mr Thorpley passed through the buffet car en route to his first-class seat two carriages beyond. He nodded to Paton and stopped at the service entrance to the bar to smile his arrival at Maurice, who replied with a conspiratorial nod.

'Better put out two tonight, Maurice—a multitude is about to board the train. You'll be rushed off your feet.'

At the Bank of England complex of roads, Harris again felt the touch of the gun on the back of his neck.

'Drive east—right at the Wellington statue—drive—go on—drive east!'

'I don't know—look, I—'

'Right through the City—the East End—keep going!'

'Who are you? Why me?'

'Just keep going east. Don't ask questions—I know how to use this gun. I'll tell you what to do. You take orders. Keep driving!'

The taxi bearing the Peartrees to Liverpool Street Station made heavy weather of the journey. It pulled into the station entrance at twenty minutes past six. With Harry fretting and grumbling at her side, Peggy Harris ferried them to Platform 9 and on to the crowded train.

'Shouldn't 'ave come,' the old man grumbled. 'Not comin' next year. Why couldn't Ted've got us 'ere.'

'I didn't want you to be late.'

'We ain't early.'

'You heard what the cab driver said—traffic's bad tonight.'

Two seats were hard to find. They walked the length of the train and found only singles.

'Not gooin' to bloody well stand.'

'You won't have to.'

Eventually, Peggy persuaded them to sit in separate carriages. It was not to their liking.

'I ain't agooin' ter come up agen.'

'You'll be all right, Dad. Mum'll come along and see if you're all right.'

Peggy Harris left them sitting on the edge of their seats. They were miles away from home and miles away from each other.

As she walked the short distance between her office building and Liverpool Street Station, Elizabeth felt a kind of regret at leaving London. There was an acute sense of life about the City; of leisure after work; time to be enjoyed in the company of others. A sense of—it was hard to define. It was as if a million chances lay in the City's heart and here she was walking away from it. And to what? she asked herself.

The village held no particular attraction for her. They should have moved to London years ago when the children were young. She lived in a house, that was all. The children had their friends, the parents had acquaintances and neighbours. But children are fickle; their friends could be found and lost in one short day. They were not to be considered.

She lived in a house. It wasn't a house in a village in a county in a country; it was a house and nothing more. A small, small environment and she could now assess just how minute that environment was.

Perhaps some sort of balance will come, she thought. Perhaps I shall enjoy both the day and night. It's natural to be thrown out of gear the first day. Perhaps things have gone too easily; irritations and discontents might lie ahead to take some of the pleasure out of the day and I shall be glad to get home and away from it all.

She came out of Finsbury Square and walked the last two hundred yards to Liverpool Street. The air was fresher and the rain seemed to be thinning.

A man in a hurry ducked under her umbrella to gain advantage down the station ramp. She watched his hurrying figure mingle in the crowd invading the station. A man in a hurry to get home—running away from a job he didn't particularly like but had to do. She could imagine his distress if he missed his train. It was a negative way of appreciating home and family, but better than nothing. Aware that it was disloyal to husband and children, she hoped she would never want to run away from her job and new-found friends.

She walked slowly, noticing the station clock at the end of the ramp. 18.20. There was no point in hurrying; John Paton had promised to save her a seat in the buffet car. She would show him and Martin just how brilliant she was; she had bought an *Evening Standard* at lunchtime and completed the crossword—the cryptic— and knew all the answers. She must remember to do it regularly.

She could now add deceit to disloyalty and since both seemed to be harmless and amusing, she could see little wrong in either. And never, never, would she let on about the crossword and the delight she felt at being an individual. Never.

Showing her season ticket in its new plastic cover, she passed through the barrier and walked down the platform in search of the buffet car.

Kemp said: 'You're taking me to Suffolk. You know Suffolk?'

'Why pick on me—I've done nothing to you?'

'Do you know Suffolk?'

'I've been there. Look—old man. You can have the car. Take it where you want. I've a wife and kid in London. They'll be worrying.'

'Lucky you turned up outside the house. You were God sent— you know that?'

'The police'll pick us up—what'll you do then?'

'They won't pick me up.'

'You shot a man in my street—I don't know your reasons. I don't want to know.'

'I've a wife and kid in Suffolk.'

'Then let me get out and you can drive yourself. You want to be with yours, I want to be with mine.'

Kemp made no reply. From the back seat he looked through the windscreen as the wipers repeated their arcs. A few miles ahead, Eastern Avenue would start with its endless roundabouts.

Harris's fear of the gun behind his back was disturbing his judgement. He drove erratically, pure luck averting the dangers of oncoming traffic and pedestrians asserting their rights on zebra crossings.

At length, Kemp said: 'Eastern Avenue ahead. Dual carriageway —you can go fast. What's your name?'

'Harris—Ted Harris. Look—drop me off—take the car.'

'I don't remember a Ted Harris. Alfie Thackeray—Wilfie Palmer. The Cox brothers. What happened to them?'

'I don't know what you're talking about.'

'I'm going to climb over to the front seat. Don't forget the gun.'

Kemp climbed over the seat and settled down beside Harris, who now saw a different face from that which had been dimly seen in his driving mirror. Saw too the heavy calibre of the revolver in the man's hand. Interest made a minute hole in his fear.

'That's a forty-five.'

Kemp nodded. 'I killed a rat at seventy-five yards—snap shot.'

'Are you going to kill me?'

Kemp frowned puzzlement. 'Kill you? You're taking me to Suffolk.'

Madmen had to be humoured, thought Harris. You talked them out of jumping to their deaths from tall buildings. Criminals were something different. The man sitting beside him was definitely off, but which was he—a nut or a criminal?

'You're on the run?' he asked.

'Flynn never stops his bullying. Flynns are everywhere.'

'Flynn?'

'They lie and cheat and push you around. You can't live with people like that.'

Harris steered the car across the Leyton crossroads and entered Eastern Avenue. Home-going traffic streamed ahead, breaking the forty-mile speed limit.

'They're always behind you,' said Kemp. 'If your name was Flynn—I'd shoot you.'

'I'll remember that, old man. Never did like the name. Sounds Irish. Tell you what—I bet the troubles in Ireland are caused by the Flynns.'

'Do you know that?'

'Just a guess.'

'Then why are they over here?'

'I don't know. Look—why not drop me off at one of the Underground stations? Gants Hill or somewhere like that. I can get a train back into London. I won't tell anyone. I don't know what you've done and I don't want to know.'

'I'm not a criminal.'

'I didn't say you were—I just want to help, that's all. That man you shot—I bet his name was Flynn.'

'He was a Flynn. He followed me all day.'

'Then you done a good thing—one less Flynn makes the world a better place. Why Suffolk?'

'I want to go home.'

'That's the best place to be. You going to drop me off?'

'It wasn't there.'

'What wasn't there?'

'Home.'

The police car containing Greenlaw, Clay, Williams and the driver had cut its way through the City traffic, its siren whooping. Now Greenlaw ordered the siren to be switched off. Not far ahead the car they were pursuing was part of the nightly exodus from London.

The radio bleeped and Greenlaw picked up the microphone.

'Tango four—Greenlaw.'

'Car registration GWT 4967G observed approaching Leyton crossroads heading for Eastern Avenue. What are your instructions?'

'Advise ahead. Regional top priority. Do not intervene, but follow without sirens. Damp blue lamp.'

'Message understood. Timed at eighteen-ten hours.'

Greenlaw looked through the windscreen at the road ahead. 'How far are we from Leyton?'

'Two—three miles, sir.'

'Then get a move on and pick up that car.'

Clay said: 'The village constable, sir—can we get a report?'

Greenlaw shook his head. 'Not yet—we'll know later. He got it in the stomach, so it's bad. The poor devil was right about his man. We should have closed in. The whole bloody lot of us!'

'Yes, sir.'

The scene under the street lamp in Islington ran through Greenlaw's mind as he stared ahead through the windscreen. The roar of the gun had echoed up the street and, as he and Williams had run down the street to join Clay sprinting up from the bottom end, the car had scudded from the kerb before they could reach Weston lying on the pavement.

A boy had come out of the house, incoherently telling them about his father and a car. Doors of houses had opened, their occupants coming across the road to join them under the lamp as Greenlaw turned Weston over and saw the wound in his stomach. Then the Panda cars arriving and the urgent call for an ambulance. Now Weston was in the Royal Northern undergoing God knows what in an operating theatre. The pool of blood under Weston had been large and spreading. A bad wound.

'I told him he'd learn more this afternoon than a whole week of lectures,' said Greenlaw.

'Could have been any one of us.' Clay spoke from the back seat. 'If we'd all gone in he might have got all of us.'

'I told him to make identification, that's all. Something happened between them. There was no reason as far as I can see why the man should have used the gun.'

'Weston might know.'

'Perhaps—perhaps not. One thing we do know—we're after a killer—more speed, driver. I want that car!'

The driver saw a gap in the oncoming traffic and stamped his foot down hard on the accelerator, overtaking a hundred yards of traffic before swerving back into lane.

'A little more of that,' said Greenlaw, 'and we'll close the gap.'

'Leyton crossroads coming up, sir.'

Greenlaw picked up the microphone. 'Tango four to Alpha Control—report.'

'*Alpha Control to Tango four. Panda one following car along Eastern Avenue. Positive identification.*'

'Put me through to Panda one and keep open on both channels.'

'*Roger—will connect.*'

Clay said: 'What's the form, sir?'

'We follow. Sooner or later he'll have to stop. Petrol or wherever the man wants to get to. He's got a hostage and a gun. We play it as it comes. There's a regional look-out established for the next fifty miles.'

'What about guns, sir?'

'Look in the side pockets of the car, you'll find all we need there.'

Control came through again. '*Alpha Control to Tango four—putting you through to Panda one.*'

'Panda one?' said Greenlaw. 'State your position.'

'Eastern Avenue approaching Gants Hill. Car under observation three vehicles ahead. What are your instructions?'

'Keep your distance. We should come up behind you in the next five minutes. We take lead. Will flash identity in rear window. Understood?'

'Understood.'

'And follow us until next pick-up. Advise ahead.'

'Roger.'

Greenlaw had had the foresight to provide two automatics, and a rifle which separated into three parts. Clay assembled the pieces expertly. It gave him pleasure to hold the complete gun.

'I'd like to shoot that bastard,' he said.

Greenlaw nodded. 'That's understood, but we take him alive.'

The 18.40 cleared the last sections of the inner London track complex and, with all the lights ahead showing green, passed through Bethnal Green and penetrated into the suburbs with increasing speed.

Maryland and Romford stations flashed by and, as the speedometer in the cabin of H109 marked up the mid fifties, Denning advanced the throttle for the straight run to Brentwood.

The rain had lessened, the cloud breaking up to reveal patches of starlit sky beyond. Visibility, too, was clearing, the focal point of track far ahead and the signal lights gleaming bright and sharp in the cold, drier air.

In the buffet car Mr Thorpley poured his second miniature bottle of Scotch into his glass and, leaning on the counter, looked along the queue whose tail was somewhere lost in the next carriage.

At the end of the car Elizabeth Marwood sat with Paton and Martin, the *Standard* crossword finished in the record time of twelve minutes.

'It's not often you meet a woman who's not only brilliant but beautiful,' Paton said.

'Tomorrow I won't get a single clue.'

'Doesn't matter—you'll still be beautiful.'

Paton's enthusiasm shocked her a little. She smiled at his compliment, forcing back any show of disapproval. Perhaps she was inviting familiarities; or was it friendliness, pure and simple? The day had started with it, had lasted throughout the day and was now extending into the evening.

Martin said: 'How about the old quid pro quo, Elizabeth? You save us two seats in the morning—we'll save you one in the evening. Fair enough?' He spoke her Christian name without self-consciousness.

'Don't make conditions,' said Paton. 'We might lose her.'

Elizabeth shook her head. 'I'll be on the train and will save you two seats. I might even buy you coffee.'

'All this and heaven too,' said Paton.

Beyond the buffet car, in a non-Pullman carriage, Thorneycroft faced his tormentor of the morning run. Annersley had been in full spate since he had tracked down his prey a few minutes before the train pulled out of the station.

It was obvious to Thorneycroft that the Inquisition had had a good day. The man's offensiveness was now sharpened by a cocky good humour that did nothing to mitigate Thorneycroft's dislike.

Ignoring the evening paper to which Thorneycroft constantly returned and focused his interest, Annersley drove his points relentlessly home; then, abruptly, he changed course.

'I remember now—you live on the outskirts of the village—the little Tudor cottage lying well back from the road and hidden from prying eyes.'

Thorneycroft hit back very quietly.

'Not from yours, it seems.'

'Mm?'

Thorneycroft withdrew his sight of Annersley and looked deep into the evening paper. He failed to see the contemptuous smile twitch Annersley's mouth.

In his first-class compartment John Davies weighed pleasure and optimism against guilt and the evening's prospect. If Cynthia had overstepped the alcoholic mark it would need all his patience to cope with her drunken tears and unanswerable self-recriminations which, eventually, she would turn against him.

And the curses would follow; the wild hysteria and more tears as she begged for sexual comfort. One evening and one night to get through and then a bright tomorrow. He would phone one of his sons during the evening and suggest that he come home for a few days. Bruce was now down from Cambridge and could afford to lose the company of his friends for a few days. One more evening and night of hell; tomorrow and tomorrow and tomorrow were Monica's and his.

Guilt lessened and he came out of introspection sufficiently to raise his eyes from the evening paper and speak to the man opposite.

'A little brighter in the City, I think.'

'Thank God.'

'Yes.'

The rule of purchased class privilege prevailed. Davies and his fellow traveller were the sole occupants of their compartment, although the corridors were packed with second-class commuters and casuals. Later, after the ticket inspectors had done the whole train, a few brave ones would invade the first class and risk the frosty disapproval of bonafide first-classers.

In Coach 7, Helen and Edward Ferris shared frustrations.

'I envy you going home to an empty house.'

'Do you?'

Ferris didn't answer. He took her hand and gripped it. The carriage juddered over points and coffee from Helen's cup slopped over the side. They watched its overspill spreading an ochre stain on the folded paper napkin.

Ferris stated the obvious. 'The cup was too full—you should have drunk some of it.'

'I thought I had.'

Withdrawing his hand, he picked up the evening paper. 'Let's see what the stars have in store for us.' He found the amusements page—strip cartoons, crossword and horoscope—and ran his finger down to Pisces.

'Pisces,' he said. 'February 19–March 20. An eventful week lies ahead if you allow things to take their natural course. Emotional tensions should ease off in the course of the next few days. Not a good time for financial speculation and caution should be practised where money is concerned. But trust friendships, for these will prove of great value. A bright week generally for domestic affairs.'

Helen said, bitterly: 'For domestic affairs. Does that mean us?'

'You can interpret it many ways. What does mine say?'

It was their nightly practice. Sometimes their horoscopes matched their situation, either confirming it or offering hope for the future.

'Taurus,' said Ferris. 'Self-restrained impulses are inclined to take over for the next few days; while many of these are justified and you will act on them, consider the outcome, especially where financial involvement is concerned. Allow generosity to dominate your actions. Watch your health this week; of strong stamina you could exceed its limits and become exhausted. A good week for travel.'

'Ivor,' said Helen. 'Ivor's travelling.'

'Tomorrow—I know.'

'No—he's gone. This afternoon. He phoned me with an ultimatum.'

She reached for Ferris's hand and grasped it. 'There's only one answer to it—it doesn't depend on you and it's not because of you.'

'What did he say?'

'Enough. I'm leaving the house—leaving Ivor. Tomorrow.'

Ferris went silent; it was as if the hand she was holding had undergone a temperature change, had suddenly lowered in sympathy with his silence.

At length he said: 'Where will you go?'

'London—somewhere. Anywhere.'

'It's so sudden.'

'Like a miracle, Edward. Do you remember what I said at lunchtime? Don't go home tonight—we'll make it now and never go back? You don't have to go home now—this is the breaking point.'

She felt his hand tighten round hers as if reacting against a sudden pain.

'I'd have to phone her—give some excuse,' he said. 'What could I tell her?'

'The truth.'

The train was well beyond Romford; Shenfield would show up, then Chelmsford, and Helen would leave him. The immediate necessity of a decision shocked him. He wanted to say, 'Give me time—I must weigh the pros and cons,' but he knew it was a request he could not make.

He looked at his watch; another thirteen minutes or so before the train drew into Chelmsford.

'I want to come home with you,' he said. 'She'll cause trouble —you know that, Helen.'

'So will Ivor. I don't care.'

'There'll be dirt—all the dirt she can rake up.'

'Nothing could be dirtier for me than staying with Ivor.'

'I don't want you to be hurt.'

'I am hurt!' She spoke with vehemence. 'Edward—get off the train with me. Come home with me. If you decide not to stay, you can catch a later train—I'll understand. Let's just give ourselves a chance.'

A sense of relief relaxed Ferris's tension. The decision could be delayed a little longer. He could always say he'd missed the train or had fallen asleep and gone on to Norwich. The car bothered him, though; it was parked at Manningtree Station. If he didn't return, if he phoned Margaret and told her that it was finished between them, she or her brother would be down to Manningtree like a shot to get the car and it was *his* car; it had cost eight hundred pounds and was only six months old.

What an understanding person Helen was! No wonder he loved her so much—she *knew* and understood his problem. All right, he would get off the train and go home with her and if he decided to return to East Bergholt—to clear up one or two things—he would see her again tomorrow and the next day and the next; after all, didn't they work in the same office block? There was nothing to lose and he had never been really alone with her. A little more time, that was all he needed—time to protect possessions that were rightfully his. Over a period of weeks he could make certain adjustments including drawing out his share of the bank account he shared with Margaret; the Clan must have *nothing*.

Reassured, he smiled at Helen with the gentleness she knew so well.

'It's going to be fine,' he said. 'I'll come home with you. Helen? . . . It's going to be good at last.'

Three seats away, Charlie Shelley and David Blake sat together. Blake had kept his promise and held a place for Charlie.

Charlie asked: 'Have a good day?'

'Not very. I stuck my neck out and had it chopped off. I asked for it. What about you?'

'Smashing. Did some shopping—spent money like water. Extra Christmas presents. After years of cheeseparing it does you good to lash out.'

'I lashed out today—now I regret it.'

'What happened?'

It was a sympathetic pair of ears and Blake needed to talk the trouble out of his system. He began to sketch in the background to his difference of opinion with his students and Charlie listened; fascinated because it was part of the change in his life which, in one short day, had broadened like the realised promise of a travel poster advertising the seven wonders of the world.

For Harry Peartree sitting opposite Blake and Shelley the world was as alien as a moonscape. Somewhere on the train, Mabel sat alone. Somewhere to the front, he couldn't remember what Peggy had said except, 'Now remember, Dad—first stop after Colchester.'

'S'pose I can't see outa the winder?'

The men sitting opposite had smiled. The round-faced one said: 'I'm getting off at Manningtree—I'll see them safely off the train.'

That was twenty minutes ago and Harry needed further reassurance. His face showed its anxiety and the second man said: 'I've seen you in East Bergholt. Do you want a lift?'

'A lift?'

'My car's at the station.'

'There's a bus from the Skinner's Arms at 'alf past eight.'

'No need for that. I'll drive you home.'

'Don't want ter be no trouble.'

'It's no trouble. As my friend says—just sit back and don't worry.'

Harry settled back in his seat, disconcerted. He didn't know the man from Adam. He didn't want a lift—the bus from the Skinner's Arms would do him well enough.

Mabel, one coach away, was less worried. She knew when to prepare for leaving the train. A few minutes after Colchester she would gather up her small luggage and go to Harry and stir him into activity; to calm his fretful bad temper and lead walk him to the Skinner's Arms to catch the 8.30 bus. But, just to put his mind at rest, in a few minutes she would find him and reassure him that he wasn't alone.

She looked at the three boys in her compartment. Their noses were buried in the comics they had bought at Smith's; Dennis Tilling partly digesting the message of *Playboy* concealed bulkily and obtrusively in the pages of *Lion and Thunder,* Giles working his way through *Sparky, Beezer* and *Dandy,* while Paul, obeying his parents' ruling, was ploughing his way through *Look and Learn* before turning to the parentally forbidden comics, *Smash* and *Beano.*

Approaching Gallows Corner, Kemp said: 'Is the big pantry cupboard in the lobby?'

'What lobby?'

'In the house. Down the three stairs—the cupboard's on the right.'

'What house? Where?'

'I can remember sleeping in that cupboard. I was little—couldn't have been more than four. We had a dog called Toby. I got in the cupboard with Toby and we both fell asleep.'

'You can have the car—just let me out—I won't tell anyone.'

Kemp felt a sudden flow of anger. He jabbed the muzzle into Harris's side.

'I asked you about the pantry cupboard.'

Harris reacted against the pressure of the gun. The car swerved and an overtaking car braked hard.

'Don't do that again,' said Harris. He was sweating. 'There was a car behind!' He looked in the driving mirror. The car behind had pulled back, the driver too unnerved to try another pass.

'Nineteen Ringcroft Street,' Kemp said.

'I live there.'

'The lobby—the pantry cupboard. Down three stairs.'

'There's three stairs, then a door and the living room.'

'Where's the scullery? The big wooden table and the copper?'

'There's no scullery. You go through the living room into the kitchen.'

'She used to boil the clothes in the copper.'

'Who did?'

'My mother.'

'There's no copper, old man. Never was.'

Harris slowed down as Gallows Corner showed up. The rain had stopped and visibility sharpened. To the left of the roundabout and under the flyover, he saw a stationary police car.

He looked in his driving mirror. A black car had peeled away from the line of cars behind him and was coming up level. Four men in the car and three looking at him. One of them in the front made a sign he couldn't understand: an index finger pointing and urging him to go ahead. The man nodded vigorously, then pointed across the roundabout to the stationary police car, then nodded again.

Police? Harris snatched a glance at Kemp. He seemed to be lost in thought.

Harris turned the car into the roundabout and Kemp came out of thought.

'Sharp left.'

'It wouldn't hurt you to let me out. The wife will be worrying —my boy, too. After what happened—'

'Nothing happened.'

'You used that gun—don't you remember?'

'It woke the street up. Like the old days. Penny bangers were bangers then.'

'Christ!'

The black car was now on their tail. As he watched the driving mirror, Harris saw the car behind the black follower; it swerved out for a moment and he saw the unlit 'Police' sign on the roof.

'I'll have to get some petrol,' Harris said.

'We can't stop—not yet.'

'Look at the petrol gauge—just about half a gallon.'

'It's lying. I had a car—when the gauge said empty there was two and a half gallons in the tank. You'd do anything to get out of this car. You'd lie and cheat and bully!—' Kemp's voice had risen.

'No I wouldn't—honest—I wouldn't do that!'

'Just keep driving! Go faster!'

'We're doing sixty—that's enough on this road. Wet surface. It's dangerous.'

Kemp brought the gun up and pointed the muzzle at Harris's temple.

'A gun's dangerous. If I'd had one like this when I was a boy—'

'What?'

'I'd've shot him.'

'Who?'

'Flynn.' Kemp frowned. 'That was Flynn in the street. You saw him.'

'That's right—I forgot.'

'You're lying. You didn't forget. What game are you playing? Do you know something I don't. You tell me—do you hear? You tell me!'

Again the muzzle of the gun bored into Harris's side.

'You said there are Flynns everywhere. I know that. The bullies.

You get them everywhere?' The sweat was cold on Harris's forehead.

'What about women?'

'Women?'

'Are they Flynns, too?'

'You tell me.'

'You don't know?'

'There's good and bad, that's all I know.'

Kemp nodded his approval. 'My mother wasn't a Flynn, but *she* was.'

'Who?'

'From morning to night she was at it. Bully, bully, bully! She was bad. I didn't know she was a Flynn—the kid was one, too. At it day and night—both of them. Want this and want that. Do this do that. Lying, cheating, pushing me around. Bullies are cowards, Alfie, do you know that.'

'I know that. If you stand up to them they crumble.'

'We'll stand up to them, won't we, Alfie? You come up behind and kick them in the crutch. Then I'll get my own back.'

The car behind was following close. Harris could see the men in the front clearly. One of them held up something that glinted, pointing to it with his other hand, then lowered the—gun?—and made an urging forward motion.

For God sake, where? Harris thought. What was he to do? The fuel-gauge needle was flickering on 'empty'. Whether he liked it or not the car would come to a stop any moment now—the engine must be running on smell alone.

'I've cleared them out of my place,' said Kemp. 'You'll like it there, Alfie. It's five acres. Chickens, pigs. It's all right if you're left alone to get on with it. Now the Flynns have gone—there'll be peace. Real peace. Why did you come back from Canada?'

'Canada?'

'I didn't think you'd like it there. You missed the street. Is that why you came back?'

'Yes. I didn't like it there.'

'Remember *Knock Down Ginger*—bangers through letter-boxes?'

'Good times those were.'

Kemp was smiling, gazing through the windscreen at the road ahead. Sweat broke out again on Harris's forehead. What in God's name was going to happen? The car would stop any moment now. It must be the police behind. Harris almost wished they were not. The effort at humouring the murderous mad sod with the gun was taking it out of him. The police had a gun, the mad sod had a gun and he, Harris, was the man in the middle. He had to protect himself some way. He forced calm into his voice.

'What did I call you in the old days?' he asked. 'I bet you don't remember.'

'Billy. You called me Billy.'

'I thought you'd forgotten, Billy.'

'Old friends don't forget. I wish you'd been at my school. We'd've settled Flynn.'

'A good kick in the old crutch. Tell you what, Billy—when we run out of petrol I'll keep a good look-out for Flynn.'

'You won't run out of petrol.'

'We will, Billy. Look—there's a car behind—you take a look.'

Kemp twisted in his seat and looked back. 'I see it.'

'See the men in the front?'

'Yes.'

'I think they're Flynns, Billy.'

Kemp slowly raised the gun and pointed it towards the rear window.

'Don't do that, Billy!' Harris said sharply. 'Don't let them know you've seen them!' He reached out a hand and grasped Kemp's arm. 'Don't do that, Billy!'

Kemp had been on the point of squeezing the trigger. He allowed the pressure of Harris's hand to bring down the gun.

'You always said we'd go down fighting, Alfie.'

'Not yet, Billy. Not before we've got a few Flynns first.'

Ahead, the road bifurcated into the dual carriageway of the new

A12; miles of straight fast road with few bottlenecks, running across Essex and into Suffolk.

'Look, Billy,' said Harris. 'The car'll stop soon. There isn't any petrol. I couldn't afford to buy any more. You remember how broke we always were when we were kids?'

'We used to pinch pennies.'

'So that's why I haven't got enough petrol to get you to Suffolk and there's all those Flynns behind us.'

'Bloody Flynns! Bloody bullying Flynns!'

'Tell you what I'll do, Billy. When the car stops, you get out and I'll hold them off with your gun. How about that?'

'You can't have the gun!'

'All right—you keep the gun. You get away while I hold them off. I'll fight them, Billy—I'll hurt them. I'll kill them if I can.'

'Don't you die for me, Alfie.'

'It's the least I can do for an old friend.'

'When the petrol runs out?'

'That's right. Then you nip out and run for it. Across the fields. I could do it better if I had a gun.'

'It's mine—you can't have it!'

'All right, all right—you keep it, Billy, but don't use it unless you have to.'

'We'll beat them yet, Alfie. Like the old days.' Kemp twisted in his seat again and looked through the rear window. 'They're still there . . . Mum used to say that—when the bugs came out. She'd burn the mattress springs in the garden—paraffin and fire —to kill the bugs. Then a few weeks later the bugs would crawl out again.' He returned his gaze to the road ahead. 'Do the bugs still come out, Alfie?'

'Christ!' Harris put his foot hard down and edged the car up to seventy. He'd had enough and was near breaking point. Use up the damned petrol and have done with it.

He looked in the driving mirror; the two cars were close behind. Better get them back a bit.

'All right if I wave the Flynns back a bit, Billy? They're too close.'

'You do that, Alfie.'

Harris wound the window down and made frantic motions to the car behind.

Greenlaw, interpreting the signals, said: 'He wants us to fall back.'

'What shall I do, sir?'

'Try fifty yards—we'll see if that's what he wants.'

Harris watched the black car fall back then hold its distance. It wasn't far enough to give him that area of safety when the car stopped and the mad sod took off.

Again he made rejection gestures through the driving window. He wanted to scream: *'Get back! Get right back—give me a chance!'*

Greenlaw's driver said: 'He's asking for more, sir.'

'Another fifty yards—no more.'

Now the headlights of the black car were small in the driving mirror. Kemp was impressed.

'You made them go back, Alfie.'

'Yes.'

The engine coughed and missed, then coughed again. Harris said: 'Billy? You ready? This is it. I'll slam on the brakes and you make a run for it. All right?'

'All right. Thanks, Alfie.'

'That's all right. Ready?'

He directed the car to the verge. On his left and beyond the hedge he could see fields and trees in his immediate vision. What lay beyond he didn't know and didn't care. He wanted the mad sod out and away.

The engine died, and Harris pushed down hard on the foot-brake.

'Now—Billy! Quick!'

'Never forget—never, Alfie—you were always my best friend!'

Then Kemp was gone. For a second or two Harris saw him race across the stretch of grass between the road and the hedge, and then he was lost in the night.

Harris bowed his head over the wheel and fought back the over-whelming urge to fetch up.

The 18.40 bored through the night, confident in its easy run to Ipswich. A train containing twelve hundred passengers following an established routine. A crowded, hot train on a mundane journey, running at a speed a fraction over seventy miles an hour.

It happened every weekday night. The same seat-savers; steward serving behind the buffet counter; the same nerves running up and down the train; the same relationships enjoyed for the length of the journey and no more; the ticket-collectors slowly moving up the train check-clipping tickets, inspecting seasons, collecting fares. A typical scheduled run subject to normal delays and the occasional irritating incidents that made commuters late and never early.

But tonight things were running to schedule.

Mr Rae, train enthusiast and timetable pundit, looked through the compartment window as a station flashed by. He consulted his watch and said to his companion, Sellars, 'Shenfield—bang on time.'

'Wonders'll never cease.'

In the driver's cabin Joe Wellford said: 'Right on the nose, George—bang on schedule. The rain's gone and the sky's clearing —a frosty night, I reckon.'

Denning nodded, keeping his eyes on the rails gleaming ahead into infinity. Half a mile distant, he saw the glow of the headlights of an approaching loco.

'Looks like the special goods. I'll give him a blast on the hooter.'

He depressed the bugle button and the two-tone call blared out its greeting to the goods train bearing down on him.

Coates heard it and answered with a savage blast on his own bugle, expressing his hatred of a day that had frustrated him beyond tolerance.

Spencer said: 'You're well over the limit—slow down a bit, you're too fast, Ted.'

'Don't tell me what to do!'

The diesels converged at a combined speed of 150 mph. A flash-roar as they came abreast and then the coupling between rear wagons five and six snapped.

Kemp was back in the night he had left. It was less cold but it had the same feel about it. As he ran and stumbled across the field and through the second hedge, he saw that the stars in the sky were very bright and clear, the constellation Plough ahead and low down on the horizon.

Voices were calling on him to stop; voices far behind. The voices of the Flynns.

He screamed back at them—'*Catch me first!*'

Another field, a narrow one and wet. He went into a soft patch and felt the mud drag at his shoes. It was heavy going, but then the ground rose, became drier, and he made good speed through a copse of trees where the ground was dry and hard.

He could hear the sound of trains. The bugle call of diesels in the night and the thrumming of wheels. Like the sound of the morning when he had shivered in the hut.

Then he stopped dead as the world ahead of him erupted in a great explosion of sound and bright, intensely bright flame. It encompassed his entire vision and smashed at his eardrums. He watched the diesel rear up and tumble in a balloon burst of flame. His pursuers were momentarily forgotten; the scene exploding in his sight was too vast to allow anything else into his brain and vision.

Then, as the great sound dwindled, he became once more aware of the Flynns behind him and he moved forward again, forward to the great orange bonfire that roared a hundred feet into the dark sky. They would never find him in a fire that size. He would hide behind it and shoot them if they came near.

CHAPTER 9

Night, 19.00 hrs.

The first of the rescue services to reach the Willow Point disaster was the Chelmsford Fire Service. Two appliances, a Dennis-Jaguar Pump with a complement of four men and a sub-officer, and a Rolls-Dennis Salvage Pump equipped with heavy lifting gear, oxy-propane cutters and a 400-gallon water-tank capacity; the appliance held a squad of five men headed by a leading fireman.

Led by Station Officer Millard, the journey from Chelmsford to Willow Point was made in precisely ten minutes following receipt of a 999 call made by a Willow Point resident.

Faced with two decisions—to get hoses into play on the blazing part of the train and to obey an instant urge of compassion to plunge into the devastation in answer to the chilling sound of the trapped and injured, Millard directed one half of his team to control the fire, then led the remainder through the wire fencing which protected the estate from the track. He retained one man and gave him instructions.

'Send out routine call—"This is a rail crash involving a passenger train of sixteen carriages. Large number of persons involved. This is a major disaster." '

Millard concentrated his efforts as near the blazing part of the piled-up wreckage as safety allowed. Experience told him that there was little hope of anyone surviving the holocaust; he moved his men only a few yards from the blistering heat and began the search for the first survivors.

Above the roar and crackle of the burning coaches, cries for help further down came to his ears. Compassion tugged in all directions, but until the hoses could be brought into play it was his duty to stay where the greatest danger appeared to be, and that was hard against the barrier of heat.

A slight movement of air, a small breeze momentarily brought the barrier closer as it swirled the flame and heat against him. His eyes smarted suddenly and he felt his eyelashes singe.

'One here, sir!'

He helped the fireman pull out the first victim, a man, totally limp and acquiescent in death, as if every bone in his body had been broken. They dragged the body a few feet clear of the wreckage and left it—there was nothing to be done.

Millard was now deep under a cave of piled rail and telescoped carriages. Torches were not needed; the light from the blazing diesel pierced the small entrances to the caves of wreckage. He saw a face with wild eyes—wild, dead eyes, staring at him; he reached out, then drew back his hand as he saw that no body continued below it.

He heard a sound, a half-articulated cry for help, and he groped forward, hand outstretched and touched a balled fist. As he touched it the fingers opened and clutched at his hand.

'It's all right,' he said. 'It's all right. We'll get you out!'

But as he spoke he saw the impenetrable wall of steel and crumbled metal plate through which the hand was thrust and trapped.

Millard called to his men: *'Help me here—I've found one!'*

Survivors came out of the wrecked train. Some, like wounded beetles, crawled painfully out of the smashed coaches; others clambered down from those coaches retaining some semblance of their former structure and helped those unable to manage the high drop from running-board to track.

Helpless and helpful blundered into each other, the panic of the one matching the frantic efforts of the other. There was no order; chaos prevailed and clumsy, well-intentioned hands caused as much suffering as they alleviated.

The contrast between dark and light was too extreme. It was either the intense glare of the fire or the total dark of the night and shadows. Retinas closed against the brilliance of the ignited diesel fuel, widened slowly in the transition from light to dark; moments of blindness that made both rescuer and survivor inept.

All rail traffic beyond Shenfield and Chelmsford was halted and trains diverted, the lines cleared for demolition and rescue services on their way to Willow Point.

High-priority calls were flashed in all the London termini. The Sword of Damocles, ever hanging over the head of a vast and complex travel system, had fallen with a vengeance.

By 19.15, diversion signs had been erected by the police on the A12 motorway between Shenfield and Chelmsford; the dual carriageway was now single track, the blocked lane available only for rescue traffic.

The first of the hospital teams arrived; four ambulances and one vehicle equipped with emergency operational equipment; these were backed up against what remained of the wire fencing between the track and the estate. There was insufficient access and movement; imaginatively, a call was sent out to the Army Garrison in Colchester for road-making equipment—bulldozers and metal grid layers. A track cut through from the A12 would widen the scope of rescue.

Willow Point Estate emptied itself of residents. They swarmed up, over and through the fencing to lend their hands in the search for survivors. It was uncoordinated help, an anarchy of well-intentioned action.

In the confusion Charlie Shelley, the cut on his forehead no longer bleeding, helped David Blake and a confused Harry Peartree down from the wrecked coach and said to Blake, 'Are you all right?'

'I walk, I live, I breathe, I see. What about you?'

'A scratch. My lucky day.'

'What do we do now?'

'Help.'

Blake leaned against a displaced lavatory door. 'I know nothing about first aid.'

'Time you learnt, then,' said Shelley. 'It's the difference between the quick and the dead. The old feller looks shaken.'

A man came along the track; he was carpet-slippered, a cardigan over open-necked shirt.

'Any help needed? I'm from the estate.'

'Can you take this old chap to somewhere safe and warm?' asked Shelley.

'I want Mabel—where is she?'

'You come with me, old chap—we'll find her.'

'I ain't abudgin' from 'ere.'

'That won't find her, Dad—you come with me. Don't you worry.'

Peartree submitted to the pressure of the man's grip on his arm. He trod gingerly on the filling on the side of the track, protesting at the uneven, shifting surface.

'We'll get something warm into you, old man.'

Blake looked at the tangle of wreckage. A few yards to his right, a man sat on the ground, his back against a carriage wheel. 'There's one, Charlie.'

On his knees beside the man, Shelley said: 'Are you hurt?'

'My name is Rae and my blood group is O Rh Positive.'

'Are you hurt?'

'My blood group is—'

'O Rh Positive—yes I know that. Can you stand?'

'Stand?' Mr Rae looked up at Shelley, his eyes not fully focused. 'My blood—' Comprehension seeped into his shocked brain. 'A rail crash?' he said. 'A crash?'

Shelley nodded. 'A bad one.'

Now sound entered Rae's consciousness; the shouts and orders, the grinding movement of steel against steel, the harsh cacophony of voices raised in panic. 'Fred Sellars,' said Rae. 'My friend—he was with me!' He struggled to get to his feet.

'Don't move. You're in a state. You stay there. You can help by telling me how you got out.'

Rae looked puzzled. 'I don't know,' he said. 'We were talking —and then I came to.' He turned his head and looked at the impacted coach behind him. 'There—I don't know. There were others —a couple of youngsters—the carriage was full. Fred was opposite me.'

'We'll find him. You wait there—somebody'll come along and take care of you.'

Shelley straightened up, looked at the wreck and said: 'Christ Almighty! How the hell do we get through that?'

'This chap did. We can at least try.'

The first heavy-rescue stock from London arrived at 19.40. Equipped with arc-light standards and generators, oxy-acetylene cutters and cranes with a lifting power of a hundred tons, it was the complement of sixty trained men under the leadership of Chief Wilson which slowly coordinated the work of rescue.

The fire had contained itself. The fuel from H109 was barely exhausted and its shape, white-hot and incandescent, could be seen through the smoke and flame. Nothing could have survived in the first three coaches; fire had totally engulfed them.

Shouted orders, cries from the wreckage, the snap and crack of metal as the heat of the blazing loco waned, the harsh light of arcs as generators started up; it was a chaos of feverish activity, dazzling light and noise.

She came to, conscious of an ache in her groin. Slowly, the ache became a pressure, suddenly intimate. She reacted violently, her body jerking away from the intimacy.

'*Don't!*' Paton's voice was very near and urgent.

She put down a hand to push away the offending, the deeply offending, intimate pressure, but a hand stronger than hers held it back.

'Don't. Elizabeth—don't move. You're bleeding, do you understand? You're bleeding. Keep still. For God's sake, keep still!'

'What's happened?'

'The end of the world—I don't know. Please keep still. I'm sorry —my hand—my fist—must be where it is—you understand?'

'No.'

'I must stop the bleeding.'

She was in a half-world—consciousness lingering like fragments of a cobweb. She remembered laughing at something Paton had said, something gallant but amusing, something flattering. It was the last thing she remembered and now Paton was very near and his hand—

'Is it your hand?' she asked.

'Yes—it's something to stop the bleeding—please understand.' —was touching her. She shuddered, feeling cold very suddenly. 'I'm cold.'

'I know. It's what happens. But it's all right—believe me. My hand—I'm sorry. It's the only way.'

Then Paton's voice spoke away from her; loud and high in panic.

'For Christ's sake—help—first aid, for Christ's sake!'

Orders, invective, noise—all seemed to be directed at Kemp. Somewhere, back there, between the motorway and the protective hell of the blazing train, the Flynns seemed to have been lost.

But now all around him was bedlam; the few Flynns had become a multitude, a firelit legion of Flynns. They flickered and danced in the great leaping fireball, their forces growing in size with men who clambered up the bank and on to the rails.

He had to find somewhere deep and dark—utterly protective.

He edged carefully away from the screen of fire that hid him from the persecutors who had called to him as he had raced from the car, the revolver held in front of him in the way he had seen gunmen use their weapons in films.

To his left, as he moved along the track, the glow from the blazing diesel softened and darkened. He stopped at a great mound of twisted impacted coaches.

A tunnel, low down by a curved piece of uprooted rail, caught his eye. Revolver first, he went down and entered the tunnel on one hand and knees.

Sound muted as he crawled forward. The Flynn voices quietened. The tunnel of debris suddenly widened and the space beyond was the size of a small cell—a little like the pantry cupboard in Ringcroft Street.

A good place in which to wait until the hue and cry died down. Somewhere to sleep, perhaps. A hiding place.

He looked behind him for something to seal his point of entry. He found debris and began to build a barrier between him and the outside world.

Then he realised that he was not alone. As the irises of his eyes widened in the dim light he saw the crown of a head across the cave. There was little else he could see. He turned the revolver onto the head and went forward on his knees. The head grew a neck and part of a trunk, then the end of the cave cut off what remained of the man.

The head spoke. *'My legs.'*

'What?'

'Take the weight off my legs.'

Kemp shook his head. 'Why should I? You just lie there and keep your mouth shut.'

'I can't move!'

'Good.'

Kemp edged back to the cave entrance. He peered through the aperture he had left—just a jagged hole of bright orange light.

The head made a deep guttural sound of pain and Kemp crawled back.

'We don't want them to hear—you understand?'

'Help me!'

Kemp couldn't see the face. He stared at the head for a moment, then went down low, moving beyond the head to the extremity of the cave whose wall covered the rest of the man.

His eyes were now accustomed to the dim light; he could discern the features of the face below the head. It was strange to him.

'I don't know you.'

'Have you come to help me?'

'That's a laugh,' said Kemp. He brought the gun round so that the eye of its barrel stared at the man's face. 'You just keep quiet till they go away. You'll be all right if you keep quiet. No calling for help.'

'What happened? The train—'

'They were at me again. Behind—in a car. I gave them the slip. I'll be safe here for a bit.'

'Help me.'

'Why should I? Nobody's helped me.'

Kemp's knees were hurting against the uneven ground. He stretched out and lay down, resting on an arm. The man's face was upside down, dim and pale in the darkness.

'What are you doing here?' he asked.

'Trapped.'

'Like the rest of us. You want me to help?'

'Yes. My legs—I can't move them.' The face contorted with a sudden spasm of pain. A peculiar aaargh! of sound came through the mouth and Kemp's brows knitted as if the pain had been communicated to him.

He raised a hand and groped among the tangled wall of wreckage, working down until his hand came to rest on the man's hip and then against a straight hard length of metal. He passed his hand along its length, noting its width and gauging its weight. Both ends disappeared through the sides of the cave. He shook his head.

'I'll never move that.' He spoke aloud, but to himself. Bunching up his knees, he manœuvred his body so that he knelt, his back bent, and looked at the man's face. He took his lighter out and thumbed it into flame. Eyes glittered in the light.

'I can't move what's holding you down,' Kemp said.

'Who are you?'

'Billy Kemp.' The name sounded foreign to him; sudden and alien. 'William Arthur Kemp,' he amended and added: 'Sallows Farm, Claybourne.'

'I want you to look—see how bad it is—down there.'

'You don't want to know that.'

'Yes. I want to know how bad it is.' The voice suddenly firmed. *'You will look!'*

The flame of the lighter was bright, but Kemp thumbed the control and the flame enlarged. He obeyed slowly, reluctant to look at what lay under the metal.

He took it in slowly, observing the ridge of broken flesh rising up from under the edge of what he could now see was an H-shaped girder. It was hard down a little below the man's genitals. The bone underneath the girder must be smashed into a paste, thought Kemp. The blood flow wasn't noticeable. Kemp put the lighter flame nearer the girder; there was blood certainly; it glistened in the light, but it wasn't the pool he expected to see.

'You'll live.' Kemp spoke callously. 'Looks like your legs are broken. You haven't lost much blood. I know what I'm talking about. I've killed pigs.'

Because the man's eyes had closed, Kemp moved closer to him.

'Did you hear what I said?' he asked.

The eyelids slowly opened. 'I heard you.' The flame from Kemp's lighter had shortened. He thumbed down the jet-control and the flame died. 'Mustn't waste gas.'

It took a little time before Kemp's eyes adjusted again to the darkness of the cave. He noticed that a different light was seeping through the aperture: a white light.

'They've put lights on us,' Kemp said. 'It's me they want.'

He stared at the light coming through into the cave, then added: 'There's hundreds of them out there. They know I've got a gun. I'll shoot the first one that comes through the hole. They know that, too.'

He brought the gun up and looked at it affectionately. The trapped man saw it, too, and Kemp noticed his interest. He moved it nearer the man's eyes, holding the revolver by its barrel.

'It's a forty-five,' he said. 'I kept it after the war. I've looked after it. It's a real killer.'

Kemp thumbed his lighter into flame again. 'Look,' he said. 'You can see it's real.'

The man's lips moved, but made no sound, and Kemp said: 'What? What did you say?'

'Please—'

'Please what?'

'Kill me—please kill me.'

Outside, help had come to Paton as he crouched beside Elizabeth Marwood, his clenched fist hard pressed into her groin.

Paton said to the St John's man, 'I think she's gone.'

'Not yet.' The man straightened up from the tourniquet he had applied and gave directions to the stretcher party. 'There's time yet.'

'The blood,' said Paton. 'There was so much blood.'

'You've done your best—a good best.'

Paton watched her laid on the stretcher and borne away to the ambulance parked at the end of the blind road on the estate. She was being taken out of his hands—into more capable hands. With the realisation, the pain in his shoulder throbbed and increased its bite into his nervous system.

The St John's man said: 'You're hurt?'

'My shoulder.'

'Let's have a look.'

Paton's jacket was torn just below the collar and the left shoulder-blade. The cut was deep, the muscle showing through the gash, bunched and dark red. His jacket was sodden down to the waist.

Paton said: 'Is it bad?'

'Bad enough. You want to know the score?'

'Yes.'

'A deep cut. Muscle exposed. You'll be laid up for a few weeks. I'm putting a pad on it, okay? Can you walk?'

'I don't know. It's as if I've been crouching down here for hours.'

'I'll give you a hand. This won't take a minute.'

Paton felt the pad laid on the wound. It caused no extra pain.

He felt adhesive plaster secure the pad and then the man said: 'How about trying to stand?'

Paton had never known his legs to be so weak. The man supporting him was like a rock.

'I'm giving you my full weight,' Paton said.

'No, you're not. You're one pint under, that's all. State of shock —it all combines. Let's walk.'

'One pint under—I sound like a drunk.'

'They say it's like that.'

A few yards away from the track, something inside Paton snapped. He seemed soaked in blood; as if he had taken a virginity and burst a dam. He felt himself going and clutched at the St John's man.

'All right, old chap—let yourself go—I've got you!'

Seeing her eyes slowly open, the ambulance attendant said: 'Just keep still—everything's under control.'

There was a blank in Elizabeth Marwood's mind between all she could see and hear in the ambulance and Paton's face opposite her in the buffet car. Hand? Paton's hand and the pressure in her groin . . . Paton's hand—*his?*

The attendant laid a hand on her forehead as if to smooth away the frown that had entered her face.

'You're not to worry—do you understand? The pain in your leg —high up—a tourniquet. I know it hurts—it won't for long.'

'Why—'

'The train crashed. You were lucky—a man helped you. He knew what to do.'

'Paton? John Paton?'

'Is that his name? We want more people like that. Don't talk any more. Rest easy and don't move—we're nearly at the hospital.'

She wanted to ask if it was literally the end of a perfect day; if it was the end of all the perfect days she had planned, but vision went in an odd, swirling motion, like a whirlpool. She fought against it with a sudden clenching of muscle, then unconsciousness claimed her and she went limp and acquiescent.

The attendant felt her pulse, lifted one of the closed eyelids, then drew the blanket up to her face. It was touch and go whether the journey between Shenfield and Chelmsford had been fast enough. He had done all that he could do.

By 20.00 hours the tally of those recovered stood at 56 dead and 159 injured and rescue work seemed only to have just begun. Many passengers in a state of shock had been taken into the estate houses; it was impossible to number those commuters and travellers who had made their own way from the wreck and no attempt to keep a record was attempted. It was sufficient to know that the massive piled-up mound of telescoped coaches still contained many dead and injured, and that tons of material had yet to be moved before it could be stated that every passenger had been accounted for.

News travelled quickly and relatives, knowing kith and kin to be on the 18.40, rushed to the accident area from points as far away as Ipswich. It soon became essential for the police block on the closed section of the A12 to harden their hearts against the anxious and forbid entry into the radius preserved for the work of rescue.

From Colchester Garrison, the Army bulldozers and grid track-layers had cut a clearway from the A12 across the half-mile grassland from the motorway to the main line. The work was accomplished quickly; by 20.55 ambulances were using it. The first of these were two mobile operating theatres, which parked on either side of the grid-laid cut-through where it touched the immediate disaster area.

This was foresight of the first order. The seriously injured received life-saving attention before the ordinarily equipped ambulances rushed them to Chelmsford hospitals and the numerous emergency centres.

Sounds had changed. Now the night air was full of shouted commands and counter-orders, the clank and whine of machinery, the occasional crash as some heavy piece of debris was lifted, swung away from the wreckage and dumped to the side of the track.

Arc-lights blazed down on the mountain of tangled metal; harsh truthful light that pierced into crevices and chinks and told those buried but alive there was a world outside and hope existed.

Mr Thorpley and Maurice were two of these. They lay in what remained of the buffet car. As far as either could tell they were uninjured, although it was difficult to move. Mr Thorpley had retained consciousness since the world had up-ended so suddenly. One moment all was light and he was raising his glass of Scotch to his lips and then—an incredible explosion of sound and darkness so black that it seemed like a visitation of total blindness.

It had been, as far as Mr Thorpley could tell, fully half an hour before a groan very near to him told him that he was not alone.

'Who is it?' he had asked.

'Bloody hell!' The response was mumbled, almost unintelligible.

'Is that what it is?' said Thorpley.

'Who—where are we? What happened?' The man's speech was clearer now; Thorpley recognised that voice.

'Are you hurt, Maurice?'

'Head hurts.'

'The train's crashed, Maurice, and God knows where or how we are. The smell of liquor's comforting. Can you move?'

'A bit. I can't see a bloody thing. Am I blind?'

'I can't see either, so I doubt if you are.'

Thorpley found he could roll on his side. He reached out a hand and groped; found broken glass and bottles intact and then, mysteriously, he touched something human.

'Maurice?'

'Is that your hand?'

'Yes. Can you move?'

'Not very far. There's nothing holding me down. There's this effing pain in my head—I'm closed in on all sides.'

'A bit like a coffin,' said Thorpley, 'but there is one consolation.'

'I don't see it.'

'Can't you smell liquor?'

'Yes.'

'Then let's see what we can find. I've no doubt we're both alive and probably unhurt. Use your hands—see if you can find a bottle.'

'I don't want a bloody drink!'

'I do. I'll see what I can find.'

Thorpley's groping hand selected a bottle. With difficulty—for there seemed to be no head room—he drew it toward him and across his chest. It had a screw top; he removed and sniffed at the contents, groaned and replaced the top.

'Orange squash!' Thorpley made a sound of disgust and allowed the bottle to roll away from him.

Maurice said, without humour, 'You're a funny bastard.'

'Is that what you really think of me?' Thorpley groped again and used his hands more sensitively. A collection of small bottles came to his touch and he recognised them as miniatures.

'Ah!' he said. 'That's more like it. Since we're no longer patron and steward, Maurice, why do you call me a funny bastard?'

'I'm sorry—I didn't mean it. I'm frightened and I don't like it. There's all those on the train—you just seemed a funny bastard thinking about drink.'

Thorpley unscrewed the cap on the miniature bottle; it was Scotch. He reached out his hand and found Maurice's.

'Drink this, Maurice. In the circumstances, it's on the house.'

He felt Maurice's hand close round the bottle and take it from him. 'In actual fact,' he said, 'you're quite right. My father and mother were never married and I'm sure I've a sense of humour. So I am a funny bastard. How's the Scotch?'

'It's all right, but I don't like spirits.'

'Then don't waste it. Give it back.'

'No—I'll drink it. I might be in a state of shock.'

Thorpley groped again and found a miniature gin.

Nothing existed below Annersley's consciousness. He knew he was dying; there was no escaping the fact. What surprised him was the absence of pain.

It was dark in the cavern of compacted metal. Only Thorney-croft's voice near to him acquainted him with the fact that he was still in the land of the living.

'Are you there, Thorneycroft?' he asked.

'Yes.'

'Do you hurt?'

'Yes. My shoulder.'

'Do you think you're going to die?'

'No.'

'I am—and I don't hurt at all. I can't see a thing—it's very dark. Is it as dark as it appears?'

'It is dark. There's a glimmer—a chink.'

Annersley was utterly unaware of his body—sans feet, sans legs, arms, body—sans everything but mind and soul.

Thorneycroft grunted against the pain in his shoulder.

Annersley said:

'Can you reach me? Can you touch me?'

'Yes—just about.'

'Then touch me.'

A few seconds later, Annersley said: 'You can't reach me?'

'My hand is on your leg.'

'Is it? Then I have no feeling—no feeling left at all. Reach up, if you can, and touch my face.'

'It hurts my shoulder when I move my arm.'

'Try.'

Only Annersley's head communicated feeling. He said: 'Now I can feel your hand. I exist only in my head. King Charles walked and talked half an hour after his head was cut off . . . You were never a priest, Thorneycroft.'

'I was ordained.'

'In what? A reformed travesty of a Church—nothing more. Must a Protestant perform the last rites on me?'

'Make your own peace with God—if that's possible.'

'You don't like me, do you.'

'No.'

'It's immaterial. Shall I tell you what every Catholic child is taught to do in an emergency like this?'

'If it gives you pleasure.'

'It does—of a sort. Once a child is received into the Church and confirmed that child is empowered to administer last rites if a priest cannot be obtained. A priest cannot be obtained, and there's no Catholic layman available but myself. A predicament exists—do you understand, Thorneycroft?'

'I have enough charity to give you my blessing and commend your spirit to God.'

'Not good enough. Will you let me instruct you according to Roman Catholic practice?'

'I'm in pain.'

'Since you're for the land of the living and I'm not, mention of your pain is selfish. Take your hand away . . . Is that better?'

'Yes.'

'Is anything broken—anything bleeding—internal damage?'

'No—I don't think so.'

'Just trapped—with me!' Annersley's voice failed a little. 'A moment's dizziness, if you were worried.' His voice strengthened. 'I never had the chance to perform the last rites,' he said. 'Instruction dies hard, though I die easy. That's the aphorism for the day —do you like it, Thorneycroft? . . . When a priest cannot be obtained . . . Is the pain any better?'

'A little—I'm not proud of my pain threshold.'

'And you'll do as I ask?'

'If it gives you any comfort.'

'It will, but first I must speak my mind about you.'

'Why do you goad me?'

'Because, basically, I despise you and what you did. So stupid—so indulgent. Do you know what I thought today? No—don't tell me you don't want to know because I'd tell you anyway. I summed up your position . . . I haven't time to refine it. I thought to myself that Thorneycroft embodied ninety-nine per cent of the world's attitude . . .'

Annersley went silent and Thorneycroft said: 'Speak your insult.'

'It's just that I have to use a word I don't like but no other word will do.'

'Nothing you can say can cause more hurt than I've sustained in the past few years.'

'Good—I'm glad to hear it. I thought—Thorneycroft exchanged the Kingdom of Heaven for a good fuck.'

The word hit Thorneycroft hard.

'I use the word in its very proper context. Sexual intercourse is too dignified. You fucked God out of your life, Thorneycroft.'

Wormwood, gall, the sponge soaked in vinegar—the astringent stung Thorneycroft's conscience.

'And that's all it was,' said Annersley. 'You tried to exalt the act by a silly sacrifice which was as silly as the act.'

'Words from a malicious man,' said Thorneycroft.

'But I admit to malice,' said Annersley. 'Regularly I confess its practise. I am forgiven, I do penance and am forgiven. I know my faults. I deplore them and trade on them at the same time. I'm a base human with a concept of God that will save me. But you— you're an unmitigated villain . . . you deceive even yourself . . . I'm dying, Thorneycroft—am I doing it well?'

'What do you want me to do?'

'I will make an Act of Contrition and then you will listen to my confession . . . I think it's that way round. Confusion—there's confusion in my head . . .'

A Covans-Sheldon railway crane had started its lifting operation and was now working its way up from the end of the 18.40. Recovery of the injured from the end four coaches had been easy. Most injuries had been superficial and stretcher cases easily dealt with.

Progressively up the train the wreckage became more complex, the task of rescue more difficult. An army of men now hacked and cut their way into the jungle of coach debris, now and then shouting for a stretcher party or first aid.

In some cases it was difficult to distinguish the severely injured from those uninjured but in a state of total shock. A girl, rigid with terror, eyes wide and staring, was extricated from a surprisingly intact toilet, still in the action of squatting. Without speech, without sight, she was handed over to a party of nurses who carried her down the line to a waiting ambulance.

Two coaches, their couplings intact, had angled up at their centre like an inverted V. The height of the apex was forty feet. It was essential that a prop be strutted up from the track to this apex, before heavy rescue could be attempted; uninjured and partially injured had already made their way to either ends of the angled coaches, and a heavy rescue foreman had heard ominous sounds of movement in the stressed metal of the carriages.

The Army was called in and a multiple-unit jack erected to take the strain. It was then that three small figures were noticed on the point of the apex.

'Hello—can you hear me?'

'Coming, son—hold on! Are you all right?'

'I am—so's Paul—it's Dennis's leg.'

'We're coming.'

An extending tubular ladder was run up to the apex and the boys watched rescue coming to them. Dennis Tilling, *Playboy* held tightly under his arm, lay between the couplings, his right leg twisted at an odd angle. He felt no fear, only a very bad pain below his knee.

He said to Paul: 'It's broken, isn't it? What a swiz!'

The rescue man appeared and spoke to them with forced cheerfulness. 'How'd you boys get up here?'

'We flew,' said Paul. 'Dennis has hurt his leg.'

'I'll see to that. Are you two all right?'

'We're all right.'

'Think you're up to climbing down the ladder?'

'Easy.'

'Get down then and tell them to send up a first-aid man and a hoist—got that?'

'Yes.'

'Get on with you, then.'

Crouching down beside the boy, the man said: 'If the other boys flew up here, how did you manage it?'

'They helped me—is it broken?'

'I think so. Does it hurt much?'

'A lot.'

'We'll soon have you down and comfortable. First aid's on its way—then we'll hoist you down.'

It was a clean break halfway up the shin. A splint was strapped on the boy's leg, and hoist harness clasped round his waist and under his arms.

'Don't be frightened, son,' said the rescue man. 'It's a strong rope and we'll lower you slowly.'

'I'm not scared—the whole thing's a bit of a lark.'

'Glad you think so, son.'

'Has anyone been killed?'

It wasn't until they had taken Dennis's weight on the hoist rope that the boy's question was answered: 'A lot of people, son. Too many.'

'Is it the worst accident you've seen?'

'The worst ever . . . Right—we're going to lower you down.'

'All right—thanks for the ride.'

It was exactly how Harry Peartree had feared. The day was a tragic wash-out. He had told Mabel it was a waste of time and trouble going up to London. Now, where was she?

He had refused to move from the track. Wrapped in a blanket, he sat by the Salvation Army mobile canteen and help centre and drank hot, sweet tea. He had known the day would go wrong— bloody wrong. All his forebodings had proved correct. Bloody London! He'd seen it for the last time—they wouldn't get him up there again.

Men appeared out of the night ushering a blanket-draped figure before them. 'You've found 'er?' Harry asked.

'Not yet—don't worry. The chances are she's all right.'

'Can't you git a move on?'

'That's what we're doing.'

The blanketed woman was crying. A Salvation Army officer put an arm round her shoulders and led her into the van.

What'll I do if the old lady's dead? Peartree thought. Never— never again would he leave Berg'olt and, if Mabel was all right, he'd see she didn't either.

'Only in me coffin,' he said aloud.

A St John's man superintending first-aid supplies heard him and said: 'What's that about a coffin?'

'It's the only time they'll get me outa Berg'olt.'

'You thank your lucky stars you got out uninjured.'

'What about the wife? She's in that train.'

'They'll find her. Don't worry.'

Mabel Peartree *had* been found. In an ambulance parked on the grid-laid cut-through on the other side of the track, a small cut on her cheek was bathed and dressed.

She repeated yet again, 'I'm all right. Where's Harry?'

'They're looking for him.'

'I don't like him being alone. Can't I go and find him?'

'No—I don't think so. They're doing all they can.'

'But I know where he was.'

'You told the rescue man—you've done all you can. Just rest. They'll find him.'

A little later, the attendant noticed she had gone. There was nothing he could do about it; there were more injuries to see to and the old lady hadn't been in a state of shock.

Order was slowly coming out of the chaos. The wreckage of eight end coaches had been removed from the track. Superficial search had revealed many dead and seriously injured, but miraculously, many had been found dazed and uninjured, extricated from impossible places where it seemed life could not possibly exist.

Distracted from their original purpose, Greenlaw and his men declared a halt in their rescue assistance.

'There's little we can do, now. Kemp's somewhere here—I'm sure of that. He's gone to ground somewhere in this bloody mess.'

He surveyed the noisy activity surrounding him; at the blazing arc-lights and grinding machinery; the groups of men and women working on the wrecked train.

Clay said: 'He could be any one of those.'

'Not our man,' said Greenlaw. 'He had one thought in mind—self-survival. We'll spread out and search. Keep your weapons handy and don't take any chances.'

Thorneycroft said: 'This crash—it is nihilistic. Destruction for its own sake. Without thought—without reason.'

'Wrong,' said Annersley. 'Quite wrong. If I can accept that it's God's way of summoning me to his presence and, at the same time, giving me an earthly punishment for my sins, then that's sufficient reason.'

'Selfish to the end, aren't you, Annersley?'

'No—I merely state how I'm personally affected.' Annersley was silent for a space.

Thorneycroft bore his silence as long as he could then said: 'Annersley?'

'I'm still here—though not very much. I was considering your comment on my apparent selfishness. Everyone on this train will be affected one way or another. It's what's known as a salutary experience. You realise that I am now only soul and mind? That I exist entirely in my head. My body has very little to do with me except to supply energy to my head and brain. My soul is, of course, nothing to do with either. It has lived not very comfortably in a vehicle I've never been particularly fond of. I can even spare a thought for you. Are you trapped?'

'On all sides.'

'Very apt and significant—good old God.'

'Why?'

'You're being shown in a practical way how your ambition and stupidity have always trapped you. You see what I mean when I call this a salutary experience?'

'My whole day has been a salutary experience,' said Thorneycroft. 'I have been disturbed by two good men and one devil.'

'Am I the devil?'

'You are.'

'I always thought Lucifer wasn't as black as he was painted. Assuming your injuries aren't all that bad and you will be mobile— will you grant a happily dying man a last request?'

'As long as it doesn't include kissing the Pope's big toe.'

'His Holiness wouldn't like that. It concerns my son. A bad lot, but with hope of reclamation. He needs a pair of shoes—size nine. You can claim from my estate. December 20th. Hollersley Remand Home. His name is Roger. Christmas parole. I want you to meet him at eight-thirty am with a new pair of shoes. Brown, I think—brogues—pay up to six pounds. Don't ask why—will you do it?'

'If it's possible.'

'It must be possible. If you can't, send your wife—your poor wife.'

'For Christ's sake stop goading me!'

'I can't help it,' said Annersley; 'and I think I know why—'

His voice had grown quiet, barely above a whisper.

'Why, Annersley?' asked Thorneycroft. 'Why?'

'Motives are difficult to determine,' and Thorneycroft had to wait, the sounds outside his prison diverting his attention. He bit back the desire to call for help.

Now Annersley's voice was even quieter. 'I'm failing, Thorneycroft. I'm afraid you won't hear me. Listen, please listen . . . perhaps—motives—it is possible I—goad you—because I care . . .'

'You care?'

'I said—it is possible . . .'

In the noise of chaos and death, the harsh grinding and clanking of the mechanical hoists and shouts of direction that resembled battle orders, Annersley's soul left its despicable vehicle.

The main concentration of passengers would have been centred front and end of the buffet car, the parcels car guard explained to the rescue foreman.

'There's always a queue,' he said. 'Between Liverpool Street and Shenfield you can always reckon it stretches way beyond the buffet.'

The rescue foreman nodded. 'It's a piece by piece job, then.' Judging where the centre of the train would be, he said: 'You think about there? There's Christ all to see under that pile!'

'I reckon it's about there.'

'Okay.' The foreman rapped out orders. 'Get lights and a bleeding move on! Heawood, Collins, Reid—sound the wreckage—use sounding tubes!' He turned to his second-in-command. 'And Caine—I want lights. Get them concentrated on that area!'

When it came, it was this concentration of light that penetrated the minute crevices in Thorpley and Maurice's prison of steel. Bright stars seemed to appear in the roof just above their heads.

'Let there be light and there was light,' said Thorpley. 'Can you see it, Maurice?'

'Like pin-pricks.'

They lay there in silence for a while. Thorpley found another miniature—Scotch this time—and drained it.

Maurice said: 'I keep thinking about that couple.'

'The frustrated couple?'

'That's them.'

'Perhaps they're no longer frustrated.'

'You mean, dead?'

'I mean dead . . . Time you had another drink, Maurice—you're getting morbid.'

A few miles outside Leeds, the man driving his car into York-shire turned on the radio at ten o'clock and heard the news of the rail crash. It meant nothing more to him than a reminder that his wife travelled on that line.

An expression of dislike crossed his face as he remembered the weekend and his telephone conversation with her earlier in the day.

He said: 'Bitch!' and turned the radio dial until he found Radio Two with its programme of pop.

At 22.15 it seemed that there was nothing more Blake and Shelley could do. They had worked together since they had emerged from the wreck of their carriage. There was blood on their hands and clothes, and black oil-dirt streaked their faces.

'I never thought the day would end like this,' said Shelley. 'I don't know what the wife will be thinking. She'd've got the message over the nine o'clock news.'

'A lot of wives and families got the same message.'

'There's nothing more we can do here. How do we get home?'

'There'll be transport somewhere.'

They walked down the track and found the information centre. Coaches were waiting on the A12, they were told. At Chelmsford a shuttle service was operating to Colchester, Manningtree and Ipswich, stations normally served by the 18.40.

Blake asked: 'Is there a phone we can use?'

The information officer shook his head. 'Not here—it's all two-way radio. You'll get a chance at Chelmsford.'

They took the grid cut-through to the A12. On the way, Shelley said: 'What did the crash mean to you, David?'

'Mean? I don't get the idea.'

'It's like this. I've had a good day. I've enjoyed the job—everything went well. Then this crash comes and I'm all right. Lucky again, you see. It's my lucky day. Some of the sights back there —they were unlucky. Not just the dead but some of the injuries we saw—that man's friend—'

'I know what you mean,' said Blake.

'You feel singled out. Before the crash I thought I loved my wife and family, now—I'm crazy about them. I want them more than anything else in the world. I took them pretty much for granted a few hours ago and now—I don't want them out of my sight.'

'I was going to throw in teaching because I couldn't connect with the students. I'm not so sure now.'

'Why should you want to do that,' asked Shelley. 'Throw it in, I mean. It's a good job, isn't it?'

'It's well-paid. The point's this, Charlie—you get the feeling that students are a race apart—that they have all the answers, despite the logic you can bring to bear to prove them wrong. Maybe it's their advantage of youth. But that boy and girl we brought out— you saw how badly injured they were—they were as fallible as anything living; just as capable of dying as an old man. And just as capable of being wrong.'

'So what do you think now?'

'Tolerance. Not to judge them by the splendid example of myself.'

They found the coach and boarded. It was brightly lit and Blake saw the dried blood on his hands and raincoat.

He said: 'Those two—the boy and girl—do you think they'll live? I've their blood on my hands.'

'Hospitals can work wonders,' said Shelley. 'They were alive— we did all we could.'

They looked back at the constellation of lights marking the accident area. The last mound of impacted coaches were surrounded by the mechanism of rescue and demolition.

'I wonder how many are still under that lot,' said Shelley. 'Poor buggers—thank God for life!'

Later, as the coach bore them away from the Willow Point crash, he said: 'Funny thing—I'll catch the train again as if nothing has happened. I wonder how many regular faces will be missing. That chap Ferris who gave me a lift this morning—I wonder if he's all right?'

Chelmsford Station was in a state of siege. Relatives had driven from Colchester and their cars choked all entrances to the station. Police commands were ignored, their authority denied by the sheer force of anxiety.

The coach stopped a short distance from the station. 'No chance of getting nearer than this,' the driver explained. 'I'm sorry. It's not far to walk.'

Blake and Shelley found a telephone booth, miraculously empty, and Blake put in a call to his wife. She was unaware of the accident. She had wondered at David's non-appearance and had not looked at the nine o'clock news.

He said: 'Look, Pat—it was terrible—many, many dead. I want you to phone East Bergholt 892—speak to Mrs Shelley. Tell her that Charlie—that's her husband—is safe and well.'

'How will you get home?'

'There's a train laid on to Manningtree. I don't know what time. I'll drive Charlie home first—okay?'

'All right—are you hurt?'

'A bit bruised. We are lucky, Pat. Phone Charlie's wife right away. I'll get off the line.'

He left the phone booth and said to Shelley: 'Pat will phone your wife right away.'

'Was she relieved?'

'She hadn't heard a thing.'

'It's just as well,' he said. 'What the eye doesn't see, the heart doesn't grieve over—I can never get that right.'

'It doesn't matter—I know what you mean.'

Down the line, abreast of the goods locomotive, a railway accident-control centre had been set up. Also, in the same centre, preliminary investigation into the cause of the accident had begun. A defenceless, inarticulate Coates faced the calm face of his questioner.

'Just tell me what happened, Mr Coates—as far as you can recall.'

The enormity of the accident had rendered Coates tongue-tied.

He remembered Spencer's warning, *'You're well over the limit —slow down a bit—'* But it wasn't his fault. It was a straight stretch, a safe stretch, and you could push up the speed with safety; no curves or difficult sets of points. It wasn't his fault, yet he felt the burden of guilt.

His interrogator prompted him into speech.

'It appears that some of your end wagons derailed. At least, that's how it seems to judge by the state of your train.'

What would Spencer say? Coates thought; he's got it in for me, I can tell that. He'll say I was doing seventy and I wasn't taking proper care. But I don't know what happened. All I know is, I kept on the rails and the other train didn't.

He found speech at last. 'I was making for the Shenfield sidings. There'd been special clearance. I saw him approaching. I answered his hooter call—and that's all I know. We passed and I felt a drag. I braked and stopped.'

'What was your speed—when you came abreast?'

'Seventy.'

'That's above the permitted speed.'

'I know.'

'I see.' The calm face regarded Coates silently for a moment. 'Any reason why you should go above the permitted speed?'

'No—it's just one of those things. We know the safe stretches. You can pick up on diagrams—it's common practice.'

'But this time you had bad luck?'

'I don't know what it is—ask the driver of the other loco.' As he said it, Coates realised the mistake he had made.

An expression of distaste flickered across the examiner's face. 'As you well know,' he said, 'that isn't possible. I doubt if we'll find much trace of him or his second man.'

'I'm sorry,' Coates said. 'I didn't think—I'm sorry.'

The excuse fell lame and flat; guilt pressed heavily down on him and he felt the burden was unfair. He had gone above the maximum, that was all.

'If you think it's all my fault—' he began.

The examiner raised his eyebrows. 'I made no such judgement. This enquiry has only just begun. No conclusions have been reached.'

Coates jerked his head towards the accident area. 'That mess back there—it's been a bad day. Everything's gone wrong. They started messing up diagrams this morning. No London stop-over was mentioned when I started out—I've been messed up all day.'

'Every goods driver knows diagrams are likely to be changed. You're paid for stop-overs and overtime. I fail to see what it has to do with the accident.'

A flush of anger stained Coates's face. 'You blame Control! They cleared me from the Chelmsford sidings to Shenfield.'

'Knowing it to be a safe run,' said the examiner. 'The Up line was clear for more time than was needed for you to reach Shenfield. Why the haste, Mr Coates?'

'I don't know!'

The examiner leaned back in his chair and toyed with his pencil. At length he said: 'Is there anything you'd like to tell me? Something that has a direct bearing on the accident?'

'Just that I admit I was going above the limit, but it didn't cause the crash. I'll not take the blame.'

'It will take some time to determine cause or who's to blame. That'll do for now, Mr Coates. Is your second man outside?'

'Yes. Spencer. You want me to send him in?'

'If you will.'

'He won't tell you any more than I've told you.'

'That's yet to be seen. Thank you, Mr Coates. Don't go far away.'

Coates left the compartment of the accident-control carriage and found Spencer.

'He wants to see you,' said Coates. 'I told him I was doing seventy. Don't say too much, Len. Just give him the facts.'

Spencer's face showed neither friendliness nor sympathy.

'I'll give him the facts, all right. You've been a bastard all day. I'm not saying you caused the crash, because I don't know.

I'll tell you this, I'm not second-manning you again and I'll tell him that and why.'

'We worked well together, Len. You learned something from me. We've got to stick together—we're both in this!' Coates gripped Spencer's arm. 'You do see that, don't you, Len?'

'I've told you—I'm not driving with you again.'

He turned away, out of Coates's grip. At the entrance to the interrogation compartment he hesitated and looked down the corridor at Coates. He saw a man he didn't want to see again. He had no proof—no proof at all—that Coates had caused the crash yet he was convinced that it was the culmination, the natural culmination, of a black day. He would tell the examiner everything: the bad temper, the hasty, clumsy shunting at Acle, the high speed along the straight run, and none of it would be positive evidence. He and Coates were the only witnesses if he was to believe on-the-spot rumours and reports. Yet so convinced was he that Coates was as guilty as hell, he wished he could report signals disobeyed and infringement of every golden safety rule in the book.

He opened the door of the investigation room and went in to tell his story to the investigator.

Maurice and Mr Thorpley lay in a drunken, black as pitch prison.

His speech slurred, Maurice said: 'How long we been here?'

Thorpley took his lips away from the miniature whisky and said: 'A thousand b-b-b-bacchanalian nights, Sharlie—I mean, Maurish. We musht . . . number ourselves 'mong the fortunates.'

'Blind thdrunk,' Maurice said. 'I can't see a bloody thing an' I'm pissed as a newt.'

'A problem there, Maurish,' said Thorpley, and recognition of the problem increased the sting of his desire. 'I wan'—want to pass water and can't see—way out of wetting myself.'

'Just let it go.'

'If I could roll—over to th' left—all well . . . but I can't, Maurish.'

'Then piss to th' right.'

'Trouble is, Maurish—you'd get th' lot.'

A little later, Thorpley said: 'How—how very uncomf'table. I've wetted myself . . . Firs' time since I left off wearing nappies.'

Rescue workers seemed to have no time for Mabel Peartree as she wandered up and down the line. She was given brusque replies in answer to her unanswerable questions.

'Ask up the line.'

'Try the first-aid stations.'

'For God's sake, missus—I've got a dying man here!'

She sat down on a piece of wreckage, the blanket draped round her shoulders, feeling cold and alone. She was miles from home; miles from her daughter and, the thought struck with deadly impact, she would never see Harry again; not the live, grumbling but always-there Harry. Somewhere in that great pile of wreckage he lay dead or badly injured and suffering, if he was still alive, because he couldn't cope on his own and wanted her near him.

An even deadlier thought struck her: perhaps he thought she was dead and wouldn't come to help ease his pain or help him die.

She began to cry, very quietly, alone in her grief and concern. The night was getting colder, the stars sparkling frostily in the dark clear sky. She would never get home; she had no way of assessing the distance to East Bergholt and the warm cottage. She was in a cold no-man's-land.

The harsh sounds of rescue activity made little impact on her. It was only when the tall figure of Thorneycroft came out of the darkness and destruction and stood before her that she raised her eyes and held back her tears so that she could see him clearly.

'You shouldn't be here alone.'

'I can't find Harry,' she said. 'I asked 'em but they couldn't tell me.'

'Your husband?'

'We was in different carriages.'

'Are you strong enough to walk? To come with me?'

'I'm strong as a horse.' The old cliché came out with customary ease.

'We'll try the first-aid stations and accident control, Mrs—'

'Peartree,' said Mabel.

'I know the name,' said Thorneycroft. 'Yours is a village name —East Bergholt, isn't it? There's more than one Peartree in East Bergholt.'

She rose from her seat of debris and felt the man's reassuring arm round her shoulders.

'We'll find him, Mrs Peartree. We'll go together and find your husband.'

The pain in Thorneycroft's shoulder throbbed. He had refused transit to Chelmsford Hospital but had accepted first-aid dressing. The death of Annersley, sardonic to the end, had had the effect of minimising the injury to his shoulder. The source of pain had been quickly analysed by a doctor working in an improvised shelter: a large bruise area and superficial cuts. Thorneycroft had remembered his selfish preoccupation with his own discomfort when Annersley had spoken to him out of the darkness; it was a microcosm of all the troubles that had affected him in the years that lay behind. Vanity, selfishness, egotism—self, all the time. He'd had a terrible injury which had slowly lessened to a small pain as Annersley died. How well that man had died!

The old lady stumbled and Thorneycroft tightened his grip round her shoulder.

'All right, Mrs Peartree?'

'It gets light, then it gets dark—you don't know where you are.'

'Not far now. There's a first-aid station and a mobile canteen not far away. We'll find your husband and a hot cup of tea.'

He didn't know if his words were hollow. The desire to comfort and inspire hope had little to do with reason; just add the water of tears and pain to the human mixture—instant compassion.

He suddenly felt a warm affection for the old lady. He wanted to go beyond reason and tell her that he knew old Peartree was safe and sound. Instant compassion. The other sort—the abstract— would insist that he utter no false words of comfort but buffer future shocks sensibly by suggesting the worst that might have happened. It gave more room for the best to turn up.

Carter was a man of instant compassion, thought Thorneycroft. Carter could see no political, economic or philosophical reason why millions should starve and die in a world rich enough to feed all its inhabitants. Carter had resigned himself to the impossibility of the Kingdom of Heaven ever being realised on earth and the improbability of it happening in the after-life.

The abstract religiosity of Annersley with its Jesuitical understanding of ends justifying the means gnawed at Thorneycroft's sense of guilt. The harshness of Annersley's judgement lingered in his memory with particular bite because a dying man had made it.

What would Aline's reaction be if he told her what Annersley had said: Her rejection would be complete. She would see in the message the very essence of St Paul's attitude to women.

And he, Thorneycroft, hadn't even thought of Aline waiting in the lonely house until this moment. Somehow he must get word to her.

He steered Mabel Peartree across the lines beyond the last of the wrecked carriages and round to the cluster of mobile first-aid posts. A single arc-light, strung high on a cable gantry, cast a cold light on the Salvation Army van.

'We'll try here,' Thorneycroft said.

To the left of the van, a police constable used his two-way radio. The language of radio communication came to Thorneycroft's ears.

'Roger—over and out.'

He should get a message to Aline to say that he was held up and would be home when a half-baked Christian had done all that he could do.

The solitary, miserable figure of the blanket-draped Harry Peartree still sat on the folding chair outside the entrance to the SA canteen.

Relieved, so that good humour loosened her tongue and inhibition, Mabel said: 'I think that's the old bugger.'

There was no tearful reunion. The old man said: 'Where you bin, girl? I been sittin' 'ere worryin' me bloody 'ead off.'

Thorneycroft left them and made his way back to the wreck.

Aline—she must wait on news of him. There was work to be done in the field—real work. To hell with dog-collars. Annersley, Chinner and Carter had revealed the truth to him and he was now in Carter's world; a world in which compassion had real meaning.

He knew one thing positively: he would go to Carter and ask if he could follow him. He would give up all possessions and follow one of the best men in the world. He also hoped that Aline would follow, too.

He went into the heart of the wrecked train and joined a party of rescue workers. He followed their instructions and harsh directives implicitly, shirking no duty and fighting back nausea as his hands touched unspeakable things. He did not call on God once.

The number of dead taken from the wrecked buffet car was as high as the accident controller had feared. As each body was brought out, identification was established and a plastic label bearing the dead person's name tied round the left wrist.

John Paton was already on his way to hospital when his fellow traveller Frank Martin was brought out. Detecting a faint heartbeat, stretchers were called for. In a mobile operating theatre doctors worked to strengthen the beat; twice it stopped and was revived, then it ceased altogether.

He was removed to another ambulance whose sole purpose was to ferry the dead to Chelmsford. Unknowingly, Martin shared with two other shrouded bodies.

They had been found together, very close, so close that each had seemed moulded to the other. But their death had not been pretty and the rescue men had seen nothing romantic in the clasped hands they had had to part. Each bore labels on their wrists: *Helen Thomas—Edward Ferris.*

Forty-two miles north, Margaret Ferris sat with her mother, father and brother. *'It is feared many are dead'*, the announcer on the nine o'clock TV news had said. Margaret was quite prepared for the worst. The value of Ted's insurance policy was known to her. *The Alliance is my shepherd I shall not want.* Ted had been fanatical about insurance; if the worst had happened she was, at least, well-provided for. And if she had to start life over again she was still young enough for marriage. The prospect was pleasing and as she thought the wish that he wouldn't return a flush coloured her face.

Further north, as he opened the door of his hotel room, Ivor Thomas wondered what the bitch was doing. He unlocked his suitcase and carefully hung up his second suit in the wardrobe. He looked at his watch. The night wasn't yet old and he felt randy. He washed his face and hands, straightened his tie, combed his hair and went downstairs to have a quiet word with the doorman; he'd yet to know one who didn't have a few addresses in the town where a man might drown his sexual sorrows.

A police car had taken the two boys to Chelmsford. On the way, more out of interest in the car's radio system than concern for Dennis's parents, Paul had asked if it were possible for the police to get a message through to the Tillings.

Fifteen minutes after the call had gone through from Chelmsford to East Bergholt via Colchester, the constable on reserve duty in Weston's absence telephoned Mrs Tilling, now returned from the station in a state of near-hysteria after receiving news of the train crash. Five minutes after the call she and her husband were on the A12 and racing to Chelmsford Hospital.

All that remained to be stripped from the remains of the buffet car was a small mound of twisted metal plate, and girders. It was tackled manually. Fifteen bodies and twenty injured had been recovered; anything could be under that mound; evidence of the miraculous or the expected.

They found Mr Thorpley and Maurice apparently uninjured but incapable of standing. They lay in a welter of smashed bottles, the smell of spirits rising strongly as the cone of the mound was removed.

Before losing consciousness, their speech was slurred, giving incomprehensible answers to questions. They were marked as severe shock cases and placed on stretchers.

Later, in the hospital, the doctor identifying their blood groups was surprised to find that each sample contained a very high alcoholic content. He went along to the ward to find them sleeping very deeply, the sleep of the totally drunk.

He could see no evidence of shock and said to the sister: 'In the morning, give these two drunks a good wash, some breakfast and send them home.'

'Drunks?' The sister in charge looked shocked.

'The devil takes care of his own, Sister. They survived the crash and got drunk in the process. From the smell on their breath I should think it's whisky—among other things.'

He turned to go, then stopped as a thought struck him. 'Incidentally, Sister, when they wake up it's likely they'll suffer from hangovers. I recommend a double Alka-Seltzer and a hair of the dog that bit them. Get some pure alcohol and mix it with blackcurrant juice eighty/twenty mixture. Hm?'

Clay said: 'I don't think our man's in this lot.'

With Greenlaw, he surveyed the last of the crumpled coaches to be searched. Only four now remained: it had been estimated that of a possible passenger tally, most had been removed.

It was now 23.00 hours and all rescue forces were concentrated on the last great heap of wreckage.

'I think he went across the line and into the estate,' continued Clay. 'He could be miles away by now, sir.'

'Anything's possible,' said Greenlaw. 'If he did he won't get far. The call's gone out—anything on foot will be picked up. But *I* think he's here.'

A stench of burnt metal and flesh filled the night air. Thin coils of smoke still writhed up from the blackened shape of the diesel. From where he stood, Greenlaw could see the winking lights of police cars and diversion signs on the A12.

'What happened to the driver of the car?' he asked.

'Harris? He made a statement and beat it back to London like a bat out of hell.' Clay grinned. 'He won't forget the experience in a hurry. Kemp had the gun on him all the time. Harris said he humoured him all the way from London. I'd like his sense of humour—it's pretty clear Kemp's a lunatic.'

'A homicidal maniac,' said Greenlaw, 'and I'm hoping he's somewhere here. How many men are posted?'

'Thirty. Some are armed. He won't get away if he is.'

'Harris—the driver of the car,' said Greenlaw; 'was he clean?'

'Virginal. It appears he owns the house the man was watching. Coincidence and bad luck it was his car Kemp had to hijack.'

'It was also bad luck Weston muffed it. We'll be closing in soon.' Greenlaw looked seriously at Clay. 'Make sure you don't repeat Weston's luck, Clay.'

'Only fools rush in,' said Clay. 'You know the rest, sir.'

Now the list of dead and injured mounted very slowly. Little sound came to the ears of those probing the wreckage. Sounding tubes, in many cases simple lengths of zinc-iron piping thrust into the debris, could not distinguish between the creak of stressed metal and human groans, but, where sound was, search had to be made.

Up the line, accident investigators nosed among the devastation at the point of collision and assessed causes. It amounted to nothing but a bag of beans. Still hot and unapproachable, H109 smoked in an almost unrecognisable jumble of metal. Somewhere, evidence of George Denning and his second man remained; some vestigial proof that two humans once drove it with experience and confidence.

As the tally dwindled, so did the number of vehicles. Now only eight ambulances and the two mobile operating theatres waited in the disaster area where there had once been three times that amount.

The Army was standing by, its road-laying trucks ready to cut new throughways if they were needed. It was now 23.20, and the last of the impacted coaches, four in number, had to be taken to pieces carefully, for it was here the borderline cases and the dead would be recovered.

The rescue co-ordinator mustered his forces; the mobile operating theatres were moved up to within a few feet of the track; St John's men stood by.

Greenlaw, too, had moved his men into strategic positions; the area now was small enough for his force to encircle the region of concentration. He explained the position to Major Beech, the officer in charge of the Army contingent.

'I may be wrong,' said Greenlaw, 'but somewhere in there a man with a gun is hiding. He's used it and killed already. I want that man. I'd like your help.'

'What do you have in mind?'

'Have you enough men to tackle him if necessary? It's a situation I imagine the Army is trained to cope with.'

The major's reply was emphatic. 'No,' he said. 'Orders given to me did not include a direction to help the police in searching for a criminal. Also, my men are not armed.' He indicated the revolver in Greenlaw's hand. 'You seem equipped well enough. It's your war—I suggest you wage it. Are there no police in the area?'

Clay watched the figure of the major walk away from them down the line. 'Snooty bastard,' he said. He raised the shotgun and fingered the trigger. 'Who needs the Army, sir?' he said to Greenlaw. 'They're amateurs.'

It seemed that his hiding place was surrounded by the enemy. Kemp listened to the sounds outside, the gun in his hand steadily aimed at the aperture.

John Davies looked up at the pale grey shape of Kemp's face and said: 'There's a case for ending both our lives, Mr Kemp.' He spoke calmly, against the chilling pain that rose from his legs to reach the peak of agony that made him grunt.

'Mr Kemp?'

'I've got a gun—I can shoot my way out.'

'You'd have done it before.'

There was so little time and so many reasons why my life should end now, thought Davies. And there was pain to add to the prima-facie case; a cold, biting agony that stretched the upper part of his body with the fierceness of the rack.

He had dined and loved as a condemned man should and it was as legendary as the last supper. He had risen out of the depths to ecstasy, only to be thrust down again. This time there was no escape.

'Born losers,' he said. 'We're both born losers. What did you do?'

'What?' Kemp took his eyes away from the jagged little screen of light coming from the cave's aperture. 'What do you mean?'

'Why do they want you. Do you know?'

'I know. All my life I've known.'

'They'll have guns, too—many guns. You won't stand a chance.'

'Why should they have guns?'

'Normal procedure when they're after an armed man. What did you do, Mr Kemp?'

It was a question Kemp had evaded all day and the night before. He had pushed it behind the screen of life-long terrors. What had he done to deserve being hunted down like a rat? The past day and night reeled back like a film in reverse. He tried to stop it because he knew its beginning, but the trapped man's voice urged the speed of its reversal.

'Remember, Mr Kemp. Go back to the beginning.'

He was back in the muddied yard. He had come out of the last stinking pig-house, put down the feeding bucket and had seen, very clearly, the mess and muddle of the house and outbuildings. It had no future, none at all and never had. He had worked like a criminal pauper on a treadmill getting nowhere but older and more desperate. For twenty years he'd trod the wheel. The future that had seemed far off had arrived, had become the present.

'I was more dead than alive,' he said.

'I know,' said Davies. 'You'd come to the end but had to go on living.'

'The bloody pigs were grunting and snuffling over the food I'd given them. I hated the bastards—I'd always hated them.'

It had grown dark in the yard. Lights were on in the house but they bade him no welcome. She would be at him again the moment he took off his gumboots and went into the kitchen. She'd turned into a sow, snuffling and squealing at him like the dirty pigs in the sties.

Anger had slowly grown up in him like a hot expanding gas; anger at his failure to get no further than a few acres of dirty land, a dilapidated house and debts that could only be sustained by working to prevent foreclosure. Working and living with pigs—living like one.

He'd wished himself dead. He'd wished all those round him dead: the pigs, the sow and the little sow in the house waiting to squeal at him.

'I wanted to blow the whole bloody lot up.' He looked down at Davies. 'They were all in my head shouting and screaming at me.' He went silent for a while and Davies listened to the sounds outside his prison. The grind of metal on metal was getting louder and voices sounded near.

Kemp spoke again, quietly, anger gone from his voice. 'I went into the house. They were sitting at the kitchen table. They said something to me, but I didn't hear them. I went upstairs to the loft and took the gun from a box of oiled rags. It's a good gun.'

He stroked the barrel with the tips of his fingers. 'I've always kept it loaded. Now and then I used to go out and see what I could hit. Five of the six chambers were loaded and I wanted to blow the pigs out of my head. I looked into the muzzle and wondered where I ought to put it. Then *she* called up the stairs. She squealed, that woman. She didn't speak, she squealed—like a pig with its throat cut. I looked at the gun and went . . . I remember going down the stairs and into the kitchen. . . .'

'They're getting nearer,' said Davies. 'There's no time.'

Kemp had gone silent again. A sudden gripping agony lanced up in Davies's body and wrenched out of him a throaty sound of pain.

'That noise,' said Kemp. 'That noise you made—she did that when I pulled the trigger . . . when I saw what the bullet did to her throat. Then the kid screamed and I pulled the trigger again.'

'*Now,*' said Davies. 'You must do it now!'

'I didn't think again,' said Kemp, and cocked the revolver. 'Not until I found myself in the wood. I was tired and I stopped in this wood. Something had happened I had to get away from. London was where—she's not there any more. Nothing's there. I thought it was. Alfie, the street, the games we played. Nothing except the Flynns. They're always there. They're outside now.'

'They won't get us, Mr Kemp—you take both our lives just to spite them.'

'Friends call me "Billy".'

'Billy—do it now—I can't afford to live. Like you, my only escape is to die.'

Kemp nodded. 'Just to spite them.'

'They'd lock us up, Ke—Billy. For the rest of our lives. Don't give them that chance. They'd make you work with pigs and scream orders at you. You don't want that. Put me down like a sick animal.'

'I've done that many times. I was never one to shirk doing what was right.'

The noise outside was loud, but over it came an amplified voice, harsh and imperative.

'Kemp! this is the police—come out with your hands raised. We know you're in there—drop your gun and come out!'

Kemp's body tensed like an animal poised for flight.

Davies said: 'Don't go—they want you alive.'

'You think we should spite them?'

'I know we should.'

And in spite of them, Davies thought. If I could get him to put the gun to my head and pull the trigger it would mean finish to the miserable trek to the end of the road and the last bet made valid. The asset wasn't a fortune but it would be Cynthia's. It wouldn't be touched by Max or the creditors. The house would have to go and good riddance to its red bricks and heritage and his sons were old enough to care for an alcoholic mother. Twenty thousand pounds insurance unless death had been caused by suicide. Murder was in. A good bet. If he could get Kemp to pull the trigger—at least a small part of conscience would be assuaged. And this grinding, awful pain, that would go, too.

But the regret of Monica. To find such a pleasure at the end of life. It was ironic and as savage as the pain that lanced up into his body.

They must not find me, Davies thought. I want no miraculous surgery, for there cannot be much left of me below the hips. Great for them to sustain a legless man, a moneyless, ruined man.

To be free of guilt and fear—the blessed relief from pain and anxiety.

'It's any moment now,' he said to Kemp.

'Yes,' said Kemp, and looked at the cocked revolver. 'It's any moment now.'

Loud-hailer held close to his mouth, Greenlaw prepared to issue another directive to Kemp. Round the perimeter of the remaining wreckage, a little beyond the sweating rescue workers, a cordon of police waited for Greenlaw to flush out the wanted man. Clay stood near him, shotgun at the ready and itching to use it.

Press photographers and television cameramen had again moved closer to the wreck. Greenlaw noticed them with irritation.

'I told those damned Press men to get back. See to it, Clay!'

Wilson, the rescue chief, came away from the debris and approached Greenlaw. 'Where do we go from here?' he asked. 'We're down to the last carriage—what's left of it. We've used mike-tubes. There's life there—we heard voices.'

'Just keep working. We've got the area surrounded. If he's there, he won't get away.'

'That's what worries me.' Wilson looked resentful. 'You say the man is armed?'

Greenlaw nodded.

'Then the best way to stop him using it is for you and your men to get out.' The rescue chief was aggressively large. He came closer and gave Greenlaw the full force of his size and authority. 'My concern is for my men and the job they're doing. I don't care if it's Crippen under that wreckage—this is a rescue operation. I want you and your men to move back—right back. I won't have any shooting.'

Greenlaw said, stonily, 'I cannot accede to your request. The man's wanted for murder—a triple murder if the police officer he shot dies.'

'It's different if a copper gets hit—is that it?' Wilson was belligerent. 'I don't care if fifty coppers got shot—anything that impedes rescue work is a breach of my peace. I can get higher ruling than you, copper. So what's it to be?'

'Let's be reasonable,' said Greenlaw. 'I can see your point well enough. You must see mine.'

'And I can see wild bullets flying.' The rescue chief shook his head. 'It won't do. My men will be the first to reach him. I wouldn't give a tuppenny damn if you got there first. I'm not having any of my men shot. Unless you have any other ideas, I'll have you moved—then I'll reassure the man, if he's there, that he's got a clear run—and I'll see that he has.'

'I've one idea,' said Greenlaw. He handed his gun to Clay. 'I'll join your team and work with you—talk the man out. Let me be the first to reach him—you said you don't care how many coppers have been shot.'

Some of the belligerence faded from Wilson's face. 'What about your men?'

'I'll move them back—with the exception of Detective Sergeant Clay. He'll stay where he is—with a shotgun. There'll be no wild shooting—Clay knows how to use it.'

'You think you can talk the man out?'

'I know how to lie,' said Greenlaw.

He turned to Clay. 'Use your initiative, Clay. I'm going over to talk to Kemp—if he's there. Whatever happens, don't let him get away.'

Clay curled his finger round the trigger of the shotgun. 'The bastard won't get past me.'

The aperture was suddenly blocked, and the cave descended into darkness. Then the quiet voice came to him.

'Kemp? I know you're there. I am Detective Chief Superintendent Greenlaw—can you hear me?'

Kemp rested the gun on his forearm and aimed at the blocked aperture.

'I hear you,' he said.

'*I want you to come out—you're in need of medical care. I understand, Kemp, do you hear me? I understand. You've had a rough time. It's all over now. I've an ambulance standing by—there's a warm bed waiting for you in the hospital.*'

'What else have you got waiting for me?' Kemp directed his voice down at Davies. 'Did you hear that lying sod?'

Davies came out of a spasm of pain. 'What did you say?'

'The police—they've a nice warm bed waiting for me. It's what the man said.'

'He's lying—Billy—do it now—they're after us both—we won't have a chance if they get to us.'

The voice again. '*You've been running for nothing, Kemp. You haven't killed anyone. Your wife and child are fine—the little girl's crying for her daddy—wants you to come home. You didn't hit the police officer, Kemp.*'

Kemp smiled in the darkness. He could discern shapes again in the faint light that entered the cave.

'He doesn't know,' he said. 'He's treating me as if—. I'm *not* mad. I know I killed them—I wanted to kill them. I fired the gun again in Ringcroft Street. I'm unbalanced, I admit that, but mad, no!'

'*You're not well, Kemp—I'm here to see you receive proper attention. You'll be charged with the attempted theft of a car and carrying an offensive weapon. That's all. Will you come out?*'

'No,' said Kemp. 'Neither of us will come out. When you reach us you can have what's left.'

'*What do you mean, Kemp?*'

'I've made a good friend. He knows what it's like to be hunted and bullied.'

'*There's someone with you?*'

'A friend.'

'Can I speak to him?'

Davies shook his head. He slowly raised a hand and reached for Kemp. 'No, Billy—no more speech.'

'No more words,' said Kemp. He took the gun away from his forearm, found Davies's hand and gripped it.

There was urgency in the voice outside. *'Look, Kemp—let me speak to him. Is it someone trapped—injured? We can get you both out. I promise you I'll go away—I'll take my men with me. There's a rescue party standing by—they're good men—they only want to help. . . .'*

'You want me to do this?' asked Kemp.

'Yes.'

'We'll go out together—that's the idea, isn't it?'

'We won't be alone.'

'That's right—we'll go where no one can touch us.'

Exterior sounds had changed. Above Kemp's head there was the hard chink of metal and the rasping, grinding sound of debris being moved. He looked up at the ceiling of the cave. More chips of light had appeared, like stars, one of them very bright. A draught of cold air wisped down from this bright star and stirred his thin hair.

A guttural sound of pain came from Davies and Kemp said: 'All right—it's all right. I was never one to let an animal suffer.'

Greenlaw heard the faint rustle of speech. He beckoned Wilson to crouch down beside him.

'He's got someone in there with him. Probably a casualty. Christ knows what to do now.'

'I thought you knew,' said Wilson. 'You wanted to be the first to reach him.'

'I'm concerned about the person he's with. He's taken one hostage already tonight.' He put his mouth close to the aperture. 'Kemp—the man you're with probably needs urgent medical attention. Will you let us get to him?'

There was no answer. Greenlaw waited, then said, 'Clay?' He

straightened up and looked round. Clay had gone. He called loudly, '*Clay!*'

The two shots were spaced a bare second apart. When they came, Greenlaw reacted and ducked to the side of the aperture. But no bullets pierced the jagged entrance to the mound of debris. He stood very still for a moment, then turned to Wilson. 'I think we can get to them now,' he said, 'and I'll lead.'

CHAPTER 10

Tuesday, 14th December, Morning

Detective Sergeant Clay, sitting beside the hospital cot in the intensive-care unit, yawned and wished he could be sleeping as peacefully as the anaesthetised man he had been watching for the last two hours. He looked up from the white face to the plasma hook-up beside the bed and followed the plastic tube down to where it entered the man's arm.

A nurse came into the room accompanied by a doctor. Ignoring Clay's presence, they examined the unconscious man, taking pulse then sounding his chest and heart with a stethoscope.

'Doctor?' Clay interrupted the doctor's concentration. 'Any sign of him coming round?'

Irritation showed in the doctor's face. 'No. I told your superior it's a waste of time. This evening, perhaps. Why don't you go away? Wait downstairs. You'll be told when he recovers consciousness.'

'I thought it was *if* he recovers.'

'Very well—*if* he recovers.' The doctor again listened to the man's heart-beat, nodding approval. 'Heart's stronger, Nurse.'

'Good news?' asked Clay.

'More than we hoped for. If you had seen his injuries—'

'I did,' said Clay. 'I helped get him out. You don't have to tell me how badly hurt he is—sir.'

For a moment the doctor was silent, then he said: 'You were there?'

'I was in at the kill. All I want now is a statement. Your patient had a man with him. I want a few facts, that's all.'

'Sleep is what you need.'

'It can wait. It won't be the first time I've missed a night's sleep. You think he'll live?'

The doctor nodded. 'He has a good chance.'

'I want that man to live,' said Clay.

'We all do—that's why I'm here. You want him to live for different reasons, I imagine.'

Clay nodded. 'A statement—to justify certain actions taken by the police last night.'

The doctor shrugged. 'The ways of the police aren't my concern.' He turned to the nurse. 'Stay with him, Nurse. At the first sign of any change—good or bad—call me.'

'Yes, Doctor.'

Clay watched him out of the room and said: 'Is he always like that or doesn't he like coppers?'

'You look incongruous in a sickroom—and you are.'

'I'm sorry. The whole night has been incongruous. The innocent were killed and injured when I wanted only the guilty to suffer. It's what we all wanted—what I wanted, anyway. I did what I thought right. Now I've got to justify it.'

Interest replaced indifference. The nurse looked at Clay, puzzled by his introspection.

'I could hear him down there. I'd climbed up on the wreckage—I thought I might distract his attention from the super who was talking to him. I had a shotgun . . .'

Clay went silent, staring across the bed and into the distance.

The nurse said: 'Why?'

'The man was a killer. He'd killed twice and shot a constable. . . . I pulled away some of the debris—there was a great mound of it and he was underneath. I made an opening—it wasn't very big. I heard his voice. I saw a movement—the light coming in from the rescue lamps must have caught his face. I pushed the barrel through the hole and fired. There was another shot, but it didn't come from my gun. Later we found that a dead man had pulled the trigger of the revolver.'

Clay stopped and looked at the nurse. It was good to tell his story to a sympathetic listener.

'I was right to do what I did,' he said. 'Now I've got to justify it. Your patient was his hostage—he's got to be. I can't plead self-defence. If your patient's life was in danger, then I was justified. That's why I want a statement from him.' Clay grinned. 'No copper likes a manslaughter charge brought against him, even though his action was justified. Your patient can clear me—just for the records, you understand.'

'I see.'

Clay's grin had sent the nurse back into hostility. She looked at her watch and Clay said: 'What time is it?'

'Nine-thirty. You're wasting your time, you know. He won't come round yet. Perhaps midday. Certainly not before.'

'I've bedside-waited before. *And* lost the chance of getting a statement because I've been told what you've just told me.' Clay suddenly switched the subject. 'What about next of kin—have they phoned through?'

'There's a wife. Her doctor phoned. She won't be coming, but he will.'

Some unconscious instigation moved a set of muscles in Davies's face; a slight momentary frown and movement of the lips and he was still again.

'Assuming he survives the shock,' said Clay, 'what are his chances?'

'He was lucky and unlucky. Fractured pelvis, multiple fractures of the legs. We think his legs can be saved—after a lot of operations. We see it as a challenge.'

'That old word,' said Clay. 'Everest, the Atlantic, round the world in a small boat, now it's legs. Last night was challenge.'

'For whom?'

'Me—him—the man we wanted. Everyone, I suppose.'

'And you shot your man because he was there?'

Clay nodded. 'Like Everest—also, he didn't deserve to live.'

At 11.30 Dr Mansell arrived at the Chelmsford and Essex Hospital. He had made the journey from East Bergholt for two reasons: John Davies was his patient and friend and Mansell was concerned with his condition. Also, he had a reluctant duty which could not be performed until he had assurance that Davies could be told.

The second reason was that two more of his patients were occupying beds in the hospital.

He spent fifteen minutes in close consultation with the surgeon who had performed initial surgery on Davies before putting him into the intensive-care unit in a private ward.

'He'll have to face more than a series of operations in the future,' Mansell said. 'Sometime, I've the unpleasant duty of telling him that his wife has died.'

The surgeon shook his head. 'Not yet. We haven't determined depth of shock. Was her death expected?'

'It's been in the cards for a long time. A toss-up between heart and liver. Drink, depression, insomnia—a killer syndrome.'

Later, sitting beside the bed, Mansell studied the face of John Davies and wondered what the death of Cynthia would mean to him. She had died alone in a chair facing a television set. At 1 am the police had failed to contact her by telephone. After a series of calls they had assumed the house was empty. At 9 am Mrs Clark had arrived to do her morning's cleaning; letting herself in with her own key, and had found her watching a bright television test card with sightless eyes. At 10 am Mansell had examined the body and estimated that time of death could have occurred round about nine o'clock the previous evening. Mansell remembered the television headline news. *'It is feared that many lives have been lost—'* Perhaps her death had struck simultaneously with the implication of that item of news. But who would ever know? It was heart failure and that could happen both in exultation and grief.

An unhappy woman had died. Alcoholism had become an irremovable factor in her life, and his friend, lying there with a strangely composed and peaceful face, had to bear much of the blame.

There was nothing he could do at the moment. John would find his own injuries and their treatment in the next few months harder to bear than the death of Cynthia. It was not a cynical observation. One had left her misery for ever, the other had only just started his.

He rose from the chair and smiled at the nurse. 'You'll find him a good patient, Nurse. Very polite, stoical and strong.'

'We know that already—strong, that is.'

'He'll want to know just how badly he's injured. Don't flannel— give him all the facts—he can take it.'

'The doctors will do that. The important thing is—there's a good chance his legs will mend. I can tell him that.'

'He'll probably smile and tell you that he's heard artificial limbs are indistinguishable from the real thing.'

Acknowledging the presence of Clay standing with his back against the door, Mansell asked: 'Why are you here?'

'Line of duty, sir. Police. Mr Davies was in a difficult position last night.'

'That sounds like the understatement of the year,' said Mansell. 'I gather he wasn't the only one.'

'You'll read all about it, sir—in due course.'

Mansell gave his attention to the nurse. 'I shall stay in the hospital for some time. If I'm still here when Mr Davies comes round, will you let me know? Sometime I must give him some bad news.'

'I'll send out a call, Doctor, but I don't think he'll be in a condition to take bad news.'

'He's the sort of man who can take hard facts.'

Mansell had two more Bergholt patients to visit: Mrs Marwood, who had survived the crash by retaining the minimum amount of blood to sustain life until the hospital could begin the process of replacement, and the devilish Dennis Tilling in the children's ward.

Hugh Marwood would be at his wife's bedside; Mansell hoped that the shock wouldn't set him back after the months of care and medication he, Mansell, had given him. On the credit side, there was a possibility that the shock of his wife's accident could do some good. Someone near and dear to you and in a worse condition than yourself can work wonders. In any case, a severed artery heals quickly and blood transfusions were a mere formality. She'd be up and about in no time at all. The doubt in her case was the possibility of traumatic shock. Mansell had studied her case history before leaving Bergholt; on the evidence, the chances of any real nervous disturbance were slight.

Dennis Tilling. A broken leg would keep the little devil out of mischief for the Christmas holidays and that was nice for the neighbours. You could see where that boy was going. He'd grow tall and successful—as confident of his abilities as John Davies. A sense of humour and a strong constitution—great gifts. John and Dennis had them in equal measure.

Monica Inchbald had made a small dent in her fortune to the extent of three hundred thousand pounds. As she drove from Aldgate into the main thoroughfares of the East End she felt a little uneasy that she knew so much about John Davies.

The news of the rail crash had made small impression on her sight and hearing the previous evening. She had seen the pictures before.

'*It is feared that the casualty figure is high,*' Robert Dougall had said, or something like that. The crash had meant nothing to her; it was something that happened at regular intervals—was the last in Yugoslavia—or Japan? It had happened many times before, like the repeat of an old film.

A few minutes later, with the same casual attention, she had heard, '*Mr John Davies, Secretary for Trade and Industry, today agreed to meet the Clydeside workers for talks following the death of . . .*'

Some time later, she realised that certain words from the news lingered in her mind. *Train disaster—many dead—John Davies—following the death of—*

She had tried to dismiss their portent, following the pattern she had planned for the evening; the long luxurious bath when she would think of John Davies; the bed into which she would climb and relive the events of the afternoon.

At 1 am she could stand the insistence of the words no longer.

Directory enquiries had given her his telephone number in East Bergholt and she had dialled it and waited on the ringing tone until it seemed obvious that it was not to be answered. She then began a series of calls and, at 2.30, exasperated with frustration, she had been rewarded. A man bearing his name had been admitted to Chelmsford Hospital with serious injuries and was now in the operating theatre.

9.30 had seen her at Viscenti's. She checked with John's secretary that he had memoed and recorded the advice that the firm would now handle the Inchbald holdings. Further questioning of his secretary revealed that a good secretary knew more than her employer imagined—and kept it to herself. In any case, the secretary told Monica, in a firm of brokers money ceased to have any real meaning, if Miss Inchbald understood what she meant. Miss Inchbald did understand. It was only when the figures were turned into hard cash did money become a reality. That was why she was concerned about Mr Davies and his terrible accident.

'Who are his bankers?' Monica asked.

'Lloyds.'

'Do you know which branch?'

'Leadenhall. I shouldn't be telling you this, Miss Inchbald.'

'But you are—and helping Mr Davies. You realise my interests are vital to Viscenti's?'

'Oh, yes.'

'Then you'll tell me if Mr Davies is in any sort of difficulty.'

The secretary hesitated; loyalty was deeply engrained in her. She had no right to know so much. She had supposed that, like most brokers, there were bad days and good days. The City Index fluctuated and clients' money was lost and won, but over the last few weeks little scraps of information, inadvertently heard fragments of telephone conversations, questions asked by Mr Viscenti—all had suggested that Mr Davies was in some sort of trouble and in the context of the company's business that could only mean financial difficulty.

'In what way?' Monica had asked.

'Mr Davies, like the other partners, buys and sells for clients.

I don't mean the careful clients—the low-per-centers—but those who want their money doubled overnight. That means playing the markets. Sometimes, if a client's money is in trust under the company's name, a broker might use the money for his own benefit. It's called "pledging client's stock". You raise a bank loan on the stock, you see, so that you can speculate. It's dishonest of course, but it's done.'

'And you think Mr Davies has done it?'

'I don't know. In any case—it's all right if the broker can meet Accounts Day—that's the twenty-first of this month.'

'How do you mean?'

'If he's bought on the first day of dealings—that was on the thirteenth, he must pay the jobbers on the twenty-first—Accounts Day.'

'And if he can't?'

'He's hammered.' The secretary looked worried. 'Please don't think I'm saying Mr Davies is in that sort of trouble. It's just that after Mr Viscenti told Mr Davies that he'd be away in Bonn until after the twenty-first, Mr Davies seemed to cheer up. I've grown to know his moods. What I do know is that he's worried.'

'And you don't know why?'

'I think he's speculated too heavily. In fact—I know he has. On his own account.'

'And lost?'

The secretary nodded. 'That's just what I think. I wish there was something I could do.'

'There is,' said Monica. 'He's badly injured. If he's in trouble it's up to us to get him out of it. Will you help me to go through his papers?'

'I don't know.' The secretary hesitated. 'I'd want a good reason.'

'I love John Davies. I think that's a good enough reason, don't you?'

At 10.30 am Monica used the privilege of wealth and made a small dent in her fortune. She visited John Davies's bank and paid into his account three hundred thousand pounds.

It was now 11.30 and she was closing the distance between London and Chelmsford. She drove the white Volvo 1800 carefully through the East End, frustrating the urge to push the car into high speeds. She had acted calmly and efficiently all morning; now, she questioned her motives with the same calm. Was it sheer possessiveness, to hold him by a great debt of gratitude, that had induced her to back him to the extent of three hundred thousand pounds? The money meant nothing to her. The ability to help was of monumental value, but would he see it in that light? He had accepted her decision to come to Viscenti's with gratitude and pleasure; by the same token he should receive the money she had paid into his account with similar emotions. That is how it should be, she told herself.

There was an envelope in the dashboard pocket; an envelope containing a statement made out that morning at her imperative request. How marvellous it was to have money and the authority it commands: *'Normally, Miss Inchbald, I couldn't possibly allow you to act for Mr Davies, but I can see the urgency of the situation. A statement will be prepared immediately and you can take it to him.'*

And she had opened the envelope containing the statement and read his very personal history. How ridiculous it was that he had no money when there was so much of it.

She would ask him for powers of attorney if that would help, or he could instruct her what to do to wipe the slate clean. If three hundred thousand wasn't enough there was very much more where that came from.

I am not just a rich bitch, she told herself. I love a man and what is mine is his. And his, mine. If I am on an errand of mercy, why the hell not? I want that man.

She entered the dual carriageway of the Eastern Avenue, following the sign directing her to Chelmsford.

She had questioned love so often; nothing tarnished so quickly, and the more you expected the less you got. They had told her that his injuries were severe. Remembering their love conversation, the Anthony Rowley lines came into her head: *'A frog she would a-wooing go—'* Errand of mercy, claiming what was hers, vanity, the suspicion that money could buy anything, even love; these were the motives energising gear change, clutch, brake and accelerator control.

Also, she told herself, he has a wife. Don't forget that, you poor, little rich bitch. Here you are on the way to a hospital bed which, in all probability, knew the presence of a grieving, unhappy wife, exhausted by the vigil that lasted throughout the night.

A signpost turned her left through the Harold Wood Industrial Estate—sixteen miles to Chelmsford. Sixteen miles between conjecture and reality. One thing was certain, she had made a small down payment on the extension of a life she dearly wished to continue.

And that, she told herself again, is the attitude of a truly bitchy poor little rich girl who seldom considered the fact that some people actually had pride.

Should she not turn back and use third parties to inform John that he was safe? To go back and wait on events? With Viscenti's now controlling her interests; with John's personal account standing at three hundred thousand, he was safe. He had to be told and soon. Unable to take evasive action his torture would be unbearable. Only his pride could stand in the way.

'Damn pride!' She spoke aloud and stamped her foot hard down on the accelerator. 'Damn his wife and damn all considerations! He's mine and I'll rich bitch my way completely into his life!'

Ahead, diversion signs directed her off the dual carriageway into single-line traffic. On her left, as she dropped speed, the residue of rescue and demolition vehicles indicated her proximity to the rail crash.

She caught a fleeting glimpse of the wreckage, the cut-through bull-dozed by the Army showing up like a scar across the half-mile of meadow. A road sign loomed ahead: five miles to Chelmsford.

Clay said: 'How are you feeling, sir?'

Davies had come out of oblivion slowly, reluctantly. It was the third time Clay had attempted his question. The doctor, one more sympathetic to police needs than the night houseman, had examined Davies and commented favourably on heart and general condition. 'Ask your questions,' he had told Clay. 'Make them short—I don't want him worried.'

'Sir?' Clay said.

A dull pain suffused Davies's body from the waist down. With clearing vision he saw the hump in the bed that covered the lower half of his body. Clay's face came into his vision, then, feeling a touch on his wrist, he turned his head. The face of a nurse smiled at him.

'You're doing fine,' she said.

'Fine?' Davies frowned and memory stirred, fragmenting the anaesthetic-induced fog clouding his mind.

Clay said: 'You've had a nasty experience, sir. I don't want to bother you longer than is necessary. Just a few questions.'

'Who are you?'

'Detective Sergeant Clay, sir. CID.'

'Am I a criminal, then?'

'Criminal, sir?' Clay shook his head. 'Not you, sir—it's the other man. You remember the man with you in the crash?'

Davies nodded. 'I remember him. He was going to do me—a great service.'

'He was holding you as hostage, wasn't he, sir? He had a gun and would have used you as a shield to get away.'

'No.' Davies closed his eyes. 'I was using him. We were both going to die.'

Clay looked at the nurse, who shook her head. 'I expect things aren't very clear, sir. I'm sorry to bother you like this. If you can give me a yes or a no to a couple of questions, I won't bother you further.'

'I've nothing to tell you.'

'Just a couple of questions. Nod or shake your head—that'll be enough. Did he have a gun on you, sir?'

Memory was now sharp in Davies's mind. It had been seconds off the merciful act. An ear-splitting explosion and—nothing. Death would have been like that.

Eyes still closed, he said: 'I didn't die.'

Clay shook his head. 'You were lucky, sir. I got to him before—well—no need to go into that.'

'There was a shot.'

'It came from my gun. It was you or him. He'd killed twice before.'

Davies turned his head away from Clay. The nurse looked worried. 'Can't you leave it till later?'

'A couple of questions and I'll go. I'm sorry, sir.' Clay bent down and spoke close to Davies. 'Would he have killed you, sir? Was your life in danger. Do you believe he might have killed you?'

The multiple questions boiled down to one question. Motives were private to Kemp and himself, but Davies had one question he wanted answered.

'Is he dead—did you kill Kemp?'

'Yes—he's dead.'

'A fortunate man.' Davies opened his eyes and looked into Clay's heavy face. 'You asked me would he have killed me?'

'That's right, sir.'

Davies nodded. 'If you hadn't interfered—yes—he would have killed me.'

'The gun was trained on you?'

'Yes.'

'And the action of the police prevented it?'

'Yes.'

Satisfaction showed in Clay's face. He closed his notebook and rose to his feet.

'That's all, then, sir. When you're feeling more yourself we'll ask for another statement. Just confirmation of what you've just told me.'

At the door, Clay turned and said: 'If anything else occurs to you, sir, regarding last night, I'd be glad to hear it.'

'You can hear it now,' said Davies. 'Your killer would have done me a great service. You have not.'

Clay shut the door quietly behind him. Pain and shock did strange things to people. Possibly the poor devil thought he had no legs under that protective cage in the bed and who'd want to live without legs?

As he walked down the corridor, Clay felt the rhythmical action of his own legs; the feel of whole bone, whole muscle and nerves co-ordinating perfectly to intention. Given time and many operations with a bit here and a bit taken there, grafted and pinned, and atrophied muscle exercised into some semblance of normality, maybe the poor devil would enjoy—if that was the word—a normal life.

As he came through the main doors of the hospital, he noticed a white Volvo 1800 enter the parking area. He watched the woman climb out of the driver's seat and slam the door shut.

She passed Clay without a glance and went through the doors. He pursed his lips in appreciation. It wasn't often you saw a woman like that; she carried an aura of beauty, authority and wealth.

And she hadn't locked the doors of her car. As he walked to his own four-year-old A40, he looked in the driving window of the Volvo. She'd left her keys in the ignition lock. Obviously she could afford to have it pinched.

He yawned deeply. Back now to London to make his report and then to bed. What a night—what a goddamned night it had been! And now all was well. A pity Mr John Davies hadn't been more appreciative.

CHAPTER 11

December 20th, Monday morning

As the 08.20 from Manningtree pulled out of Chelmsford Station, Mr Thorpley laid an envelope containing two five-pound notes on the counter of the buffet car.

'A Christmas token of my appreciation, Maurice,' he said.

'Thank you, sir. Very kind of you.'

Thorpley looked round and down the car. The scene had changed. A few lightly bandaged heads and hands suggested the presence of 18.40 regulars, but the thinning-out had been enormous; so many familiar faces without names were missing.

'Do you notice the change, Maurice?' he asked.

Maurice nodded. 'I thought people stepped in dead men's shoes quicker. Remember what this bar was like after the Chelmsford stop? Look at it now.'

'I saw Dresden immediately after the war,' said Thorpley. 'It was unbelievable. You had to search for a really habitable dwelling. The place was gutted. A hundred thousand people died in one night of bombing.' He emptied his glass and put it down on the counter to be recharged with Scotch. 'I went back to Dresden not many years after. It was more incredible than the result of the blitz. The place was crammed with busy, bustling people and you could hardly find a trace of the night of terror.'

He looked round the half-empty buffet car. 'And in no time

at all, Maurice, you'll be worked off your feet after the Chelmsford stop. There'll be other solicitor bores and frustrated lovers—the ground's thick with them. It's an unhappy fact of life.'

He picked up the refilled glass and looked at it. 'That was a real bender we had, Maurice. Do you regret it?'

'Haven't touched a drop since. My head ached for two days.'

'I didn't feel too good, either.'

'Is it the difficult aunt today, sir?' asked Maurice.

'Yes, but she's much less difficult now. She's a good woman, but needs looking after. As a matter of fact—' Mr Thorpley paused. 'I intend spending my working days in London from now on. Home for the weekends only.'

'I'm sorry to hear that, sir. I'll miss you.'

'Someone tiptoed over my grave last week,' said Thorpley, remembering the shudder that had run up his spine. 'Next time hobnailed boots might be worn. I'm getting too old for commuting. In any case, the Monday aunt is a sort of home from home. She tolerates my bad habits and I'm her favourite nephew.'

Thorpley hadn't taken his eyes away from his inspection of the buffet car.

'Only two regulars can I place,' he said. 'The artist and the train-spotter.'

Four seat banks away Mr Rae sat alone, hands folded on the tabletop. He was thinking of Fred Sellars recovering from multiple injuries in Chelmsford Hospital and the journeys they had made together. They would never share trains again. What was the point of Sellars trying to take up from where he left off? Five years off retirement and a permanent cripple—what employment future was there in that? And Fred hadn't liked trains. He'd had good reason, and Rae found that his own enthusiasm had died. On that day—the morning of that day, he'd sermonised on the laws of chance. Jumbo jets had been his text. But the laws of chance had selected a train, not a Boeing 747.

He raised his hands to his face and covered his eyes with his fingertips. He was tired, very tired, and had been since that night of hell. It had taken something from him; not just the friendly

Sellars but part of his life's force. Like Sellars he, too, was five years off retirement. He'd had enough and would exercise freedom of choice. A little less pension, perhaps, but it would be worth it. When Fred came out of hospital he could spend days with him; help bring him back to health with friendly disagreements. Today he would announce his retirement to the office.

Across the aisle David Blake attracted Charlie Shelley's attention and directed it to Mr Rae.

'Remember him?'

'His blood group's O Rh Positive,' said Shelley. 'He doesn't look well. I wonder how his friend is. Do you know—when he got on the train I nodded to him and said "Good morning"—he didn't recognise me.'

'Did you expect him to?'

'Half and half.'

Shelley looked through the window. 'We're coming up to it now.'

The side of the track was piled with remnants of the wrecked train. Much of it had gone, but another two days' clearance remained. It was totally unlike the scene imprinted on Blake and Shelley's minds. Then, it had been a mad visionary's dream of the torments of Hell. Now, the shortly risen sun in a clear blue sky glittered on the piles of twisted metal stacked along the line.

As the 08.20 crawled past the accident area, the day-glow orange jackets of the track-workers working on the track showed up brilliantly in the morning light.

'It's as if the train's going slow out of respect,' said Shelley. 'I know that sounds soft, but you know what I mean.'

'More out of fear.' Blake withdrew his gaze from the window. 'Whenever I pass an accident on the road I drop my speed down to the minimum. Mr Blood Group didn't look through the window —did you notice?'

'That's because he's seen it before. Oh—well,' Shelley rubbed his hands together. 'It's another Monday and lightning never strikes in the same place twice. Christmas next Saturday and that's good. Did you hear about the village bobby?'

'No—what's the latest?'

'He'll be all right. A few bits missing.' Shelley grinned. 'They took out his appendix at the same time.'

They sat in silence for a while drinking their coffee. The crash had had little effect on them apart from sharpening Blake's appetite for life. He had accepted the school's offer. As Head of Painting he would now have put the cold hand of death on those whose usefulness to the school had come to an end. He wished he could do it as anonymously as the instigator of the rail crash.

He expressed this to Shelley. 'I don't know what they'll do. They've been protected for years at the expense of the students.'

Shelley summed it up in a cliché. 'You've got to be cruel to be kind. Anyway,' he said, using another, 'if you want good flowers in your garden you don't look after the weeds. Life can be bloody cruel—we saw that last Monday. You do what you think is right—you can't do more or better.'

The train picked up speed; the driver had lost a few minutes in the slow-down between Chelmsford and Shenfield. With the memory of the Willow Point crash behind him, the driver said to his second man: 'Let's hope we get a clear run to Liverpool Street. If all goes well, we should be dead on time.'

Five minutes late the train came to a stop on Platform 9 and the commuters swarmed across the concourse of the station. Under the Christmas tree Santa Claus rattled his collecting-box at slow-moving, trappable commuters: *'Don't forget the orphans—only five shopping days to Christmas!'*

Overhead, in the vast cavern of the station, loud-speakers carolled seasonal music.

> *'Jingle bells—jingle bells—jingle all the way*
> *O what fun it is to ride*
> *In a one-horse open sleigh . . .'*

The last passenger to leave the train was Mr Thorpley. He directed a porter to take his two suitcases and carry them to the taxi-rank.

On his way up the platform, Maurice leaned out of the buffet-car window and caught Thorpley's attention.

'Happy Christmas again, sir. Thanks for the present.'

Thorpley shook the extended hand, 'The same to you, Maurice, and many of them. Second Monday morning after Christmas—right?'

'I'll have it poured and ready for you, sir.'

Alone in her kitchen, May Denning heard the two-tone call of a homing diesel. It came across the bright, sunlit town of Ipswich; a facsimile of the sound she had heard for many years, but its message had changed.

It no longer said, *'Denn-ing!'*